BERKLEY UK

MADHOUSE

Rob Thurman lives in Indiana, land of rolling hills and cows. Lots and lots of cows. *Nightlife* and *Moonshine*, the previous novels in the Cal Leandros series, are also published by Penguin. Visit Rob at www.robthurman.net.

Madhouse

ROB THURMAN

BERKLEY UK
PENGUIN

BERKLEY UK

Published by the Penguin Group
Penguin Books Ltd, 80 Strand, London WC2R 0RL, England
Penguin Group (USA) Inc., 375 Hudson Street, New York, New York 10014, USA
Penguin Group (Canada), 90 Eglinton Avenue East, Suite 700, Toronto, Ontario, Canada M4P 2Y3
(a division of Pearson Penguin Canada Inc.)
Penguin Ireland, 25 St Stephen's Green, Dublin 2, Ireland (a division of Penguin Books Ltd)
Penguin Group (Australia), 250 Camberwell Road,
Camberwell, Victoria 3124, Australia (a division of Pearson Australia Group Pty Ltd)
Penguin Books India Pvt Ltd, 11 Community Centre, Panchsheel Park, New Delhi – 110 017, India
Penguin Group (NZ), 67 Apollo Drive, Rosedale, Auckland 0632, New Zealand
(a division of Pearson New Zealand Ltd)
Penguin Books (South Africa) (Pty) Ltd, Block D, Rosebank Office Park, 181 Jan Smuts Avenue,
Parktown North, Gauteng 2193, South Africa

Penguin Books Ltd, Registered Offices: 80 Strand, London WC2R 0RL, England

www.penguin.com

First published in the USA by Roc, an imprint of New American Library,
a division of Penguin Group (USA) Inc. 2008
First published in Great Britain by Berkley UK 2012
001

Printed in Great Britain by Clays Ltd, St Ives plc

ISBN: 978-0-718-19277-8

www.greenpenguin.co.uk

Penguin Books is committed to a sustainable
future for our business, our readers and our planet.
This book is made from Forest Stewardship
Council™ certified paper.

ALWAYS LEARNING   **PEARSON**

As always, for my mom

ACKNOWLEDGMENTS

I would like to thank, as always, my wonderful editor, Anne Sowards; thanks also to Tina, Erica, and Cam—Penguin's Charlie's Angels of kicking publishing ass; Dr. Linda James for her assistance in the medical areas; Jeff Thurman of the Federal Bureau of Investigation for his weapons advice; the unequaled art and design team of Chris McGrath and Ray Lundgren; my agent, Jennifer Jackson; Shannon and River—forever the twins; Jordana, friend and inspiration for the Nature Channel reference; Shawn and Beth, for keeping my Web site up and running; and fellow writer Mara.

I have taken great liberties with the tunnel system at Columbia University, as well as with the interior of Buell Hall. It was all in the interest of the plot, I promise you, but as a result, reality has suffered. My apologies to reality.

Then again, what has reality ever done for me?

1

I hated kidnapping cases. Hated them with an unholy passion.

And trust me, unholy was something I knew about—hell, I wore it like a faded old T-shirt. One I'd had since birth. There were those who said I couldn't let go of that, and that it was long past time I did. But hey, if you can't bitch about your monster half, what can you bitch about?

As for kidnappings, no surprise there on how I felt about them. Several months before, someone I knew had been kidnapped—two someones, actually. Although the second taking had lasted less than an hour, the first had lasted two weeks. Despite the difference in time, they had both left their mark, physically and mentally. My shirt and jacket hid the first. I wasn't sure anything hid the second, but I gave it my best shot with caustic sarcasm, brittle bravado, and good old-fashioned denial. That was a triple threat that had done well by me for a long damn time, and I had no plans to give it up now.

I was briskly swatted on the back of my head. "I'm curious, Cal. Do you plan on paying attention any time soon or would you like to have the kidnappers reschedule? I'm sure they'll be amenable. Kidnappers so often are."

Niko Leandros. He had been one of those who had disappeared on me, even if only temporarily. As brothers went, he was a good one, despite a horrifying obsession with health food, meditation, and things generally not revolving around pizza and beer. But we all have our crosses to bear. . . . Mine was to be smacked when I wasn't with the program, and his was to be overeducated, as self-aware as the Dalai Lama, and to keep my ass alive. Poor bastard.

"I'm paying attention," I lied instantly, rubbing the back of my head and giving him a wounded glare.

He snorted, but didn't call me on it as sharply as I deserved. Apparently the swat was punishment enough. "Then let's move on before you pay so much attention that you fall asleep where you stand."

Like I said, a good brother, and good brothers, besides keeping your ass alive, also don't let it get away with much. But there was no denying he was letting me slide a little. Why? Because he knew me, and he knew a case like this wasn't going to trigger any good memories. Grunting in reply, I moved along at his side. "So they kidnapped the mistress of a vampire," I grumbled. "She's a lamia. I've seen lamias and I don't know why the hell anyone would want one back." Like vampires, lamias fed on blood. These days most vampires had found a better way, but lamias weren't looking to improve themselves. And although they fed on blood, there the similarity to vampires ended. A lamia's bite, usually on the chest—or if they were really into you, other, more sensitive parts—had a chemical in its saliva that paralyzed its victim. Like a leech they would stay fastened to you and drain your blood . . . very, very slowly. It could take days—days in which you couldn't move, couldn't scream, couldn't beg for a faster death.

Sure, that's *my* dream girl. Bring her on.

But obviously a vamp felt different and here we were.

"I think it matters less about his taste in bed partners and more about us getting paid." I didn't see his dark blond head move, but I knew Niko was scanning the area unceasingly.

"I keep telling you, if you'd go with the whole trophy boyfriend thing, life would be a lot easier," I pointed out helpfully.

From the narrow-eyed look shot my way, apparently I wasn't as helpful as I'd thought. Niko was tight with a vampire of his own, Promise. Promise was, to say the least, loaded. Five excessively rich, as well as excessively elderly, husbands in the past ten years had her set up for . . . well, not life—after all, she was a vampire. But it would keep her comfortable for a long, long time. And Niko absolutely refused to take advantage of it, not that he had some sort of macho hang-up. He simply would make his own way as we had all of our lives. Right now, making our way revolved around an agency we'd set up with Promise. Kidnappings, bodyguard work, cleaning some killer clowns out of a carnival . . . we were up for all of it. The fact that it didn't quite cover our expenses yet had us working second jobs. Niko was a teacher's assistant at NYU (pity the kid who walked late into one of his classes—decapitation is a big deterrent for tardiness). As for me? I tended to move around a lot. Mainly bars. It wasn't good to get attached. I'd learned that from a lifetime of running from my relatives . . . the ones with claws and hundreds of teeth. And although the running had stopped, habits were hard to break. Which, I guess, is why we'd made monster hunting a career instead of an occasional necessity.

And Central Park was full of them.

They liked the park. It was big, and it was full of snacks. No one notices if a mugger, murderer, or rapist goes missing. It was a good place to hit the human buffet and not be noticed. We'd once had an informant here of the very same opinion. He was gone now, dead by Niko's sword. Somewhere to the north lay a mud pit empty of a boggle with the worst New Yawk accent I'd ever heard. I kind of missed him sometimes. If nothing else, he'd been entertaining. Bloodthirsty and homicidal, but amusing—up to a point. Trying to kill Niko had been that point.

"Are we there yet?" I checked my watch. We had about five minutes until the meet.

"Did you look at the map that was sent with the instructions?" Niko looked down his long nose to ask in a forbidding tone that said he already knew the answer.

"That's what I have you for." I grinned. "I'm just here to carry the heavy stuff. The union says thinking rolls me into overtime."

Niko pulled his katana from beneath his gray duster, looked at the moonlight glimmer of it, and then looked at me with an eyebrow raised.

"Yeah, right," I dismissed, unfazed.

"You're assuming I wouldn't paddle you with it like the child you are."

Okay, that threat I bought. He could do it all right, and he actually might during one of our sparrings just for his own personal amusement.

"And yes," he added, "we are almost there." He took another three steps. "And now we are."

I looked around, but didn't see anything even in the bright moonlight. Shoving my hands in the pockets of my black leather jacket, I took a whiff of the cool November air. Instantly, I grimaced. I might not have seen anything, but I damn sure smelled it. The scent was dank—stagnant water with the ripe and rancid taint of day-old fish beneath it. "They're coming." I freed a hand and rubbed at my nose. "And they stink like you wouldn't believe. Something from the water." A fish of the day you definitely didn't want to order.

"Aquatic," Niko murmured. "That narrows it down to a few hundred in the nonhuman pantheon. Very helpful."

"Hey, I tried." Getting accustomed to the smell, I shifted impatiently on the grass and checked my watch again. "Crooks, monster or human, they're all the same. No damn consideration."

I suppose that's how my gun found its way into my hand as the first figure appeared out of the trees. "Bishop-fish," Niko murmured. "Nothing extraordinary. Easy to kill."

If I was a little disappointed at that, I kept it to myself. As creatures went, it wasn't that impressive. I'd seen someone more grimly unnerving in a mirror. Sometimes I wasn't sure who I meant by that. It could've been the creature known as Darkling, who a year ago had crawled out of a mirror to put my body on like a snazzy suit and take it cruising on the road to hell, or it could've been my own mundane reflection. Either way, there was no denying the both of us had our moments and either of us could eat fish boy for lunch. Although dead Darkling, every molecule the monster to my half, might've enjoyed it a little more.

Maybe.

Dappled here and there with the ghost of scales over nearly transparent pale skin, the bishop-fish had the form of a human. Sort of. The shape of his head was a little off. Hairless and only lightly scaled, it was oddly flattened and the mouth had thick, rubbery lips and tiny triangular teeth. No kelp eater, this one. He wasn't wearing a stitch—not a damn thing, which told me he didn't rub shoulders with the local New Yorkers much. I looked down. Even they would give that a glance. Yeah, *that*.

Now I knew where fish sticks came from.

I decided keeping my gaze on his eyes was the lesser of two evils despite their unblinking bulge. Guess you can't blink if you don't have eyelids. Round pupils took us in and the mouth opened to gurgle, "These are the demands. First—"

That's when I shot him.

My patience with kidnappers was long gone before I had even taken a step into the park. I put a bullet in his chest, which exploded like an overripe tomato and splattered fluid in a wide arc. With his impossibly wide mouth gaping, he teetered and began to fall. I stepped forward and slipped the paper from the fleshy claw as Mr. Fish Stick crumpled to the ground with a disturbingly wet slapping sound. "I can read, asshole," I muttered.

Niko said from behind me, "Really? When did you learn?" Raising his voice, he asked mildly, "Is there anyone here we could negotiate with that my brother would find less annoying?" Like me, he knew there was someone else in the trees. I smelled them and he heard them. Rustle one leaf, step on one frost-brittle piece of grass, and he would hear it. He was all human, Niko, like our mother, Sophia Leandros, but when he did things like that you had to wonder.

The smell I was picking up from a distance wasn't as bad as that of the fish. It was the scent of old things and attic must and hundreds of abandoned spiderwebs. In other words, it smelled like Niko's library of books. Knowing Niko would be watching its approach, I squinted at the paper in my hand, ignoring the damp slime on it. If the moon hadn't been so bright and plump in the sky, I wouldn't have been able to see anything. I might have monster smelling—whoopee . . . what a superpower—but I had human vision. As it was, I could make out only a few words. Money wasn't mentioned. I wasn't that surprised. Very few monsters were into the material world. Vampires, pucks, and werewolves liked to live high on the hog, but most of the nonhuman world was more interested in eating. Lots and lots of eating.

The ransom mentioned people. Nice, plump people. Nice, juicy children. The kids. Why was it always the kids?

Some kidnappers don't want to earn their money, and some don't want to catch their own dinner. Trade one lamia for a truckload of humans—what a deal. In the end they were all lazy psychotics and the one that finally came to Niko's call was no different. You could all but see the waves of craziness coming from her, shimmering like heat off a summer road.

"Black Annis." Niko sounded almost pleased. "I thought she was a myth."

She scuttled with the back and forth motion of a

poisonous centipede. Part of the time she was on two
feet, the rest on all fours. She looked like an old
woman, but not a sad wraith in a nursing home or
cheerful crocheting grandma—unless it was one
who'd have no problem picking her teeth with a
sliver of Hansel's gnawed leg bone.

Now, this was a little more disturbing than the
fish. And it became more disturbing when six more
of her appeared to race across the grass.

"You thought *she* was a myth. She. Singular. Is that
what you were saying?" I dropped the paper to the
ground. I still had my gun in my right hand and I
drew my knife with the left from the double holster
under my jacket. Ugly and serrated, the blade had
been a constant and faithful companion for a while
now. Niko did give damn fine Christmas presents.

"Apparently the myth is incorrect. It only makes
things more interesting," he said blandly. "Surely a
few old women don't concern you?"

Old women, my ass. The seven of them were covering the ground with freakish speed. Long, thick
fingernails scored the ground, sending dirt and grass
flying, and their teeth . . . let's just say they weren't
the kind that got put in a glass on the bedside table.
The Annises, Anni, Black Annies . . . whatever—they
weren't identical, but they were so similar they may
as well have been. They all wore the same ragged
black shifts too. Torn to streamers in places, the cloth
fluttered and tangled as they ran. I saw flesh through
the holes, flesh I suspected was cyanotic blue although it appeared gray in the glow of the moon.
Whatever color it was, I didn't want to see it.

"Fine. You play shuffleboard with the grannies and
I'll cheer you on from the sidelines," I retorted. Not

that I would have, but one of them made sure I didn't have the option. She went from scuttling to leaping. From nearly thirty feet away, she launched off the ground and propelled herself onto my chest with a force I didn't expect from her spidery frame. I hit the ground hard. Unable to get the gun between us, I buried the knife in her back. I was hoping to sever the spine or at least put a serious dent in it, but the blade practically bounced off the bony structure. "Goddamn it," I gritted, and went for another target instead. With her teeth snapping at my throat, I plunged the knife in the side of hers.

"Leave one alive, Cal, to lead us to the lamia."

Thick and bitter fluid flooded out of the Annis's throat and across my face. Trying not to retch as it worked its way into my mouth, I spat with revulsion and shot back, "I'll try and show some self-control." Then I stopped tasting the blood and caught the scent of it . . . or rather what was in it. "Oh, hell. We are so not getting paid."

I tossed the thing off me, its teeth still feebly gnashing, and saw Niko, who had moved a distance away to get a little elbow room. He was surrounded by four of them. "Forget the restraint," I called. "They ate her." I smelled it in the one twitching beside me . . . in the blood, on her last breath . . . hell, leaking out of her damn pores.

Niko shook his head. "Annoying." He swung at the nearest Annis to decapitate it, only to have his sword repelled by that unbreakable spine. I heard the grating clash of metal and impervious bone. He frowned. "Even more annoying." Stepping back with a deceptive speed of his own, he sheathed about nine inches of his sword through the Annis's single eye.

Niko turned to present his side to her and lashed out with a foot to propel her off the blade and into another Annis.

He had things, as always, under control, and I decided to take care of my own business. Two more of them were circling me, wary of the knife. What they weren't concerned with was the gun I had hidden behind my leg. One snarled, I swear, just like the cranky old woman we'd lived next to in one of the trailer parks where our mother had set up her fortune-telling scam. That old biddy had sicced her yappy, ankle-biting dog on us more times than I could count. The Annis didn't need a dog, yappy or otherwise.

"Shouldn't you be baking cookies or playing bingo, Granny?" I gave her a black grin, tapping the muzzle of my gun on the back of my thigh. She crabbed closer, her hands bent into claws in front of her.

"You are no little boy." Her grin was so broad I could see the black gums gleaming slickly. "Your flesh will not be soft." It was gloating, the words rolling around her tongue as though she were already savoring the meat in her mouth. "We will eat it anyway."

I'd heard it all before.

I shot the mouthy one. I nailed her in mid maniacal, choking laugh. She saw the gun as I whipped it from behind me, and she'd already started to move. It didn't do her a damn bit of good. Despite the one second it took, the other one was already on me. Like I said . . . quick.

It hit me from the side. I'd already been turning to prevent it from getting behind me. This time the teeth did reach me, fastening on the junction of neck and shoulder. Like the ragged edge of a saw, they

ground in and locked. And there went the chunk I'd
been so sure that I wouldn't lose tonight.

As with the first one, I used my knife, but this
time opened the belly. Whatever spilled free slithered
down my hip and leg. Slithered . . . not fell. That
was some serious motivation to get granny off my
neck, and to hell with the mouthful of flesh she might
take with her. Ripping her and her death grip off of
me, I spun her and threw her as far as I could, and
then I took a look at what was twining its way
around my leg.

Holy shit. I mean, really . . . holy *shit*.

The bright pain and blood flowing steadily under
the collar of my jacket to stain my T-shirt took a
backseat just like that—because what felt like snakes
wasn't. Not that that wouldn't have been bad
enough, snakes falling out of someone's gut. But I
couldn't get that lucky, could I? Nope. What I got
was a crawling combination of worms and intestines
with a little barracuda tossed in. They undulated
slow and sure like the worm, were ropy and dripping intestinal fluids, and had the bear trap mouth
of a barracuda. Did I shake my leg like I was having
an epileptic seizure? Yes, I did. Did I scream like a
B-movie bimbo? No . . . but it was a close thing.
Niko never would've let me live that down.

I stepped back from the seething mass. "Jeeesus."

"Problems?" Niko was already peeling my jacket
off one shoulder to examine the wound.

I swiped it with my hand. The pain was subsiding
to a sharp ache and I decided the Annis had gotten
away with less than the mouthful I'd thought she
had. It had been an appetizer at best.

Past Nik I could see one Annis still alive. Her
wrists and ankles were handcuffed, and she was

writhing, hissing, and biting the ground like a rabid dog.

A monster wearing handcuffs—it was a little reality-jarring at first. We'd started carrying them months ago when we needed to restrain a werewolf, one who really didn't care to be restrained. He normally might've shattered them—I wasn't sure how strong Flay was—but he'd been injured and was barely alive. He'd been incapable of lifting his head, much less ripping apart steel. Still, it was a useful learning experience, and we'd carried them with us ever since.

Niko was still frowning at my neck. "It's more messy than fatal. They have the teeth of an adolescent crocodile."

"Didn't feel like a baby one to me," I grumbled as I felt the punctures and slashes. The blood was slowing and I dug in my pocket for something to hold pressure with. Of course there was nothing but a flyer for a Chinese restaurant.

Exhaling in resignation at my lack of preparation, Niko pulled a package of gauze and a roll of tape from inside his coat. With quick, efficient moves he had the wound covered and taped up in seconds. "It's amazing how hard I work to keep you from bleeding to death on so many occasions, and for so little reward." He finished and stepped over to the tortuous twining of the bile-dripping creatures on the ground. "Do you want a pet? One would fit nicely in a terrarium."

"Yeah, and I'm just one giant nummy num on the other side of the glass. Thanks, but no, thanks." I pulled a repulsed face.

"'All things bright and beautiful, all creatures great and small,'" he quoted.

"Right," I said drily. "God"—making the huge assumption there was one—"did not make those."

"Perhaps you're right." He pulled yet two more things out of his duster—a small container of lighter fluid and a pack of matches. Once the barbecue was started and the air stank of roasted barracuda, Niko made a call and we went, picked up the surviving Annis, and moved on. A vampire met us near the edge of the park. He stood among the trees; could've been one of them as he blended into the darkness. Black hair, black eyes, and an equally dark Armani suit. At least I assumed it was Armani. It was the only expensive brand I knew. To me, all fancy suits were Armani.

We dumped the snarling, spitting Annis at his feet, and I considered but decided not to stick my hand out for the money. I had a feeling I might draw back less than I put out—a few fingers less. Vampires mourn too, apparently even over lamias. Niko had already delivered the bad news over his cell phone. Now all he said was, "She is the only one left. The others are no more."

"And they suffered?" His voice was cool and empty. It didn't bode well for the Annis. At least with rage you would go quickly. It would be messy, but it would be quick. Icy retribution could go on for . . . shit, it didn't bear thinking about. My appetite for dinner had already been ruined by the smell of cooking intestines; I didn't need to kill it altogether.

"Yeah, they suffered," I confirmed. "And the god-awful things in them suffered too." The Annis hadn't really suffered, not the way he meant, but it was going to have to do. A job was a job and torture wasn't on our menu. Not for pay anyway. But there was no point in disappointing him. Cranky vampires are a pain, and I'd had enough ass-kicking for the night.

Despite what I'd said earlier, we did get paid. An envelope thick with cash was passed to Nik. Living off the radar, we didn't exactly have the ID to set up a bank account. We could've gotten the fake stuff and Promise had offered to keep our share of the payments for us, but once again, we fell back on the ways we'd always known. We'd bought a safe and stuffed what we made in there. Unfortunately, it was still pretty damn empty.

As we left, we heard one sharp scream after another. It seemed like torture was on someone's menu. I wondered if it sounded like the screams of the people that the Black Annis had killed over the years, because you know they'd screamed too.

Karma, she is a bitch. But in this particular incident, not my karma, not my problem.

We moved on. We were nearly to the edge of the park and for a few moments the night was perfect. Cool and crisp with the rustle of falling leaves. Perfect. Right up until we saw what was hanging in the last line of trees. Heavy and ripe like fruit, the color of a nectarine . . . pale salmon blooming with red. Lots and lots of red.

In the trees.

Bodies.

2

We'd pulled off the job. Maybe not with complete success, but with enough to get paid. We'd heroically fought the powers of darkness. So stalwart and brave that virgins tossed rose petals in our path and strong men wept at our courage. Did life get any better than that? Minus the dead people in the trees of course. Yeah, definitely minus that.

"You're scaring the customers again."

It was later that night and I was leaning my elbows on the bar of my current place of employment, also known as the Ninth Circle. It catered to the strictly supernatural crowd. That's not to say a human wouldn't wander in on occasion, but one good look at the crowd who was giving no kind of good look back had them running for the door. Everyone in the bar could pass for human—they had to walk the streets after all—but they exuded enough bad atti- tude and ass-kicking vibes to get rid of stray humans without even trying.

With my chin propped in my hand, I rolled my eyes in the direction of the stern voice. With his pale blond hair to the shoulders, straight slash of dark brows, gray-blue eyes, and white wings barred with gold, the only thing that kept him from being a figure straight out of a stained-glass window was his weapon-calloused hands and a long scar along his jaw from chin to ear. Ishiah, who owned the bar, was one kick-ass angel if ever there was one. You could all but see the flaming sword, not to mention the nonflaming boot he'd be happy to put up your ass. Of course he wasn't really an angel. As far as I knew, those didn't exist. Ishiah was a peri, and no one quite knew what they were. They were rumored to be the offspring of angels and demons, but how could that be? The first didn't exist. As for demons . . . open your eyes. Demons are everywhere. They're us.

"And how am I doing that?" I snorted. I'd decided against bringing up what Niko and I had found in the park. He might be my boss, but I didn't really know Ishiah, and I definitely didn't trust Ishiah. Not yet. Not that I had any reason not to trust him. Trust simply wasn't an emotion I was very good at. "By slinging drinks and making change because the cheap-ass bastards don't tip? Yeah, that's scary shit right there."

The wings flexed, shimmered with light, then disappeared. It was a neat trick. I didn't ask how he did it or how any of the peri did it, for that matter. We all have our secrets. Everyone in this bar had their secrets because there wasn't a human among them. Ishiah, now looking like just a man, albeit an unusual one, said in a lower tone for the two of us only, "You're being Auphe."

Auphe. The other half of my gene pool—my inheritance from good old Dad. The Auphe were what mythological elves would be if they were born in the ninth circle of hell and passed through the other eight on their way out. Because hell couldn't hold them—nothing could. Most had pale, nearly transparent skin, pointed ears, molten red eyes, white filaments masquerading as the flow of hair, and what seemed like a thousand needle-fine metal teeth. So fine that when they smiled, never a good occasion, you could see your hazy reflection.

Mirror, mirror, on the wall, who is the most malevolent of us all?

"And how," I asked, annoyed, "am I doing that?"

The twilight eyes studied me. "Let us say you don't precisely look happy. And when you don't look happy . . ." He raised eyebrows in the direction of the clientele, some who knew through the grapevine and some who could smell the Auphe in me, who were either clustered on the far side of the room or at closer range silently snarling. "That happens. It's not good for business."

"Happy? I'm happy." I bared my teeth in a fixed grin. "See? Happy."

"Gods save us. I haven't seen an expression like that since Medusa went through menopause." Robin Goodfellow dropped on a stool and shook his head. "Quick. Brandy before you destroy my will to live with your catastrophically bad temper."

Ishiah immediately drifted off. He and Robin had some sort of problem with each other. I had no idea what it was, as both were silent on the subject. But with Robin's mouth, if one of them didn't leave, there'd be little left of the bar for me to terrorize with my inner Auphe. They would pull the place down around our ears.

"Catastrophic temper?" I reached for the good stuff I kept under the bar just for Robin. A hundred years old, it was still barely fetal in age to his point of view. Yet another mystery: why Ish would stock it for him. "Come on."

"Kid, everything about you is catastrophic. Your temper, your fighting skills, your attitude, and let's not even discuss your look. Simply put on the eyeliner and join the rest of the Children of the Night knockoffs at the local Goth bar."

And that was Robin. Otherwise known as Rob Fellows—car salesman without peer, Robin Goodfellow—trickster extraordinaire, and, oh yeah, our favorite puck. Considering I'd killed the only other one we'd met, it wasn't much of a contest.

"I don't need the eyeliner." I gave him a glass and the squat bottle.

"Yes, yes. Child of the Night is on your birth certificate. Six-six-six is tattooed on your infant ass. I believe I've heard it before." He poured a drink as I gave a quirk of my lips, but it was more genuine than the grin I'd flashed a few moments ago. Robin did have a way of pulling me out of a mood. It was hard to moan and groan about my bogeyman heritage when he treated me less like a monster and more like Bo Peep with a gun. I appreciated it, because there had been times he had seen what I *could* be. And it didn't come out of any nursery rhyme.

"So, did the case not go well?" He held the pregnant glass—all curves—sniffed the liquid, clicked his tongue, and shook his head, but took a swallow anyway.

"Eh." I shrugged. "We got paid. The lamia got eaten. Really a win-win in my book."

"And the fact that it was a kidnapping case, that doesn't even bear discussing?"

I ducked my head, letting my longish hair swing

forward—black to my brother's dark blond. My skin fair to his olive. All we had that showed our common mother was our gray eyes. And I knew mine, peering through the dark strands, were now opaque. "It was months ago. Let it go, okay?" I warned.

He took another swallow. "Months. Millennia. A veritable eon. Whatever was I thinking?"

"You weren't," I said stiffly.

A werewolf came slinking up to the bar, ears flat and nose wrinkled in disgust at the Auphe tinge to my scent. It was hard to ask for a brewski with his half-human face contorted around a mouthful of teeth straight out of *The Call of the Wild*, but he pointed just fine. He was obviously not a fine-bred, but part of the wolf population breeding for recessive wolf genes, not that I had any prejudices about that. How could I? I gave him his beer and kept my chew toy jokes to myself. Ishiah was right. It really wasn't good for business, and he'd given me a break with this job.

I didn't know if it was as an unspoken favor to Robin or to piss him off. I had asked Goodfellow once which it was, and he had declared smoothly that if I didn't want the job, I'd make a great junior car salesman and he had a place for me waiting at his lot. Hell, no. I didn't know if I had a soul or not, but if I did, I wasn't giving it away that easily. If there were a surer path to damnation than being a car salesman, I didn't know what it would be.

"I always think. You might not want to hear what I say, Caliban, but that's your problem." He poured another glassful. "Thinking and talking are what I do best."

"I'll give you the last one all right," I grunted.

He smoothed his wavy brown hair, straightened

his suit jacket, rich brown over a deep green shirt. Just the fabric of one of them probably cost more than a week of my pay. Picking up the bottle in preparation to leaving, he said soberly, "You should try talking to her."

Her being Georgina—George. She was the one who'd been kidnapped. We'd gotten her back. She'd survived. Although it had been a very close thing—for all of us. George was the local psychic, but she was the real thing . . . and this girl, this special girl, had thought we could be together. I had known better. And although she'd proved to be as stubborn and hardheaded as me in her own way, I still knew it.

"I talk," I countered defensively.

He stood, the amber liquid in his bottle not sloshing even a millimeter. When you'd been alive as long as he had, you tended to be pretty damn graceful and controlled in your movements. "I mean really talk to her as opposed to flapping that useless mouth once in a blue moon and saying absolutely nothing. But I wash my hands. Please, ruin any chance of a love life that you have while I go expand mine." He winked rapaciously. "Do you want to guess? Male or female? Other? One or three? I'm willing to gift my knowledge to the less fortunate."

"Yeah, thanks anyway," I refused. "I like being less fortunate." Although lately that wasn't precisely true. "Gives me something to bitch about."

"As if you need an excuse," he snorted.

"Wait," I said as he started to move off. "Niko and I came across some bodies in the park. Five. Hanging in the trees like goddamn ornaments." And wasn't that creepy as fucking hell? "Would a Black Annis do something like that?"

Niko and I had discussed it. If they were willing to catch their own food, why bother with kidnapping the lamia? We couldn't investigate for more than a few moments—the inner edge of Central Park wasn't the safest place to be pawing over bodies for clues. "Two men, three women." One had been more a girl . . . sixteen maybe . . . with long hair that had dripped blood in a gentle rain to the grass. "All were . . . shit . . . chewed on, I guess you'd say. Ripped and torn."

He considered it. "A Black Annis? It's conceivable. They're not much for delayed gratification, so taking a bite or two while waiting on you and Niko would be something they would do. Hanging them in a tree?" He seesawed a hand back and forth. "They're more for caves, but in a pinch?" He shrugged. "They are adaptable." Pausing, he added soberly, "Five people? Unpleasant." Setting the bottle back in front of me, he advised, "Just this once. Bacchus was a doctor in his own right." He then waved a hand and was gone.

Less than a moment later, Ishiah returned and watched Robin disappear out the door. He looked exasperated. Scratch that. Not exasperated—highly, profoundly annoyed. And intent, very intent. It was a peculiar combination. "Oh, hey. I get it." I grinned, pouring a small amount of Robin's gift into a glass. I wasn't a drinker, to say the least, but he was right. One wouldn't hurt; it could only help. "You have a thing for him."

He turned his gaze to me. It was still annoyed. "Insolent bastard."

"True enough, but it doesn't change the fact." I tossed the bar towel over my shoulder. "You were watching his ass, don't lie." I had no idea if Goodfellow had a good ass or not. That wasn't the way my boat floated, but *Robin* had told me and everyone in the free and not-so-free world that he did. Could be Ishiah had an opinion on the subject. "By the way, is it a good . . ."

He turned and walked away before I had a chance to finish. In reality, I kind of doubted that's what it was all about. If it were, Robin would've been walking out of here with feathers in his hair, down his pants, and a smug grin on his face.

I shrugged. Not my business. At least, as long as Robin wasn't in trouble. And he usually wasn't. He'd gotten very, very good at avoiding that since before the human race was born. I wasn't sure how old he was exactly, but I was guessing that he had probably served up one of mankind's wriggling water-going ancestors on a nice wheat-berry bread at some point or another.

At four I closed up the bar. Swept up the feathers, fur, and scales, locked the door, and headed home. The apartment was relatively close to the Ninth Circle on St. Mark's Place, but every time I had to think I might not make it . . . I had every night for the past four months, but I always had my doubts. Spine tense, shoulders set, I searched every dark nook and every roof for the Auphe. I never saw my relatives during that period, but it was only a matter of time.

They'd kidnapped me and kept me prisoner for two years when I was fourteen. They'd done the same again last year only with a little more of a twist. They'd had me possessed and planned to use me to remake the world in their image. When we'd returned the favor by destroying the remains of nearly their entire race, they had been a little put-out. We'd thought they were all dead, destroyed by a collapsing warehouse, but we'd been wrong. And when you were wrong about the Auphe, you might as well cut your own throat and get it over with. It would be a helluva lot less painful.

The Auphe had torture down to a fine art. They'd roamed the earth with the dinosaurs—before the dinosaurs. It had given them a long time to perfect their technique. And the Auphe had technique out the ass. I still didn't remember what they had done to me in the two years they'd had me. I doubted I ever would . . . not without ending up in a place where people shambled in paper slippers and considered lunch to be a cupful of happy pills.

Unfortunately the Auphe were determined to make me pay for betraying my own kind. Months ago when I'd had the one thing in my hand that would bring George back to us, one had snatched it away and told me in excruciating detail just how I would pay. They'd make the others pay too, Niko and Robin, who had helped in their destruction. They'd also take anyone I cared for, simply because I did care for them. My friends, my family, they would all go first, long before I did.

Like I said, the Auphe had torture down to a science. And that they were taking their time about it only made things worse. The only thing that kept me moderately sane was the fact that Niko, Promise, and Robin could take care of themselves, and I avoided George whenever I could. The Auphe would never know she existed if I had anything to say about it.

Of course, all that sanity rested on the fact that I was living in denial about how amazingly good at killing the Auphe were. God knew that they'd almost killed Nik and me on more than one occasion. We were good. They were better.

Trudging up the stairs to the apartment, smelling of secondhand beer and worse, I unlocked the door, opened it, and dropped my jacket on the nearest surface . . . the floor.

"You may as well pick it up. We have someplace to be."

"Christ. It's four thirty," I groaned as I took in Niko waiting with arms folded. His face was amused but serious nonetheless. His hair was pulled back into a bare inch and a half of ponytail. Once it had been a braid that trailed down his back, but I knew he didn't begrudge its sacrifice. It had been for me, and he hadn't expected to survive long enough to walk around with the Kojak look.

"Yes, it is four thirty and the longer we stand here the later it will get, but I'm sure the basic mechanics of time are understood even by you."

"You're in rare form tonight," I sniped. "Rare shitty form."

"Yes, keeping us in rent payments, how inconsiderate of me." He tilted his head and frowned slightly. "How's the shoulder?"

I'd moved only with the slightest amount of stiffness, but he'd still noticed. I rotated it and did my best not to wince at the pull of torn flesh. "Bearable."

"I told you serving drinks would aggravate it. You should've told Ishiah that you were injured and couldn't work." He stared pointedly at the jacket, and I picked it up with an annoyed groan.

"I was afraid he'd turn me into a pillar of salt. Besides, he's pretty iffy about me working there, period. Apparently when I'm grouchy, I exude Auphe." I snorted. "And I'm guessing they don't make a roll-on for that."

We were already out in the hall and moving as I

yawned heavily. "It's only because the clientele already know thanks to the loose-lipped werewolves." Niko focused on the bandage, visually checking for blood as I pulled on my jacket. Satisfied that it was unstained, he continued. "If it weren't for them, no one would know."

Niko tried hard, he did, to make me believe I really wasn't that different. And even though it wasn't true, I was grateful as hell for the effort. "The peri would know," I said absently as I zipped the jacket. "They know, shit, everything as far as I can tell. At least everything that has to do with who or what passes through their bar. Although Goodfellow seems to have them bamboozled."

"Bamboozled?" Niko's eyebrows went up.

"I'm trying to expand my vocabulary." I grinned. "Just for you. Now, where the hell are we going?"

"The Metropolitan Museum. Promise is meeting us there. She's on the board of directors through one of her late husbands. There's been a difficulty of some sort. The curator is a good friend of hers, the supernatural kind, and doesn't want to call the police in on this one. She says it's more up our alley."

"Kicking ass and taking names?" I yawned again, ready to let the images of crazy old women and dead bodies fade with sleep.

"We so rarely ask their names that I'm not sure the last counts."

A half hour and a ride on the number 6 train later, we were at the Met and I was hammering on the huge double doors. No one came. "Don't get a lot of pizza deliveries here, do they?" I grumbled, before pounding again.

"How about I call Promise to come let us in? It's

an audacious plan, I realize, but don't dismiss it out of hand," Niko said dryly. He had his cell phone in his hand when Promise and another woman opened the door. The woman, the curator, was a foot taller than Promise . . . at the very least. She was also taller than Niko and me. Her hair was the color of bronze and pulled back into a tight French braid. Her eyes were a fierce ice blue, her breasts an entity unto themselves, and I could practically see the horned helmet and breastplate she should be wearing instead of a gray suit.

"Valkyrie?" I murmured to Nik.

"Missing her crow feathers," he answered in the same low tone, "but yes. Very good. You are learning, no matter how reluctantly."

Along with Niko, I took a few steps closer and looked up at her. I was going to offer my hand to shake, but decided I needed it for fighting and other . . . ah . . . nocturnal activities and hers looked as if it were capable of ripping off my arm to use as a back scratcher. Niko was braver and held his hand out and said gravely, "A friend of Promise is a friend of ours."

The large hand shook Niko's firmly. "Sangrida Odinsdóttir."

"Niko Leandros. My brother, Cal." To this day, he refused to call me Caliban. The meaning behind the name given to me by our ever-adoring mother had never escaped me. Even before I could read See Spot Run, much less Shakespeare, she'd been all too eager to tell me a monster deserved a monster name.

Mom did find ways to get her kicks. I was slowly getting used to the others, who knew the meaning of my name but not the intent, using it . . . just as I was still getting used to there *being* others. For years it had only been Niko and me on the run. Now there were friends and lovers and goddamn if that didn't still warp my reality on occasion.

Promise was one of those. Niko and her—hell, they'd been made for each other, the few hundred years' age difference aside. Despite the deep chocolate and pale blond stripes of hair pulled back into an Amazonian braid that reached the small of her back and eyes the color of spring violets, she was a quiet beauty. The exotic coloring didn't make her flashy, and it didn't touch her inner stillness, her innate tranquility. Of course under that tranquility she could be deadly. She and my brother were two of a kind that way. Now she curved her lips gently in a smile meant only for him. "Thank you for coming, Niko. Cal. I realize it's already been a long night for you both." She laid her fingers on Niko's arm for a fleeting moment, and then stepped back into the museum.

Sangrida moved with her as we followed. The inside of the museum was pretty much as I remembered it from the last time Niko had dragged me there for arts and crafts, art education, history stuff. Whatever. I liked the Natural History Museum better, myself. Dinosaurs. Who doesn't love dinosaurs? I remembered seeing an exhibit with a re-creation of a T. rex towering tall. Robin had once said the Auphe used to hunt them in packs . . . not so much for the meat as for the fun.

Yeah . . . the *fun*.

"So, Promise, what's up?" I asked, my voice echoing against the marble.

Sangrida answered instead. "There has been an incident with one of the exhibits."

"It couldn't have been stolen," Niko commented.

"Promise would know that is not our area of expertise."

"No, it was not stolen." She walked with long, muscular strides. "Not exactly." There was a faint glottal flavor to her words, but barely noticeable. "Best for you to see."

We entered the Arms and Armor section and walked past an exhibit of suits of plate armor. One of the galleries was labeled with a red and black exhibition sign that read FAMOUS SERIAL KILLERS THROUGHOUT HISTORY AND LEGEND.

"Entertaining," Niko said wryly. "It puts impressionism to shame."

Sangrida sighed in annoyance. "It's a traveling exhibit of horrors. The board of directors, curse them, are responsible. Not you of course, Promise," she added gruffly. "Just the vultures and hyenas on the board. They are of the opinion that sensationalism keeps attendance high. The first exhibit to your right will be, of course, Jack the Ripper."

Promise gave a hint of a satisfied smile at the mention of the name, and I thought how Jack had disappeared, never to be heard from again. Not many serial killers stop, unless they're caught or someone does the stopping for them. In a time when vampires still relied on blood, it could be that Promise had taken from those who in turn took from others. As I stopped to take a look through the glass at old letters, photos, and period blades that could've been similar to the ones used, Promise took my arm and gently urged me on. "He liked attention then. Let us deny it to him now." Considering what I'd seen of the photos, I wasn't sorry to move on. I'd seen similar in living color just hours ago.

A few exhibits down, Sangrida stopped. The glass

of this display case was blackened . . . scorched by what looked like a small explosion. Glass shards were lying everywhere.

"The case burst from within," Niko pointed out, obviously intrigued. "There is no glass within the exhibit itself, only on the floor."

Also on the floor was a stone box, the lid broken into pieces and scattered far and wide. I toed a piece with my black sneaker. Historical or not, I damn sure couldn't do any more harm to it. "What was in that?"

"Ashes. Fragments of bone." Sangrida shook her head, high forehead knit with worry. "Sawney."

"Sawney?" I repeated curiously, only to be instantly overridden by Niko.

"Sawney Beane? The Scottish mass murderer?" He sat on his heels to get a better look at the box. "The cannibal? I knew the women and the children of the clan were supposedly burned, but the men were executed differently."

"No one is quite sure what really happened. No one who wasn't there." I made a mental note to ask Goodfellow. If he wasn't there, he probably knew someone who was. Sangrida went on, "Of course, mankind doesn't know if Sawney was fact or fiction, but we know better. And although he ate close to a thousand people, he wasn't strictly a cannibal, as he wasn't human." She looked at the shattered box and corrected himself. "Isn't human."

Five words fought to be first out of my mouth. A *thousand* people and *isn't* human. I went with the one most pertinent to the immediate situation.

"Isn't?" I repeated. "He came back from ashes and bone? No goddamn way."

Sangrida didn't blink at that language. I guess if

you hang around warriors for a few centuries, you get used to it. I had no doubt she could curse me under the table . . . probably while bench-pressing me with one hand and swilling ale with the other. "I'm not sure. I've never heard of such a thing in regards to him, but it is a chance I don't wish to take."

The explosion from within, the missing remains—I could see her point. "Was there anything else in the exhibit?"

She frowned. "His scythe. Or what was claimed to be. It was a handheld one, his weapon of choice. It is missing as well."

And that was the definition of didn't bode fucking well, now, wasn't it?

3

There was no way to search the entire museum in-cluding the rooms below where the unused collections were stored, not in the two hours before the staff would start arriving. We searched the first floor, found a metal exit door that was crumpled and askew and that said it all. At least the Cliff's Notes version. Either someone had taken Sawney's bits and pieces out of there or Sawney had taken himself.

With that good news under our belts, we left so Sangrida would trigger the alarm that would bring the police. The security, her special security, had turned off the alarm system the instant it went off, benefiting from the five-minute lag built into the system that most of the board of directors definitely didn't know about. There were a lot of old things in the place and not all of them were known to be completely "inactive," so to speak. There was checking to be done before the authorities showed up. With that now accomplished, Sangrida was ready to play the distressed curator. Well, with Sangrida's backbone, the mildly concerned curator.

When Niko and I finally got back to our apartment on St. Mark's Place, I was wishing I had that iron rod running bolted to her spine because I was teetering on the edge of exhaustion. Something to hold me up would've been nice. I yawned heavily. "You think what we saw in the park could be Sawney?"

Niko was stripping off his weapons onto the kitchen table. "I think we don't know enough to make suppositions. There are many creatures that could do what we saw. Perhaps even one not so powerful as to be responsible for the deaths of over a thousand people." He dropped his last blade onto the surface. "But to reintegrate from ash and bone, that would take enormous energy, enormous sustenance. And he wouldn't have had time to take the bodies with him, not when he was on the run."

"In other words, who the hell knows?"

"In other words," he confirmed with a quirk of his lips.

"It'd be nice if there was only one mass murderer to worry about. Hope springing eternal and all that shit. I'm grabbing a shower, then bed. I'm tired of smelling like a leaky keg."

"Convenient. I'm tired of smelling a leaky keg." He headed for his own bedroom, adding casually, "The bathroom is taken care of."

He never forgot, but he usually told me anyway, and it was always said as if it were perfectly natural to secure the bathroom like an enemy encampment. As if I didn't have one helluva weird phobia—even if it were a slowly resolving one.

When I went in, the bathroom mirror was covered with a towel just as he'd assured me. I knew Darkling was gone. He wasn't coming through any mirror ever again, but the fact that I could have a mirror in the apartment, even a covered one, was an accomplishment. The Auphe had stolen my body and tried to steal my mind. Darkling had possessed me and gobbled up my soul. Temporarily, thanks to some help from Niko and Robin, but it wasn't an experience you forgot. Or got over, not completely.

I knocked the glass through the towel and muttered, "Rot in hell, you bastard."

After the shower, I slept for about five hours and then staggered up. Niko and I had already discussed what our next move was. Or, rather, who it was. And at noon we hit Robin's place in Chelsea just as he was rolling out of bed.

He answered the door wearing silk pajama bottoms, an untied matching silk robe, and a shitload of morning cranky. Blinking in sleepy ill humor over a steaming cup of coffee, he mumbled, "Who . . . what . . ." Giving up, he snared a hand in his tangled curls and took a drink. Green eyes clearing with the addition of life-giving caffeine, he managed to get out an entire sentence. "Why? Why are you wretched creatures here at this hour even Apollo himself would spit upon?"

"We're here to pick your brain." I immediately flopped on his couch, an affair so massive that it could host an orgy. Hell, this was Robin we were talking about. Just go ahead, give the benefit of the doubt, and say it *had* hosted an orgy. "And by the way, Bob the doorman said the condo association shot down your idea of a condom machine on every floor."

"Puritan bastards," he muttered. "Even I, on occasion, run out." I wasn't sure why he used them to begin with. He couldn't get anyone pregnant. Pucks don't reproduce that way. In fact, I didn't know how they reproduced, and quite frankly, that was fine by me. As for the condom's other use . . . I wouldn't have thought Goodfellow would be too vulnerable to STDs . . . at least not the human kind. That train of thought led me to places my mind had no desire to go . . . vampire gonorrhea, glowing pixie herpes, who knew what the fuck else. As I hastily mentally kicked those thoughts to the curb, Robin closed the door behind Niko and waved a careless arm at the kitchen. "Coffee. Tea. There." With that eloquent invitation, he collapsed on the couch next to me and immediately dozed off. Miraculously, the coffee cup remained firmly upright and balanced.

I shook my head and flicked his earlobe. "Rise and shine, Sleeping Beauty."

"Talk about your worst lay ever," he murmured, and then swatted at my hand, leaving me with fiercely stinging fingers. "And I've yet to hear why you are ruining a perfectly good morning of postcoital lazing about."

"Sawney Beane," Niko announced as he leaned against the marble countertop that separated the kitchen from the living area. With arms folded, he ignored the burbling cappuccino machine and focused on Robin. "He may be back."

If we were expecting a big reaction, we were disappointed. Sighing, Goodfellow opened his eyelids to half-mast, grunted, and drank more coffee. "So," I said, relieved, "not such a bad thing, huh? Totally overrated, right? No way the son of a bitch ate a thousand people."

"A thousand?" he snorted. "Hardly. Six hundred most likely. Seven hundred tops."

Ah, shit.

I was about to drop my head in my hands when there was a rattle at the door—a very prolonged rattle. One that said "here I come" as clearly as if the person had shouted it through the door.

"Ah, my housekeeper," Robin said with amusement, rocketing to complete alertness in a heartbeat—the kind of alertness that seemed to spring straight from the son of a bitch's crotch. "Seraglio is reluctant to be a spectator to some of my more exotic entertainments. She doesn't seem to approve of nudity either, certainly not mine anyway." He put the coffee mug on the slab of rock crystal masquerading as a table and stood. "Considering her name means harem, that's rather curious, but to each her own. If one cannot appreciate the muse-inspired work of art that is my body . . ." He held his arms out to indicate the glory of it all. "Then I must respect their mental pathology and get on with my life."

He tied up his robe and flashed Seraglio a brilliant smile as she came through the door. It bounced off her impenetrable facade without effect. "You're looking . . . professional as always, ma'am. Why, the very air sparkles with your unmatched efficiency." He gave Niko and me a wink. "Seraglio has always made it very clear that compliments of a personal nature are not welcome and that she has four protective brothers who would be ecstatic to tutor me on the concept. So, as difficult as it is, I behave myself."

I could tell he thought it was a pity, though, as he watched her begin to work. With her flawless peach-colored skin, enormous ageless black eyes, and glossy dark hair that she wore piled high on her head, Seraglio was beautiful in all the ways there were to be beautiful. I would've guessed her to be thirty-five, but I could've been a decade off in either direction. She was also a little person, but not Goodfellow's kind of little person. She was a human one, barely four feet tall—medically speaking, a person with dwarfism. And if she wasn't proof positive that once in a while Mother Nature got something right, I didn't know what was.

"Why, are you looking at me, Mr. Fellows?" Her voice reminded me of orange blossom honey, Spanish moss, and the thorns of a wild blackberry bush. Georgia or somewhere down that way. We'd lived in a trailer park there once; I recognized the broad drawl and faded *R*s. Her words drifted over her shoulder as she bent over to retrieve cleaning supplies from the bottom half of the pantry. Robin's lips curved into a wicked grin as he watched her uniform pants pull taut over her rounded backside.

"No, ma'am," he lied gravely. "I would sooner pluck my own eyeballs out than show you such disrespect."

As I rolled mine, other skeptical ones pinned the puck. "Well, sir, if any assistance is needed in that area, you just let me know. I have ice tongs that would be just the thing," she offered matter-of-factly before turning back to her task. "Now, run along, children. I have work to do." A bejeweled hand flapped impatiently to hurry him and us on our way.

So we went elsewhere for the whole seven-hundred-tops discussion. After dressing, Robin decided lunch would be a great forum for cannibal tales and picked the restaurant, because after one three-ninety-nine buffet, he would never let me choose again. This place seemed interesting, though, and I let the thought of a tasty twenty-five-cent eggroll go. The restaurant didn't look too fancy from the outside, a few dingy windows and a faded striped awning, but the inside made up for it. The tables were old,

dark wood with mosaic tile tops, and the chairs . . .
they were just ugly as hell. With claw feet and worn
velvet seats, they looked like props from Count Dra-
cula's castle. From the ceiling hung several non-
matching chandeliers. Some were looping metal, some
whimsical blown glass, and some looked like they'd
been banged together by kindergartners with a lot of
enthusiasm and absolutely no talent. Everything in
the place did have one thing in common, though—it
was all old. Antique, and I could see how Robin
would like that.

He ordered for us, some dish called Tavuk Gogsu,
and then got down to business. "Turkish." He waved
off the waiter before Niko or I could even take a look
at the menu. "It's magnificent. Trust me. You'll bring
offerings to my altar in thanks. Now, what about
dusty old Sawney? Oh, and by the way, he wasn't a
cannibal, as he wasn't—"

"Human. Yes, we're now aware," Niko interjected.
"Promise's acquaintance at the museum filled us in
regarding that, at least that he wasn't human. She
didn't say precisely what he was."

"A Redcap," Robin said absently as he accepted a
drink from the returning waiter. "Try this. Kahlua,
soy, honey, very much like a mead I had in pre-Nero
Rome. Quite tasty."

Niko and I exchanged looks of tolerant resignation,
gave in, and drank. Robin operated on Goodfellow
time and mere humans, or human-Auphe hybrids,
couldn't change that. After a polite swallow, Niko
put his glass down. "Sawney's a Redcap? I didn't
know they were that powerful. And why the human-
style name?"

My own swallow barely made it down and I
pushed my glass away with a curled lip. Pre-Nero

Rome could keep that crap. "What's a Redcap? Some sort of goblin, right?"

"A Scottish-English legend," Niko elaborated. "They were said to murder travelers and then stain their caps with their victims' blood, hence Redcap."

"And once again, the folklore monkeys got it wrong. Caps stained with blood." Robin gave a foamy snort into his drink. "Yes, how frightening. A capering evil wearing a *hat*. Maybe he wears suspenders and short pants as well. Will the terror never end?"

"No caps, then?" Niko said mildly.

"No." He finished his glass and promptly reached for my discarded one. "They use the blood on their hair. They have this mess of twists and tangles, matted together with gore and stinking to high heaven. They're unpleasant, filthy, nasty creatures, but only dangerous to the unwary or simply stupid. However . . ." He tapped my now empty glass against his and frowned. "Sawney Beane was quite a different thing altogether. *Is* a different thing, I guess, if what you say is true and he has come back. That's quite the trick, and one I wasn't aware he was capable of. I'm still doubtful." Sighing, he leaned back and linked fingers across his stomach. "Besides, what he was capable of was more than enough to begin with. As for the human name, who knows? Familiarity? They deal with humans. Fool humans. Eat humans." He shrugged.

"Then the legend of Sawney Beane as we know it is mostly true?" Niko was flipping the serving knife from wrist to palm and back again. Lunch was no excuse to let a practicing opportunity pass by. "He and his incestuous clan robbed and murdered travelers during the fifteenth century. They dragged their victims back to their cave in Bannane Head, hung them from hooks, dismembered them, and ate them. You put the body count a few hundred lower, but do the basic facts hold true?"

"Except for the incest." Goodfellow beamed at the waiter who had chosen that particular moment to appear with our food. "They're brothers," he said to the server, shaking his head woefully. "I tell them that close is good, family is good, but don't be so quick to limit your options."

I lashed out with my foot, but only succeeded in banging the shit out of my toes on his chair leg. Both Robin and Niko gave me a look of disappointment— Robin's mock and Niko's more genuine. "Later we spar in the park," my brother ordered. "If we can find you a worthy opponent from the playground."

By that time the waiter had made his escape, the lucky bastard, and Robin continued. "Redcaps aren't into incest. That was a typical human soap opera addition, because mass murder and cannibalism simply weren't juicy enough."

I swirled a fork through the pale mound on my plate dubiously as he went on. "In reality, Redcaps don't much care for one another's company. Loathe each other. The male and the female even more so. Consequently, they have the quickest mating habits one could possibly imagine. In, out, handshake, see you next year—this is how much they hate one another. Which is what made Sawney so unique. He brought over forty Redcaps together. They killed together, dwelled together, and didn't try to eat each other during it all . . . astounding." He took another bite.

"And what of the rest of the legend?" Niko asked, ignoring his food for the moment. "How they came to their end."

"Half true. In the original, the women and children were burned and the men bled to death after having their hands and feet chopped off. In reality there were no women or children. They were only male Redcaps and the humans burned them all. I heard that Sawney, as their leader, was given special attention and burned separately. If his remains were gathered and put in a cask, then I suppose that was true." Unfazed by the subject matter, he continued to make his way through lunch with enthusiasm.

"How the hell did a bunch of humans manage to capture and kill these guys?" I finally broke down and took a bite of the weird stuff in front of me. It looked and smelled like chicken pudding. That's what it tasted like as well, but cinnamon sweet. It wasn't half bad.

"How did they manage?" He gave a little shrug. "They had an army. Literally. If you have some bizarre fascination with taking up with where they left off, you're a few short."

"Even counting you?" Niko had gone back to playing with the knife. Palm to the back of the wrist, back of the wrist to palm. The waiters were watching the show from across the restaurant—some giving silent whistles in awe at the sight, some looking a little perturbed.

"I'd advise you not to get ahead of yourself," Robin said with a jaundiced air. "Is anyone offering to pay you to chase after what may end up only being a phantom? Anyone? Hello?" He cupped a hand to his ear. "What? No answer? Quel surprise."

"And if this is real? If Sawney is back . . . if he

isn't the phantom you hope, what do you advise then?" Niko countered, flipping the knife to tap the table lightly with its handle.

Robin went back to working on his meal. "Perhaps he'll be dieting. He is older now. Age wages hell on the waistline." He looked up to see Niko's patient eyes on him. "Oh, fine," he grumbled. "I don't have any further information on Sire Beane, but I have a friend who may—Wahanket. Well, friend is rather a strong term . . . an acquaintance. He tends to gather facts, has a desiccated finger in many a pie." He added smugly, "I do know people."

"Yeah, you know people," I commented sourly, remembering another of his informants, Abbagor, who'd tried to kill us . . . twice. "Too many god-damn people."

Wahanket, though, turned out to not be nearly as bad as Abbagor. Equally as freaky, but nowhere near as homicidal. And he lived in the museum we'd left only hours ago, which made him more likely than anyone to know about Sawney and his Great Escape.

The Eight-sixth Street station was starting to seem awfully familiar. After exiting and walking over to Fifth Avenue, we were back where we'd started. The Met was packed when we walked in. There were drifting couples, hordes of tourists from every country imaginable, people wandering alone, and a school group of screaming rug rats from hell. They must've left their indoor voices on the bus; even the empty suits of armor looked pained as they thundered by. We kept moving past them as Goodfellow murmured something about the lost art of child sacrifices. In one wing, he stopped before a bust with blind marble eyes and the sneer of white stone lips. "Caligula, you dumb son of a bitch." He shook his head. "I told him horses weren't the monogamous kind, but did he listen? No, not for a second. Insanity, tyranny, and one screwed-up love life, that was Little Boots for you." He sighed, "Threw some great parties, though."

Shrugging off the nostalgia, he led us to a corridor off the exhibit hall, and that in turn led to another corridor and a locked door marked AUTHORIZED PER-SONNEL ONLY. Niko offered, "I'm sure Sangrida Odinsdóttir would be able to provide us with a key."

"Please. You insult me." Robin slid a bright green glance back over his shoulder as he slipped a kit of small metal tools from his pocket. "Not that that can't be arousing in certain situations."

Niko had left the restaurant knife behind and wasn't practicing with any of his at the moment, but the shimmer of metal was embodied in the minute rise of his eyebrows all the same. "No fun," Robin muttered and got back to the job at hand. "An entire absence of revelry whatsoever."

Within seconds we were on stairs and heading downward into the gloom. The steps ended in a rabbit warren of storerooms. "Wahanket or Hank as I like to call him used to be up top, mixing and mingling, so to speak, but eventually he was shuffled off down here with the other passé exhibits. I think he much prefers it here. Dark, cramped, musty . . . much more like home."

"Where the hell was home?" I turned sideways to move between a row of crates. "A gopher hole?"

"Not quite." Robin had produced a small flashlight and switched it on. Either the overheads didn't work or his friend wasn't into a lot of light. We moved along and entered an open area encircled by a Stone-

henge of piled crates. There weren't any signs of hab-
itation, but that's where he stopped, voice echoing
in the empty area, "Hank? You up for a visit?" he
called cheerfully.

There was a long stretch of silence, and then a
sibilant hiss, dry as dust and abrading as sand, came
out of the darkness. "A long time, Peter Pan. It has
been a long time, long time."

"Get the guy a VCR and some Disney movies and
this is the thanks I receive," Goodfellow grunted.
"I've brought friends, Hank. Let's reduce my emas-
culation in front of them and call me Pan, shall we?"

A brown figure materialized out of the dark into
the dim white light of the flashlight. He seemed to be
made entirely of sticklike bones and resin-hardened
bandages. A gaping pit of a nose and empty eye
sockets were all that could be seen of his face. He
looked like the title villain from every bad mummy
movie I'd watched when I was a little kid, come to
life. But he wasn't slow like they were. He wasn't
slow at all. He slipped in and out of the thick shadows, scorpion-quick and snake-silent. It was the cowboy hat, though, that was the crowning touch. I
wondered if Sangrida knew about her squatter. Or
knew that he was raiding the . . .

"The lost and found, eh, Hank?" Robin settled on
a crate and tilted his head. "It's a good look for you.
Very rugged."

Covetous fingers of nut-brown bone touched the
brim of the cowboy hat. "It is a crown for a king."
There was a gaping grin of blackened stubs that revealed a leathery curl of tongue and the taut ligaments of a disintegrating jaw.

The thing was it should have been funny, a
mummy called Hank wearing a cowboy hat, but we

were looking at what was basically a corpse made of jerky. Not beef, mind you, but human jerky. Not funny. You could've dressed him in drag and it still wouldn't have been funny. Like roadkill dressed in a tutu. It was spooky and more than a little repulsive.

"The closest you got to a king in ye olden dynasties was stealing their dusty mummified genitals to make your potions," the puck scoffed before promptly contradicting himself. He was never one to let logic interfere with a good insult. "Niko, Cal, this is Hank . . . Wahanket. He's a scholar, like they used to make them in the day when knowledge translated to power. He was the high priest of some cranky Egyptian god or another. He was also the teacher of a minor pharaoh or two. Or five or six. Maybe even ten or twelve. Only Hank knows for sure how many dynasties he pulled the strings on, and he's not telling." He clucked his tongue reprovingly at the stinginess of it. "I don't believe he was ever human, although he's not telling that either. But he's the only walking, talking mummy I've come across in my lifetime. The human ones just tend to lie there like a bad date."

Wahanket's jaw snapped shut rigidly and a yellow glow roiled to life in the hollow eye sockets of the brittle skull. It wasn't a sunny light—more like the luminescence of a creeping cave creature. Dim, flickering, and *cold*. I could hear a buzz vibrating his throat—it could've been the rattle of petrified vocal cords or a plague of enraged locusts swarming from within the hollow cavity of his chest. I didn't have the slightest urge to know which.

"What have you brought me, Pan?" came the displeased rasp. "Where are your offerings? Lest I find you most unworthy, lay them before me."

"Offerings, eh? Once again, I steer the subject back to dusty, unused genitals." Goodfellow's heel kicked the crate and the beam of his flashlight danced over my face mockingly.

"Shut the fuck up, Loman," I snapped. I'd used the name for him from the beginning. Although Goodfellow was a much better salesman than Willy Loman had ever been, it was a good name for him . . . mostly because it pissed him off. Much, say, as he was pissing me off now.

"We are here for a reason," Niko reminded us both, his patience a little less than it had been in the restaurant. "And I'm sure that Wahanket has better things to do than entertain us. So let us move things along. Now."

"Fine, fine. I would think regular vampire nookie would mellow you out, but apparently not," Robin mumbled as he doffed the strap of his shoulder and dug the "offering" out of its black leather case. It was a laptop, the very latest with all the bells, whistles, and technophile crap that you could possibly want. That's what Wahanket was, the puck had said, a technophile of the highest order. If it was bright, shiny, and it plugged in, then he wanted it, and thanks to the seekers of his info, had it. "The latest and the greatest, O Son of the Sun. Its RAM is as plentiful as the waters of the Nile," he promised, flashing that blinding salesman smile. Pure shark. No bark, all bite.

Greedy claws snatched it up and began to examine it. "Ahhh, how can one worship gold and jewels when the knowledge within this makes you unto a god?"

"Yeah, that's great," I said dismissively. "Enjoy. So, what do you know about Sawney Beane? Ate a

lot of people, was supposed to be dead. He was upstairs, now he's not. What's going on?''

"Sawney Beane." The seething eye sockets looked
up from the computer. "Six hundred and eighty-
seven humans consumed. For a Redcap, mildly impressive. But reconstituting from bone and ash . . .
ah. That is quite impressive indeed. Pity there were
no security guards between him and the way out
or it could have been six hundred and eighty-nine.
Crawling back from one's molecular shore must cre-
ate a prodigious appetite." The fragments of teeth
clicked together. "Unbelievably prodigious."

I had a feeling he was speaking from personal
experience . . . personal hunger. "It was him, then?"
Niko verified. "Sawney has returned?"

"Yessss." The wheeze carried with it a scent that
drifted across the space . . . it was full of desert
heat and spice. It sounded pleasant; it wasn't. It was
repugnant, floating over dry rot and out of the empty
carapace of a long-dead cockroach. The cockroach
might still be walking and talking, but there was
nothing in there but the stink of death. Stuff it to the
brim with all the myrrh and fucking oregano you
wanted; it wasn't going to change a thing. Dead
was dead.

"Sawney is gone and Sawney is here and soon
things will become more interesting in this city of
gloom." Ligaments stretched and popped to accom-
modate the predatory gape of jaw. "Exceedingly
more interesting."

Bodies in trees, dead girls with empty eyes and
mouthfuls snatched from their flesh—if that was interesting, I could do without it.

4

We survived the mummy without a scratch. When dealing with an informant of Goodfellow's, that was an accomplishment. Robin knew pretty much everyone, and when you cast a net that wide, you're going to scoop up some crazies, some killers, and, if you were really lucky, a happy combo of the two. Compared to that crowd, Wahanket was practically serving up supper down at the Mission. He hadn't tried to mutilate, kill, or eat us. In my book, that made him good people. Creepy, dead, weird as hell with the hat, and not too fragrant, but good people all the same. Granted, he seemed anxious to see what havoc Sawney was going to wreak, but, hell, he was a monster, and for a monster, that was serious restraint.

It didn't make me any less glad to show him my backside. There's only so much talk of genital stealing you can hear before, damn, it's time to go. And this basement . . . there was something about it. If you stood still and closed your eyes, New York would fade away. There would be low guttural chanting, a choking lack of air, and the desperate scrape of fingernails against bloody desert stone. Wahanket had made this place his own, and it wasn't a place where I wanted to spend a lot of time. Unfortunately, it didn't work out that way.

We were three rooms away from the stairs when Niko and Robin stopped simultaneously with weapons drawn. That's when I heard it too: the faintest unidentifiable rustle. I might not know what it was, but I did know what it wasn't—it wasn't human. There was no aftershave, no shampoo or soap, no wool or synthetics—no people smell at all. Not fresh anyway. There were thousands of other smells down here . . . animal, plant, mineral. Some strong, some not, and no way to tell which was packed away in a box and which was out and moving around.

With the hundreds of crates, it was close quarters for my gun and I drew my knife. It wasn't a sword, but at twelve jagged inches it was close enough. "Is the flashlight just a special effect," I asked Robin, "or do the lights work down here?"

"In this section, no. Wahanket disables them on a routine basis." Goodfellow had placed the flashlight on a dust-coated, empty display case and cautiously stepped away from it to keep from giving away his position in the darkness. Niko moved several steps in the other direction, and using his free hand on the top edge, vaulted onto a five-foot-tall crate.

And he immediately came crashing back down under several hundred pounds of scales and surging muscle. For one brief second, I saw the snapping of dinosaur-sized jaws, the flare of orange eyes in the glow of the stationary flashlight. I saw a yellowed ivory grin.

Then reality slid into place, and I slid with it, sinking my blade into the eye of the writhing monstrosity on top of Niko. Not a dinosaur—hell, the Met didn't even have dinosaurs—but something just as horrific in its own right. It was a serpent, the size of a man and half again as long, with the powerful legs and feet of a jungle cat. The inky black of its underbelly was spotted with the palest finger smudges of gold, and it blended into the darkness so efficiently that once it flowed off Niko, it disappeared instantly. But first, there was the grate of its bony eye socket against my knife as it ripped its massive head off the blade, the twist of a heavy tail that slammed me against a crate several feet away, and a steam-whistle screech that had my ears ringing.

"Caliban?"

I could see only the faintest smear above me, a pale oval to go with Robin's distant call of my name. I blinked. It didn't improve things any. If anything, it made things worse. Orange, black, gold—a hurricane rush, and then the oval and the voice were gone. It was just me and the darkness. Shit. I tried rolling over. Once, twice, three times was the charm. Three times was also a faceful of floor, but it was still progress. I managed to get my hands under me and push up. I was halfway there when a hand under my arm boosted me the rest of the way.

Nik. I steadied myself with a hand on his shoulder, then pulled it back when I felt the wet warmth. "Shit. You okay?"

"It's not mine. Have some faith, little brother." He'd vanished under something that could've been a baby T. rex, showed up dripping with blood, and I was supposed to have faith. I looked at my hand briefly before wiping it on my jeans. It was hard to tell with only the reflected glow of the flashlight, but the liquid on my skin looked pale gold, not red. That, more than Niko's denial, halted the twist in my gut.

"Where's Robin?" My knife was at the base of the crate I'd impacted and I moved to retrieve it.

"I think it took him." He was already moving, following spatters of the monster's blood, and I came up hard on his heels. We were silent from that moment on. It would probably hear us coming nonetheless, but we didn't have to make it easy for it . . . because we would find it. We would get Goodfellow back. This was nothing compared to the shit we'd all gone through together. A big lizard—a pissed-off giant gecko. So what? Hell, Robin would make a belt out of it by the time we caught up.

Boxes and boxes, a labyrinth of them every which way I turned. I clipped several as we ran. We'd left the flashlight behind. It would give us away quicker than my nose would. There was some light now—small emergency lights up in the corner juncture of ceiling and wall. Hank hadn't gotten to these yet, but they were dim enough to do more harm than good. They created impenetrable pits of black shadow that looked as thick and sticky as tar and just as capable of sucking us into suffocating depths. They'd make good places for a serpent to hide and wait for its next meal to wander by.

Or to leave what was left of its last one.

I saw his sword then, lying on the floor half in and half out of the shadow. Robin didn't treat his weapons with the reverence Niko did, but neither did he discard them carelessly like trash. "Niko?" I said grimly.

"I see it." He disappeared into the blackness to investigate, and I kept following the blood. As I passed a stagecoach, fake trees, and a massive stuffed bear, the spatters turned into an unbroken trail.

"Follow the Yellow Brick Road," I muttered as I

careened around a corner into the next room, slipped, and nearly fell in a lake of lizard fluid. It stretched almost seven feet across and was still flowing sluggishly from the belly of the serpent. Minute tremors ran under the scaled hide, but it lay on its side with its mouth open and unmoving. The remaining eye stared at nothing as a putrid stench began to seep from the hundreds of slices that bisected the stomach.

There were leaves in the blood, courtesy of the fake trees stored nearby. A bright and artificial green, they floated serenely on the golden surface. It was a bizarrely peaceful and strangely beautiful scene, and I hovered warily on the edge of it. "Robin?" The serpent was still alive . . . dying, yeah, but there was life in it yet. And it only took an ounce of life to make a ton of murderous purpose capable of impossible vengeance. No one likes to go out alone, not even snakes. "Goodfellow?" He was there somewhere. Had to be. What could possibly kill that smug, vain, irritating son of a bitch? "Robin, where the fuck are—"

"Here."

He slipped out of the night forest of fake trees to my right. Like Niko, he was covered in blood that wasn't his own. It stained his expensive clothes, slicked the equally expensive haircut, and coated the blade he carried. He'd lost the one, but he had others—which was why he'd lived so long and why he was still here right now. "Christ." I scowled instantly, shoving the relief down. "I thought your worthless ass was a footnote. Ancient history."

"From a sirrush?" He sluiced a handful of yellow fluid from his face and slung it to the floor. If that hand shook, he would claim it was from exertion. Considering how many slashes had been needed to take down the lizard, it might even be the truth. "Do you mock me? On my best day, I could take on an entire nest of them and barely work up a sweat. I might even have time to squeeze in a margarita and massage, happy ending of course."

He was still talking, but I'd stopped listening. It wasn't only monster blood after all. There was red mixed in with the gold. Puck red. "Robin?"

Stopping in midsentence, he met my gaze and followed it to the red staining his shirt and pants. "Ah. Yes." His sword dropped from his hand as he swayed slightly. "Not exactly as gentle as a cat with her kitten, was it?"

It had carried him away, either in a clawed grip or in its massive mouth. Definitely not gentle. I didn't carry the first aid supplies Niko did, and I wasn't as good with them either. I took Goodfellow's arm to keep him upright and turned my head to call for my brother. I didn't get the opportunity.

Impossible vengeance, and here it came.

Goodfellow had called it a sirrush. That sounded like something that could fly. This one didn't have wings, so in reality it couldn't. But it soared through the air regardless. With the same grace and power as a spring-propelled cougar, it catapulted toward us. I only had the time to get the impression of a kaleidoscope of teeth, claws, and scales before it was on us. The wounded can be dangerous—the dying can be almost invincible. There was no time for a blade. No time for a gun. There was time for only one thing.

I built the gateway. In the past, I'd created them several feet away . . . made for walking through. This one I built *around* us. I'd never done that before. I'd barely built a handful of gates in my life, and trying something new wasn't the brightest thing to do. It was the boldest, though, and bold was all that could save us now. Gray light outlined us, a tarnished and tainted silver glimmer. I felt the turn in my stomach, the burn at the base of my skull, the twist of reality, and then we were one room back. Behind Niko. And ahead of him came the sound of the sirrush slamming into the wall where we had been standing a fraction of a second ago.

"*Skata*," Robin gurgled at my side before he hit the floor. I would've held him up, if I could've stayed up myself. As the gateway popped out of existence, I went down as well. While Goodfellow fell flat, I managed to stop my descent at my knees. My head was a tight ball of agony and my face felt warm and wet. I swiped at it and came away with a blood-coated hand. I'd learned some control over the traveling several months ago when facing down George's and Niko's kidnapper, but I hadn't made a gate since. It didn't come as easily as I remembered . . . not that it had been easy before, but it hadn't hurt. It had nauseated and terrified but it hadn't hurt. It hurt now.

I felt the warmth at my ears too. From nose and ears, I was apparently a faucet and that couldn't be good. "Cal." I looked up from my dripping hand to see Niko's face before mine. It was a little blurry—not quite double vision, but almost. The sirrush was blurry as well . . . blurry, enraged, and coming toward us. A little more slowly now, but still coming.

Niko heard it before I had a chance to open my mouth to warn him. Flashing a hand under my jacket, he pulled my gun, whirled, and fired. Two shots careened off the skull, but seven more went through the remaining eye with exquisite precision.

Niko wasn't particularly fond of guns—he felt they lacked grace and technique—but that didn't mean he wasn't good with one. If it could kill, Niko knew how to use it and use it well. The sirrush went down when the bullets hit, and this time it stayed down.

My weapon was reholstered smoothly, and Niko continued calmly. "You're a mess."

There was no arguing with that. "Yeah," I verified, and wiped at my face again, this time using my sleeve. Leather wasn't good at sopping up blood and I could feel it smear things to a much worse degree. "Robin's worse." A sick groan from the floor confirmed it.

"Don't do that again." The puck curled on his side and gave a nasty dry heave. Apparently, it was less his wounds and more a profound case of motion sickness. "Don't ever, *ever* do that again."

"Right. Being eaten would've been better. What was I thinking?" My knees decided enough was enough and I sat hard on my ass. Dropping my head in my hands, I clenched my fingers at my temples and aimed a muffled query at Niko. "Tylenol? Aspirin? Morphine?"

"Head?" I felt his fingers below my ears, checking the flow of blood. I didn't nod. I couldn't begin to imagine what that would feel like, but it wouldn't be pleasant. Luckily, Niko didn't need the confirmation. While one hand rested lightly on the back of my neck, he used the other to pull out his cell phone. Within seconds he was informing Sangrida Odinsdóttir that she had a dead sirrush in her basement as well as two wounded warriors and he would appreciate whatever help she could offer that fell short of a trip to Valhalla.

A half hour later we were back at Niko's and my

apartment courtesy of Sangrida's private car. By that
time, Goodfellow could walk, more or less, and I'd
stopped bleeding. The headache hadn't eased any,
though, and I let Niko lead me along as I covered
my eyes with my hand. The thin glow of the hallway
light was suddenly a hundred times worse than staring directly at the sun, and it felt like molten lava
pouring directly into my eyes to fry my brain with
laser thoroughness.

Inside our place, Niko steered me to the couch,
pulled the blinds, and turned off the lights. "I'll dress
Robin's wounds in my bedroom. Rest."

As a sign of how truly miserable he felt, Goodfellow didn't have a word, rapaciously sexual or otherwise, to say about being in Niko's bedroom. Fifteen
minutes later Nik was back to settle onto the couch
beside me. I'd slid and slouched down enough that
my head rested against the back of the sofa and my
legs sprawled wide. "Robin?" I asked, turning my
head cautiously to look at him.

"It wasn't as bad as it appeared at first glance.
Several penetrating claw wounds to his arms and
legs, but they're fairly clean. No ripping. I believe
traveling with you through your gateway affected
him more. Pucks don't take well to it is my guess."
He handed me a wet washcloth for my face. I'd
cleaned it up as best I could in the car using the front
of my shirt . . . just enough to get me into our building without people stopping to donate money to the
axe-maniac survivor fund.

"Probably no one does." I scrubbed at my face,
careful not to jostle my head too much. If it weren't
for my Auphe half, the nausea I felt when opening
and traveling through the gate would be a helluva
lot more debilitating. "No one normal."

Niko frowned, a slight downturn of tightened lips. "You know better." He'd spent a lifetime, mine at least, telling me that I was normal, that I wasn't Auphe, wasn't a monster. Though he could save my life, my sanity, and everything in between, it was the one thing he couldn't fix, couldn't change. But I'd finally come to realize that as long as I could remain *who* I was, I could survive what I was. It was only bad genes. Alcoholism gene, cancer gene, monster gene, choose your poison and work around it. Thanks to Niko, I was doing that. And when I faltered in that belief, he was there to kick my butt back on the path.

I dropped the washcloth on my leg. In the past opening a gate would drain me, exhaust me. Goodfellow had once said that he thought that would pass with practice. He was right. I was tired, damn tired, but not like I had been in the past. But the headache . . . shit. What the hell was with that? And the blood? The last time I'd used the ability months ago, I'd opened a gate and *kept* it open for nearly a half hour. Maybe a full-blooded Auphe could do that with ease, but I didn't think so. Ripping a hole in the world or between worlds—it wasn't something meant to be long-term. "I think I broke something." I grimaced, massaging my forehead with the heel of my hand.

Niko picked up the cloth and pulled my hand back down to fold my fingers around the damp material. Steering it to the area on my jaw by my ear, he released me and agreed, "I think you may have." He waited until I'd wiped at my skin again for a few seconds, then took the bloody cloth from me and put it aside. "Or strained it. How is the headache? Improved any?"

We'd thrown some Tylenol at it. We may as well have thrown it down the toilet and flushed. "It'll pass," I evaded. "On the plus side, I can still hear." Through the open door in the hall came a nasal snore more suited to a constipated moose than a puck. "But on the downside, I can still hear."

"You didn't rupture your eardrums, then. Do they still hurt as well?"

"Let's write off the entire area above the neck. It'll save some time." I knew what he was thinking. CAT scans, MRIs, all the things that weren't possible for me. Our mother, Sophia, had never been one for doctors or anything that cost money. We got our shots at whatever local clinic we were living near at the time, but only because the schools demanded it. If I got hurt or Niko got sick, we toughed it out. And when we were older, Niko and I had come to the realization that hospitals . . . any place with imaging equipment, any place that would want blood tests . . . were out. I was human on the outside, but it might not be the same on the inside. We'd eventually met a healer and when he'd found out the truth about me, he'd confirmed it. I was different. Subtly, but noticeably different. I didn't ask how. I didn't want to know.

The bottom line was, no hospitals for me. And as our healer hadn't answered his phone in a while, we had to make do. This was another make-do situation.

"No more gates, Cal," Niko said uncompromisingly. "None."

"Maybe if I give it a few months," I hedged. I didn't like opening them. It only reminded me of a part of myself I'd sooner forget. But there was no denying that if you had your back to a wall with a giant serpent leaping at you, it came in handy.

"It's been several months already." He stood and headed into the kitchen. "Next time it might be your brain that comes out of your ears. I'd like to avoid that." Returning, he handed me a soft pack from the freezer. "Although it would be proof there was something in your skull besides laziness and inept swordsmanship skills."

With the pack covering my eyes and the cold seeping through, I relaxed minutely. "You forgot my blinding charisma and stunning popularity."

This time he didn't play along. "No more gates, Cal. I mean it."

I gave in for the moment, peering out from under the pack at him, but I had a feeling I was making a promise I couldn't keep. More honestly, didn't intend to keep. "Okay. No more gates." I'd survived nearly my whole life without them, but there was no denying that an emergency exit like that could save my life. Something to think about . . . maybe later when Nik wasn't studying me so suspiciously. Sliding down another few inches, I pulled the pack back in place and waited for the cold to kick in and lessen the headache. "Robin said it was a sirrush, whatever the hell that is. So, what was it doing in the basement trying to eat us? Do you think Wahanket sent it after us? That'd be about par for the fucking course with Goodfellow's buddies."

"I asked him while dressing the puncture wounds. He said no, that it wasn't Wahanket's 'style.' "

"But did the wizened son of a bitch *know* it was there?" I pressed.

"That, Robin said, would be entirely his style," Niko said sardonically. "And a sirrush is a Babylonian creature—part snake, part cat. Why it was hunting in the basement of the Met is anyone's guess."

"Everyone makes it to the Big Apple sooner or later, huh? See the sights." The cold was beginning to work, easing the pain somewhat, and I yawned. "The Valkyrie going to pay us for the extermination on the side?"

"I've always enjoyed your sunny optimism, little brother."

I was glad someone did.

5

As much as I hated kidnapping cases, I wasn't a whole lot fonder of the extermination ones, but work was work, and money was money. And truthfully, extermination came up about as often as kidnapping did. Where's the cool factor in that? No-damn-where. We'd also done babysitting, and babysitting something that can eat you if you try to give it a time-out makes exterminating a fun gig by comparison. Usually. Mostly. On the whole.

Other times you just get screwed.

And that morning we ended up so very, very screwed. After three hours out on Staten Island, we'd taken the ferry back to Manhattan and made our way home with clothes singed and hair covered in bird shit all courtesy of an Aitvaras, otherwise known as a demonic chicken from hell. A fire-breathing, crap-slinging half rooster, half serpent that weighed all of sixty pounds had nearly served our asses to us on a silver platter. It'd also burned down one-third of the house of our less than completely satisfied client. And a less than completely satisfied gargoyle isn't a pretty sight. A satisfied one isn't either for that matter, but they hawk up less granite-sprinkled phlegm when paying the bill.

After cleaning up and changing, we jumped on the 6 train and headed up to Promise's penthouse for some brainstorming. I tended to not be so good at that type of thing, but I sucked it up. And there was food there. That always helped. Promise had a turkey and bacon club sandwich for me and some sort of vegetable soy cheese thing for Niko along with an antioxidant carrot-cranberry juice mixture. I could smell the healthiness of it from across the table and gave an internal *blech*. Taking a huge bite of my sandwich, I wondered who made the food. I never saw a cook there, but the thought of a vampire slaving over a skillet wasn't an image I could wrap my mind around. Especially an extremely wealthy vampire. They did eat food, though apparently not very much, along with massive doses of iron and some kind of other supplements, but Promise making a casserole? Nope, couldn't see it.

Niko took a drink of his red-orange stuff, ignored the face I made, and then said, "Sawney can't go on the way he has. He's going to be noticed. The police will certainly suspect a serial killer at some point. Although there's been nothing in the paper about the bodies in the park." He frowned, puzzled. Niko didn't like to be puzzled either. It tended to interfere with things like surviving. "They've disappeared, apparently." Puzzlement could also lead to annoyance when you were as anal-retentive as my brother, but he tucked it out of sight and went on. "But that's a mystery for another time. It's not the fifteenth century anymore and eventually Sawney will realize he can't just kill whoever he wants. Once he settles on a territory, he'll be even more wary. He won't want that home to be found and I think he'll start to go after victims who won't be missed."

"Like those that don't have families to raise a stink with the police." I chased a bite of sandwich with Coke. About as un-antioxidant as you could get and I was damn happy about that.

"Such as the homeless." Promise sat down next to Nik at the polished dining room table. An actual dining room in NYC, could you believe it? "But how would we track something such as that?"

"Goodfellow would say I had the clothes for the undercover work," I snorted. "But those guys aren't so trusting of strangers, I'll bet. And, hell, it's New York. How would we cover all of the city asking if any of them had disappeared? There's no way."

"True." Niko pushed his plate away, finished. "There's the shelters, the encampments, the streets themselves. There's bound to be gossip among them if there have been disappearances, but as you say, they're not going to talk to us."

"A big waste of our time and for nada." I was still hungry and eyed what was left on Niko's plate. Nah, I wasn't *that* hungry. Then I had an idea . . . it happened occasionally . . . and it wasn't from any antioxidant crap making my brain cells sit up and take notice either.

"Hey, I know a guy." I leaned back in my chair. "Ham. He comes into the bar sometimes and plays the sax. Just for kicks. He doesn't get paid or anything, but he's damn good. He says he plays the subways and streets too. Not that he needs to from the looks of him. Wears some pretty flashy clothes."

"And if he plays the subways and the streets, he may be familiar with some of the homeless." Promise gave a nod of approval, wrapping a string of dusk-colored pearls around a finger.

"If he's amenable to helping us. Not too many are." He was right. A human and a half Auphe weren't going to ever win any popularity contests. "What exactly is he?" Niko asked.

I frowned. "I don't have a clue. He looks human. Doesn't smell human, but he seems okay. Drinks whiskey, plays the sax, has a thing for pretty women, especially vampires . . . seems fairly laid-back to me." And considering what I'd done to a few customers that had pissed me off, that was saying something, not to mention my automatic suspicion of anyone I first met. "I don't know how the hell we'd get in touch with him, though. He comes and goes at the bar. Sometimes I won't see him for weeks. There's no predicting it."

"Perhaps Ishiah knows his last name," Niko suggested.

Nonhumans didn't have last names or if they did I hadn't run into one. "You're kidding. And so what if he did?"

Nik shook his head. "One idea and your brain shuts down for the day. It is a pity." He went on to explain, "If he is that good a sax player, he probably plays at clubs as well. And if he plays at clubs, I imagine he'd want to be available for gigs." He gave that faint smile of his. "In other words, he'd be in the book."

Jeez, the phone book. Maybe there was something to that carrot-cranberry juice after all. "I'll give Ish a call."

Luckily he was at the bar, and he did know Ham's last name. I didn't need any brain cells at all to think it was maybe more than coincidence. "Piper," I said after shutting off the phone. "Now, I know I'm no genius, Einstein." I gave Niko a mock glare. "But even I can guess that one."

"The Pied Piper of Hamelin." Niko stood and began to clear his dishes. "If nothing else, this should be interesting."

Ham was in the book and home when I called. He remembered me fine and said in a deep, mellow voice to come on over. If I worked for Ishiah, then I was good in his book. He gave me the address: Park Slope in Brooklyn. I winced, knowing we had a transfer at Fifty-third Street and a ride on the F train to look forward to.

When we arrived, he opened the door and immediately gave a blinding smile . . . to Promise. Niko and I were waved in absently. "If I'd known you were bringing such a fine lady with you," he said cheerfully, "I'd have cleaned up some."

The place wasn't that messy. There were a few instruments lying around, two saxes and a guitar, and a couple of flashy suit jackets tossed over a chair and the couch. Dark red, bright blue, and the most subtle one, brown with finger-width neon yellow stripes. I looked away before my retinas were burned out of my eyes and took a look at the rest of the place. It was a loft, bigger than a musician should've been able to afford, and painted . . . never mind how it was painted. It made the suits look like pastels in comparison.

"Pull up a cushion." He tossed one jacket to join the others, his eyes still on Promise. He was a tall, thin black man with unusually pale brown eyes. He kept his hair in short dreds and was dressed casually in a shirt patterned in a mixture of black and dark green and black pants. It was nice to give my eyes a break from the rest of the place and I kept them on him.

"Hey, Ham, thanks for talking to us."

He patted the couch for Promise, giving her another wide smile before turning to Nik and me. "No problem. Like I said, if Ishiah lets you work in the Circle, then you're good by me. He's not one for slackers or troublemakers."

Unless you happened to be a friend of Robin's, because I fell in both of those categories. But I kept my mouth shut on that and got to the point. "There's this thing in town." It damn sure didn't qualify as anything else. "A Redcap. Sawney Beane. He's been killing some people and we'd like to chat the bastard up." Chat with a sword, a gun, a cannon . . . whatever it took.

"With his history, 'some people' will soon become many people and we'd like to stop that before it happens," Niko added.

It was a tricky subject. There were monsters and then there were nonhumans. Monsters ate people and nonhumans didn't—they just lived their lives. There were crossovers sometimes. A wolf could be either or. I knew both kinds. Some others qualified as well. No matter what Promise said about vamps and their vitamins, you couldn't tell me there wasn't the occasional rogue out there bleeding people for all they were worth. But the tricky part was that some nonhumans had a policy of keeping their mouths shut. The way they saw it, they weren't going to get between a monster and his meal. That was dangerous, maybe deadly, and not their job.

It was ours, though.

The smile faded as he sat down beside Promise,

slinging a casual arm on the top of the couch behind her. Great. Another Goodfellow. I didn't check to see if Niko was jealous. If he was, he wouldn't show it anyway, but I doubted he was. He trusted Promise, five dead husbands aside. And if he trusted her, then she deserved it. Niko didn't often make mistakes when it came to trust. "Sawney Beane. I heard that son of a bitch was dead a long time ago."

"He was. He's back. And if you do not remove that arm, I will. Permanently," Promise said coolly.

It wasn't the type of thing to build up goodwill and useful conversation, but I didn't much blame her. Ham only flashed a smile and pulled the arm back. "No harm in trying. Didn't know one of these pups was yours." No harm, no foul. If he was the Pied Piper, we were pups to him. "That'd be the only thing that'd have you resisting my skills."

"Yes, of course that's the reason," she said dryly.

Niko steered the subject back. "We were thinking that soon enough Sawney will begin to prey on the homeless. They're more vulnerable in that they'll be less likely to be missed. He was burned at the stake once. I doubt he'll want to risk getting caught again."

"We thought you might know a few of the guys from the subways and the streets. All kinds of people hang around to hear you play at the bar. I figured it wouldn't be much different on the streets."

"Yeah, people have always lined up to hear me play." The smile was more sly than friendly now. "And for professional jobs I always get paid. One way or another."

Such as having children follow his piping out of a town some six or seven hundred years ago when he got stiffed on a job he'd done on their rat problem. But he did give the kids back once he got paid. So the story went at least. That kept him off the monster list. Barely.

"But, yeah, I know some guys and those guys know some guys. Some of them are cool enough—for humans. Just fell on hard times." His smile disappeared this time. "And if they have a nickel, hell, even a quarter, they always toss it in my case. Good guys who appreciate a little entertainment." He drummed long fingers on his knee. "Let me ask around. See what I can find out. These guys do come and go, so it may take me a few days, maybe more. Disappearing for a while isn't so unusual for them and Sawney's not the only one who thinks they're easy prey."

That was true enough. I'd seen the Kin try to take an entire busload of them once. That took balls. Furry ones, but balls all the same. Yeah, the homeless were easy prey all right, but if Sawney was still shopping around for his new "cave," he might not be as careful about not taking a lot from one place. Most monsters know better than to hunt in their own backyard. Sawney would too, but if he was still hunting around for a place, he might not be so cautious. I doubted he'd settle on the first one he found. It'd have to be just right. Deep, hidden, safe to eat your human pork chops. You know what they say: It's all about location, location, location.

6

The next morning I called the car lot looking for Goodfellow only to find out he'd called in sick. Sure, he'd been injured, but too hurt to lie, cheat, and steal from the masses of clueless consumers? Knowing Robin, that freaked me out a little and had me at his place checking on him. From the way he was going on about our visit to Ham, I might've been wasting my time. Then again, he was in bed. Unless it was for sexual acrobatics, seeing Robin in bed was damn rare. So many orgies, so little time.

"Ah, he wanted to be Promise's *special* friend, eh?" Robin said gleefully. "Tell me more. Did Niko actually emote? Did righteous jealousy cause a slight twitch of one eyebrow? I cannot wait to . . . *skata*." His face grayed as Seraglio efficiently ripped the bandage from his upper arm. The revealed puncture was knitting but still puffy and reddened. It looked painful as hell.

"I'm no nurse, Mr. Fellows," the housekeeper said as she swabbed the wound with a mixture of half peroxide, half sterile water. "And I never claimed to be, now, did I? But it's either me or this tale-carrying young man."

"Sorry, ma'am," I drawled. "Healing's not exactly where my talents lie."

"Ma'am, is it? Don't you have the sugary tongue." She applied an antibacterial ointment with a slightly gentler touch than the one used to remove the bandage. "At least your mother taught you proper manners."

No, but my brother had. I waited until she finished up dressing all the wounds, helped clean up the leftover supplies, and then closed the bedroom door behind her. "She makes me feel like a kid." Which in a way was rather nice. It was a feeling I hadn't had too often in my life.

"She does have the essence of the Earth Mother about her." There was a weary quality to the satyr quirk of his lips. "Soft hands, sharp tongue, and breasts like sun-warmed velvet."

"Like you'll ever know." I grinned. "You've finally found the one woman who's too much for you." I watched as he slowly pulled the pajama leg down to cover the last bandage applied. I was torn between mocking his choice of sleepwear and asking a question. I went with the question. "Why are you lying around in bed anyway? Why aren't you at work stealing some poor guy's last dime?"

"I like being waited on hand and foot. It is only my due." He pulled the covers back up to his waist and leaned back against the pillows.

That was true enough . . . as far as it went. But with his face still the color of clay, there was obviously further to go on the subject. "Niko said it wasn't that bad," I said, oddly irritated, although I wasn't sure if it was at my brother for not being right or at Robin for proving him wrong. Not that I was worried.

Ah, shit.

I shot a brief look at the door and escape . . . escape from concern and emotional entanglement. Applying these things to others outside of Niko was still new and scary as hell to me. I didn't know if I even knew *how* to do it.

But, in the end, that was nothing but piss-poor cowardice. Goodfellow, who'd saved my life at least twice, deserved better. I looked away from the door, shoved hands in jean pockets, and scowled. "Something's wrong. Tell me." And quick before I bolted.

"It's nothing." He closed his eyes and laced his fingers across the mound of covers.

"If it's nothing, then tell me, goddamn it," I demanded, "before I kick your horny ass."

He cracked an eye. "Can you feel my waves of unadulterated terror from there? I'm doing my best to suppress them, but I fear I'm wholly unsuccessful."

"Fine." I gave him the finger and headed for the door, making my escape. "Screw you."

He sighed and untangled his hands to push up to a more upright position. "Wait."

I already had one hand on the doorknob, brass and cold, and I could've kept going. An object in motion tends to remain in motion. It's physics, that's all. It can't be cowardice or the easy way out if it's physics, right? I let myself believe that for several seconds before I dropped my hand to my side and turned, exhaling, "Damn it."

"I do have that effect on many, many people. And I'm not used to any of them wasting worry on me. I've not built up a habit of gracious acceptance." He gave a tired grin. "Although in all other aspects of etiquette, I am without parallel. The Don Juan of decorum."

"Yeah, right, and I'm not worried. Just . . . gathering all the facts," I said with obstinate wariness. "Now give them to me already."

He did. It was poison. The sirrush was venomous with toxic claws and fangs. It could be fatal, but pucks were extremely resistant to poison, so for Robin it was only painful and slowed recovery by a few days. Now, there were some nice mutated supergenes for you. What'd I get? Super-smelling. No wonder I didn't have my own comic book.

"And it's a rare excuse to have Seraglio mother me and to catch a glimpse down her polyester shirt at the Promised Land. That's worth a little pain." He reached for a half-empty glass of wine on the nightstand and added smugly, "I told her I was injured saving a nun from being mugged. There were orphans involved as well. I'm quite the hero."

"I'll bet." Seraglio was far too sharp to swallow that, I knew, but it was possible she had a soft spot for her employer. "You're okay, then? A few days in bed and you'll be annoying the hell out of us as usual?" The relief was sharp. This whole having a friend thing, damn, it was work.

"It's my calling in life, and, yes, I will." After draining the glass, he rolled it between his hands. "Now that you're done *not* worrying, shall we hug? Isn't that what one does in emotionally fraught situations as this? I'll keep my hands above the belt. I am still mooning after your brother after all. Blonds, they always break my heart."

He seemed ridiculously pleased with himself, grinning despite the lines of pain creasing his forehead.

I strongly considered grabbing handfuls of sheet and blanket and yanking his ass onto the floor, but that was before I figured it out. Robin had said it himself: He wasn't used to people worrying about him. Concern—I wasn't in the habit of giving it and he wasn't accustomed to receiving it. He wanted to be, though. That was plain to see in the grin, the humor-lightened eyes, and the quirk of eyebrows under wildly curly bed hair.

"I'm not hugging you. So shut up. Jesus." But I did stay and filled him in about Ham and how he was going to investigate the homeless situation for us. Naturally, it wasn't the homeless theory that he concentrated on.

"A musician," he said with interest. "Wild and willing groupies, how can one go wrong?"

"About that . . ." I was sprawled in a chair by the window. "Remember what we talked about before George was taken?" It seemed forever and it seemed like only yesterday. And wasn't that a trick? "About me not passing on the family name?"

The Auphe might not have a family name—I'd never bothered to ask—but they did have genes. They'd given them to me, but that's where it stopped. I wasn't taking a chance of making any more like me . . . or worse than me. And worse than me was definitely a possibility. It was one reason George and I weren't for each other. Robin had given me the usual options—rubbers, the big snip—but I didn't have the faith in them that I had in the Auphe will to be born.

"I remember." He leaned toward me. "Don't tell me. You're finally casting aside celibacy and embracing the nasty, oily arts. Thank the Minotaur's massive member. It's about thrice-damned time."

Facing down a sirrush was nothing compared to the level of predatory attention now aimed my way. "Hold up. I don't want orgies or sadomasochistic role-playing weirdness," I said cautiously. "I just want to get laid, pure and simple. Being half Auphe doesn't mean I want to spend my whole life not getting any." No one with a dick, working or not, wanted that. And I was twenty. You could *make* little blue pills out of what was running through me. I wanted George more than I'd ever wanted anyone, but I couldn't have her. Maybe, though, I could have someone else, even if they meant so much less. And if anyone knew someone it would be impossible for a human-Auphe hybrid to reproduce with, it would be Goodfellow.

Robin nodded and laced fingers to crack his knuckles in preparation—the mental kind, I fervently hoped. "Actually, I've been contemplating your horrifying, nay, catastrophic situation for a while now and I'll be happy to—"

I interrupted hastily, "Yeah, thanks, but no, thanks."

He snorted, "You should be so privileged. No, you braying ass. As I was saying, I'd be happy to introduce you to some open-minded females." Leaning back, he relaxed. "Let me think on it. There are those out there who would fit your situation. However . . ." He paused and the sly cheer faded. "Some would know about you and some wouldn't. Both come with issues."

I answered the unspoken question. "I'll stay in the Auphe closet if I have to." Some would know and some wouldn't, he'd said. The ones that did know wouldn't fuck me on a bet. The ones that didn't know were my only chance, and if I were stubborn about hiding what I was, Robin would have a real challenge ahead of him. Stubborn and stupid, I knew the difference between the two.

"Then take your vitamins and get ready, Forrest Hump," he ordered, cheer reignited. "You're in for a wild ride."

I wasn't thinking about that wild ride when I left. Okay, that was a lie and a half. I was thinking about it all right, but I was thinking about something else too. I was thinking about how the sirrush came out of nowhere, and what if pucks weren't resistant to poison? I was also thinking about all the times things could've gone very differently for Niko and me. The close calls, the near misses . . . we were good but we'd had them. And how one day a near miss might not be a miss at all. Niko was one of the best out there, and I was good enough. But I thought about the revenants. The best, the good enough, someday that wasn't going to get it. Get thirty or so really pissed-off revenants or fifteen wolves or just one nearly un-defeatable troll, get cornered by that, get boxed in and that very well could be all she wrote.

Unless we had an emergency exit, a way out.

And we did have it. If my Auphe ability saved Niko or Robin, if it could save us all, I didn't care about headaches or if I bled like a stuck pig. It was worth it, and if Niko was right and my brain did go down for the count, hell, it was still worth it.

Robin's stairwell was empty. Not surprising. It was daytime; most were at work. I took advantage of it, and sat on the landing off Robin's floor and let the door close behind me. When I'd built the gate around Robin and me to escape the sirrush, I'd done it in a mixture of effort and instinct. I didn't have a monster charging me now, so I was going to have to depend on effort. Every gate I'd ever seen or built had been big enough to walk through. But maybe if I started small there'd be fewer nasty side effects.

I held out a hand, tried not to think about the pain from last time, and focused. It came, a little slowly, but it came. It was small like I'd concentrated on— the size of an orange. Gunmetal gray, the light of it was a sluggish whirlpool—spinning as if it wanted to suck you in. It was an ugly thing. Ugly and repulsive. And it lived in me. Hard to come to terms with that, but I was going to have to.

Gateways had to lead somewhere, so this one went to the tiny closet in my room. No one would see it there. Not Nik, who would be highly unhappy about my breaking my word . . . even if I'd never meant to keep it in the first place.

I felt the touch of liquid warmth on my upper lip, but the headache that began to throb was bearable. So, okay, the bigger the gate, the worse the side effects. Maybe easing up to a size we could get through would help. A slow and steady progress.

And think what I could do with it besides escape. I could do what I'd done to Hob, the puck kidnapper who'd taken Niko and George. I could build one between us and our attackers and let them rush into the Auphe home away from home. Tumulus. Hell. They'd be ripped to shreds there. Turned to a pile of blood and guts and I imagined they'd live for a while as it happened. Strangled with their own intestines. The Auphe did like to play with their food. Why not get them to do the dirty work? Why not let them murder and maim? Why not let them mutilate . . .

I blinked and let the gate go. Now, where the hell had that come from? If you were attacked, if someone wanted you dead, you did what you had to do.

But maim? *Mutilate*? I wouldn't do that. Wouldn't send someone to that god-awful fate. That wasn't me.

Never mind that I'd done it to Hob. That was different. He'd defeated Niko and hung him up like an animal to be slaughtered. He had George tied up across the room. I couldn't get to them both to get us out of there, and Hob would've defeated me. *Was* defeating me, slicing me to ribbons. Niko, one of the best. Me slightly less. I'd had no choice. But to do that when I did have a choice . . . no.

No.

I felt the blood drip down my chin, catching it at the last minute with a wad full of paper towels I'd shoved in my pocket before I left Robin's place. I'd known then what I'd planned to do. I mopped up the blood and held the stained towels to my nose until the bleeding stopped. With the paper saturated, I pulled off my jacket and carefully scrubbed my lower face with my sleeve. It was black; any leftover blood wouldn't show, which in turn would keep me from a Niko ass-kicking of righteous proportions.

Half of me thought I deserved it. Half of me knew I was doing what I had to. All of me thought the same thing over and over.

That wasn't me.

Not me.

Never.

7

While Robin recuperated, plotting and planning things for me that would make Hugh Hefner cry for his mommy, I ended up in an abandoned warehouse. I'll say it again. . . . It sounded trite, and, hell, it was, but one phone call from Promise had sent Niko and me to one. According to any mystery or cop show, these rat-infested, echoing places are a dime a dozen. They're not, but you can find one if you put your mind to it. Sawney had. How did I know?

Bones.

Chains and bloody bones.

Like wind chimes, they hung high from the rafters. But no wind would make them sing. The skeletons were held together with ligaments and thin stretches of overlooked flesh, just enough meat to keep them intact. Either Sawney had planned it that way or he hadn't been as hungry as he'd thought. And they weren't bodies of the homeless. He wasn't being careful. Not yet. He was still enjoying himself way too goddamn much.

I looked up to see a stained bike that hung beside a small skeleton. There was a silver sparkle banana seat, a basket blooming with bright plastic flowers, and shiny brown hair tied around the handles like streamers.

That had had nothing to do with hunger. That was evil, pure and simple.

"How did Promise know this was here?" I dropped my eyes to the floor and the large dried patches of brown on it. It had been hours at the very least, this morning or last night. Three sets of remains, two adults and one child. A family . . . a bike. It had probably been the previous evening. A mom and dad taking their little girl for a bike ride in one of the parks. Katie, Sarah, Maddie . . . Katie. Yeah, Katie, a tomboy with freckles and brown hair in a long ponytail.

"A friend of a friend." Niko had knelt to touch a light finger to the largest pool of dried blood as I wrenched my thoughts back to the here and now. "A relative of a friend rather. Flay's sister told her."

Flay was a werewolf acquaintance of ours. Once an enemy, he was now . . . hell, I had no idea what he was now. Not an enemy, but not precisely a friend either. He was long gone from New York anyway, so it didn't much matter what label you slapped on him. He was on the run from the Kin, the werewolf version of the Mafia. If he showed his furry ass in the city again, he was dead—the kind of dead that would have the human La Cosa Nostra sitting up in admiration and taking notes like a dedicated college freshman.

"Flay has a sister?" I drifted away as I began to look for more bodies. Sawney might not have hung them all up. He might've gotten tired of playing his festive little games. "A scary proposition." Flay was many things—unbelievably strong, murderously quick, a talented fighter—but he was one homely son of a bitch. No, that wasn't true. He wasn't ugly, but he was unusual, damn unusual. Exotically strange enough to draw anyone's eye.

"Do not judge." Gray eyes mocked. "We cannot all be the vision you are." He stood. "They've been dead awhile, that is clear. What isn't as clear is where they came from."

The warehouse was near the piers. It wasn't the most likely place for little girls to ride their bikes. And transporting three bodies some distance in the city would be a trick for even a homicidally clever bastard like Sawney. He couldn't put them under his arm and shamble along. Even in this city, that would be noticed. I shook my head. "No telling." There were several islands of stacked crates, but no other bodies that I'd seen yet. "Why is Flay's sister helping us? For that matter how'd she know we needed help?"

"Promise put out the word in the community with Sangrida putting up some of the museum's money as a reward for information. They can't justify a fee for tracking down a supernatural serial killer of course, but can offer rewards for the damage done to the exhibit. Creative accounting." Nik kept scanning the area. "Some wolves stumbled across the bodies a few hours ago. Kin wolves. This is a Kin warehouse, although they only use it off and on. Delilah is Kin in good standing, unlike her brother. Once she heard what had been found, she contacted Promise. As to why?" He headed toward the other side of the interior. "Money, and we did save her nephew's life or did you forget?"

Not likely. I still had the little fuzz-butt's bite marks scarring my calf to remember him by. It did surprise me that this Delilah would be grateful enough to act on it, but there was the money. The Kin did love their money. It was still risky for her, though. We weren't loved by the Kin any more than Flay was, but while Nik and I were considered ene- mies of the Kin, we didn't hold the special place in their vengeful hearts that Flay did. Flay had betrayed his Alpha to outsiders. If there were a worse crime to a wolf, I didn't know what it was.

"Kin will be back to clean up the area soon enough, so we need to be quick." The Kin didn't like their territory violated or conspicuous. And it didn't get much more conspicuous than bodies hanging from the ceiling. Niko had moved out of sight behind a far tower of crates, and seconds later he rapped out my name, "Cal."

The tone was enough to let me know he'd found something interesting. My gun was already in my hand and had been since I'd entered the building. I loped after Nik, seeing what he'd found so intriguing the moment I rounded the crates. It was a van. With its side door open and dried blood within and with- out, we'd discovered how Sawney had transported the bodies. It was so mundane, not to mention inex- plicable. "Okay, Cyrano, riddle me this," I said. "How the hell does a Redcap from the fourteen hun- dreds know how to drive a goddamn van?"

He frowned under his hawkish nose. "That is an excellent question." As he clambered into the back, I opened the passenger door and leaned in the front for a whiff. Huh. Now, that was damned peculiar. "Revenant," I announced aloud. Revenants weren't what legend made them out to be . . . legend never got it right, but I could see how easily it had been to go wrong with these slimy pieces of shit. They weren't the dead returned to life—unpleasant, rotting life—but they did give an amazing imitation. Revenants weren't human and had never been, but they looked damn close to a man . . . if that man had been dug from a not-so-fresh grave. It wasn't difficult to see how someone had made the mistake. With milky white eyes, clammy slick flesh, and a black tongue, they weren't nature's prettiest or proudest moment.

"It seems Sawney is recruiting a new family." Niko finished examining the van and vaulted back out. "Logical. There are no other Redcaps in New York, and revenants, like Sawney, do not particularly care if their meals are alive, dead, or decomposing."

"And revenants can drive." They'd been around New York nearly as long as there had been people. With a coat and a hat or a hooded sweatshirt, they could pass to the casual glance through a car window. I'd seen them do it, and it was the last cab ride you were likely to take. Finding nothing in the front, I stepped back and shut the door. "I wonder why they didn't stick around here. It's not a cave, but it's empty and there's plenty of room to keep leftovers." To keep more little girls and their mommies and daddies. "Even if the revenant knew it was Kin, I can't see Sawney giving a shit. A few wolves would be a snack and rug combo to him. Dine and decorate in one shot." Something glittered by my foot and I crouched to pick it up with my left hand. It was a barrette, gold and yellow. The little girl's last touch of sun. It had the caustic humor lying like lead on my tongue.

"The revenants may have known. And they would've known that if a few Kin wolves went missing here, the rest would come en masse," Niko conjectured as he watched me put the barrette in my pocket.

"Too much light."

It came from above. The words.

"Where is soothing darkness?"

In the shadows where the stray rays of sunlight didn't penetrate.

"Where are the sheltering arms of stone?"

A bright slice of winter, sharp as ice and white as a fatal blizzard, bloomed.

"Where is Sawney Beane's home? Not here."

As my eyes adjusted I saw more . . . up in the rafters. An unnaturally wide killer grin. Tangled ropes of hair, white stained with red and brown. There was the impression of a sweeping bulk of a cloak or coat, but face and hands . . . they were nothing but blackness. Inky shadow come to life.

The impossible stretch of smile widened. "I see you." Tiny embers sparked to life, the cheery red of an autumn fire. "Travelers."

Travelers. And we knew what Sawney Beane did with travelers.

I fired instantly. The bullets hit. I knew that although the monster didn't move. There was no attempt at evasion, only the echo of gunfire and that ever-present leer. The bastard didn't flinch, didn't shift under the impact, didn't register the blows at all. If I didn't have the confidence of my aim, I would've wondered. But I hit him. . . . It simply didn't matter one damn bit.

"Educational," Niko mused.

"Glad you think so," I grunted as I slammed another clip home. Just another day at the office . . . until the late afternoon sun chose that moment to shift to twilight, plunging the warehouse into a dusky purple gloom. What few lights had been on joined the sun in disappearing, deepening the gloom to the impenetrable.

And then it began to rain blood.

The color was impossible to discern in the thick murk, but I knew the smell, knew the slick consistency against my skin. "What the fuck?"

There was the sound of rushing air and then a meaty thump inches from me. Another body, and from the sound as it hit, this one had most of its flesh intact. There was another thump and another as the charnel house above continued to fall. I didn't know how Sawney had kept them up, and I didn't care. I only wanted to get my hands on the son of a bitch.

"I'm going up," Nik said grimly. "You cover him here if he tries to escape." There was no sound of departing footsteps—this was my brother after all— but he was gone.

I moved my own foot a few inches to one side to place the first body. As my eyes adjusted I could make out a vague outline, a crumpled form . . . arms, legs, a mound. Pregnant. She'd been pregnant. I couldn't make out any more than that and I didn't want to. She'd been alive; now she wasn't.

When the next body fell, I thought I was ready for it. How much fucking worse could it be? Stupid goddamn question. Sawney was the stealer of mothers, children, and babies. The taker of lives, flesh, and hope, because in New York everyone was traveling. From place to place, everyone was on the move. And to someone who preyed on travelers, that meant everyone was fair game.

Sawney hit me from above . . . the one body that

wasn't dead, but we weren't done yet. Not by a long shot. He hit hard and with a weight I wouldn't have guessed. He was an avalanche—not one of rock, but of ice. Cold, wherever he touched me. The burn of dry ice on my neck and jaw as he tasted me. I felt the slide of the tongue over my carotid artery as hands pinned my head. "Different, traveler. You taste different."

I struggled to pull breath back into my lungs that curled abused and beaten beneath bruised ribs. But I didn't need to breathe to pull a trigger. I jammed the muzzle of the 9mm into the mass that squatted on top of me and emptied the clip I had just put in. Like before, I got jack shit for my trouble.

"Full of sulfur spice and ancient earth and a world far from here."

Auphe, he was tasting it in me. That stuttered my lungs to painful life. I wheezed and used the oxygen to propel my body into motion under him. I tried to roll, dropping my gun and pulling a knife from the calf sheath. My fingers passed through the slit in the denim and fastened around the rubber hilt. My roll was less successful. Flickers of scarlet light still burned into mine. Hanks of knotted hair smelled like a slaughterhouse and felt like rope against my skin. And that grin, that goddamned grin, was still inches from me.

Then it was in me.

Teeth went through jacket and shirt, into my chest, and ripped a piece of me away. Sawney had succeeded where the Black Annis had failed, and he had done it so easily. Had made me food, and I hadn't been able to do a damn thing about it. Food. There's a special horror in that, a particular twisted terror in a part of you being *eaten.*

It hurt, but not as badly as it should. The shock of it muffled the pain, wrapped it in cotton, and let me plunge the knife into his back without hesitation. What it could do that the gun couldn't I didn't know, and when his grin widened, I got my answer. And with that answer came other things. There was blood on my face—my own blood—and the sound of a purring swallow.

"Soft and sweet, your flesh, traveler." The cold tongue lapped blood from the wound. "Sweet and spiced with madness." He laughed then. It wasn't dark or deranged, deep or demonic. It was happy as a child with ice cream, and that was worse. So much fucking worse.

If ever there were a time for a gate, promise or not, this was it. But even if I could have managed one the size I needed, and I had head-splitting doubts that I could, Sawney would only have gone with me. Eat me here, eat me somewhere else, I didn't know the difference. I did know panic, though. Sheer, kick-in-the-gut panic, and I used it. I twisted the fear into energy and momentum and I tried again to throw the bastard off. This time, I did it. I didn't take the time to get to my feet. It was time I didn't have. I got to all fours and scrambled backward with all the speed I could muster. When you can smell your blood on someone's breath, that's pretty damn fast.

He was fast too. Faster than I was. Faster than anyone I'd seen. He was ten feet away and he was directly in front of me, yanking me up with a hand on my throat. Up, not to my feet—my feet weren't touching the floor and neither were his. We hung in the air, the goddamn *air*, three feet of empty space beneath us. He had two smiles now, one sheened with my blood and one the gleam of metal. It was the scythe from the museum. Sangrida had taken good care of it. It was as capable now of carving human flesh as it had been six hundred years ago. I'd seen that in Sawney's recent victims and I was about to feel it as well.

"Traveler, abide with me." Red light blazed to bloody suns. "Abide *in* me. Special boy with the special taste. The taste of madness, the taste of me." The cheer, the horrifically affectionate cheer, was the silken touch of a spider's fatal web, and I wished he would shut the hell up. I wished I weren't so sure it was Auphe madness he was tasting in me. I also wished I had brought my Desert Eagle with the explosive rounds. Wish in one hand and shit in the other and hope you aren't facing Sawney fucking Beane when you do it.

I was reaching for another blade, knowing it probably wouldn't do any good, but doing it anyway. Because you don't give up and you don't give in. Niko taught me that. If they're going to take you down, you make them pay. It was good advice. I'd been taken down before; I'd always made them sorry as hell. This bastard wasn't going to be any different.

And I wasn't a *boy*—special or otherwise. I wasn't a lost little girl or terrified pregnant woman either. When he sliced me up with his scythe, piece by piece, I would take the same from him. It might not kill him and it might not even hurt him, but I would take it anyway. I damn sure gave it my best shot. My knife punched through cloth that felt like flesh . . . could have been flesh for all I knew. This thing had come back from bone and ash. He remade himself; who knew the limits to that remaking? The blade slid into flesh, scraped bone, and kept going. This time I twisted it, viciously and with all the force I could manage. And he let me. Guests go first, right? It's when you're the guest and dinner all in one that you run into trouble.

I twisted again. The bastard was *cold*, like ice, and I could feel cold creeping up the metal to the hilt and into my hand. My knuckles cramped, but I wrenched the blade one last time. Sawney's patience had run out, however, and so had that of his scythe. It flashed toward me. They were like those paintings—Sawney and the scythe—the ones from the museum, the abstract kind. A metallic glitter of iron, scarlet light, a jet gloss of flesh, all fogged by thick darkness—a jumbled bit of art in motion as the scythe slashed. I couldn't see the whole, but it could see me.

Too bad it didn't see Nik.

The blade of the scythe missed my stomach by millimeters. It tore through my leather jacket as if it were no more substantial than an illusion as Niko hit Sawney from the side and carried him away from me. The icy clamp peeled from my throat and I fell. Landing in a crouch, I coughed against the air that had curdled in my frozen throat. Niko and Sawney had landed ten feet away: Niko on his feet and Sawney on his back with a sword pinning him to a wooden pallet. Dead center through his gut . . . or what I guessed to be his gut. The sword blade disappeared into the darkness that was Sawney, but Nik didn't stop there. His hand a blur of motion, he slammed a dagger into the Redcap's neck to pin him further. Then, because he was loaded for bear, he drew his second big blade. He'd seen how much effect my gun and my knife had had, but he swung the machete anyway. When I saw where he aimed, I knew what he was thinking. If you can't kill it . . .

Disassemble it.

My brother in action; it was something to see. When he lifted his blade, he had the grace and elegance of Lancelot on the field of honor, and when he brought it down, he had the efficiency of the family butcher down the street. The metal bit through the shoulder joint of the arm that controlled the scythe and then Nik kicked it away. Not the weapon—the entire arm. Yeah, safe to say that when Niko disarmed someone, he didn't fuck around. Proof positive was in the next blow. He'd seen how quick Sawney was with that scythe, and he'd taken care of that first. Now the second step was to end it. Sawney's head was the next thing to be kicked across the floor or it should've been, but things were never that easy.

Before Nik could take that next blow, Sawney exploded upward into the air above us, suddenly upright and with his feet at least three feet above the floor. The surge tossed Niko backward with the force of a vicious, storm-driven wave. Impaled by a sword and dagger, the legend hung suspended. Hung and gurgled. It was only when he pulled the dagger from his throat that I recognized the gurgle for what it was. Laughter.

I lunged at him as his hand, the one he had left, moved to the hilt of Niko's sword to pull it free. I reached him as the blade came loose and the wooden pallet clattered to the floor. "Pretty." Sawney held the sword high. "A fetching blade. Bonny. Bonny-bonnybonny." The laughter ratcheted higher and higher into the crazed cackle of a hyena—bloody-mouthed, full-bellied, and happy. Two of a kind, because Sawney was that, through and through. When I jumped up and hit him, the laughter didn't stop. It kept on and on, all I could hear.

My tackle didn't move him, not an inch. How he managed to float there, I didn't know. Or care. I just wanted him dead, down, or both. With my arms wrapped around his torso, he and I hung suspended in the air, like flies in amber . . . until Niko joined us. He didn't add the weight of his body, though. He was smarter there than I had been. He used a more effective weight, that of a baseball bat. At least that's what it felt like, even from the other side of it. A massive blow was slammed across Sawney's back. It did what I hadn't. We tumbled through the air and hit the front of the van, the hood, and then the windshield. It cracked underneath us, but held—just barely. I grabbed for the sword in Sawney's hand, but he was already gone, disappearing upward into the darkness. Niko was in his place almost instantly, a black metal rod in his hand. Telescoping and two feet long, it wasn't a baseball bat. It was an illegal version of a police baton and a helluva lot more vicious than your average Louisville Slugger.

"New toy?" I asked hoarsely.

"I like to treat myself once in a while." He held out a hand and pulled me out of the hollow my impact had formed in the safety glass. I made it to my knees, considered trying for my feet, and decided against it. Bracing myself on the hood of the van, I looked up and saw nothing. Not a damn thing.

"Shit." I had his smell now, up close and personal. Ice, bone, and insanity. I hadn't known the latter had a specific scent. It did. "He's gone." It was true. The taint in the air had faded a fraction, from present to past.

"I'm not surprised." Nik slipped off the hood and away to return seconds later. "He took his arm and scythe with him."

"So much for souvenirs." My chest was beginning to hurt, the cotton wool ache migrating to a raw acid sear. It burned so savagely that I didn't want to look at the damage Sawney had left behind. Setting my teeth against the pain, I eased my way from the hood down to the floor. It wasn't graceful, but it wasn't a drunken stumble either. It didn't matter; Niko spotted the hesitation immediately.

He didn't waste time asking if I was hurt; he went straight to the heart of the matter. "Where?"

"He . . ." I gave a reluctant dark laugh as I laid the flat of my hand on my chest. It was too strange, too goddamn weird. And terrifying. It made it hard to find the words and harder to put them out there. "Jesus. He ate me."

Niko didn't laugh in turn. He didn't see the humor, dark or otherwise. Truthfully neither did I. With a pen flashlight from his pocket for the examination, he pushed aside my hand and spread my jacket. He didn't have to lift my shirt. I guessed the hole in it matched the one in me. Straight-shot viewing. For him . . . I didn't bother to look, not yet. Nik's face, calm, became even more so. It wasn't a good sign. "I suppose I get to be the pretty one now," he said lightly. Minutes later, I had a thick bulk of gauze taped to my upper chest. There wasn't much blood soaking through and that didn't necessarily seem a positive. And when Niko's hand fastened onto the back of my jacket to urge me into a walk, that didn't seem like one either.

"I'm okay," I insisted. I was. It hurt like hell, but

I was all right. I certainly could walk. One foot in front of the other—it's not that difficult.

"I know," he said agreeably. Far too agreeably, and he didn't let go as we walked outside and hailed a cab.

"You lost your sword." He'd lost it only once before . . . to Hob. Hob the kidnapper. Hob the megalomaniac. Hob the shit-head. It wasn't a good memory. The homicidal puck had nearly killed Nik, and I'd used Nik's sword to return the favor. "You lost your sword," I said again, oddly shook-up over it. More than I should've been. After all, Sawney wasn't Hob and Niko was right here.

"I'll get it back or I'll get a new one. It doesn't matter." His grip on me tightened as my legs went a little rubbery . . . developed a mind of their own. Yet one more thing to add to the "not good" list.

"You know," I said with a sudden dawning of truth, "Mr. Goldstein would've kicked Lancelot's ass."

"The butcher?" He gave it the solemn consideration it deserved. "I believe you're right." Damn straight I was, but there was no denying I had a new empathy for the cows that Mr. Goldstein chopped into steaks and rump roasts.

Being the cow wasn't much fun.

8

We made it home in record time for New York traffic, which was nice. I liked home. Home was good. Sawney wasn't there and massive painkillers were. It was a win-win.

"We need a healer. Now."

"Yes, I *know* we need a healer, Niko," Goodfellow said with a strained patience. "But we don't have one."

We'd had a healer. Rafferty Jeftichew. He'd saved my life once upon a time. Twice upon a time actually. But he'd disappeared in the past month. Closed up his house and vanished. When your healer took off, it was bad news, especially if you didn't know if your insides matched your human outsides. And a hospital would know, Rafferty had told us, either from imaging or blood work.

"A doctor, then." It was said with determination although Niko knew better . . . knew it wasn't possible.

"And what?" Robin shot back. "Tell them Caliban was attacked by a small bear in the park or perhaps a large homeless man with a voracious appetite and a taste for the other white meat?"

I opened my eyes. "It's not that bad."

Goodfellow stared at me incredulously while Niko pointed out, "You haven't looked at it yet, Cal." His mouth tightened. "Reserve judgment."

"Ignorance is bliss." I closed my eyes again and let the fuzz of codeine carry me along as the discussion went on without me. After the cab had dropped us off, we still had to get up to the apartment. I almost hadn't made it. Once he'd half carried me upstairs, Niko had called in reinforcements and then turned to cleaning my wound. Or attempting to. It didn't sound as if it had gone well. When Robin had arrived, there had been talk of possible muscle damage, surgery, skin grafts. All impossible for me. While the discussion went on, I lay in bed and drifted; there wasn't much else to do. I suggested once that Robin and Nik help themselves to a few pain pills too. It really took the urgency out of things. They didn't take me up on it. Their loss.

"He can't heal like this," Niko declared emphatically. "Infection alone would kill him. We'll get a doctor, a surgeon if necessary."

"And by 'get' you mean . . . ?" Robin asked dubiously.

"You know what I mean," Niko said flatly.

That cut through the happy-pill hoedown. "Jesus, Nik." This time I struggled to sit up. The pain swelled for several excruciating moments, then receded as I made it upright and stopped moving. I sucked in a breath and held it until I could speak without a ragged edge shaking my voice. "You can't kidnap a doctor. That's the kind of trouble we can't deal with." Monster trouble, yeah. That we could do. Human trouble was to be avoided at all cost. At best, we'd have to leave New York. We had lives here.

Niko and Promise had a life. I wasn't going to cost them that.

"It's trouble *I'll* deal with. Lie back down." It was said in a tone that brooked no argument. I argued anyway—go figure.

"No way." It was cold. Our landlord wasn't above skimping on the heat. What landlord was? I grabbed a handful of blanket and pulled it up toward the large bandage on my bare chest. Or rather I tried. My left arm was weak, functional but only barely. They'd said it and I hadn't listened. Muscle damage. Nik's eyes darkened as he watched my slow progress. "No goddamn way," I repeated stubbornly as I finally got the blanket up. "Loman, you have to know a doctor. One who'd keep his mouth shut. You know everyone, right?" The codeine helped with the discomfort, but it didn't do anything for the weariness, the bone-deep exhaustion. I slumped back against the headboard despite myself, taking the blanket with me.

"One would think." He was still pale from his own wounds, but he looked better than he had. The poison was passing out of his system. That was some good news anyway. "I met Hippocrates once. I wouldn't have let him treat a pig. Cross-eyed, fond of the bottle, and desperately searching for a cure for his own personal crotch rot." That breezy, cocky smile he was so very good at faded. "I'm sorry."

Knuckles rested on my forehead and then my jaw. "Give him more Tylenol in an hour." Niko's hand was as icy as the room, as icy as I felt. It didn't take a genius to know that meant I was running a pretty good fever. And codeine, as helpful as it was in other areas, wasn't going to bring it down. "I'll be back," he went on, unbending in his goal. It was easy to translate. Niko was going someplace where he could snatch a doctor. Hospital, probably. And that would be the beginning of the end.

I'd done the same for him once. I'd struggled against that same damn dilemma. Although at the time, I doubt I knew dilemma was even a word. I'd been seven and Niko eleven, back before the Auphe had snatched me and I'd lost two years in their dimension while only two days had passed in ours.

I didn't get sick much when I was a kid . . . only once in my life that I remembered and it had been Niko who'd taken care of me. I'd have died long before Sophia ever noticed I was ill. Bourbon and whiskey are great for glossing over the annoying events of a parent's daily life. When Niko got sick, it wasn't any different.

What started out as a cold became bronchitis and finally pneumonia. With that came the dilemma. We didn't have insurance, and we didn't have a mother willing to take Nik to the doctor. If you show up at the doctor sick as a dog and without a parent, they notice. They notice enough to get Social Services involved. Maybe foster care would've been better than what we had. It couldn't have been much worse, but there were no guarantees they wouldn't split us up. Niko was old enough to know that and he made sure I knew it too.

We weren't going to be split up. Period.

But when you're seven and the brother who's your whole damn world is too sick to get out of bed, you have to do *something*. Anything. I was too young for kidnapping, but there were other things I could do. We lived in a trailer park then and we had a few elderly neighbors. Old people had medicine, lots of it. But those same old people hated to leave their trailers. Hated it like poison. I'd wanted Nik to tell me what to do, but he was so desperately sick and even more stubborn. He didn't want me doing anything stupid. At seven years old, that was about all I *could* do.

Old people make an exception about leaving their homes when there's a fire. I'd torched an empty trailer two rows over with Sophia's lighter and a half-empty bottle of Old Crow. When everyone had run or hobbled over to watch the bonfire, I'd raided medicine cabinets. I wouldn't have known an antibiotic from blood pressure medicine, so I'd taken it all. Shoved bottle after bottle in my backpack, and after hitting four trailers, I'd run home to pour them in Niko's lap. They had cascaded down onto the blanket, bright and shining plastic reams of them.

"Which one?" I'd demanded desperately. "Which *one*?"

It had worked out then. I didn't have faith that the same would hold true now.

I made a grab for his arm, using my right hand this time. Between the drugs and the fever, it still wasn't much of an attempt. I missed. Promise didn't. She'd entered the room as quietly as she entered all rooms. Laying a hand on his arm, she slid it down to curl around his own hand. "I've brought assistance." She released Niko to move closer and rest a hand on the blankets over my leg. "She's not a doctor, but she can help." Glancing over her shoulder, she called, "Delilah?"

She appeared in the doorway. Flay's sister. I could see the resemblance instantly, although they were more different than alike. She was of better breeding, which would make her Flay's half sister. Flay could barely manage a half-human form. He was plainly a werewolf for anyone who had the eyes and the intelligence to look. With Delilah you would never know. She also had a hint of Asian features in her almond-shaped amber eyes. Where Flay had albino white hair, hers was silver-blond, very nearly as pale. It was pulled into a high ponytail at the crown of her head and hung ruler straight to midback. A stylized necklace was tattooed choker-style around her neck. The jewels set in Celtic swirls were eyes, wolf, all of them. Gold, red, green, brown, pumpkin orange . . . and the softer amber of her own eyes. An unbelievably talented artist had imbued them with emotion. Some were full of laughter, some curiosity, some hunger, all of them astonishingly real.

She wore low-slung black jeans, a matching jacket, and a snug amber-colored shirt. Both jacket and shirt were cropped to reveal a good seven or eight inches of midriff, which was as decorated as her neck. But where the one decoration had been made of ink, the ones on her stomach were composed of scar tissue. Multiple slashes, thick and cruel. As a wolf she'd be as proud of those as she was of her tattoo, maybe more so. Ink was ink, but scars were badges of survival. They said, "I'm here. I'm alive. And I buried the son of a bitch who did this."

"You can help? How?" Niko said with rigid control.

Fine blond eyebrows quirked and she raised a hand, palm to her mouth, to bite the heel of it hard. Then she licked the wound and turned the hand toward us. The bite was healing already. The blood had stopped flowing and the flesh was knitting slowly.

"Of course," Goodfellow said. "Werewolves have a natural propensity for healing, but their saliva speeds the process."

Delilah gave a single regal nod, then moved over to me and removed my bandage. Light flared behind her eyes, turning amber to brilliant copper. "Ahhh." She sounded impressed. When a wound impresses a wolf, it doesn't bode well for the guy sporting it.

For the first time I looked. Impressive was one word for it. Horrific was another. A hunk of flesh nearly as round as a child's fist was gone from my upper chest, just . . . gone. Left behind was a ragged red crater deep enough that I could imagine I could see the shine of muscle. "You were right." I swallowed, looked up at Niko, and gave him a crooked smile. "You get to be the pretty one now."

"News flash, little brother, I always have been," he retorted as he rested his hand on my shoulder to squeeze lightly.

From Delilah's snort, we were both fooling ourselves. In that moment I could see the impatient Flay in her clearly. Climbing onto the bed, she straddled my thighs and stripped off her jacket. "Go," she ordered to the room in general. "Now." It was more of Flay. I'd been wrong about Delilah; she wasn't what the old-school wolves considered pure breeding after all.

The community was divided among the wolves who cherished the old ways . . . pure human to pure wolf and back again, and the ones who thought the more wolf you were, the better. And they meant all wolf all the time with no taint of human. Those were the ones who bred for the recessive qualities. Flay and Delilah had come from a pack who had embraced that.

She had the normal teeth of human form, white, even, and straight, unlike Flay's mass of wolf teeth crammed into a human mouth. But while her teeth were normal, her vocal cords weren't. Talking was difficult, not garbled or coarse, but raspy like the tongue of a cat and thick as butterscotch pudding. Your average person would've pinned it on a heavy accent. Those in the know would hear it for what it was—a she-wolf from the wild doing her best to talk.

"Go?" Niko shook his head and refused adamantly, "No."

"Imagine it, Niko," Promise said simply. "It will be rather . . . intimate."

On that note, Goodfellow promptly offered to stay. Promise marched him out without any apparent sympathy, but she did place a supportive hand on his back. They might have their differences, Robin's thing for Niko being a big one, but Promise did care for the puck, which seemed to shock the hell out of him.

"Call if you need me."

I raised my gaze to Niko and quirked my lips. "If being licked gets to be too much, I'll yell."

"Smart-ass." A last firm clasp of my shoulder and he left.

Delilah turned her head to watch him go, then looked down at me. "Still nursing?" Rusty and slow, but understandable—the canine version of a purr. It was soothing in its own way.

"He's a good mom," I responded, unoffended. "Oh," I added diffidently, "sorry about my scent." Wolves weren't wild about the Auphe smell, and, considering the reaction I'd gotten from Flay and the Kin, I had my fair share of it.

"Auphe? You?" Her mouth curved, dismissing me as an Auphe cublet at best. "Cocky pup. Close your eyes."

I started to protest, but between the anchor of narcotics and a lack of desire to see the gaping pit in my chest any longer, I went ahead and obeyed. I felt the touch of her tongue against the wound. It was warm, moist, and gently methodical as it moved. It was also odd as hell, and, as Promise had said, intimate.

It hurt as well, but only in the beginning. Her saliva must have numbed as it healed, because the pain faded, even the residual pain that had broken through the pills. It wasn't long before I drifted, not asleep and not awake. There was an incredible heat growing in my chest, chasing away the chill of fever. There probably would've been an incredible heat in a lower location too, but it had been a long, hard day. Even twenty-year-old hormones couldn't fight against this day. Soon enough, half sleep became the genuine deal and I dreamed. Long silver hair turned to short red waves, amber eyes to deep brown. The warm weight on top of me—Delilah to Georgina.

It was a nice dream. Hot as hell and very nice indeed. And then the dream changed. There were clothes involved this time.

It wasn't the only difference. When I thought of George, I usually pictured her, depending on the state of my willpower, in the same dress. A brown silk sundress . . . cherry chocolate. I'd seen her once in it and never forgotten the image or the feeling I'd had. So it didn't matter that it was fall and far too cool for that dress, I still thought it, dreamed it. Except this time. This time George was wearing a finely knit sweater, deep crimson, and filmy skirt of gold, bronze, and copper. She also had a tiny ruby piercing in her nose. It made her look exotic, a priestess of a far-gone time and place. A prophet, and wasn't that what she was?

"A ruby," I said in a voice thick with sleep. "Like your hair."

"It's a garnet," she corrected with a smile. "A practical gem for a practical girl."

Her hand was holding mine, our fingers linked. "I miss you, George." It was something I could only say in a dream, because admitting it in the waking world wouldn't do either of us any good.

"You don't have to." She leaned to kiss me. We'd kissed before, but not like this. Our first had been with the relief of rescue, the second a bittersweet good-bye. This was the kiss of a different life. Heat and hope and all the time in the world. There were only the two of us. No monsters, without or within. Dreams can be that way, the good ones. Then you wake up. You always wake up.

Because they are only dreams.

"Stubborn."

I opened my eyes as George's voice still lingered in the air. I actually heard it—heard her. She wasn't there, yet I knew if I saw her . . . if she showed up at my door at that moment, she would be wearing crimson, gold, and a garnet.

But that was something I wasn't going to think about. Couldn't think about. I touched the small plait of copper hair tied around my wrist, a memento of times past. Of doubts present.

No, I'd made my decision, and it was the right one. I knew it. In my gut, I knew it, even if no one else did. I sat up and waited for the pain to distract me from useless thoughts. It didn't come. I looked down. The bandage was still gone; it hadn't been replaced. There was no need to. The raw crater was gone. In its place was an indentation, still fist-sized, but more shallow, about a quarter of an inch deep—

as if that fist had been gently pressed against soft clay. The scar tissue was purple and thick and ugly as hell. I couldn't have cared less. When I was a kid, Sophia had once told me that, while I was a monster, I was a beautiful one. I'd known from that moment on that what was on the outside didn't count for anything. Our mother had been beautiful too, physically, but inside she was as ugly as any Annis or revenant. Uglier in some ways. They had their excuse. She'd had none.

There was a rustle of paper as I pushed the covers aside. A note started to fall to the floor and I caught it before it could . . . with my left hand. The weakness was gone, the muscle damage repaired. Unfolding the paper, I read words in an unfamiliar hand. *Now you are pretty.*

Yeah, the wolves did appreciate a good scar. Delilah was no exception.

9

Niko had fixed the kind of food for breakfast that was normally banned from the apartment. Pancakes, bacon, greasy potatoes. Good, *good* food—not the soy, wheat, egg-substitute crap he normally tried to convince me to eat. "I should be dinner for a supernatural pit bull more often," I said around a mouthful of syrup and blueberries.

"Or not," he said matter-of-factly, turning a glass of juice back and forth between long, calloused fingers.

"Or not," I said apologetically. I didn't see the evidence of a sleepless night in his face, but I knew it was there nonetheless. I shoveled in another forkful of potatoes. "You tell the others about Sawney's new family?"

"The revenants? Yes. No one was precisely thrilled." It wasn't a surprise. Revenants weren't popular with anyone or anything. Dumb, smelly, and mean.

Leaning back with my belly full, I considered burping, but my knee gave a phantom twinge with the memory of the last time I'd had that idea. Nik enjoyed good manners and he enjoyed them in others . . . with great and occasionally painful enthusiasm. Painful for me anyway. Patting my chest lightly through the T-shirt I'd slipped on, I said, "Delilah did good work."

"Amazing work." He drank the juice in several smooth swallows and then pushed the glass away. "She was here nearly the entire night, but what she accomplished . . ." He shook his head. "She was worth every penny."

"I thought she was helping us because of Flay." I decided I could fit in one more piece of bacon and sat back up to reach for the plate.

"Yes, but she *is* Kin. Family is important, money is important. There's no reason she can't honor both. I admire her initiative. Your initiative, however, is a different story." A foot rapped my ankle briskly. "I cooked. You clear."

"Hey, I'm wounded," I protested. "Have a heart."

"You *were* wounded." His foot impacted again, this time with a little more English on it. "You *are* lazy. Let us work on making that past tense as well." He stood. "I teach three classes today. I'll be home by six. We'll go hunting then."

There was a barrette on the dresser in my room, all that was left of one of Sawney's victims. Katie the tomboy's sunny hair clip. "I'm ready for a little hunting trip," I said with determination. I could call Ishiah and ask to get my shift switched from tonight to this afternoon. He wouldn't have a problem with it, and if he did, I'd sic Goodfellow on him.

As it turned out, Ishiah wanted to speak to me, the sooner the better. I showed up at the Ninth Circle an hour later, wondering, not for the first time, if it was Ishiah's dark sense of humor or if there was more to peris than Robin knew.

"Good. You're here."

I continued to wrap the bar apron around my

waist and nodded. "Here I am," I confirmed, puzzled. Ishiah wasn't usually one for berating the obvious. "Although, trust me, I deserved a sick day."

"You found the elusive Sawney Beane, then?" His wings were out in force and rustling impatiently.

"Rumor mill's already working overtime, huh?" The bar was mostly empty, but last night it would've been full, and monsters like to gossip the same as anyone else. "Yeah, we found him, and he pretty much kicked our asses." I poured myself a glass of tomato juice. Not as manly as a slug of whiskey, but better at replacing iron from blood loss. "So, what'd you want to talk to me about? Am I going to be employee of the month? Is there a plaque involved?"

"After impaling that Gulon with a beer tap? It seems unlikely," he said with annoyance.

"He brought in outside appetizers. It's against the rules." Not to mention that the appetizer had been a dog. A big playful mutt who hadn't had a clue what was in store for him. The beer tap had cleaned right up when I'd finished with it. No harm done, although the Gulon probably wouldn't agree with that assessment. "How is Rover doing, by the way?"

"That is beside the point," he said, eyes stony. I wasn't buying it. One of the other bartenders, a peri named Danyeal—Danny to me—said Ishiah had kept the dog, which was now fat, happy, and a veritable fountain of urine whenever his master's back was turned.

"And what was the point again?" I asked innocently.

"Never mind." He got out while the getting was good and folded his arms. "I want to talk to you about Robin."

"Goodfellow?" I said curiously. "You're not going

to ban him from the bar, are you? He'll only show up more often if you do. Probably move the hell in."

"No." The wings were spreading now. It was the unconscious reaction of peris to stress or danger. Danny flared his wings at even the hint of a bar fight, but as the steely Ishiah was about the furthest thing from high-strung as you could get, I was betting that danger of the big and bad kind was the option here. "I'm hearing things," he announced quietly.

"What kind of things?" I prodded.

"There's word that Robin is being targeted. I heard it just today." Catching a glimpse of feathers from the corner of his eye, he hissed in exasperation and the wings wavered like a heat mirage and disappeared. "I don't know who's behind it. I don't know if it's true, but the rumor is out there. I would tell him myself, but his harridan housekeeper won't put my calls through. And if I showed up at his home in person, I might have to tell him over crossed swords."

I still wanted to know what had led to the peculiar animosity on Robin's side versus the vexed watchfulness on Ishiah's, but now wasn't the time. "Targeted?" The museum. "He was attacked two days ago by a sirrush. We thought it was a random thing. Shit." I grabbed my cell phone. "You don't know anything? Who's behind it? Why?"

"No. Nothing. It's the flimsiest of hearsay, the source of which I can't determine." His jaw set as his eyes narrowed. "And I've made the effort." His hand clenched into a fist. "An extensive effort."

Damn. If Ishiah couldn't get to the bottom of it, it was going to be a hard nut to crack. Goodfellow's answering machine picked up and I swore again.

"I've got to go." I ripped off the apron as I came around the bar and tossed it on the counter.

"Make sure the son of a bitch watches his back," he commanded.

"I'll do one better," I responded as I hit the door. "I'll watch it for him."

When I arrived, I was sweaty and breathing hard from my run up twenty-five flights. I didn't take elevators. A good fight was about defense and offense. It was hard to get a good defense going in a steel box—a giant mousetrap, for all intents and purposes. And I wasn't fond of anything with the word "trap" in it.

After I'd pounded my fist against the door, Seraglio opened it and looked up at me with disapproval. "You most surely are a loud young man."

"Sorry, ma'am. I need to talk to Rob." I felt as if I were six and asking if my friend could come out and play.

Smelling of cinnamon and honey, she pursed full lips painted a glossy burgundy and shook her head. Her long, cascading silver earrings rang like church bells. "He's not here." But she stepped aside to let me in. "He may be at work or he may be out debauching the innocent. Lord above, I cannot keep up with that man's schedule."

"Who can?" I muttered. Robin had kept his non-human origins from the woman, but there was no way he could conceal his sexual and alcoholic exploits. He didn't even try. Hell, why would he? He was as proud as if there were a Nobel category for high living and he was up for consideration. Seducing, swilling and just proud to be nominated.

I tried his cell again. Nothing. "Do you know his office number?"

Clucking her tongue, she went to the kitchen and opened a drawer to pull out a leather notebook. She then pointed out a number with a long nail the same color as her lipstick. It was amazingly pristine for her profession, I thought as I called the provided digits. He wasn't there either. "*Goddamn it.*"

Fathomless black eyes pinned me disapprovingly as those startlingly immaculate nails tapped against the counter. "Sorry, ma'am," I said again. In the past year I'd fought against an army of Auphe and a massive two-headed werewolf and yet this woman had me bobbing and weaving. "I just need to find Rob." I remembered to use his "human" name with ease. What Sophia hadn't taught us about lying and dissembling, a life on the run had filled in.

The trouble was I couldn't tell her that I was worried about him. She would ask why and Robin wasn't here to come up with one of the brilliant and utterly false stories he was so good at spinning. I tended to go with the "What's it to you, asshole?" response to questions I didn't want to answer. And I could only picture which of the household appliances around us would be inserted in me if I used that line with Seraglio.

Her eyes were still marked with maternal disappointment at my poor etiquette, but she relented enough to say, "I can't help you, sugar. I am not psychic, and, in this house, thank the heavens above for that."

No, she wasn't, but I knew someone who was. This "goddamn it" I kept silent and within.

George didn't carry a cell phone, so I needed to

show up with the rest of the supplicants at the ice cream shop near Pier 17 on the East River. As usual, I was fresh out of cash for cab fare and it took two trains and a hike to make it there from Robin's place.

George used to hold court at the ice cream shop after school. Once she had graduated, she kept the same schedule. People needed to be able to find her, to depend on her, she said. She hadn't yet decided whether college was for her or not. Service to others came first. Of course, if she'd look into her own future, she'd know if college was there. But she didn't look and she wouldn't. That would be cheating and George didn't cheat. Things happened as they were meant to, and while the little events could be changed, the big ones never could. Trying would be not only a waste of time, but also an insult to existence itself. She could tell those who came to her the small things and keep to herself the unchangeable, but she didn't see any reason to tempt herself by looking past the distant turnings of her own path. Besides, she'd once said with cheeky smile and earnest heart, it would ruin the surprise.

The ice cream shop was run by a partially blind, mostly deaf codger whose name I remembered only half the time. George kept him in business. She didn't take anything from the people who came to her, but she did gently suggest people buy an ice-cream cone or soda as thanks for having a place out of the weather. I'd yet to see a person say no to her.

Except for me.

I didn't have time to mess with ice cream and I slapped a few bucks on the counter. "Treat the next couple of kids," I ordered to the old guy half dozing behind it on a high-backed stool, and headed for George's table. She sat serenely, hands folded on Formica. The Oracle of Pearl Street. Brown eyes warm, wide mouth softly curved, she was crimson, gold, and garnet . . . just like my dream, just like I knew she would be. "Cal." She reached out as I sat opposite her and took my hand as easily as if she'd done it a hundred times before. "Mr. Geever has missed you."

"I'll bet." He was completely asleep now, head pillowed on the counter by my money. I looked down at her skin against mine, sunset amber against moon pale.

Monster pale.

I slid my hand from beneath hers, missing the warmth of it instantly. I didn't look at her eyes or her short cap of wavy red hair or the faint freckles that spilled across her nose and the tops of her gold-brown cheeks. I didn't have to—I had them memorized. "I need to find Robin," I said abruptly. "He's in trouble."

"Trouble?" Her brow wrinkled. Never one to back down, she left her rejected hand on the table as if it were only a matter of time before I changed my mind.

"Yeah. Something is after him. I have no idea who or what, and now I can't find him." My own hands I dropped into my lap to rest on my thighs. Get thee behind me, Satan, or get thee under the table. Whatever.

"Robin." She said it as if she were calling him, as if he were around the corner. Out of sight, but still within earshot. Closing her eyes, she frowned, eyes moving behind the copper-brushed lids as though scanning the page of a book. Several seconds passed and then her eyes flew open. I thought it was with distress or fear, but then she flushed. "Oh."

I got it immediately. This *was* Goodfellow she was trying for a peek at. "Oh," I echoed sheepishly before apologizing. "Shit. Sorry. I didn't think about that."

"He's very . . . limber." She parted her lips, showing small teeth in a gamin smile. "I'm impressed and educated."

"He's okay, then?" I leaned back in my chair, tried not to think about the word "limber" and that knowing smile she'd flashed, and exhaled in relief.

"He's fine." Eyes bright, she tilted her head. "And very happy right now. Among friends—the friendliest of friends."

"You're laughing at me," I snorted. "Go ahead. Someone should get some enjoyment out of this besides Goodfellow. Can you give me his address? He's safe now. He might not be after he leaves." She would know if he would be or not, but I wasn't going to ask. If she'd been willing to look that far, she would've told me. Besides, I refused to believe in that whole "everything happens for a reason" bullshit. Any universe that would actually *plan* my being born of an Auphe wasn't a universe I wanted any part of. Destiny and fate could kiss my ass.

"Yes. I can give you the address." She did and watched as I stood up. "You *are* stubborn, you know."

Just as she'd said that morning in my dream. "Some things are worth it," I said quietly. And they were . . . worth being stubborn, worth the sacrifice. Like keeping her safe. Like letting the Auphe line die with me.

"Cal."

I shook my head and stood. "Thanks for the help, Georgie." I made it to the door before she spoke again.

"You've run all your life, Caliban. You have to

stop. Sooner or later, you have to." The bell overhead rang as I opened the door, but it didn't drown out the next words. "Please make it sooner."

Significant words. They deserved to be thought about, to be considered carefully. I pushed them out of my head the moment I passed through the door. I needed my resolve, which wouldn't be helped by mulling over what she had said. Or by the fact that every time I turned my back on her felt like I was turning my back on a good portion of my life. Those things couldn't matter. Not if I wanted to keep her safe, and in my life she never could be.

It was the way it had to be.

The address was in the East Village, not too far from the fifth-floor walk-up Niko and I used to live in that barely deserved to be called an apartment. Good times. I had a feeling there would be wildly colored hair, tattoos, and lots of black in the near future. Goodfellow had always liked artists—they were open-minded, adventurous, and willing to worship him in many mediums, and what better place to find them than the East Village?

Robin even had a fresco of himself hanging on his apartment wall, though the artist who'd painted that had done that for the love of a beautiful form in general, not for the love of Robin's form specifically. He'd been the brother of the woman Robin was going to marry. Goodfellow wasn't one for talking about his past—a statement not as ridiculous as it seemed. He would talk without end about every casual encounter, every historical figure he'd ever met or screwed from the birth of time on.

The key word was "casual." Robin wasn't quick to share the things that truly touched him. I thought in the beginning that it was because nothing did touch him. When Niko and I had first met him, I didn't think there could be a creature more superficial, shallow, or self-absorbed. I'd been wrong.

The puck had the depth of a long-abandoned well, and if those depths were desolate and murky, that was the result of outliving everyone you cared for. Robin was a human-lover, not a nice turn of phrase among monsters. So not only was he despised for a puck's natural trickery and thieving ways; he was scorned as well for the company he kept. His human companions would die, and the nonhuman would have little to do with him. Robin boasted of his vast circle of acquaintances—how many he knew—but knowing and being accepted are far different things.

I didn't know when Robin gave up on humans, when letting them go . . . when watching them die got to be too much, but I suspected it was around the time of that painting. It had been created in Pompeii days before he lost his chosen family, and now that hunk of ancient wall hung on a modern-day one—a constant reminder.

Why he'd made an effort to connect with Niko and me, I'd not yet figured out. Why he picked that moment to break a solitary pattern of almost two thousand years was still a mystery. I wasn't sure I could've been brave enough to take that chance. Hell, I knew I wouldn't have been.

I was brave enough, though, to knock at the door where George said he would be, but only just barely. I couldn't begin to guess what might be behind the door, but if I saw one donkey, I was gone. Robin could face certain death on his own. Two girls, naked except for their body art, opened the door, human

female, and from the twining of arms and pressing
of flesh, they were *very* close. I swallowed thickly
and took a closer look. I mean, Jesus, who wouldn't?

One was painted in blues and greens with waves
and leaping fish. The other was all over raging flames
with the yellow scales of phoenixes shining through
the red fire. As art went, it was pretty cool. As for
the nudity, that was damn cool too.

"Is . . . ah . . . Robin here?" I asked, forgetting his
name for a second as my brain decided to send my
blood south for the winter.

The red girl looked blank and the blue one
wrapped her arms around the other's scarlet neck
and her legs around a waist painted with the eternal
fire lizard. Her lips were busy sucking lightly at an
earlobe and nipping the soft skin behind. It was dis-
tracting. I did need to find Robin, but how often did
you get a show like this and not have to pay a big-
ass cable bill for it?

"Boom chika bow wow."

Robin slid up, patterned head to toe in green leaves.
He was a forest and in the forest were eyes—the cagey,
wise ones of foxes peering through the foliage. "Someone has you down pat," I snorted. "Who's running
around here painted like a henhouse?"

"They're resting." He grinned shamelessly. "They're
very, very tired." The grin widened. "But you, on
the other hand, are wide-awake. Care to help yourself?" He waved an arm toward the inside of the
apartment. There were thirty people at least, all
brightly colored and most of them horizontal.

"Are they all human?" I asked.

"Yes."

"Then no." I took his arm and pulled him into the
hall. "I need to talk to you. There's trouble."

"Isn't there always? It's exhausting. Perhaps I should dress first?" he suggested dryly. "I'm perfectly comfortable as Zeus made me, but not everyone is as amenable."

With the two naked girls holding my attention, I hadn't even realized Goodfellow was wearing the same party attire as everyone else . . . absolutely nothing. "Crap," I groaned, blinked, then looked away hurriedly. "Goddamn, Goodfellow. You have a permit for that?" Talk about your weapons of mass destruction. Jesus.

"Now you know precisely why I'm so smug," he said with mock hauteur. "Give me ten minutes." He disappeared back into the interior of the apartment. I waited in the hall, a lack of faith in my own willpower keeping me there—not to mention a healthy dose of survival instinct. It wasn't only lamias that could drain a man unto death. The girls still framed in the door looked entirely capable of doing the same. Not necessarily a bad way to go, though.

"All right, kid, I'm cleaner than a nun's pair of Sunday panties. What trouble are you speaking of?" Robin, dressed with damp hair, had stepped back into the hall to close the door behind him. The red and blue girls were still intermingled close enough to be only seconds away from making purple, and I craned my head to catch one last glimpse as the metal swung to block them from sight.

"Ishiah." I straightened and said seriously, "He said someone is targeting you. He doesn't know who or why, but the word is out."

"The sirrush," he announced after a short stretch of silence as we walked.

"Yeah." The building had the typical flavor of artist tenants . . . old, decrepit, and smelling of pot.

There was one lonely light overhead and it flickered uncertainly. "So who's after you? Who'd want to kill you?" I waited a beat and added, "Besides me, I mean."

"You must be joking," he said incredulously. "I couldn't begin to guess. Ex-lovers, ex–business partners, ex-marks . . . there isn't a PDA in the world big enough to compile that list."

The light gave up the ghost entirely as we reached the stairwell. There was still illumination from the street coming through a distant, dirt-filmed window, but it was gray and wispy—a ghost among us. It reminded me. "It can't be Abbagor. He's dead." Abbagor had been one of Robin's acquaintance/informants. A troll the size of a Lincoln, he'd lived and died under the Brooklyn Bridge. And Niko and I had nearly died with him. He'd been one malevolent, flat-out *evil* son of a bitch and every time I passed the bridge I flipped it off in his memory.

"Even if he were alive, it wouldn't have been him. Abby did his own dirty work. He enjoyed it far too much to farm it out." He started down the stairs.

"The Auphe." I hadn't wanted to say it, because I didn't want it to be true, but burying your head in the sand was only going to leave your ass up and chewed the hell off.

"No," Robin denied. "They're not above subcontracting, but they would be more subtle than a sirrush. Auphe are insidious, cunning, all the things a poor, simple sirrush is not." He sighed as he moved downward. "Thinking about my own horrific end, what a way to ruin a good orgy."

"Sorry about that." I followed him. His hands were empty, but mine were not . . . one of them at least. I held the Glock against my denim-covered outer thigh. "I assumed you'd want to know you've been marked for death. I don't know what I was thinking."

"When it comes to murder and assassination, it *is* the thought that counts. I appreciate the effort." The words were sober, the expression anything but . . . until he moved on. "It's hardly the first time. Or the hundredth for that matter," he said absently as he looked back at me. "You're well? Before she left, Delilah said you were recovered. Do you have full strength in your arm?"

"Normally I'd flex, but after what I saw upstairs, I'm keeping the sexiness to a minimum." The stairs were concrete and slick from years and years of pounding feet. "And, yeah, I'm fine."

"Good—that's good, because your chest looked . . ." He grimaced. "Never mind." Hitting the landing, he paused to say slyly, "I think she was attracted to you, our wolf girl. The situation was too dire for the customary ass-sniffing and leg-humping that is so prized on the wolf social scene, but there was definitely a look in her eye."

"Do you want more than one person trying to kill you?" I drawled. "I don't really have the time, but the inclination is no problem whatsoever."

He didn't have time to take me up on the offer. Someone . . . some*thing* else spoke in his place.

"Give me drink."

Goodfellow had been about to move down another step. He stopped, set his mouth tensely, and held up a hand before I could open my mouth. I turned my head and looked up past the spiraling box pattern of stairs, then down past the same. There was nothing to see or hear other than a faint dripping sound and the flicker and buzz of elderly lightbulbs.

The words were raspy as sandpaper against rock and utterly devoid of humanity. And then there was a clicking sound . . . nails against concrete. A slow, patient tapping, silence, then the clicking again.

A rustling started . . . scales or feathers, I couldn't tell.

"Give me drink."

"Go." Robin grabbed a handful of my jacket and hurled us both toward the landing door. I didn't stop to protest or ask who was so damn thirsty. If Goodfellow said go, then going was a damn good idea. I slammed into the door and flung it open.

It was waiting for us.

It was a bird. Gray as ash, round black eyes, and the size of a half-grown German shepherd. It used jet claws to score the dirty tile, sending chunks of it tumbling aside. The black beak, sharp as a sword, gaped to show an inner maw the plague yellow of jaundiced flesh. *"Give me—"*

"Drink," grated the one behind us.

Identical to the other, it came up the stairs toward the door propped open by Robin. It didn't waddle like you would expect from a bird. It stalked with the smooth gait of a creature used to running its prey into the ground. The flattened head cocked to one side. There was red on this one's beak and staining the feathers of its chest black. Now I knew what it had a hankering for, and it wasn't lemonade. I turned. The one in the hall had snaked closer, one clawed foot held in the air like the weapon it was. The talons were four inches long and, if they were capable of punching through the floor, they were capable of punching through flesh.

"Bad?" I said over my shoulder.

"Bad," Robin affirmed tightly.

That was all I needed. I raised my gun and fired at the one in the hall. The gray head exploded, feathers filling the air. Some, coated with black blood, stuck to the wall and floor and me. The body poised motionless for a second, then fell sideways, talons still extended in either a last-gasp pursuit of prey or from postmortem pissiness. Take your pick.

I heard the scrape of metal against scabbard as Goodfellow pulled his sword. Following that was a gurgle of someone not getting the drink they so desperately wanted. I turned just in time to see the feathered head bounce down the stairs. "Bad," I commented, "but not that bad."

"Wrong." He started down the stairs at a run. I was starting to follow when I saw something stirring in the pool of blood that had spread from the neck of the bird I'd killed. No, it wasn't something *in* the blood; it was the blood itself. Thick and viscous, it crept along the floor, curled up into a ball, and began shifting from red to gray. Began to sprout feathers . . . began to *grow* and grow damn fast.

"Give . . . me . . . drink."

The faintest of whispers, a garbled croak from incomplete vocal cords, but I didn't wait around to hear it improve. I vaulted the other dead one on the landing and clattered down the stairs after the puck. "What the fuck?" I yelled as he sprinted ahead, hit the next landing, then disappeared around the turn. Robin was one helluva fighter, but when it came to running for your life, he had absolutely no equal. I sped up, trying not to tumble my way into a broken neck. I did manage to shorten the distance between us . . . slightly. "What are those things?"

"Hameh. The story goes they arise from the blood of a murdered man and take revenge by drinking the blood of the killer. Blah, blah. Idiotic tale." The bastard wasn't even breathing hard as he bolted, taking three and four stairs at a time. "They actually arise from their *own* blood and attack whoever their master chooses. And as staying dead isn't a particular hobby of theirs, they're very difficult to escape."

"Give me drink," echoed from above us, full-voiced and implacable.

"We should've stayed at the orgy," Robin groaned as he hit yet another landing. "Bacchus would never get himself in this situation. He'd still be face-deep in topographical mounds and I don't mean the Seven Hills of Rome either."

Above us the cry came again and it didn't come alone. A weight hit me hard, taking me down. I hit the stairs and rolled but caught myself before I went down farther than three steps. I ignored the pain of banged elbows and ribs and raised the gun, but the Hameh was gone. It didn't want me. I'd just been in its way. I twisted my head to see it dive-bomb Goodfellow. Talons were spread and a razor beak was aimed at Robin's throat. Where better to drink? Where better to start the flow of blood?

I opened my mouth to warn him, but he didn't need it. He whirled at the sound of air rushing through feathers and speared the Hameh through the chest. It didn't squawk; didn't screech. It screamed— a human scream. A child's scream. That's what it sounded like, as if a child had been run through with Robin's blade. It was disconcerting as hell and I unconsciously tightened my grip on the Glock. And it didn't stop. The screaming went on and on as the Hameh thrashed, sending blood splattering.

"Christ, make it stop," I hissed. We could scream our guts out all day long and no one would poke their head into the stairwell, but a kid screaming? Someone was going to show up, and that someone might get a beak jammed through their eye. Not much of a reward for being a Good Samaritan.

"Stop? But I'm enjoying it so much," Robin snarled as he whipped another blade from his brown leather duster and slashed the throat of the bird. The blow was forceful enough that the head was almost completely severed. The good news was that it stopped the screaming. The bad news was that it didn't do a damn thing about the other Hameh stooping on us like a falcon on a mouse. I shot, missed, and shot again. This time I nailed it. It veered, hit a wall, and plummeted onto the stairs above us. In the seconds that took, the blood of the first was already twisting in on itself and changing colors.

"This is annoying as hell." This time I took the lead, moving past him as he took the time to extract his sword. "I've seen Hitchcock movies. I don't want to live in one."

"Did you know he wore women's—"

"I don't want to know!" I growled, cutting him off. I kept going until I reached the door to the first floor and threw it open. Only it wasn't the first floor and it wasn't the lobby. It was the basement. We'd overshot by one when racing downward and ended up in precisely the sort of box I avoided in elevators. It wasn't an empty box either.

"Give me drink. "Give me drink. Give me drink. Give me drinkgivemedrinkgivemegivemedrinkgivemedrinkgiveme-drinkgivemedrink."

It was utterly black except for the soft reddish blue glow of eyes . . . ten, no, twenty eyes. I didn't hesitate. I emptied the rest of my clip blindly into the room, slammed the door, and headed back up, meeting Goodfellow on his way down. "You don't want to go this way. There's some seriously thirsty pigeons down there."

"Give me drink," from above answered the question to what lay in that direction as well. And in case I missed the point, let's hit it one more time—*"Give me drink."*

"Shut up, you flying shit-heads," I spat as I slapped another clip home. "Just shut the hell up."

"Yes, I'm sure that will clear the matter right up. In the diplomacy of predator and prey, you dominate the field. You are without peer. A veritable Kissinger of the circle of life."

"You know what? Take the flying part out and it applies to you too, Loman." I shot the next Hameh that came spiraling through the air. It somersaulted past me and, in a mass of blood, ruined flesh, and feathers, landed on Robin. Mortally wounded, it stabbed repeatedly at Goodfellow's neck with its black beak. I grabbed it from behind before it did anything worse than superficial damage and threw it to our feet, where it was impaled by Robin's bloody sword.

"Okay," I panted. "There has to be a way to kill these things for good. What is it?"

"Bathe them"—he was finally beginning to get a little short of breath himself—"in the blood of a virgin. Care to open a vein?"

I snarled soundlessly, wiped handfuls of gore-covered feathers from my palms onto his shirt, and then bolted for the first floor. The pounding at the basement door was beginning to warp the metal, and I wasn't waiting around to play games with the group of parched blood drinkers that were seconds away from coming through. "I can't believe I hauled my ass over here to warn you, and all you do is give me shit." Still pounding up the stairs, I looked back over my shoulder at him with narrowed, dubious eyes. "You *are* giving me shit, right?"

"Trust me, if it were true, I wouldn't be trying so hard to get you laid. I'd be selling you by the ounce instead," he retorted.

We both hit the door simultaneously and burst out of the stairwell. The building didn't have a lobby; it wasn't that sort of building. What it had was a lounging area for artwork and those who made it—an informal art gallery. There were people sitting on the floor drinking weird teas and paint-thinner-strength coffee. Canvases were piled against the walls, funky twisted bits of metal and chunky pottery were grouped here and there, and there were naked, painted people posing like living statues. I guessed that's what they did before they went upstairs to orgy central, because your paint was bound to get smeared all to hell up there.

I vaulted one guy who was lying flat, stargazing at the cracked and yellowed ceiling. I wove in and out of a few more and then I was outside. Behind me, I heard the mild wonder of: "Cool. That's one motherfucking big parakeet."

It wasn't what I wanted to hear, to say the least. Another thing I didn't want to hear was the thrum of massive wings, but I heard it nonetheless. It was raining as I hit the sidewalk. There were sheets of heavy, gray water and black clouds that brought twilight several hours early. Into that twilight flew Hameh after Hameh. I looked up as they circled. They were the color of the rain almost exactly, lost against the sky. As for hearing them . . . you could make out their voices over the hiss of the falling water and the blaring horns of cabs, but only if you listened hard. No one in New York listened hard.

Beside me, Robin looked up, the inhuman perfection of his profile washed clean. "Baal of the Winter Rain," he said softly. "The fortune that is finally due us."

"Yeah, it's great for the crops and all, but what the hell is it going to do for us?"

"Watch," he ordered with vengeful anticipation.

The Hameh soared, circled, and one by one they began to explode. It wasn't loud. Muffled by flesh and feathers, the *whump* was barely audible. From the inside out, they ruptured, and pieces of them fell along with the rain.

"Blood is the only thing they can drink, the only liquid they can even touch." Teeth flashed in the pelting water as he stepped back under a dingy awning and out from under a very different kind of rain.

There was the scent of burnt feathers and scorched flesh in the wet air as I followed him. It wasn't a pleasant smell, in the ordinary sense, but at that moment I didn't mind it at all. It was apple pie and fresh coffee to my nose. Sweet and fragrant roses all the way. I continued to watch the fireworks show above. *Boom*. There went another one.

And the rain continued to fall.

10

"I'm not sure which disturbs me more—that you could have been killed or that you could have been killed at an orgy. What precisely would you have me put on the tombstone? Here lies Caligula Leandros?"

"Oh, Jesus, that reminds me. You should've *seen* the size of Goodfellow's . . ." From the annoyed twist of Niko's eyebrows, I decided it was a subject for another time. "Anyway . . . bottom line is Robin's in trouble." I finished loading the Glock and holstered it. "Someone is pissed as hell at him and apparently has a zoo in their backyard to pull from."

"That in itself is curious." Nik had just made his fifth blade disappear under his coat and now had numbers six and seven in his hand. "The Hameh and the sirrush are from the same general geographical area. Sirrush are Babylonian and the Hameh are mentioned in Arabic mythology, but they are more like animals, not intelligent entities. It's as if someone sicced a guard dog on him. We should ask who in that part of the world Goodfellow has managed to so thoroughly annoy."

"That could narrow it down to a few thousand." I leaned against our kitchen table. "If we're lucky."

"When have we ever been especially showered with luck?" Niko asked dryly as he disposed of knives number six and seven and considered number eight before flipping it high in the air. It didn't come down again as far as I saw. His hand flashed and it was gone.

I snorted. "No comment." Actually I had plenty of comments about the rather bitchy Lady Luck, but we had things to do and Scottish assholes to kill.

Robin had declined an invitation to our hunting trip, but Promise had come along. The three of us spent the night combing the parks, the piers, and any condemned and abandoned buildings we could locate. The parks were good hunting grounds and any large empty structure could function as a substitute for a cave. It was a reasonable plan . . . if this wasn't New York City. A city this size? We were whistling in the wind and we knew it. But we kept it up. It was better than doing nothing and we hadn't heard back from Ham yet.

Yeah, it was the best we could do right now, but that didn't change the fact we came up empty—that night and the two nights following that. We didn't run across a single Redcap or revenant, which was unusual. Revenants were plentiful in the city. A few of them worked for the Kin doing jobs that the wolves considered beneath them. The others worked for themselves, eating what they could catch. They weren't bright, but they were fairly quick. They didn't go hungry too often, and it was unusual to go through the park at night and not spot at least three or four. We didn't see a single one . . . anywhere.

But at one park we did run into several sylphs cocooning a lowlife for later consumption. They were smaller creatures, the size of a seven-year-old child, with pale gold skin and hair and the amazing wings of giant butterflies. Purples, blues, greens, red, orange, yellow . . . any color you could think of. Their eyes were huge and the same gold as the skin. Beautiful, like the fairy tales in books . . . not the fairy-tale reality that stalked our streets. When you saw a sylph, it was enough to make you believe in Peter Pan, Tinkerbell, and a place built solely on magic.

And you'd keep believing it right up until they ate you.

It was at that same point you'd probably notice they had eight multijointed golden legs and were more spider than butterfly. And like the spider, they didn't drink blood or eat flesh, not separately. After cocooning their prey, they injected a chemical that dissolved the internal organs to soup. Eventually there would be nothing but a dried husk hanging in a tree that would disintegrate in the first brisk breeze.

Frankly, I didn't care if the homicidal butterflies ate a hundred muggers or drug dealers. New York could use a little cheap crime control. But, as Niko logically explained while smacking the back of my head, it might not always be a petty criminal they snared.

There were many things I'd done and many things I'd killed, but there was something about killing a giant butterfly, even one with spider legs, that wasn't going to leave any fond memories. I'd never been one for pulling the wings off something smaller than I was. But when they opened their mouths and I saw poison-dripping pincers and a circular gullet lined with tiny triangular teeth, I changed my mind. Tinkerbell took one in the gut, and, as it snarled with sizzling poison gushing from its mouth, the only thing I felt was gratitude I was out of spitting range.

Other than leaving scattered wings like ludicrously colored autumn leaves, we accomplished nothing. Not a damn thing. The only positive was there weren't any further attempts on Goodfellow's life. And I kept thinking it was positive up to the point he showed up at my door with a plan of his own.

Goodfellow tapped his watch when I opened the door. "Tick-tock. We have places to go and cherries to pop." He looked me up and down. "Could you change into something a little less . . . homeless-friendly?"

It was five in the afternoon and the last two hours had been spent working out with Niko. That wasn't anything I couldn't do in sweats and a T-shirt. Getting my ass kicked by my brother wasn't a black-tie event. I ducked as a lamp came hurtling from behind to bounce off my shoulder and shatter against the door frame.

"That could've been a dagger," Niko said reprovingly. It wasn't an idle observation, because the next one was. I caught a glimpse of it from the corner of my eye and dived to the ground. Robin caught it point-first and examined the blade. "It's dull. Now, what type of teaching tool is that?"

"He's delicate," my brother offered gravely.

I growled and rose to my knees, and then tackled Goodfellow to the floor while snatching the thrown dagger from him as I did. I rolled to keep him between Niko and me and held the training blade to his throat.

"You have a hostage. Nicely done." Niko approached and held out his hand. I slapped the dagger into it. "Assuming someone cares for the hostage." His lips twitched as he extended his other hand to assist Robin to his feet. "Considering the past several days, that's not an assumption we would hold true for all. Goodfellow, are you sure you won't stay here with us until we find out who is behind this?"

"I couldn't afford the massive cramp in my style." But there was a fleeting glint of surprised appreciation behind his eyes as Robin straightened his coat and smoothed his hair. "Speaking of style or lack thereof . . ." He focused his gaze on me. "Would you change already? Even I can't get you laid looking like that."

The practice session was nearly over and I looked over at Niko. He exhaled, folded his arms, and gave the most minute of shrugs. He thought I was making a mistake—that Georgina was for me, and that I was too stubborn by far for my own good. But while he thought I was wrong, he understood why I'd made the decision I had. He'd also seen it had actually given me some small measure of peace to have made *any* decision. I'd spent most of my life on the run. You don't get to make a lot of decisions doing that. You react and brace yourself in case it isn't good enough. But giving up running meant standing your ground . . . on all things. I'd made my choice—I was sticking with it, because I knew, even if no one else did, it was the right one.

The only one.

Niko had suggested I wait. That there might be a nonhuman who could come to mean something to me. Someone safe to care about. The thing was, I didn't want to care about my first. If it couldn't be with George, then I didn't want it to mean anything. If I couldn't care for her in this case, then I didn't want to care at all. I wanted it to be just what it was, sex and nothing else.

"Yeah, okay," I said slowly. "I'll change."

Niko lightly bumped my shoulder with his as I passed. I'd say that was the good thing about family: they supported you whether they agreed with you or not. But that was a lie. None of my other family had been remotely capable of that, and I was referring to the human half. I guess it would be more accurate then to say that wasn't the good thing about family; that was the good thing about Niko.

I dressed in jeans and a black pullover sweater. I imagined Robin would be massively unimpressed. I was right, but he was distracted enough by Niko that when I walked back into the room he let the clothes pass with a minimal amount of ranting and raving.

"Beau Brummell would choke himself with his own cravat," Goodfellow said scornfully as he looked me up and down, then brightened. "The whole polishing his boots with champagne, he stole that from me, you know." He extended an expensively shod foot and rested it on the coffee table as he relaxed on the couch. "See the shine? Subtle but impeccable."

"While I'm immensely fascinated by your shoe-care regimen," Niko commented as he leaned against the wall, "let's return to the discussion of who might be trying to kill you."

Robin admired the sheen on his shoe for another moment before exhaling, "You have no idea what you're asking."

"Piss off that many people? I believe it." I dropped into the chair and hooked a leg over the padded arm.

"Smart-ass pup, fetal flash-in-the-pan," he grumbled, but it was all surface. Beneath that was a dark melancholy he was usually more cautious about concealing. "I'm a puck. Pissing off lesser creatures is what I do. How can I be blamed for those who have absolutely no humor and a marked inability to hold on to their wallet? But that, while significant, is not the problem."

"Then what is?" Niko asked with the patience of a man who has all the time in the world. What we'd forgotten was that Robin was the one with that trait.

"I can't remember." He dropped his foot back to the floor. "I can't begin to recall all those I've practiced my trickery on over the years, because it is the years that are too many, not my victims. Although, to give credit where credit is due . . ." He flashed a happily predatory grin. When it faded, he added contemplatively, "I remember the highs and lows, naturally, but if I, for example, stole a boggle's treasure trove some ten thousand years ago, that I won't remember."

"But he would remember you," Niko stated.

"Yes, I would definitely be a low for him and I'm sure it would stick quite clearly in his muddy speck of a brain cell, but for me?"

"Not so much?" I said.

"Yes, not so much," he responded impassively. "I have no idea where I was born or when. I've forgotten more of my life than I remember. There simply isn't a way to make a list of the usual suspects."

"Perhaps if we concentrate on the attempts themselves." Niko straightened, pale eyes razor sharp in their persistence. "The Hameh birds and the sirrush are all from the same general area. Did you do something memorable down Babylon way? Were you someone's rough beast?"

Robin met that gaze with an unwavering one of

his own. He was either remembering something or doing his damnedest not to. "Poetic." He stood. "But nothing that could pertain to this, I'm sure."

I could see Niko wasn't buying it, and neither was I. But what we believed didn't matter, because the conversation was over. Goodfellow made some noise about how he'd think on it, mull it over, keep his head down, and thanks so very much for our input, care, and concern, and he was out the door. And there I sat, leg still dangling.

"Your ride on the debauchery express is leaving without you," Niko informed me blandly.

"It looks that way." I heaved myself up and grabbed my jacket.

"You're positive about this?" he asked as I shrugged into it. "You should let Georgina make her own decision when it comes to this. She's stronger than you give her credit for."

"I know she is." I shoved my hands in my jacket pockets and curved my lips without humor. "Hell, she's stronger than me. She can live with the uncertainty. I can't."

He dipped his chin and said only, "You're strong enough, just in all the mulishly obstinate wrong ways." Tilting his head toward the door, he continued. "Tell Goodfellow if he gets you in trouble, he can look forward to a few more attempts on his life."

"Come on, Cyrano," I said lightly, "people get laid all the time. What could go wrong?"

More to the point . . . what could go right?

Not a goddamn thing.

The first stop was a penthouse apartment on the Upper West Side. Other than the door being painted black, it was an impressive place. Doorman. Soft, deep carpeting in the halls with subdued lighting.

Very pricey. I looked around, feeling a little out of place. "You're sure she won't know I'm half Auphe?"

"If she does, she won't mind," Robin assured me. "She's quite open-minded, a wonderful species, totally without judgment. And they absolutely cannot breed with Auphe, or humans for that matter. In fact, they lay eggs, which requires fertilization at a much later date. She looks very human, though, so don't pull a groin muscle worrying over that one. I know you're new to the nonhuman dating scene." He checked his watch. "Good. We're right on time." He knocked lightly on the door, then mentioned casually, "Oh, I nearly forgot. She may . . . *may* . . . try to eat you afterward, but it's rare. Only if she finds you very, very charming, and with your personality I think we know what the odds are on that."

On that note, I turned and headed back down the hall away from the door . . . at a slightly faster clip than when I'd approached it.

The next stop was Central Park and the lake. Goodfellow stood on the shore, careful of his champagne-scrubbed shoes. "Lyrlissa. She's a limnade, a lake nymph. Once again, eggs, requiring the sperm of not one but *two* . . . well, that's neither here nor there. You're good to go."

The moon had turned the water into ripples of silver against black, a spill of platinum chains against velvet. It looked beautiful. It also looked cold as hell. I crouched down and slid a finger into the water. "Huh. Is she coming out?"

"She's a lake nymph, you uneducated child. They don't do that."

"Well, here's something I don't do," I countered, irritated, "get it up in fifty-degree temperature water."

"No?" Robin frowned.

"Jesus Christ, no! At least not and keep it there. I might be only half human, but the dick? That's all human, okay? It has its limits."

"As if you haven't suffered enough." He shook his head and squeezed my shoulder sympathetically. "Perhaps it's for the best. You would have to hold your breath for the duration, but I figured with your phenomenal lack of experience with the female of any species, you could manage to do that for the forty-five seconds that it would take for you to finish anyway."

"You are such an ass." I scowled.

"I do my utmost to live up to expectations." He grinned, before turning away from the water. "All right. Third time's the charm, which is apt, because that's her name. Charm."

"And she doesn't live in freezing water or will try to eat me?" I asked suspiciously.

"The most she will do is plait flowers in your hair. She's a leimakid, another kind of nymph. Meadow. Grass, trees, flowers." We walked up the path until we hit the Great Lawn. "And reproductively speaking, she spores. However, practice safe sex. There have been cases of moss growing on the north side of the wood afterward, if you get my drift. And termites are not your friend either."

"Thanks for making the experience so painless," I growled.

He slapped my back. "Goodfellow Enterprises—we aim to please." Then he drifted back into the trees. "I was never one much for monogamy," his voice floated out, "but . . . it's not too late to change your mind. If anyone is worth it, it would be Georgina."

"Good-bye, Robin," I said quietly. There was a deep silence and then I heard the rustle of leaves as he left, a courtesy—ordinarily he wouldn't have made any sound.

Charm came to me. If she knew I was Auphe, she didn't say. She didn't say anything really. She sang words I didn't understand and brought blankets woven of supple grass. She was nude and had what I suspected was green hair, although it was hard to tell for sure in the moonlight. Her hands were sure, her skin was soft, and she smelled like clover.

Everywhere.

11

While I'd been doing other things, very interesting things, Niko had been thinking. I got the results of that the next morning as I yawned. I was not a morning person, to say the least. "The subway?" I finished applying the gun oil and reassembled the Desert Eagle at the kitchen table. I was done playing with that cannibal son of a bitch Beane. Big gun, explosive rounds, and one vengefully pissy attitude—if that didn't take care of him, I might have to check out the going price on a rocket launcher.

"Miles and miles of tunnels, some of them even abandoned and unused, it's as close to a cave as one can get. More and more, Sawney seems to be a creature of habit. But Ham may have narrowed down a location for us. He called last night while you were out becoming a man." His lips twitched, but he went out without any more ragging on the subject. "He turned down our invitation to join us for any battles with Sawney, as expected, but he did have some information. Several of the homeless have disappeared. All of them have been the more 'out-there' ones. The schizophrenics, the mentally ill. And all of them had been using the Second Avenue Subway construction project for shelter."

All the SAS construction and mess going on there—it made sense. Easy access to the lower abandoned levels for both the homeless and Sawney. Those poor bastards could've walked right into his cupboard.

What also made sense was him going after the ones who were a little off. "You know," I said diffidently, "Sawney's made it pretty clear he has a thing for the nuts. Madness seems to be a turn-on for him." And I tasted just fine.

"I've heard what he said. You know it's not true. And considering what you've been through in the past year, the fact that you're not is a testament to just how strong you are." He fixed me with a sharp glance. "Don't make me emphasize that. My hand gets tired from swatting that hard head of yours."

Niko was at the table opposite me doing a little cleaning of his own. I wasn't the only one breaking out the big guns. He was rubbing a cloth across the metal of a double-bladed axe. It was a somewhat smaller version than seen in your average barbarian movie, but not by much.

"How the hell do you hope to walk the street with that?" I asked as I carefully slid the clip home. When an accidental discharge can take out a two-by-two chunk of the wall, it pays to put safety first. New York landlords are not especially understanding of homegrown ventilation systems.

"I've taken up the cello." He hefted the axe and measured it with approving eyes. "And this should fit quite nicely in the case." Laying it on the table, he began to wrap it in soft felt far more gently than was required. To me a gun was a gun, a hunk of expensive metal—nothing more. To Niko a weapon was an object of respect. "Musical aspirations cover a wide number of sharp-bladed sins," he added with an undercurrent of dry humor.

"I'm all for seeing you sin away on that son of a bitch Sawney." There was nothing quite like catapulting out of sleep with the absolute certainty there were teeth in your chest and hunks of your flesh being torn away to be eaten while you lay paralyzed. It really put a damper on the whole goddamn morning, let me tell you. "Promise coming with us again?"

"Yes." He tied a cord around the felt with a simple slipknot. "I think she worries that two helpless creatures such as us need a bodyguard." Normally, that would be a joke. I wasn't so sure it was this time. "And she feels a responsibility. It was she and her friend that drew us into this."

"Responsible enough to take Robin in and keep an eye on him until we figure out who's after him?" Whether it was the survivor or the Rom in me, I'd never been one to overlook an opportunity.

"Believe it or not, very probably," Niko allowed. "However, Goodfellow seems extremely loath to give up his independence, even with his life at stake. He's as stubborn as you."

Okay, maybe he wasn't done ragging on me after all about the previous night, but it was said with acceptance. Exasperated acceptance, but acceptance still. I'd made my decision, gone through with it, and Niko was going to stand behind me on it. The swat he delivered to the back of my head as he stood and circled the table didn't change that. Gave it a helluva punctuation, though. "My hand's not quite as tired as I thought," he informed me.

I rubbed the area and scowled, "You can't smack out stubborn."

"Oh, I think you'd be very surprised what I can do when I put my mind to it. Promise will meet us here this evening and then . . ." He looked down at the swaddled axe and smiled. It was something Niko rarely did; he was usually more subtle in exhibiting his emotions—head-smacking aside. This smile, however, had its share. Anticipation, retribution, and an icy anger. Niko would walk out of here carrying a cello case, but it didn't look like music was going to soothe his beast, not until Sawney was back where he belonged. Dead and in minute pieces. Not surprisingly, I didn't have a problem with that. And the more old subway tunnels we ended up splashing through and the more rats we dodged, the less problem I had. Even if Sawney hadn't killed the people in the park and warehouse, even if he hadn't tried, fairly successfully, to turn me into dinner, I would've long lost any tolerance for him.

That night, as planned, we made our way into the tunnels through the SAS. The extension of the Q train to Second Avenue and Ninety-sixth Street was a great idea—and the city had been having that same idea for longer than I'd been alive. After all the false starts and financial disasters, there were enough half-built and abandoned tunnels to hide a hundred Sawneys.

Now, that was one crappy thought. One of that son of a bitch was plenty.

The water was thigh high in the latest tunnel we hit, a maintenance one long out of use, and cold enough that I'd lost the feeling in my feet and legs. This tunnel itself was inky black except for our flashlights, and the rats were big enough that at some point they must've mated with dogs. Great Danes from the looks of them. None of this was the worst I'd come across in my life, nowhere near. But after hours and hours of it, I was losing my patience, and I had considerably less of the commodity than my brother. It wasn't something I was good at.

"That last rat had a subway conductor in his mouth," I grunted. "You saw that, didn't you?"

"Don't exaggerate. It was a dead coyote and only a medium-sized one at that."

I rolled my eyes in Nik's direction to see if he really thought that made it better. From the raised eyebrow that met my gaze, apparently he did, and I sighed and sloshed on.

"The wildlife is varied and interesting." Promise was doing the same, to my left and slightly ahead of me. Although she didn't slosh when she moved through the water—she didn't make any sound at all. Even Niko, quasi-ninja extraordinaire, caused the faintest ripple now and again, but when Promise moved, you wanted to rub your eyes to verify that she was actually there at all. Then again, dressed all in black as she was, without the paleness of her hair and skin, your eyes would've let you down too.

I didn't know whether moving that silently was a skill vampires were born with or one they gained over the years of their long lives. While I was curious enough to ask, the cockroach as big as my hand that fell from above to land on my shoulder distracted me. The dead body that came floating by distracted me even further.

The mass slowly drifted toward us speared by our flashlights . . . a tangle of clothes and limbs, pallid white hands with fingers curled like the legs of drowned spiders. As the body came closer, I got a better look, and said with a grimace, "Leftovers?"

It wasn't a body. It was pieces of one. Two bloated arms and a leg ripped off from below an absent knee were wound up and trapped in sopping cloth as the entire mess of it floated along. It wasn't pleasant to look at and less pleasant to smell. There was no way to tell if Sawney's scent was mixed in this toxic soup somewhere. I had a good nose, but I wasn't a bloodhound.

"I guess 'waste not, want not' isn't a concept Sawney embraces." Niko bent for a closer examination. "Death occurred somewhere around two days ago from the looks of the decomposition."

It wasn't just a guess. There was a book sitting on one of our shelves that spelled out the stages of decomposition in a corpse . . . dry corpse, wet corpse, soggy . . . whatever you were looking for. I knew because I'd once used it to prop up one leg of the coffee table. Nik, on the other hand, had read it, memorized it, and on occasion the knowledge had come in very handy. Despite that, I still had no desire to crack that book.

"Two days, give or take, yes," Promise gave a confirming nod. Considering she was old enough to have lived through a time when vampires still fed on humans, she would probably know. She aimed her flashlight down the tunnel. "The question now is the distance they've traveled. How far is the larder they slipped from?"

There was only one way to find that out and we moved on. Promise had her hair in an intricate twist that was wound tightly around her head. Despite the delicacy of it and her large shadowed eyes, she didn't look out of place in this hellhole. She . . . I don't know . . . fit, in some strange way. From day one, if you'd asked me to picture her life, I would've imagined that every day of it was spent in elegance and quiet luxury. That she was to the manor born, as they say.

But she'd once given me the hint that that wasn't the truth, not her truth anyway. She hadn't gone into any detail, but I got the impression Promise had been born to dirt and hardship rather than silk and satin. Not all vampires had lived in a castle with bug-munching flunkies to wait on them hand and foot. I didn't know Promise's age, but it was possible she was old enough to have been born into some pretty rough times in history . . . for vampire or human. It would explain all the rich husbands with fastly approaching expiration dates she'd had. Our bodies might escape the conditions that made us, but our minds rarely do.

Whatever her origins, she moved through the tunnel as if it were an aisle in Sak's—boldly and comfortably. I followed and Niko pulled up the rear. Every fifteen minutes or so, Nik and I would switch off, but we kept Promise, her flashlight now turned off, in the lead. Vampire night vision was better than both of ours put together. When the revenants came, she spotted them several seconds before we did and raised a hand to halt us in our tracks.

To look at, they weren't so different from the body parts that had been carried our way—decomposing and hideous to behold. Nature's imitation of a corpse—slick putrid-appearing flesh, white-filmed eyes, and yellowed, rotting teeth framed by bloodless gums and a dead black tongue. Some of them wore filthy clothing; some of them wore nothing at all. An

anatomically correct revenant is nothing to write
home about . . . literally. With all their smooth mottled flesh, I had no idea how to tell the difference
between male and female. But knowing how to kill
them was info enough.

It wasn't too difficult . . . killing them. Although,
if you just chopped a piece off, it would grow back—
given enough time. Simple minds, simple nervous
systems, Niko had explained disparagingly. Upright
salamanders with an attitude, that's what I said. Bottom line, not that hard to kill, but if you didn't finish
the job, a revenge-seeking revenant would show up a
few months later sporting new limbs and a hard-on
for a little mutilation of his own. The motto is "Make
sure the imitation dead are the genuine dead."

So, when the first revenant appeared into the weak
orange light ahead of us, I wasn't worried. When the
next five showed themselves, I only pulled my Glock.
I wasn't wasting the .50 and expensive rounds on
these guys. But when the following sixteen slunk into
sight, I did spend the time to be grateful that I didn't
see Sawney with them. A revenant was a walk in the
park, a couple of revenants . . . cake, but twenty-
two? I'd been accused of being a little cocky, but I
wasn't stupid. Certainly not *that* stupid. Twenty-two
was going to be a workout, no way around it. Because revenants, when they wanted to be, were fast.
They weren't the cheetahs of the preternatural world,
but they were the hyenas. Their asses could *move*.

Niko, always up for a little aerobic exercise, had
left the cello case behind at a junction of several tunnels and now hefted his axe. "How unfortunate for
them that they can't regrow their head." Which was
the place to aim on a revenant. If they had a heart,
I had no idea where it was. Their circulatory system

was a lot more primitive than a human's. Whatever pumped their vital fluids didn't seem to be centralized, and taking out the brain, à la every zombie movie ever made, was your best bet.

They were unusually quiet as they came. Revenants weren't the biggest talkers around, but they weren't above the occasional dinner conversation . . . of the usual "I'll rip you to shreds and enjoy every mouthful" type. Not these, though . . . they were silent and completely on-task. Sawney appeared to be a monster who valued discipline in his clan. There was no speaking, only determined white eyes, and a random jagged laugh here and there.

Which was disturbing in its own right. Because that laugh . . . that crazy, nerve jangling, completely over-the-edge-and-dogpaddling-in-the-pit-of-insanity cackle . . . was pure Sawney Beane. "Sound familiar?" I murmured to Nik.

"Yes," he answered flatly. "Yes, it does."

That's when they spoke. Every last one of them . . . simultaneously.

"Travelers."

Okay, that was creepy. I'd seen a lot of shit in my day, but that was definitely pretty damn freaky, but worse? It was Sawney's voice . . . almost. Not exactly, but like a distorted echo of it.

I shot the lead one in the head and heard another echo—this time in my mind. He'd said I tasted like insanity. And I wasn't. I wasn't like that. Wasn't like him or the Auphe. I gave a silent snarl and fired again, the flashlight in my other hand. After that they were on us and the gun was no longer the best option. They were too close, moist skin against my clothes. Niko was swinging his axe with devastating effect and Promise had a sword—silver, slender, and deadly. The one I drew was more along the lines of a Roman short sword. Long enough to take off a head, short enough for close quarters. Ugly, but functional . . . much like the revenants themselves.

I pushed hard at the one on me, shoving it away before slicing open its gut. That didn't kill it, but the wound distracted it long enough to let me whirl and take the head off the one coming from my other side. Partially anyway. Another two chops and then I flipped the first one over my shoulder. I could feel the drench of whatever fluid escaping his sliced guts hit my back. It was hot, slick, and that was more than I ever wanted to know about the internal juices of a revenant.

From the corner of my eye I saw Promise take the head of one revenant with her sword while tossing another of the creatures fifteen feet straight up to smash against the ceiling of the tunnel. A third hit her as she handled the first two and took her down to disappear under the water. I only had time to take one step toward her before she surfaced . . . alone. Three for her, three for me, at least six for Nik, which left only ten.

Unless you counted the next twenty that appeared from the gloom.

And behind those . . . I stopped counting. When it came to mathematics, there were three numerical concepts I was interested in: barely worth the time, doable, and strategic fucking retreat. I didn't need a calculator to know we were looking at the latter.

"Promise, go," Niko rapped. "Cal, cover us."

"Got it." The big gun was coming out after all. I pulled out the .50 and emptied the clip. I hit the revenants in the lead and concentrated the rest of my fire on the ceiling. It didn't fall, but chunks of it did.

Between that and the heads of their companions exploding like a Fourth of July event gone catastrophically wrong, they did hesitate slightly. It was enough to give us a head start and we took it. I stopped once more in my headlong rush to slide another clip home and fire again. Normally this would've been enough to put off a group of revenants, even one this large. They weren't bright, but they weren't usually suicidal either.

These were different. Sawney, not their own instincts and intelligence, controlled them. I didn't know if it was through sheer force of his maniacal personality or through something more unnatural in its domination. And in the end, the "how" didn't really matter; it was the results that concerned me. The ones that were left kept coming and coming, no matter how many I dropped. There were probably close to thirty-five to forty of them still remaining by the time I ran out of the explosive rounds.

"Cal."

"I'm coming." I turned and ran again. Niko was waiting a short distance ahead as I splashed along. The revenants weren't far behind me . . . like I'd said, they were fast. "All out of the good shit," I panted as we both raced along. As we approached, Promise stood still in a sickly pool of yellow light by a metal door she'd pried open. I saw the remains of the lock hanging, shattered by her deceptively slim hands. It was nice having a vampire on your side when it came to breaking and entering, especially when the breakage involved was fairly high.

"This way," she said, seemingly untroubled by the horde behind us. As the three of us passed through, she slammed it behind us and turned the handle with a flick of her wrist. That flick led to a creaking of metal and one seriously jammed door. Body after body hit it behind us. It held, but it wouldn't for long. We didn't wait around to time it. This tunnel was higher than the other, the water only ankle deep.

"Think Sawney is making this his permanent head-quarters?" I asked as we moved. We needed him to settle in, to choose his territory—the one he wouldn't be able to abandon. The one he'd be forced by his own nature to stick around in so we could kick his ass, the home he'd defend to the death . . . hope-fully his.

"Difficult to say. He's long-lived and the long-lived tend to be cautious. Especially, I imagine, those who've been burned to death." Niko had slowed to a fast lope and Promise and I followed suit. "Even if that death was only temporary. I think it's more likely he'll try several locations before choosing the one most suited to his particular lifestyle."

If you could call eating random strangers a lifestyle—cannibalistically inclined seeks open-minded cave dweller. No vegetarians please.

Nik's conclusion wasn't what I wanted to hear, but he was probably right. Sawney was cunning. He wasn't going to pick a place without checking out all his options. As for the revenants . . . "We're going to need more firepower or more hands or both," I pointed out. "I swear, that son of a bitch has every last revenant in the city working for him. The line at Monster Manpower must be short as hell now."

In the distance, I heard the sound of a metal door slamming back against concrete, and it was time for more serious running—not to mention a little serious cursing. By the time we reached one of the tunnels close to the surface, I was torn between barfing up a lung and lying down to die of a welcome heart attack. Damn, those bastards could run. They'd pulled back at the last second when we'd finally reached the lights and sounds of civilization. It was a good thing we weren't in active tunnels. Vaulting off the rail followed by a mob of ravenous revenants would've ruined the evening of any average commuter who happened to be standing on the platform.

I sat on the floor and leaned against a square pillar. "Enter"—I wheezed—"taining."

Vampires did breathe. They weren't dead, undead, any of that—a common misconception, no matter how much it made for good literature. They did have a larger lung capacity than humans, though. Promise was barely breathing deeply. At least Niko, who thought the New York Marathon was for those without the commitment for genuine exercise, was pulling in the occasional heavy breath of his own. It made me feel a little better about my burning chest.

"So . . ." I sucked in a breath and the oxygen deprivation spots began to fade around the edges of my vision. "What now?"

"That is a good question." Niko looked back toward the tunnel. "A very good question indeed."

12

Charity work in the tunnels didn't mean I got to skip the "day job." Two hours later I'd cleaned up after the tunnel battle, was back at the bar, and facing something worse than a horde of hungry revenants. A whole lot damn worse.

"Let me tell you a story."

Goodfellow was drunk. Not buzzed, not a little loose, but absolutely shit-faced. I'd long lost count of the number of drinks he had. What was the point? He never paid for them anyway—another way of thumbing his nose at Ishiah.

"How about I tell you one? It's about the moron who got loaded when there was someone out there trying to kill him." I kept my eyes on the rest of the bar. I always did, but this time I did it with a mental target branded on every patron's vulnerable areas. Robin seemed to have forgotten about the attempts on his life, but I hadn't.

"Why don't you stop serving him?" Ishiah said at my shoulder before finishing acidly, "Although the alcoholic fumes emanating from his pores should drop any creature in its tracks."

"I tried. He threatened to go somewhere else and

guzzle." I checked my watch. It was nearly three thirty a.m. I'd gone to the apartment to change after the tunnel fiasco, then had come to work. I'd been dead on my feet before I even got there. Now I was wondering just how difficult it would be to drag the puck back home with me, because it was doubtful he was up for fighting off a foot fungus, much less your generic inhuman killing machine. The thought didn't make me feel any less beat. "At least I can keep an eye on him here."

"And why do you bother? Most do not. He's an extraordinary amount of trouble. He always has been. He always will be." It was said without anger or accusation. Ishiah said it as if it were nothing more than the truth—the sky is blue, the earth is round. Neither good, nor bad. It simply was what it was. Although there did seem to be a trace of more personal observation of this particular puck than simple general knowledge of the race at large.

"He saved my life." I caught the glass that came tumbling through the air across the bar, refilled it, and set it back in front of Robin. "He stood with me and Nik against some pretty nasty shit when he damn well should've run the other way." I would have. At the time I didn't give a shit about anyone but Nik and myself. Goodfellow, the ultimate self-serving creature, had risen above in a way I know I wouldn't have. Not then.

"Robin's changing. After all this time." I couldn't read the emotion on Ishiah's face. A coma victim wasn't as deadpan as my boss could be when he wanted. Whatever lurked behind the current stony facade was well hidden, but from the phrase "after all this time," I could guess. "And I do have many years of perspective on our friend," Ishiah apprised us as he studied Goodfellow's slumped form. "More than he would probably like, and I don't mean that in a neg—"

He didn't get a chance to finish. Robin had started talking again, seeming oblivious of both Ishiah and the crowd noise that swelled at his back like a wave. "Let me tell you a story," he muttered into his glass.

Second verse, same as the first.

"Yeah," I groaned. "You've been telling it awhile now." And he'd yet to get past the word "story."

"*This* story"—his gaze meandered up, then in an uncertain circle until it managed to find me and attempted to scorch me with a fuzzy glare—"features a god of unparalleled charm, unsurpassed wit, with a male beauty unseen in this or any other world. . . ." He took another swallow of his drink. "And who was hung like the Trojan horse."

"No relation to you, I'm sure," I commented blandly.

Ishiah had moved from my back to beside me at the bar to say with quiet intensity, "Robin, you don't want to tell this one."

It was rather serious talk for what sounded like one of Goodfellow's usual cock-and-bull stories— heavy on the cock, light on the truth. His glare expanding to include Ishiah, he ignored the warning and went on. "And this god, so very perfect in every damn way as he'd be the first to tell you, met a people. Warm, friendly, open-minded . . . always a plus . . . and too unbelievably stupid to possibly kn—"

"*Enough!*" Ishiah's hand slammed down on the bar with a force that temporarily halted all conversation in the room. If he had actually been feeling some sort of satisfaction, it was gone now. His wings were visible as well and that wasn't a good sign. "Caliban, take him out of here now. Do not let him near another drop of alcohol. And"—as he leaned in toward Robin, the scar at his jaw blanched bone white—"if this seems to be a problem for you, Puck, if you wish to be difficult, I'll be happy to help your friend carry your shiftless, corrupt, and *unconscious* body out of here."

The next few minutes proved to be a learning experience.

First: Bar fights are the same, human or otherwise. The enthusiasm is identical; only the level of violence changes. Second: Peris can fly. Really. Third: Peris, flying or grounded, have hellacious tempers. Four: Pucks don't let anyone tell them what to do. Five: Even blind drunk, said pucks can kick some serious ass.

Before it was all over, there were chunks of fur, scales, feathers, and some things I didn't recognize littering the floor. There were also pools of blood and splatters of vomit, all covered with the glitter of shattered glass in an unpleasant kaleidoscope that I had no intention of cleaning up. Finally, there were Ishiah and Danyeal. They were flinging drunken fighters through the door while hovering in midair with wings fiercely beating, and it was something to see: The biblical exit from Eden meets a caged death match. I pushed up, sat on the bar, drank half a beer, and enjoyed the show. Meanwhile, Goodfellow took on two wolves with a bar stool and a glass mug. One fur ball ended up choking on ground glass, while the other poor fuzzy bastard ended up impaled with a wooden stool leg. Both would live . . . werewolves were sturdy.

"I challenge you all." One of the remaining legs of

the stool was waved aloft, Excalibur in the hands of Arthur. After all, if anyone could've seduced it out of the Lady of the Lake, it would be Robin. "Every last one of you impotent, parasite-ridden, Yeti-toe-loving . . . yes, I said it. You suck their hairy toes. You suck them with enormous relish. Now come to me! Come to me, you . . . *gama mou*," he abruptly cursed, and ducked.

I was taking another swallow rich in hops when I deciding ducking wasn't such a bad idea. As I did, Danyeal came hurtling over my head. He hit the wall behind the bar wings-first and slid down. He twitched once, then lay frozen, copper head tilted to one side, but eyes still blinking slowly. The Amadán who'd done the throwing started toward the bar to finish the job. Amadán, some sort of faery if I remembered right, were nasty. They excreted a venom through their skin. One touch and you'd be paralyzed for at least an hour. It made hand-to-hand combat rather tricky, as Danyeal had been so helpful in demonstrating. Hand-to-hand combat always had been seriously overrated in my book. I pulled the Glock, pointed it between opaline almond eyes, and peeled my lips back in a welcoming grin. "Interesting fact. I get paid whether the customers are alive or not."

With shining waves of silver and black hair, lithe figures, and ever-changing eyes, the Amadán were the supermodels of the unnatural world. Skinny, hungry as hell, and couldn't buy a brain cell with a bucketful of credit cards. Fortunately for this one, he was capable of wrapping the empty space between his ears around the fact that a bullet bouncing about in the confines of his skull might be undesirable. He faded back into the seething mass of the crowd, everyone he touched skin to skin falling at his feet as he moved.

Goodfellow, who had fallen during his lunge to avoid Danny, was staggering back up and still looking to defend King and Country. "Come to me. . . ." Then as Camelot fell, so did Robin. I caught him by the back of his shirt before he hit the floor. His head hung as slackly as that of the paralyzed Danyeal with his chin resting on his chest. He was out cold, but unconscious or not, he still kept talking. "I was a god," came the barely decipherable murmur.

"I'm sure you were," I snorted as I pulled him up and over the bar. Depositing him in relative safety beside Danyeal, I went to help Ishiah shut the place down. What was left of it.

Two hours later I was home, Goodfellow was on the couch, and I barely made it to bed. I paused only to touch the barrette on my dresser. A reminder . . . a promise to a dead little girl. Neither Nik nor I had ever gotten to be a normal kid with a normal life. Ours had been taken away before we even had one. This girl's had been taken away too, and in a far more brutal fashion. I wasn't going to forget that and I wasn't going to forget her.

I stripped, fell into bed, and five seconds later was listening to Niko explain his plan. At least it seemed like five seconds—six, if you were generous. Definitely not the hours it had been. Blinking against harsh daylight, I felt the cool rub of the sheet against my face and rocked a little at the firm nudge to my shoulder. "Then we're clear?" Niko said.

"What? Yeah. Clear," I mumbled. "Crystal. Bye."

"You've committed every word to memory?"

"Right next to 'The Road Not Taken.' Swear." I rolled over and pulled the sheet over my head. I hadn't heard Nik come in or the door shutting. It didn't worry me. I hadn't heard him precisely because he was Nik. The door would've been shut with complete silence, and I tuned out the sound of the key turning in the lock as only he, Promise, and Robin had a key. If I'd heard a different sound, the stealthy one of claws skittering against wood or the scrape of a metal pick against the lock, I'd have woken up instantly. I wouldn't have answered that door alone either. I slept with a knife under my pillow, a gun under the mattress, and a sword under the bed. If I could have litter-box-trained an alligator, I would've had one of those under there as well.

But since my subconscious did know it was Niko— here we were. I'd slept through the plan and was attempting to sleep through the post-game. I knew better, but hope and laziness spring eternal.

"Good. Then I'll leave the recruiting the boggle up to you."

That woke me the hell up. A bucket of ice water and a shot of adrenaline couldn't have done it any faster. I rolled back and propelled up to a sitting position. "No," I refused as quickly as I could snap the word out. "We agreed. No more boggles."

"Did we?" He had showered at Promise's. Damp blond hair, closely shaved face—the goatee of several months prior had disappeared not too long ago. There was the smell of a different shampoo, but the scent of the soap was the same as what we had in our bathroom. Some sort of all-natural herbal, goat-milk concoction without the faintest tinge of artificial chemicals. I didn't know where he got it. I just used it and went on with my life. Promise obviously did know which store sold it or Nik had started taking stuff over with him. Either way . . .

I gave him a crooked grin. "You're nesting, Cyrano. That's cute as hell." The desire to yank his chain faded as quickly as it had come. "And, yeah, we did agree. No more goddamn boggles." I'd once hired werewolves to kill George when I was "under the influence" so to speak. And I'd done the same to Niko and Robin, under the same influence, using a boggle instead. Nine feet of scales, mud, and killing fury, a boggle didn't have to be pushed very hard to do what was already natural instinct. That I'd personally known that particular boggle had only made it easier.

"It wasn't you," my brother said, knowing the twisted lane my memories had traveled down, "and this boggle won't be that one."

"Why are we talking about boggles anyway? Shit." I swung my legs to the floor and rested my head in my hands. "What was that plan again?"

As plans went, it was simple. Niko had never felt the need to overcomplicate. The more tangled the approach, the equally tangled your body parts were likely to be when it all went wrong. There were more revenants in the tunnels than we could handle; therefore we'd do a little recruiting. There were those who wouldn't mind snacking on a horde of revenants . . . that would be pay enough for them. Then there were a few species who happened to like money and expensive things.

Boggles, for one, were suckers for jewelry. Gold, silver, precious or semiprecious, as long as it was bright and shiny, they coveted it. It was rather amusing to see a huge hulking figure caressing chunky gold chains that would barely fit around one of his enormous fingers. Good for a chuckle, right up until

you remembered where the jewelry came from:
people.

"Since when do we depend on anyone but ourselves?" I looked up. "And what are we going to
pay? We going to hock your tofu collection?"

"Since doing it alone could take us months or get
us killed. As for financial incentive, Promise says she
has far more jewelry than she could wear in two
lifetimes. Vampire lifetimes," he added with a quirked
eyebrow.

A boggle would definitely demand a good chunk
of Promise's collection. Seemed fair. She had gotten
us involved in this bit of community service. Once
it was determined Sawney was out of the museum,
Sangrida hadn't seemed to consider it her problem
any longer. She'd washed her Valkyrie hands and
turned her attention to cleaning up her sirrush-
splattered basement. And Promise couldn't justify
anything to the rest of the *human* board of directors
other than the "reward" money for information, and
the reward money wasn't really enough to make it
worth our while following Sawney's slaughter from
beginning to end. Yet here we were.

Back in the old days when we were on the run,
we'd been right along with Sangrida—not our responsibility, not our problem.

When had that changed?

"We can also enlist a few wolves. We're not popular with the Kin, but not all werewolves are Kin."

True—though the better fighters tended to be.
"Okay, wolves are fine. Wolves, I get." I hadn't had
the opportunity to avoid wolves in the past year like
I had boggles. Wolves were everywhere. Let a problem with them get to you and you wouldn't be able

to leave the apartment. "But there's probably only one boggle in the park." They were tremendously territorial. Central Park would only be big enough for two, and Niko and Robin had already killed the one we knew of. "Just one isn't worth the trouble." It was a lie. One boggle alone could take out his weight in revenants.

"It's worth the trouble," Nik corrected with patience, but as his patience tended to be of the ironclad variety, it didn't do me much good.

I tightened my lips. The boggle had nothing to do with the revenants. We could hire double the wolves, hsigos, or whoever else we came across. No, this was about me. I was getting over Darkling and it was time to do the same with boggles. "Jesus, fine," I surrendered with ill temper. "I'll deliver the invitation. Happy?"

"Actually smug would be more precise. Now"—he tossed me a shirt from my bureau—"there is a pool of puck vomit on the living room floor. Enjoy."

I did not.

I neither enjoyed it nor cleaned it up. I slapped a scrub brush in the slack hand of a bleary-eyed, swearing, and painfully sober Goodfellow before showering, and taking off into the late-morning sun. It was an unusually warm day for November and I would've been able to get by with only a T-shirt as long as I didn't mind my holster showing. I minded, and I thought New York's finest probably would as well. I ended up wearing the lightweight weathered denim jacket that I wore in the summer for the same purpose. As for Niko, as accessories went, I wasn't sure if he counted as summer or fall. I wasn't the type of guy into lugging around extra crap unless it was a weapon, although Nik definitely did fall into that category. "I'm trying to think of you as a back-pack or a little dog in a ninja outfit," I said finally, "but it's not working. I thought I was supposed to do this myself. Tough love and all that shit."

"Cal," he responded with vast tolerance for my idiocy, "it is a boggle."

"Je-*sus*," I growled. Threading through the crowded sidewalk, I planted a rib-cracking elbow into the ribs of a well-dressed pale man with a satchel, a Rolex, and hungrily twitching fingers who was following with voracious intent an oblivious thirteen-year-old girl. He stumbled, snarled, and faded back. He could've been human; he could've been something else. Sometimes you can't tell the monsters from the maniacs, and sometimes there's no difference at all.

Boggles came down on the monster side. They weren't smart, but they weren't stupid. They were driven by logical needs: greed and hunger. You could reason with a boggle . . . as long as you were on equal footing. We'd laid that groundwork with our boggle, although in the end it hadn't worked out too well for either party, but this other boggle—he was new territory. Friend, foe, or food, we'd have to prove it all over again.

We took the 6 train uptown from Astor Place, got off near the park, and walked east, enjoying the sun. In the park, free of the city's crush of humanity during the week, I'd be able to smell the boggle out. It might take a while and more exercise than I cared to invest, but I could do it. That was the easy part. After that, it was hard to say what would happen. An invitation to party with revenants in a subway tunnel, that wasn't necessarily a universal passion, whether you got paid for it or not. Boggles were homebodies as well. But if baubles were what got you through the day, Promise could offer far more variety than the boggle was likely to get from random victims.

I could see it going either way—if, and this was a big if—he wasn't pissed about what had happened to his fellow mud-dweller. It's one thing to be territorial; it's another for the only other member of your species in three hundred square miles to end up dead. Very thoroughly dead. If I were a boggle, I knew I'd be wondering how long it would be until whoever had done that came after me. He was about to get his answer, just not in the way he probably would've guessed.

"You think boggles have names?" I stepped off the path into a wide grassy area and shaded my eyes from the sun. We'd called ours Boggle and he'd never offered up anything else. It wasn't surprising. Snitches don't love their cops, and Bog had certainly never loved us. We hadn't exactly loved him either, but I'd . . . hell, gotten used to him, I guess.

"I imagine they do. I doubt they call themselves Boggle One and Boggle Two as in the highest level of literature you care to pick up." Niko still hung back in the trees, his black on gray blending in with the shadows.

"You were the one who homeschooled me, Cyrano. If I'm afraid of big words, you have no one to blame but yourself." I inhaled deeply and after an hour of roaming the park I finally caught a whiff. Mud and boggle. "Got him."

I'd long passed Charm's particular meadow. It was impossible to distinguish her scent from that of yellowing grass and the dried remnants of clover warming under the sun, and I hadn't seen or heard her as we'd gone by. I took it as a sign. As with Ishiah's opinion of the pucks, it was neither good nor bad. It was what it was. The bittersweet regret had nothing to do with her; that all belonged to me. I knew I had fucked up, but I'd meant to. Aimed to. Amazing how for the best reason, you do the worst thing. And George was my reason, in more ways than one.

"Which direction?"

I pulled the sunglasses out of my pocket and slipped them on. "Past the far end." There were more trees there. Through those would be a small area, about twenty-five by twenty-five. Big enough for a wallow, but hidden by the trees—that's how boggles liked it. "Maybe Ham would help us out with Sawney. I don't know if he's a fighter, but we could ask. If you trust him around Promise," I added with a grin.

"You know I trust Promise." I did trust her too, at least when it came to Niko. She'd do anything for him, and I meant it. Anything, and God help you if you got in her way. "There's not much she wouldn't do to save your neck. But she doesn't seem too fond of Ham." I grinned wider.

"That would be Promise's business, and, as we've seen, she is very good at business. If Ham ignored her threat . . ." A millimeter slice of white teeth flashed, then disappeared. "I only hope I'm there to see the end result."

"Yeah. I'd buy that ticket." But his feeling for the homeless or not, I doubted Ham would go down in the tunnels with us. He'd met us once. No way was he that invested in our problem.

Just as we went beyond the next line of trees, we came across a whole mess of them. Or it might've been more accurate to say a litter of them—boglets . . .

seven of them, sunning themselves around the edge
of the muddy water. They were mud-encrusted creatures the size of a full-grown bull alligator, minus
the tail. With lazy yellow eyes, flickering tongues,
and claws stained with old blood—they were predatory toddlers in a wide-open playpen. "Great," I
muttered as over a half dozen sharklike heads turned
toward us with a curiosity that was becoming more
and more avid by the second. "Where's she going to
get a babysitter?"

The more important question—the truly pertinent
one—would be whether the boggle we'd killed had
been their father. I couldn't recall any information on
boggle mating habits off the top of my head. Did
they have two sexes? One? Seven? I didn't know. If
they went with the usual two, I already knew this
female didn't have much of a dating pool to choose
from. As odds went for our boggle being her
boggle . . . shit.

"About boggle birds and bees . . . ," I said, moving
a casual hand toward my holster. "Care to do a little informing?"

"Boggles mate for life."

It didn't get more informative than that.

As avid curiosity began to change to avid hunger,
the boggle offspring began to shift. The slit pupils of
their eyes dilated as they rose to muscular crouches.
And as they moved, so did the muck on the edges
of the water. The surface quivered, then abruptly exploded upward.

She was big. Easily the nine-foot standard, the
same flat head and backward curving rows of teeth
that I remembered from Boggle. If there was a difference in superficial appearance between the male and
female, I couldn't see it. Classic brown dappled scales

glinted here and there through the coating mire, and the claws were identical as well. Over a foot long and the black of volcanic glass, they could cut a tree in half with one swipe, and if they could do that to solid wood, it didn't take much imagination to picture what they could do to less sturdy flesh.

When the Great White mouth opened, liquid mud streamed from between the teeth and became a brown mist in the air as she roared. The smaller ones immediately echoed the roar, over and over again, until the air was full of the reek of the half-digested flesh of their last meal.

"Guess what, Nik," I muttered, squeezing the grip of my gun with whitened knuckles, "I'm now even less over boggles than I was before."

It was like before too, only this time the boggle wasn't fighting simply for the sake of the adrenaline-pumping violence; this one was fighting for her children. Eyes as big as human fists focused on us, and a clawed foot came out of the mud and water to slam onto solid earth. The ground shook under my feet, and I brought my gun up. We had options, sure. We could run. But mama boggle could run too, and as quickly.

We could stay and fight. Niko and Robin had been able to take one boggle. Niko and I could do the same. But there wasn't just one—there were eight. Seven were only half the size of what had spawned them, but that didn't change the fact that they were killers, or that from their stealthy sideways slither, they were already practiced ones.

Run or fight.

Live or die.

Or we could just give them a present.

I had to admit, I hadn't thought of that. As choices

went, it had sailed cleanly under my radar. The result was that I was almost as mesmerized as the boggles by the dripping cascade of diamonds and rubies that hung from Niko's hand. The jewels blazed in the sun like rain-drenched poppies. My sunglasses dimmed the colors and sizzling glory by barely a fraction.

"Pretty." "Pretty." "Shiny." The boglets had stopped moving and were staring at the necklace with rounded eyes and unconsciously grasping claws. Mom wasn't as easily impressed. Her other foot hit the ground and she thrust her head closer with brutal force. The gems were reflected in the cold sheen of her eyes and she gnashed her teeth repetitively. Finally, the lethal weapon that was her hand was held out.

"Tiffany's?" The question oozed out with splintered shards of bone and more remnants of mud.

Niko stepped forward and deposited the necklace across her scaly palm. "Of course. We would not insult you with anything less."

She brought it closer to study it. Held it near to her eyes, up to the sun, let it dangle in the air, and then finally . . . she purred. Or maybe it was only the grinding of more bones caught in her throat. As sounds went, they were remarkably similar. "You have more?"

"Many more. Anything you can imagine." Nik looked up at her and added without hesitation, "You should be aware, however, that we did kill the other boggle here in the park."

There was no softening of the blow, no attempted explanation . . . no "He tried to kill us first. It was self-defense. Sorry for your loss and I'm positive he's in a better place." He simply gave her the information and waited to see what she would do with it. I think for every lie our mother had told in her fairly short life, Niko had racked up an equal number of truths . . . often in situations where deception would've been the easier and far safer choice. Considering how many years we'd spent on the run and literally living a lie, it was a peculiar dichotomy. Nik had done a lot of things to keep me alive that cut across the natural grain of who he was. He'd told the truth when he could. When he absolutely couldn't, he'd used lessons Sophia had unwittingly taught us to keep me from the hands of the Auphe, and he'd not once hinted he'd regretted what he'd done for me.

I did. I regretted the hell out of it, but right now? Wearing a fine spray of boggle mud on my jacket, smelling old blood and decomposing flesh, I honestly wished he'd picked this moment to lie like a fucking dog.

"You." Transparent lids blinked over her eyes as the head began to weave slowly. "You killed him. You." Not a question, but a tasting of the words and the reality behind them. "My mate. Their sire."

I still had the .50 up and the trigger halfway home when she clacked her teeth again and said abruptly, "Opals. Black opals. Do you have black opals?"

And that was that. Boggles might mate for life, but apparently they didn't mourn for it.

Although I'd been dispatched to extend the invitation, Nik did most of the talking. I'd say he'd planned for that the entire time. I had certain talents and skills, but negotiation of the nonviolent kind wasn't one of them. So while the discussion of price went on, I played with the kiddies—which meant I hid in the trees while they tried to eat me. Fifteen minutes later, I was soaked with sweat, hanging in the lower limbs of an oak, and pistol-whipping two boglets who were about to take chunks out of my legs.

"Cal, playtime is over. Let's go."

The juvenile killers, who'd been shaking off what they considered love taps, moaned in disappointment and loped back toward the muck at their mother's beckoning snarl. I dropped to the ground and did some snarling of my own as I holstered the gun. "You know, Cyrano, as a therapist, you suck out the ass."

"It's a hit-or-miss process," he responded solemnly as we wove through the trees. "Constantly changing and developing. Jung once wrote . . ."

What I had to say about Jung wasn't hit or miss at all. It was very precise, graphic, and involved Niko's intestinal tract.

"You didn't enjoy yourself? Why not? Children are always enamored of you."

Yeah, kids loved me. Loved to eat me. Werecubs, boglets, I was walking milk and cookies for them all, but I wasn't thinking about that, and I wasn't concentrating on Niko's dry teasing either. Seeing boggles again had brought up some buried emotions all right, but not the one my brother had planned on. No, that wasn't true. It was the emotion . . . guilt . . . that he'd hoped to resolve, but this time the guilt was focused elsewhere. Niko and Robin hadn't ended up the casualties as intended a year ago, but someone else had.

"I miss Boggle," I said quietly. And I did in a way. Not for who he'd been, but for *what* he'd been. He'd been our informant and like Robin's tended to be, he was homicidal as hell, but he'd been a piece of our lives. When you lived life on the run you didn't have many constants. Boggle had been one for two years and I'd gotten him killed. He'd deserved it, no doubt, but I didn't have to like the fact it had been because of me.

Nik, like Bog's mate, didn't waste any tears as he said without a trace of doubt, "He was a killer, Cal. Through and through, a killer."

I looked away, said, "Not the only one," and kept walking.

13

Recruiting isn't as easy without the glossy pamphlets and television ads. I'd been thrown out of so many wolf bars and social clubs that night I was beginning to lose count. I never would've thought the boggle would be the easy part. It was seven in the morning when we finally dragged ourselves to Robin's place in Chelsea, choosing it only because it was closer than ours. I had a black eye, Robin was limping again, and Niko had a hair or two slightly out of place. Normally I would say it was because he was the better fighter, but the reality was it could well be a toss-up between him and Goodfellow. Niko's abilities were nothing less than astounding, but Robin had had many more thousands of years of practice. It wasn't a lack of skill that had Robin on the short end of the stick this time.

Wolves had only scorn for humans. They were nothing but sheep . . . weak and existing only to be preyed upon. It wasn't an attitude you wanted to be on the receiving end of. Then again, when it came to pucks and the Auphe-tainted, being a sheep was a step up.

As Nik settled on the couch, long black-clad legs

stretched out and crossed at the ankle, Goodfellow asked him acidly, "Could I get you a comb perhaps? At least until the paramedics arrive?"

"I told you eight breasts in a sequined halter was not our top priority," Niko offered mildly as he clasped hands across his abdomen, "did I not?"

"Monogamous sex is rotting your brain." Robin flicked both arms in a gesture that wasn't quite obscene, but definitely full of outrage. "They were all on the *same* woman."

"We were there to enlist wolves, not grope them. And offering to include her mate in on the exercise did not improve matters any."

I ignored them both and went to the freezer for ice. Applying a towelful of the crushed stuff to my eye, I leaned against the counter as the discussion continued. "Oh, don't let him fool you. He was completely into it. He simply feared he'd be overshadowed by my prowess and endowments. Although, to be just, his seemed impressive behind the leather. Male wolves." Green eyes gleamed. "They do love their leather."

Truthfully, the fight hadn't had much to do with Robin hitting on two wolves, but it was easier on the stomach than discussing how our two kinds were so loathed. Not all wolves felt the same, about me at least, but enough did to make things uncomfortable. To be hated was one thing. To be considered a worthless, utterly detested thief or a mixed-breed abomination that inspired disgust and revulsion . . . it was less uncomfortable to talk about the results of gawking at wolf boobs.

Then there was the fact that we'd killed a Kin Alpha.

Yeah, none of us were too popular. Niko just happened to be a little less unpopular than Robin and me. So far we hadn't found a single wolf willing to work with us, no matter what the pay. And Goodfellow trying to include himself as a bonus wasn't helping. If he kept it up, he wouldn't have to worry about a mysterious assassin ending his life; Niko would handle that himself.

It was a good change of subject because the lingering image of eight lightly furred, seismically bouncing breasts was still making me mildly motion sick. "Anyone try to kill you in the past three days?"

Robin draped himself over a chair and rubbed a calf that I assumed was just bruised. No blood showed through the expensive slacks. "Only that new restaurant on Columbus. The chef there is far deadlier than any Hameh bird."

"I thought we agreed you'd stay close to home until we discovered who's behind this." Niko didn't move or change the tone of his voice, but the heavy weight of disapproval was evident nonetheless.

Goodfellow gave him a brilliant smile in return. "Your concern warms." He didn't say specifically what or where it warmed. "I also have a pair of leather pants. I can go change right—"

The door opened and Seraglio entered, saving either Goodfellow or Nik. I wasn't at all sure who would come out ahead in that contest. At the sight of us, she shook her head and, touching a small hand to the immaculate piled hair, sighed in resignation. "If I feed you, will you leave? I can't possibly work with your lazy bodies piled about." She passed Robin and ruthlessly shoved his leg off the arm of the chair. "And you all are skinny as they come. Whoring and drinking will keep you that way. A man—a real man—should have flesh on his bones."

Standing, Robin—who had never been a human

man, real or otherwise—shook his head. "Thank you, but no. Bed is what I need, unless you care to join . . ." Already in the kitchen on a step stool, Seraglio, at his words, traced a contemplative finger over the handle of a knife embedded in a butcher's block. "Ah, that would be a no? Your inconsolable loss, then."

As he disappeared down the hall, his gait uneven, I asked politely, "Do you make pancakes, ma'am?"

An hour later, my stomach was pleasantly full of peach waffles, and my eye ached somewhat less. Seraglio had given me a plastic bag full of ice and another towel to wrap around it. It had lasted until we made it to the subway before becoming nothing but an empty bag and a damp towel. I'd shoved the cloth in my pocket, and now I was leaning my head back against the window of the subway car, ready to take what I'd known was coming.

"Ma'am? You called her ma'am?"

"Like I told her, you taught me good manners." I kept my eyes shut, on the verge of dozing to the rocking of the car. Then I flashed my left arm up to block the blow. There had been the faintest rustle of cloth to warn me, one that Niko wouldn't have given anyone else. The training never stopped, and it never would. It was what had kept me alive this long.

"I taught them, yes, but I had no idea you'd actually incorporated them into your daily life." I felt his arm drop away. "I've seen you interact with humans and nonhumans, and I've not seen you show anyone the respect you show Madame Seraglio."

"She scares me," I admitted frankly. "I've yet to see her more than three feet from a butcher's knife. And I show you respect, Cyrano. I respect the hell out of you."

"For the same reason?"

"Pretty much," I confirmed, this time protecting my ribs with a quickly sheltering forearm. Opening my eyes, I added, "A healthy dose of humiliation doesn't hurt. That you changed my diapers when I was a baby isn't something I'll ever get over."

"Trust me, it wasn't that memorable." He snorted as he penetrated my guard and slapped my abdomen with just enough stinging force to make the lesson stick. "I would bring up the size of the excessively large guns you carry, but that would be unnecessarily cruel."

"Ass," I grumbled.

After that, we rode in companionable silence until the train made a stop. When the doors closed again, I said, "I'm guessing it's the four of us and the boggle in the tunnels, then. Flea-free." Nobody liked the smell of wet dog anyway, and I personally thought the she-boggle was enough to worry about keeping track of.

"We're not there yet. We have one more avenue yet to try." Niko leaned his head back as well, but he didn't close his eyes. He didn't take chances, big, small, or in between.

"Yeah?" I asked. As far as I could tell, we were standing at the end of the road. It was time to cope with the lack of asphalt and grab the hiking boots. "What?"

"Wait and see, little brother. Wait and see."

The wait and see turned out to be Delilah, and we met her at a strip club in Chelsea conveniently located a few subway stops from Robin's condo. She was the bouncer. The dancers were all male, muscle-bound, and bored. I was relieved that Niko hadn't told Robin that's where we'd been heading. He was probably a regular, and it had been a long night. I wasn't ready for a longer morning of dollar bill waving and more discussion of leather pants or the removal thereof.

White-blond hair still in the high ponytail, Delilah was wearing leather herself. Pants and a scoop-necked top, both the amber of her eyes, clung to her lithe figure, but it was the type of snug fit meant for fighting, not for show. "Pretty boy," she said with lazy recognition. "Twenty dollars."

"We've no interest in the show, Delilah," Niko explained with a slight bow of his head. "We're here to speak with you."

"Ah." She nodded and held out an unrelenting palm. "Twenty dollars."

We paid the ten apiece and went in out of the morning light. Nine a.m. and some guy was already onstage. That early and normally I was still in bed, but this poor bastard was up there shaking . . . whatever you had to shake for ten bucks' admission. The place was dark and small with red spotlights and a few glassy-eyed patrons. We sat at a table close to the door, but with a good view of the room as well. Delilah could keep watch for customers and trouble simultaneously.

"Your chest? Doing well?" A finger with a natural, unpolished nail touched my shirt.

"No problems." Which was true. It wasn't much to look at, from a human point of view, but it was healed and mostly painless. There was the occasional pull of skin that was tighter than it should be, but it would loosen up eventually—stretch like the majority of scar tissue came to do. If I did have a problem, it was drifting awake in the middle of the night with the distinct sensation of a soothing tongue rasping at my chest and a warm weight pinning me firmly to the bed. And that—well, that wasn't really what I'd call a problem.

"Good." Satisfied, she propped a booted foot on the table. "You are healed. You are pretty. So why come here?"

"Yeah, well, about that." I shook my head at the shirtless waiter as did Nik. "We're not too popular with wolves, and we need to do some hiring."

"Not popular." She smiled with those perfect teeth. "Puck, Aupheling, human. Kin killer. Not wanted, not embraced. So misunderstood." Throwing back her head, she laughed. The bar was dark and only a fourth full, but everyone turned at the sound to look at her with faint expressions of surprise. She caught them staring, pinned them with oval eyes, and the men hastily looked away, concentrating on their drinks or the stage. Dominance, humans picked up on it as quickly as dogs, whether they wanted to admit it or not. "Human sheep," she said scornfully. "Barely prey."

Tilting her head, she leaned in and smelled Niko. She didn't get close enough to touch, but sampled the air around him. "But not you. You are as they say. Warrior." Then she was at his throat in a movement so fluid and quick that I doubted the identified sheep caught the shift in position. I know they didn't see the edge of Niko's knife between Delilah and him or her teeth click purposely against the metal.

"Alpha," she identified decisively as she settled back. "You lead your pack. Protect your pack."

She wasn't wrong. Niko had been born an Alpha. If you screwed with him, screwed with his own, there wouldn't be much left of you to regret that decision.

Niko flipped the blade and made it vanish under

his coat. He didn't comment on her conclusions. Alphas had no need to brag. "We would like your help. Yours and anyone else you could convince to accept our pay."

She dropped her booted foot to the sticky floor and licked away the single drop of blood on her upper lip. "You come about Sawney Beane?" His presence in the city was evidently not a secret, not anymore. "He kills." There was a shrug that said clearly, "Who doesn't?" "He wastes." That was entirely different from the haughty lift of her chin, a sin seen only with contempt. I remembered the body parts floating in the water, disgusting to us, squandered to Delilah. It reminded me. She had helped us, she might help us again, but she also was a wolf. Some wolves didn't eat people, but she was also Kin. Kin ate whatever the hell they wanted. I wanted to like her, and I rarely wanted to like anyone, but liking involved trust and truth, things I'd only started to put into play in the past year. I wasn't good at either one yet, and I didn't know that Delilah even deserved either one.

But this was about Sawney and the revenants. If and how she could help us now was what was important, not wondering about the ethical implications of her diet. "He's in the subway tunnels," I said, hooking a leg around the chair leg and wearily resting my elbows on the table, "with a whole shit-load of revenants."

"We saw at least forty." Niko picked up the story. "And there could be more. They're oddly organized. They act as one with none of the usual revenant squabbling and infighting. We've enlisted a boggle, but I don't believe that even she will be enough. Not if Sawney is there with them this time."

Delilah tapped her foot against the floor with eyes distant for several seconds. "Sawney is Sawney. Not Kin business. But . . ." Her upper lip, now blood-free, lifted with distaste. "He is careless. He brings attention. Bad attention. Kin will not help, not you." Tracing a reflective finger along the tattooed wolf eyes around her neck, she said, "But I will help." She took a drink from a passing tray and popped a slice of orange in her mouth. "If price is acceptable."

"I thought the Kin wouldn't help us. You are Kin," Niko pointed out, gray eyes focused with skeptical caution. It had been his plan to ask for her assistance, but while he was capable of trust and truth, you had to earn it.

"I am Kin, but I am also free," she announced as if it were common knowledge.

"Free being?" I asked.

She tossed back the rest of the drink and gave a sly smile. "Not caught."

14

Delilah was a wolf of her word. She took the pay, and two days later she showed up in the tunnel as shown on the map of the Second Avenue subway project Niko had sketched on a bar napkin. She also brought four other wolves with her. Big ones, all half-and-halfs and wearing hooded sweatshirts to cover the fact. It didn't stop an experienced eye from spotting the glitter of golden-brown irises, thickened black nails, and jagged teeth made for the ripping out of throats.

Niko, Promise, Robin, Boggle, Delilah with her wolves, and me, if we couldn't take care of the problem, we might as well grab a walker, move south with the snowbirds, and let Sawney have New York.

"Did you leave the kiddies with a nanny?" Robin asked as he looked up at the boggle. He didn't have any better memories from the fight with her mate than Niko or I did. It showed in the wary distance he kept from her.

From the contemptuous snap of her jaw and gale-force snort of rancid air, she managed to say without words that the boglets would do just fine on their own. I wasn't sure where she'd gotten into the tunnel system to eventually meet us, but I doubted it had involved a MetroCard.

"This is quite the mix." Promise's hair was in a braid this time, one woven with black cord, then wrapped in a thick club at the base of her neck. She smiled to show the tips of pointed canines. "The very best parties always are."

In contrast, Delilah was already frowning in impatience. "We go now. Skipped dinner. Mealtime is now."

"You didn't eat simply to work up an appetite for this?" Niko had brought his axe again and raised it slightly in respectful salute. "*You* are the warrior."

"Devious and ravishing." Robin sidled closer. He'd made the sacrifice called for by filthy tunnel water and wore jeans. My jeans. He didn't own any. Hit men after his ass he had plenty of, but casual wear for revenant hunting—that he was lacking.

"Devious, ravishing." She snuffled his hair, neck, and shoulder and it wasn't in what I would call a sexual way. "*Hungry.*"

"All right, then. Moving along. Let us return Sawney to the hell from whence he came." Goodfellow was in the lead and moving with alacrity. He was armed with a sword, as was Promise. I had my guns, and the wolves and the boggle had what nature gave them. As we moved, Boggle . . . if she had a name, she also wasn't sharing . . . slid under the water with the slow grace of a crocodile. When she surfaced, the mud was gone, and her mottled scales held the pattern of an entire desert full of rattlesnakes. Then she went under again. The water here had been thigh deep; now it was almost waist high. It didn't cover her completely. You could still see the ridge of her spine and the glow of her eyes in the dim light, but she moved fast. So fast that within seconds she had disappeared—past Goodfellow and gone.

"You know, I'm not quite sure she'll need the rest of us after all," Robin remarked.

She had something beyond what her mate had possessed—more speed, more decisiveness, more of a predatory nature. I'd thought how our past informant had been content to sit and wait for his prey to come to him. This boggle, she wouldn't be. I'd made an assumption that all boggles were happy to dwell in their mud until dinner wandered by to be mutilated. It wasn't true. She would range, she would hunt . . . she chased down her prey, and having seen her in motion, I didn't think she would have it any other way.

It'd be fucking fantastic if she were the answer to our Sawney problem, but I knew better. Things were never that easy. And insanity, like Sawney had in spades, carried you a long-ass way.

We found that out in less than an hour. The tunnel we ended up in was long abandoned and most likely long forgotten. The lights had gone dark who knew when and remained that way. No one had come to replace burned-out bulbs. No one came for anything as far as I could tell. Niko, Robin, and I carried flashlights. No one else needed them. The wolves and Promise got by easily on our reflected light and I didn't know if the boggle needed light at all. As for what the revenants required . . . bump into it in the dark. If it's not cold and clammy, take a bite out of it. You didn't need light for that. Revenants weren't smart, but they didn't have to be, and the fact that Sawney had somehow lifted them an IQ point or two only made things worse for us. Worse being?

They came out of the water.

I thought the massive swell was the boggle at first, because they rose as one. Boggle was what my mind expected and so for a split second that's what I saw. Then reality—at least forty more revenants, six inches from us. Six inches. They couldn't have surrounded us as at least one of us would've felt them under the water as we passed them, but this . . . this was right up there with being the next best thing. I couldn't have smelled them separately from the ever-present rank decomposition already in these unused tunnels anyway. The wolves might have, though, if those revenant sons of bitches hadn't been covered with several feet of sluggishly flowing, horrifically ripe water. Now that several feet had become six god-damn inches and we were beyond screwed.

Niko and I were in the lead, having just traded off with Delilah and Promise ten minutes ago. The four other wolves were strung out loosely behind their silver-haired Alpha, and Robin was pulling rear guard.

Six inches. I kept thinking it, but it bore repeating. I was so close to the revenant that I could see the poreless stretch of pallid skin stretched across bone. I could see that behind the thick coating of white that covered their eyes was a fine tracery of purple veins, the size of a stream of spider silk, and that the lips had no lines in them. Lastly, I saw that every tooth in every yellowed grin was flecked with dried blood like speckling on a quail's egg.

Such a short distance, and it let me see more detail than I wanted. It also let me jam the Glock in the belly of the revenant before me and blow his spine in half. Six inches . . . six miserable inches, it isn't the space you want between you and a hungry foe, but at least you don't have to aim. Unfortunately, the same was true for them. They passed over us in a wave. No specific attacks on individuals—tidal waves don't do that. They just take you the hell down. Drowning in the ocean's version of a sucker punch wouldn't be pleasant; drowning in tainted tunnel water and moistly putrid flesh wasn't any better.

I lost the flashlight. I lost the Glock too, but that was purposeful. I let it go and went for my blades. One was the serrated knife, a mercenary magazine special, and the other a kukri. Niko had shown me how to be effective with the minimachete. Now I was ready to give the same lesson to a revenant or ten. I came up from the water, the thrashing bodies, and ripped through everything solid around me. Everyone in our temporary quasi team was experienced enough to give everyone else their room. Personal space, it's yours—kill at will.

It wasn't easy getting back up to air—air to breathe, air to slash metal through. It was a process of clawing and stabbing and biting. If you wanted to give a label to something that already had the perfect one: Survive. Process. Method. Survival. When I surged upward, I was spitting out something other than water. They weren't dead, they weren't decomposing, but damned if they didn't taste as if they were.

I kept both hands in motion, doing my best to clear the area around me. The serrated knife took out one throat; the kukri did the same but with a cleaner slice. All around was . . . what? The dimmest flickering of illumination from flashlights dropped underwater, a horde of white-eyed zombie wannabes, five giant wolves leaping and sending shredded intestines spilling through the air, a soaked and bloody puck and human with sword and axe, a vampire ripping an entire head from a revenant's shoulders. What did you call that?

Hell. You called it hell, because chaos was far too pretty a word.

And where the *fuck* was our boggle?

"Travelers."

Once again, they said it as one. And, I was sorry to note, that with repetition, it did not get any less freaky. It was still wrong and unnatural, even for a revenant.

Delilah catapulted over my head as I dodged one revenant's rush and permanently ended another's ability to move at all. I recognized her as she was the only white wolf among the minipack. The silver-blond fur was a startling glow as she soared over. Her brother Flay managed about three-fourths wolf when he changed. He could run on all fours but could walk on two as well. Delilah, as far as I could see, went all the way. Wolf through and through and big as hell. When she landed, she did what Promise had done. She removed a head, but she did it using her jaws. And then she did another and another and another. The other wolves, one with the remains of a hooded sweatshirt still tangled around his neck, were cutting their own swath, and doing the job we paid them for. All except one. Whether he was a shade slower, slightly less agile, the reason didn't matter. What did was that he got caught. Several sharp-nailed hands managed to fasten on to him, and even more mouths bit through brownish fur to flesh and didn't let go.

When he disappeared under the water, he didn't come back up. I tried to make my way over in his direction and I saw Nik do the same. It was too late.

The wolf was gone. Despite that, we were holding our own. We weren't kicking ass and taking names, but we were alive, most of us, and right now that was good enough for me.

Sawney had an entirely different idea of what was good, and he brought that idea with him. Carried it along as he slithered along the wall and up on the ceiling over our heads. The knotted hair hung down over the black emptiness of his face, but the amused red shimmer of his eyes gave away his mood easily.

"Heads up!" I called to the others.

"Traveler."

The word came from only Sawney this time with just the faintest echoing murmur from his choir. "Traveler with the frenzied taste. Madness and cream and butter."

"Cream and butter, my ass" I said flatly. Auphe and insanity, maybe that went as hand in hand as it did with Sawney, but I damn sure didn't want to hear about it. "You bastard."

Over the snarls of wolves, the splashing of water, and the thudding of metal chopping through flesh, he shouldn't have heard me. My voice didn't have the carrying properties his did and I hadn't shouted it, but it didn't matter. He heard.

"Yes, traveler, cream and butter." There was a tone of lazy contentment, as if he wasn't hungry at the moment, not for an entire meal, but a casual taste would be all right. He wouldn't be above that, not a connoisseur like him. Whether he would've tried for it or not, I didn't find out, as another connoisseur, one of gems and metal, finally showed up.

She came through the wall. Brittle tile shattered as concrete shook, shook again, cracked, and there she was in all her glory. And right then, that was a helluva lot of glory in my eyes. Grace as well, no matter that she'd ended up in the wrong tunnel. She flowed through the large hole and up the wall, spiking her claws nearly half a foot deep through the tile to propel herself along with more speed than I would've thought possible for her bulk.

There are moments in life to savor and cherish, to keep and warmly recall at a later date. The flare of surprise in Sawney's scarlet eyes was one of them. Seeing that smug bastard caught off guard for once— yeah, it was the goods. It was the shit. The absolute shit.

I flipped a revenant over my shoulder, pinned it with a knee in its back, and started to take his head. It took some doing sawing underwater, even with the commando knife, but the ones whose throats I'd slashed were slowly staggering back up their feet. They weren't in prime fighting condition, but they were moving, they were in the way, and there was no time for that inconvenience. When, with water up to my collarbones, I jerked my attention up from the writhing revenant beneath me, I saw Boggle lunge and cover Sawney altogether. The shine of his scythe and crazy smile vanished under the ripple of scales and surging flesh.

Maybe we were going to luck out. Maybe it was going to be that easy. She would rip Sawney to pieces and we would bathe in a rain of his blood. Maybe I'd even catch a drop on my tongue like a snowflake. See what he tasted like.

Finally, I felt the spinal discs separate under my knife, and the parting of a remarkably tough spinal cord; then I was standing with my eyes still on the boggle. She was moving. The claws of her hands and feet were embedded in the ceiling, keeping her aloft, but her head was whipping back and forth. The movement was too quick for me to see him in her mouth, but I knew he was there. The only thing that would've made this any better was if the boggle had been wearing the pearl and diamond tiara that had been included in Promise's payment. That would've been the cherry on the goddamn sundae.

"She has him."

Niko was at my shoulder, the axe dripping in his hand. "Yeah, she has his ass," I said with a warm glow in my gut that beat Christmas morning all to hell.

There was a particularly vicious snap of the scaled head, a sense of flight, and a brutal thud as a dark mass hit a far wall. Score one for Mama. "Don't notch a point in the air," came the warning. "It's crass." The axe took out one of my shambling revenants, who was sucking in air through his throat with a shrill whistle.

"I wasn't going to." An utter lie. "I do plan on punting his decapitated head like a football, though." I flung water and gore from both knives and started toward the wall where Sawney adhered like a drying clot of blood.

Niko moved with me. "Stabbing a football isn't the same as playing it, I hope you're aware."

I hadn't played well with others when I was a kid. Invitations to baseball or football games didn't often come after the "Your mom's a thief and a whore." That type of thing is hard to take from another kid, especially when it's true. It tended to lead to lashing out. Some of that lashing out was verbal; some involved a switchblade. Better to spear a football to the gym floor than some junior high asshole's poisonous tongue to the same polished wood. "I can kick. I kick your ass on a regular basis, don't I?"

"No. Not once," he shot me down ruthlessly as he swung the axe loosely, up and over. "And without vast improvement, not ever."

Not my day for getting the bullshit through. I didn't mind. Putting an end to that child-killing monster put a rosy glow over the entire scene. Dead and incapacitated revenants, whole and less than, floated in the water. There were wolves . . . eating. Robin and Promise gave them a cautious berth as they moved toward us through the water. The fur balls were on our side for the moment, but they had different dining manners than the rest of us. Get too close to their food and they might take a chunk out of you by pure instinct. Automatic and unthinking. As they were with us, they might be sorry afterward. Several sets of lambent amber eyes focused at us over mouths filled with flesh. Then again, they might not.

I turned my attention back to Sawney. The redness of his eyes was barely detectable and the scythe hung limply from the ebon-skinned hand. His back was to the wall, and how he was staying suspended there, I couldn't have guessed and didn't bother to try. I was more interested in how he was going to come down. It was going to be hard and it was going to be messy, and I wanted to be involved in both of those.

Boggle wasn't done with him yet, however. She soared across the open space—a cave-in, falling in a completely improbable direction. She hit Sawney and the wall and took both down. There was a cascade of tile and concrete, flesh and bone, and it all disappeared under the water about thirty feet away. Revenants and their parts bobbed in the resulting tidal rush.

"She's not like the old boggle, is she?" Robin was unwounded except for a long scratch along his jaw, and if Promise weren't wet, she would've been as pristine as before we'd entered the subway tunnel. "He was a lazy creature." He continued watching the water roil frantically where Boggle and Sawney had vanished. "Deadly, but content with the status quo. I doubt this one would be. She's beyond magnificent."

"Thinking of asking her out?" I asked with a snort. Not even Goodfellow had the balls for that.

"I don't date those with children." He touched a finger to his jaw and wiped meticulously at the blood. "It takes the focus from where it should truly lie."

"With you." Promise carried it with a heavy dose of irony to its natural conclusion.

"Am I wrong?" Finishing with the blood, he used his free hand to comb carefully through his curls. He was grooming himself. In the aftermath . . . hell, it wasn't yet an aftermath . . . during, he was grooming himself *during* a battle. "There are those who wish to experience me and those who wish to kill me. If that's not exclusive focus, what is? You can't be considered self-centered, if you sincerely are the center of all attention, now, can you?"

I didn't respond. The violent disturbance of the water had stopped, and as I took a step forward, Niko's hand settled on my shoulder. "Wait," he ordered. "She doesn't need us getting in her way." That we didn't particularly need to be torn apart by a blood-enraged boggle, he left unspoken. The water rippled, calmed. . . .

Then it turned blacker than it already was. The will-o'-the-wisp of our lost flashlights was slowly vanquished by billowing darkness. I didn't know what color Sawney's blood was—despite temporarily having his arm chopped off, Sawney hadn't felt it necessary to bleed a drop for us. What I did know was that boggle blood was black. A spill of octopus ink, just like this.

"I'll pass on pick of her litter. Raising carnivorous offspring does not fit my lifestyle." Robin, along with Niko, had fished a secondary flashlight from her jacket pocket and lit the place up. But the light wouldn't touch some things and Sawney was one of them.

He rose out of the water and hung inches above it. In one hand he held either a handful of cloth, a blanket, or . . . shit. Scales. The material rippled with scales and was lined with the black velvet of blood. "These caves"—drop by drop that same black fell from the point of the scythe to the water below— "they are not the chill of the sea caves of home." He shook it, his new blanket, to the rustle of the largest piece of snakeskin in the world. He'd skinned her, and, from the blood that had poured free, he'd done it while she was alive. The dead didn't bleed. I imagined, also, that the skinned didn't live long after the process.

"I shall wrap myself in it when the cold finally comes." The bright blaze of his eyes was back as he pulled the skin up to his face and rose higher in the air. "Ahhh, the sweet smell of a mother. The incomparable scent of orphans. I cherish your gift, travelers."

I'd let the Glock go, but never the Eagle—not with what it held. I pulled, fired, and with three shots,

I saw Delilah coming up behind and below Sawney. . . . I saw it *through* him. The hole was not quite the size of a grapefuit, although the rounds should've blown him in half. There should've been Sawney on one side of the tunnel and fucking Beane on the other. Whatever he was made from was as hard as stone . . . harder. Delilah wasn't deterred. She hit him. Landed on his back and wrapped her jaws around his neck with room to spare. He was man-sized. She was not. She was Wolf and Kin and she dwarfed him. Not as Boggle had, but enough that she could've torn through his throat as if it were paper. Could've.

Should've.

Didn't.

She leaped free a split second before the scythe would've opened her up. When she landed, she was shaking her head hard as if her jaws or teeth ached. Gritting my own teeth, I aimed and pulled the trigger again, this time aiming for his head. But he was gone. Between one blink and the next, he'd faded like smoke. He was fast, Niko and I had seen how fast in the warehouse, but this . . . Christ. How can you hope to kill something you can't possibly catch?

Quick or not, he could've gone in only one direction. I refused to believe he could've gone over our heads without us seeing at least a flicker of motion. I started forward down the tunnel, only to be knocked backward by a wave of water and flesh. Raw, weeping flesh. Horrifically injured, she'd been stripped of skin from neck to crotch. Flayed and still alive.

"Where?" Boggle roared, arms uplifted, fists clenched. "Where? Where? Where?" Turning, she pounded those fists against a wall to bring down another section next to the rough entrance she'd

made. "Where? *Where?* **Where?**" Whirling, she
snatched up the nearest creature, which happened to
be a wolf, and pulled him into two pieces like a tasty
piece of taffy. The lupine jaw snapped feebly for several seconds afterward, and it was far more disturbing than I wanted to admit.

"As the Irish, a brilliant people, say, a good retreat
is better than a bad stand. Also the Bard once pon-
tificated that the better part of valor is discretion. I
am nothing if not loaded with discretion. Shall we?"
Robin turned and began to sprint back the way we
had come.

I couldn't say he had the wrong idea. Attacked by
our own wounded, crazed ally and Sawney gone . . .
things weren't going as planned. One half of the
wolf, a gray male, fell from Boggle's hand and the
other was thrown against the far wall. The back legs
and hindquarters slapped limply against the surface,
then dropped into the water.

"*Where?*"

"Fortune may favor the brave, but pucks are remarkably long-lived. I say we go with the latter advice." Niko yanked me the rest of the way aloft as I
was pushing up from the water. And for the second
time in a week we were running through a tunnel.
This time we had the addition of Robin and three
wolves—as well as the world's most pissed-off
boggle.

We could have killed her. She was more savagely
fierce than her mate had been, but she was injured
and there were seven of us. It would've been enough,
but . . . she was our partner. We'd gotten her into
this. It didn't seem right to finish off what Sawney
had started. Although in the end, it wouldn't have
mattered what our moral stance was on skinned bog-

gles and their murderous rampages. If she had chased us, that stand Robin wanted to avoid would've taken place, brutally and instantly. If she chased us.

She didn't.

She chose to go after Sawney. He was long gone, I had the feeling, but I wished her the best of luck. I also hoped she lived. I couldn't spend every day tossing raw meat at a mud pit full of baby boggles. I had a job. I had things to do. I was responsible for their father's death. I didn't want to go there with their mother too. Guilt gets old. It gets so damn old.

Beside me ran the white wolf, who within six steps transformed to a naked human female. Except for the scars on her stomach and the choker tattoo around her neck, she was wet and gloriously nude. I handed her my jacket as we ran and her upper lip lifted to show her teeth in an amused smile. She also thought about patting me on the head, I could see it, but she took the jacket and slipped it on.

I liked Delilah—why, I wasn't sure. Perhaps because she was like Niko . . . if he were a completely immoral female. Lethal and laconic. The familiar is always comfortable. The fact she was sexy as hell didn't hurt.

She wasn't Georgina. Never would be—I knew that. But I'd have to learn to settle for a warm touch or a secret smile from someone else, and it would have to be enough. Or I could spend that part of my life alone. Not only did I have hormones that strongly disagreed with that, but without that wall between us, George might eventually convince me.

And then she would die. Or worse. Delilah or Charm would never die for me, not if they could avoid it.

We all ran on, slowing when it was clear Boggle wasn't following us but delving farther into the depths for Sawney. When we finally hit a maintenance tunnel, we had three half wolves—one in my jacket and two naked. None of them minded. The two males were partially covered with patches of fur here and there, one with a stub of tail and the other with a misshapen jaw and joints. Badly bred or not, they ran far faster than the rest of us did, although I knew Promise could've kept up.

They disappeared around a turn and I turned to Delilah. "Sorry about your friends."

She was wearing my jacket with casual flair. It fell past her hips and hung open enough that I saw the curve of her apricot-colored breasts. I'd already seen them in their entirety; it didn't change the fact I was still looking.

"Friends?" Her amber eyes slanted in my direction. After she'd changed back from what Wolves considered their true shape, her silver-blond hair had fallen free to hang like a wedding veil in color and sweep. "Keep up with the pack or don't. Die for the pack when needed. Pack is all. There are no friends." With that, she was gone too. Despite her sly glances and my hazily half-ass thoughts on the matter, I didn't know if I'd see her again or not. Delilah was Delilah. She lived, like most fur creatures, in the here and now. Planning ahead wasn't a priority or a concern.

"Furry women are tricky, kid." Robin was waiting for us. "I suggest a spoonful of butter before and after any snorkeling activities. Hairballs. Also, diamond-studded flea collars? They are a bitch to find for anniversary gifts." He'd put away his sword under his coat and continued with a more serious and uncertain shrug. "On the other hand, her abdomen. You know . . . she may be infert—"

I waved him off with a growl. "I think the fact Sawney got away again is a little more pressing, okay?" We were letting down a dead little girl right and left. It was in my pocket, my reminder—the sunny barrette of a girl who would never see the sun again. My social life and the lack thereof paled in comparison to that.

"And he nearly slaughtered a boggle to do it. Single-handedly." Niko had retrieved his cello case from where he'd left it, dry and safe. We hadn't been hit with a random search yet, but our luck would run out sooner or later. If Sawney stayed down here, we were going to have to find a different access. "The fact that he did it with a hole that ran the entire depth of his body isn't encouraging either." Closing the case with a snick of buckles, he looked at me steadily. "Next time, go for the head shot."

I was a good shot, not Olympic quality or anything, but competition-wise, I could've held my own. A head shot, though, on a moving target wasn't easy under the best of circumstances, and I'd yet to see anything remotely less than absolutely crappy circumstances demonstrated during our recent battles. Niko knew that as well as I did, if not better.

"Head shot," I confirmed solidly.

"No wiseass remarks?" he asked, hefting the case. There was no mockery in the comment, no faked surprise; he knew what he was asking of me.

"Too bad Halloween's over. We could use his head as a pumpkin. Stick a candle in there and scare the kiddies." I put the Eagle in its holster. "That work for you?"

It wasn't much of an attempt, a letdown of my

smart-ass tongue. But the entire night had been a letdown. Other than taking out more revenants and losing two wolves and a fair piece of Boggle, we hadn't taken care of Sawney, hadn't learned anything new. That the rest of us were alive was our only achievement.

15

The walk from forgotten to abandoned and maintenance tunnels, then to the new construction took a
while, and Delilah had peeled off after her Wolves
long before that point. Without my jacket to hide it,
I handed off my holster to Niko to conceal in the
cello case. I tucked my gun in the back waistband of
my jeans and covered it up with my sweatshirt before we hit the street level. Then minutes later it was
back underground to hit the 6 train home. We had
just stopped to stand on the platform, ignoring the
sideways glances at our soaked clothing, when I
heard it.

It wasn't loud, the bang. Barely audible over the
train that roared out. A small sound, a stumble, and
then Robin was falling face-first on the floor. It
looked as if he had tripped. Only now, instead of
bitching and groaning about scrapes and bruises, he
was unmoving.

God.

I could tell that his torso wasn't moving because
he wasn't breathing and he wasn't talking. You don't
breathe, you don't talk. Goodfellow—with no words?

Not a single one? I believed in monsters, I believed in the grimmest of fairy tales, but I couldn't believe that.

Strange that I wasn't breathing either, but I was still alive, could still feel the ragged pump of my heart, the acid burn in my lungs. And when I raised my eyes from that unmoving back to stare at Niko, I could still see. If I could do all those things without breathing, why couldn't Robin?

Niko's face was completely blank and devoid of anything . . . killing machines don't need emotions to get the job done. "Left," he said with a voice as empty as he turned and moved in that direction.

"Right." My face wasn't empty. It was full of bad things, hidden things that I hadn't let myself feel since George was taken, Niko almost sacrificed. They'd been shoved down, smothered, dismissed, but they were still there. They'd been waiting for their chance, and here it was.

With speaking came oxygen and with that came the ability to drive my body to the right through the mass of people. Some had picked up on the faint sound of the shot and run, but most hadn't caught it and were hovering around Robin. Maybe it was his heart, maybe drugs, maybe goddamn mutated pigeon flu . . . the muttering and whispering swelled. I drove through the vultures with lowered shoulders and vicious elbows as I went right.

Niko had already gone in the opposite direction. I thought I heard Promise call from behind me as she bent protectively over Robin's body, but it was lost in the sound of the crowd, the rush of the train, and the blood raging in my ears. I ran on. He wasn't getting away, the murderer who had done this. Sawney had, but he wouldn't. It didn't matter that I hadn't seen who had pulled the trigger; I would recognize him when I saw him. I would *know* him.

I tackled a cop moving toward me with wary eyes and steely intent, rode him to the ground, choked him out, and kept going. That the bastard assassin was human wouldn't save him.

And he was human.

I saw him—walking a little faster than those around him. As I got closer I could see and smell the human in the tiny beads of sweat winding down the back of his neck from his hairline. He didn't hear me behind him. It's almost impossible to run silently across concrete and tile, sneakers or not, but with people milling and stomping about like cattle, I had the perfect auditory camouflage. Perfect, yet it failed me. Although the killer didn't hear me behind him, he looked over his shoulder anyway. Professionals don't look and they don't sweat. Amateurs hold the patent on that. They also run instead of taking the offensive, as my amateur did. He bolted the moment his eyes caught mine. Not used to killing. Too bad for him I was.

Let the bastard run. Let him run all goddamn night. At the end of it, he would still be dead. A sirrush, Hameh birds, this son of a bitch—they were all the same. Monsters. I couldn't get rid of my gene, but that didn't mean I gave a shit if his were one hundred percent normal. For what he'd done . . .

He was dead.

I almost pulled out the Eagle, but that was bound to attract its fair share of attention from at least some of the commuters. As it was now, they were only clearing a path for us as we ran. The dead man, so goddamn *dead*, snatched another look over his shoulder, shoved a woman who hadn't meandered out of his way quickly enough, and then vaulted her when she fell to her hands and knees. He hadn't taken out his gun either, which led me to believe he'd already dumped it. He didn't want to be caught by the cops with a weapon, now, did he?

He should be that lucky.

The next time he looked for me I was nearly on top of him. Barely three feet away I could smell the fear coming off of him. I could also smell determination and resolve or maybe I was seeing it in his dark eyes. I was so focused on him, so ferociously aware, that I couldn't tell where one of my senses began and the other ended. The same went for my sanity and something a little less than. He'd taken my friend. He had taken the first person I'd learned to trust aside from my brother.

Months ago I'd been on the edge of losing it utterly when I'd thought George and Niko were gone for good. Robin had told me then that the frozen control I'd used simply to be able to function would come back to bite me in the ass. Told me that when you bury emotions like that, you're only pissing them off . . . making them stronger, because you're burying them alive. They don't like that, and one day they'll make sure that you don't like it either. He'd been right. But against the odds and my own screwed-up psyche, I had found George and Niko.

I'd never find Robin again.

But I'd found his killer. Right here. Right now. And restraint and composure, they were just words to me. Meaningless sounds, worthless concepts.

I've felt savage rage. What I felt now was beyond that. When he jumped down to the tracks and took off down the tunnel, I was with him. On him. I saw

only him, felt only him when I tackled him. I didn't
feel the thud of the ground rising to meet us, him
twisting beneath me or the fists that hammered my
ribs. I didn't feel the gun that I had in my hand
either, but I know he did. The matte black steel dug
into the flesh under his chin until a small rivulet of
blood welled around the gunsight and wound down
to pool in the hollow of his throat. And because I
could see only him, I could see the rapid pulse beating beneath the red with startling clarity. There was
the blood rich with copper, sweat sour with dread,
and breath heated and harsh.

"What you do to me doesn't matter. My task is
done," he panted. Somehow, outside of his fear, the
bastard had found satisfaction. "The betrayer is
dead."

I should've pulled the trigger. The clean jerk of it,
the kick of the recoil, I wanted that. But I also wanted
something else. "Are you the only one I get to kill?"
I asked, the question leaden and guttural in my
throat. I jammed the gun barrel harder into his neck
until he gagged against the pressure. "Are you? Or
is there someone else? Die hard and alone or easy
and with company. Which is it going to be, you son
of a bitch?"

He spat in my face, contorted his body, and shoved
me off in a move that I'd not seen before, not even
from Niko. I staggered as he lunged upward, but I
managed to stay on my feet as I aimed the Eagle at
his chest from six feet away. "No, not yet," I said
more to myself than to him. "Not that easy for you."
I lowered the muzzle to point at his knee. If I fired,
he'd be an instant amputee, but he'd tell me whether
he was in this alone. That was worth a leg to find
out. He was dead anyway. He could bunny-hop his

way through the Gates of Hell, for all I cared, and think of me while he did it.

"You can't make me tell you anything." He was a study in contradiction. Afraid, but proud. A murderer, but so fucking naive.

"Think again, asshole." I gave a feral grin. "I can make you do anything. *Anything*. All I need is time." I pulled the trigger, and it felt as good as I knew it would. "You don't have anywhere you need to be, right?" I finished as the echoing boom of the round faded away.

His scream was slower to wane. He should've been grateful. He still had his leg. I'd used my left hand to throw my combat knife. I wasn't as good with my left as my right, but I was good enough and good enough was all it took. Half the blade buried itself in his thigh. The gunshot and crater in the far wall a few inches over had been for emphasis; there's nothing quite like an explosive round for highlighting the six inches of steel in your body. There's nothing quite like it for emphasizing any damn thing you can think of.

The cops would be coming but good luck getting through the panicked crowd that that explosion would have milling like wild animals. It would take a while and a while was longer than I needed. We were far down the tunnel and I was motivated. Very motivated.

I watched as he fell to his knees, his hands finding and locking on to the rubber handle. Looking up at me, he swallowed the last of his harsh cry and his mouth worked soundlessly before he mumbled something too slurred to understand.

"I can't make you tell me anything, is that what you said?" I stepped forward, put my hand over his tightly clenched ones. "It's serrated, so very sorry about that. But don't worry. It'll be just like pulling off a Band-Aid." I leaned in and offered a mockery of sympathy. "I'm happy to do it for you. But if I were you, I'd try not to look at what comes out with it."

"My task is done," he repeated, my words ignored. The fear was gone; there was nothing to smell but the remnants of it now. "I will be remembered."

The tracks beneath us began to vibrate, followed by a brilliant light cutting through the shadows. Piss-poor timing—I lived for it. Or, rather, it lived for me.

"I will be honored." He managed to get to his feet and stepped back, using an untapped and desperate energy to pull his hands and the hilt from my grip. He took two more steps, looked down and back, then took that one last step. He rested his left foot on the third rail without hesitation. Immediately, his body arched before snapping back so rigidly upright and with a force so anatomically impossible that I thought I heard his back break. I also smelled the cooking of flesh and the stench of burning hair, but only for a second. I flung myself back against the wall as the train took him. After that there was only the sharp scent of ozone, empty space, and a hundred wildly raging emotions with nowhere to go.

I slid down against the concrete wall until I was sitting, the gun still in my hand. He'd beaten me to it. The bastard had gone out his own way and without telling me a damn thing.

"Shit." I pulled up my knees and rested my forehead on them. "Sorry," I rasped roughly, "so goddamn sorry." The curse was for me, the rest for Robin.

"Did you kill him?"

Niko would've quickly realized that he'd assigned

himself the wrong direction when the milling of the crowds and the yelling and screams started from the opposite end. My end. He'd caught up with me, but not in time.

"No." I straightened and leaned my head back. "A million volts and a train beat me to it."

"Dead is dead," he said with a dark satisfaction as he held down a hand to me. "And that, little brother, is quite thoroughly dead."

I shook my head and didn't take the offered hand. He was right. Dead was dead, but it wasn't enough. "Robin's gone." I looked blindly at the smoking rail. "That stupid, horny piece of shit is . . ." I dropped the gun beside me and rubbed hard at my forehead with the heels of one hand. I couldn't say the word. I picked the Eagle back up, threw it across the tunnel with as much force as I could muster, and didn't bother to care when nothing blew up from the careless tantrum. "In the back. Jesus, he got it in the goddamn back. He's supposed to be better than that. Smarter than that."

"He told us so often enough, didn't he?" Nik sat beside me. To keep it out of his eyes, he'd drawn the top half of his jaw-length hair back tightly and secured it just below the crown with a black rubber band. But without the weight of his braid to pull the rest of it straight, the damp bottom half that fell free had dried with a subtle wave where he had pushed it back behind his ears. That wave must've been there for months now, and I hadn't noticed. It seemed important, my blindness; it seemed almost momentous, because Niko was my brother. My *brother*, and I hadn't noticed. I couldn't begin to grasp the things I'd not taken the time to notice about Robin.

"Yeah," I said raggedly. "He did. Smarter than Socrates, quicker than Hermes . . ."

"With the stamina of Hercules and Priapus combined," the familiar voice croaked from several feet away. From the gloom, Robin appeared. He was leaning heavily on Promise, but he was moving under his own power. Moving, breathing, bragging . . . he was alive. The son of a bitch was *alive*. All those roiling emotions tearing through me finally had an outlet, and until I reached Goodfellow I had no idea if they would result in violence or something worse.

It was the something worse.

I'd jumped to my feet and moved in to push him hard. Then I grabbed a handful of his shirt to pull him back and shake him, and finally, growling as loudly as any wolf, I wrapped an arm around his neck and squeezed until his face began to turn vaguely purple.

Yeah, I hugged him. It didn't get any worse than that, did it?

Shoving him back again before he had time to blink in surprise, I demanded harshly, "Why aren't you dead?"

"At this rate, I soon will be." He raised a hand between us, wary at any further welcome. "I can tell you are overcome with relief at the reunion, Caliban, but, please, don't strain any hitherto unused emotional muscles on my behalf. I'm not sure my neck can stand it." Matted brown hair stuck to his sweaty forehead as he leaned back with a wince to give more weight to Promise's supportive arm. "And I'm not dead because of Boggle." His pale face became a little more animated beneath the discomfort. "Also because of that bastard Darkling. Wouldn't he have loved to know that, that wretched wad of lizard mucous?''

''I think this would be better explained in a location where our chances of being arrested''—Niko rested a hand on my shoulder—''and dissected are a little less.'' The hand gripped and then pointed. ''Gun. Only rude little boys leave their toys lying about.''

And I wouldn't want to be rude, would I? Or dissected. I walked over, avoiding the third rail that still sizzled with leather and flesh, and recovered the weapon with fingers that felt oddly clumsy. Hard fight, long night, friends dying and rising again, that sort of thing played hell on a person's nervous system. Understanding that didn't stop me from cursing my numb fingers, the suddenly much heavier than normal Eagle, and Lazarus frigging Goodfellow. After tucking the gun in my jeans, I pulled off my shirt, turned it inside out, and put it back on. I'd gone from a dark-haired maniac in a black shirt, to just an average guy in a red one. The difference was enough to fool any nonprofessional eye, and here was hoping that cop I took out was still unconscious.

We did make it out, blending into the panicked while taking turns helping Robin along. This time, we shelled out the bucks for a cab and headed to Promise's penthouse at Park Avenue and Sixtieth to recuperate. Promise had offered. I was beginning to think she was fonder of Robin than she let on. They were both long-lived, although he was much older by far. They had a common bond that Niko and I couldn't be part of. Actually, the jury was still out on whether I had inherited the Auphe longevity. It could stay out as long as it wanted. I wasn't outliving Niko; I wasn't outliving my only true family, not by hundreds or thousands of years. No. Just . . . no.

By the time we climbed out of the taxi and were ushered into the building by an imposing, silver-haired doorman with an equally imposing sweep of mustache in pure white, Goodfellow's cursing had grown louder, but his movements came with more ease. A bruised or cracked rib, that was what he'd managed to escape death with—a dark purple splotch on the left of his back . . . precisely over where his heart would be.

The key to his survival had been the memories of our boggle, which had been triggered by his mate, and by Darkling. Darkling, at one with my body and my mind, had set up an ambush in Central Park. While Boggle had attacked Goodfellow, Darkling . . . I . . . *we* had shot Niko. Point-blank range. I leaned toward guns. Knives were okay, but guns were the top of my comfort level, and Niko hadn't forgotten that. When I'd been taken by Darkling, my brother had worn a bulletproof vest in anticipation of just such an event. It had saved his life.

Robin knew that he was an assassination target of two attempts already. When we'd told him we were bringing in another boggle, it had brought the fight of the past year to mind. While Niko had expected the gun then, Goodfellow hadn't. Darkling wasn't human; he would have no particular attachment to a gun. Nonhumans rarely did. That type of thinking would've gotten Robin killed if he'd been in Nik's place. As lessons went, it had made an impression on the puck.

Hameh birds, a sirrush . . . a man with a gun was a long way from creatures such as those. Long way, long odds. But pucks, gamblers to the last one, knew all about odds and they knew their payoffs. I'd wondered how someone as long-lived as him had gone down so easily. Now I knew. He hadn't. After the Hameh, he'd bought a bulletproof vest and started wearing it under his finely woven fall sweaters. The damned things probably matched, cashmere and Kevlar.

Reclining on overstuffed pillows and a sage green silk cover, Robin was lounging in Promise's guest room with a distinctly superior smirk on his pointed face. Look at me. Look how clever. The breadth and reach of my intelligence are so unfathomable to the average brain that I must appear godlike to you lesser mortals. Whether it was only in my head that I heard it or he'd actually said it aloud, it didn't matter. My hand was already closing around something on the dresser to toss at him. Gilded French vase, crystal decanter, statue of Venus, I didn't look. I didn't care. I hefted it and cocked my arm back as if I were trying out for the majors when Niko took me by the scruff of my shirt and began to hustle me out of the bedroom.

"He really doesn't deal with the unexpected well, does he?" Robin commented as if I and my makeshift weapon weren't there. Rolling onto his stomach, he hissed at the cold as Promise, who didn't look particularly pleased to be playing nurse, placed an ice pack over the spreading bruise. Fondness only went so far. Seeing a half-naked Goodfellow was apparently the outer limits of that affection. "In his world there are no good surprises and all piñatas are filled with evil-tempered tarantulas and poison-spitting snakes." I heard the clucking of his tongue before he rested his face in the pillows for a muffled finish. "We do need to work on that attitude or he'll never be able to enjoy the true . . ."

I didn't hear anything further as the bedroom receded behind us. Promise's home had soft and gloriously woven rugs, draperies, and tapestries on the wall that all worked to soak up noise like a sponge. I looked at what was in my hand as Niko kept marching me along. A candelabra, silver and gold. It would've made a nice dent in that curly head. "He deserves it," I said, knuckles whitening as my grip tightened.

"Why?" At the end of the hall, we went down the winding stairs as the metal was deftly worked from my clenched hand. "Why does he deserve it? For being a self-righteous ass, which is nothing new, or"—he put the candelabra on the nearest table—"for scaring you?"

"I have Sawney and the Auphe to scare the shit out of me," I dismissed stiffly. "Goodfellow doesn't come close to making that list." After depriving me of my expensive puck swatter, Nik released me, and I promptly began to prowl the living room in ever-widening circles. I plunked the keys of an ivory-colored small piano, glanced at several pictures in simple polished silver frames, and kept walking.

"There is more than one type of fear, little brother. You had a not so healthy taste of that with Georgina and me, and you did your best to forget about it." His gaze drilled into mine, letting me know what he had thought and still did think of that idea. Very damn little. "To push it down where you wouldn't have to look at it, to think about it." He leaned against the wall as I shifted my wary glance away from him to the floor and kept pacing. "Or to deal with it."

I had exactly zero desire to talk about this, but I knew the difference that would make. When I passed the piano this time, I slammed a fist down instead of a few fingers. The discordant crash didn't make me feel any better, but it did make me feel like I had company in my chaos. "I deal," I gritted. "I deal just fine."

"Yes, you're dealing. You're dealing a path of destruction through a home that Promise is quite fond of." Fingers tapped lightly against folded arms as he led into what he'd said before, more than once, although he hadn't said it as often as I'd expected him to. He knew better than I that I wasn't ready to hear it. Not then. "Cal, Robin is alive. Georgina and I are alive. That is what's important—what did happen, not what could've happened."

What did happen, not what could have. Yeah, it was all very Tao and accepting and all that. But, Zen crap aside, it could easily have gone the other way. Over the past year and a half we'd been lucky so many times. That luck, sooner rather than later, would have to run out. The law of averages wasn't going to be our bitch forever.

I touched a finger to the cool keys again, this time tentatively, and then I sat down to play. It wasn't pretty music. It wasn't ugly either. Yet, in a way, it was both. It was alien—that was the best description. Dissonant and illogically strung together, wild note to wilder yet, but it hung together somehow. A symphony from swamps and caves, jeweled bones and forgotten dungeons, living tombs and empty graves—the Darkling places. He had been related to the banshees, a male version whose history had never been recorded, whose true name along with the rest of his gender was lost in time. But like his female cousins, he liked music, and he liked to sing.

On the other hand, despite inheriting our mother's honey and rum voice, I couldn't play or sing a note. That hadn't stopped Darkling from leaving me a present. Unwelcome, unwanted, and unknown up until now. It didn't matter. He was dead, chopped to the finest of pieces. I'd done the chopping. I knew for a fact he was gone.

But the reflection came before I could stop it, at least when he'd been in me, no matter who left, I wasn't ever alone. Schizo as hell, but not alone. It was a thought that left me so repulsed and exposed that I veered away from it instantly. Folding arms on the top of the piano, I rested my chin on them. "I'm used to having all my eggs in one basket." That would be Niko. One steel-shelled egg, one unbreakable basket. God, I hoped.

It was an obscure statement and coming after an exhibition of a freakish musical talent I shouldn't have had, you had to give Niko credit for catching on to it. "The more eggs you have, the more likely one is to break."

"Poached. Scrambled. Pureed in a blender for an over-the-hill boxer. Whatever." I extended an arm and touched the corner of the nearest frame. Promise and a dark-haired little girl, both colored sepia and dressed in clothes from at least a hundred years ago. For the things that I did know of Robin and Promise, there were thousands upon thousands of things that I didn't and might never have the chance to learn.

"I'm not good at this shit, Cyrano. I'm not good at caring, and I'm sure as hell not good at all the crap that comes with it." I looked up at the ceiling, eggshell with a hint of rose. It reminded me of the inner curve of a shell scoured clean by salt water. Full of dawn's purity and glow. "He made me *like* him, the son of a bitch. And I don't like . . . didn't like anyone but you. But Goodfellow made me like him and then he goes and proves he's mortal after all. It sucks. It just goddamn sucks." I pushed away from the baby grand and stood. "I'm hungry. You hungry? Want a sandwich? Great. Sandwiches coming up."

"I think you need to avoid sharp objects for a while," Niko ordered as he moved away from the wall. "I would hate for you to ram a butcher's knife in Goodfellow's leg in the hopes he wouldn't force you to like him anymore. Although the aborted attempt to brain him with a candelabra might already have him tipped off to your cunning plan."

"I am so screwed." I sat back down, this time on the floor. Dirty red shirt, damp jeans, and black sneakers, I was a definite test to the stain-repelling skills of the oyster gray, violet, and ebony rug beneath me. "Why do I like him?" I muttered, more to myself than to Nik. "Promise . . . I have to like her. I get that. She's yours. You're hers. It's a package deal. George . . ." I shut my mouth. There was no way to continue that sentence without regret, not a single one.

"We should've left New York. Even after Darkling was dead and we thought the Auphe were, we should've kept moving." I exhaled heavily as I sheathed fingers in my hair and said by rote, "You don't get attached, you never tell anyone your real name, and you always leave. Those were the rules." *You always leave* being the most important of them.

Niko sat across from me on the floor. His legs were

folded in a style that made mine ache just to see it. He loosely rested his hands on his knees. His wrists were banded with what looked like a double row of Tibetan meditation beads, except these were made of steel and would deflect the blow of nearly any blade easily. "I know," he said. "I made those rules." The corners of his mouth deepened downward briefly. "And Sophia thought I scorned the old ways."

Sophia didn't have much room to talk. She'd broken ties with her clan when she'd run off, and they'd done the same to her years later when they found out what perverse bargain she'd made with the Auphe. As for the "old ways," she had never purposely taught us a thing, not once Niko had refused to be part of her scams. As young as the age of six, Nik already had an unwavering moral compass; he was a regular Dalai Lama of the trailer park. Whether we were involved or not, though, it didn't matter—the lessons were still there for the taking. She'd run a fortune-telling con at the kitchen table while we watched cartoons four feet away. At night she'd run a different kind of con and the walls were much thinner than four feet.

"Her rules, your rules." I shook my head. "I don't care. We should've lived by them. I should've. You wanted to leave. I was the one who said we should stay in New York." I frowned at him. "Usually when I'm an idiot, you don't listen to me."

"If that were true, I would be selectively deaf every hour out of the day," he stated, hitting my knee with a not-quite-painful flick of his finger. "Besides, you were right. We thought the enemy destroyed and we had made a life here. Granted it was a life of only a few months and we both broke the rules in doing so, but it was still a life. We had an ally and friend in Robin. We had the potential for more in Promise and Georgina. Why give that up for no reason at all?''

"Sanity is a reason," I countered, scraping a bruised knuckle along the silken fibers of the rug. "Pretty good one too."

We should've known better. Seeing their destruction with our own eyes aside, we still should've known better. The Auphe were still out there, and they wouldn't stay hidden forever. Then there was Robin. Someone wanted him dead, and that was probably a fairly frequent event. Jesus. As for Sawney . . . we'd made him our problem and it was possible he could take one or more of us out. I'd managed to survive the uncertainty of George's and Nik's disappearance months ago. Managed, as in, just goddamn barely, and only by becoming the coldest son of a bitch that I could be.

Deal?

What a lie. After sitting, pacing, sitting again, and thinking of other things to bash over Robin's head while he slept, I obviously wasn't dealing.

"I have to get out of here for a while." I got up more quickly from the couch than I should have, my body groaning from multiple revenant blows.

"It's four a.m.," Niko pointed out, unmoving. "Where will you . . . ah." He gave an approving nod. "An excellent idea, if she cooperates. If she will 'look.'"

"Yeah." I started toward the door. "That's a big if." But if I had my way, she wouldn't get away with not looking.

Not this time.

16

George was sitting on the stoop of her apartment building waiting for me. For that, she had looked. Or maybe for the little things, she didn't look. Maybe she just knew without any effort at all.

She was wrapped in a robe. Hundreds of patches were stitched together in a tapestry of velvet, silk, simple polished cotton—any material you could think of. Some were embroidered, some not; the only requirement was they were all a shade of red. Scarlet, garnet, crimson, ruby, candy-apple, every hue you could imagine was there. That combined with her deep gold-brown skin and copper hair reminded me of a painting we'd passed in the museum while looking for Sawney. Some artist, the name began with a K, but I remembered the repeating pattern of squares, the vibrant colors, the tranquil face.

At almost five a.m. we were as alone as you could be in the city, and I looked at her silently. She knew. About Charm, she knew, and I didn't think that had anything to do with being psychic. It had to do with being a woman. I ducked my head and then sat two steps below her.

She rested a hand on my hair, smoothing it. "We

all have to learn our own way. Make our own passage.'' She dropped her hand and said with anger and disappointment, ''You always were and always will be one for the difficult path.'' She squared her shoulders and shook her head. ''There is the road traveled, the road less so, and the cliff. You head straight for the cliff, Caliban. Every time. Every single time.''

She tightened the robe around her and clasped hands around her knees. ''When you tire of hitting the bottom, let me know. Maybe I'll still be here. Maybe I won't, but I can tell you this: The only things that you'll find on the difficult path that aren't on the smoother one are bruises and regrets.''

Like I didn't know that.

How she knew that—now, there was a different question altogether. ''You finally looked, then?'' I asked cautiously, uncertain if I really wanted to know the answer to that and feeling like the absolute shit she meant me to. I'd turned her away once. I couldn't take a chance; I couldn't be with her if I didn't know how things would end up. I couldn't risk her like that. I had to know . . . if she were with me, did she survive the Auphe who were still running free out there? More importantly, did she survive the Auphe *in* me?

''Caliban,'' she said, her anger fading slightly to a resignation over an argument we'd had time and time again.

Of course she hadn't looked. She never looked at her own life and she never tried to change the truly monumental aspects of the lives of others. What was supposed to happen would happen. It was only the little things that could be played around with. She wasn't the only one who was angry. I'd pushed her away to save her and she wouldn't even look to tell me if it was necessary. I cut her out of my life to keep her safe, to keep her alive, and she wouldn't . . . *goddamn it*.

I looked away.

I didn't want to see the red and gold or the hurt, the anger, and the reluctant understanding that ran under it all. If I couldn't have it, I didn't want to see it. "Robin's in trouble. Someone is trying to kill him and doing a pretty good job of it. We need to know who it is." Across the street, a garbage truck rumbled. It was easier to watch than what I could sense crossing George's face. "I want to know. Robin wants to know. Even Niko, the only person more Zen than you in this world. We want to save Goodfellow, so who the hell is behind it? We got one human. Was he in charge? Was he the last one?" If she wouldn't look at the future, maybe looking at the past and present could help us.

I heard her shift and stand, her robe a rustle of warm velvet and cool silk. "Robin did something once, something quite . . ." Her voice trailed off, the anger now buried. This wasn't about us anymore. This was about a friend. "I imagine he has a lesson to learn. Life seems to be like that," she continued, her sympathy for him plain. "I can't change that, and I shouldn't try." Which was her way of saying she wouldn't try. "Try to have faith. Robin is clever and he has loyal friends. Trust that that will be enough."

That was the problem with George, one of many. She saw the big picture, and a single life was only a small part of that picture, only one of many lessons. For me, that wasn't good enough. Life might be all we got, as far as I knew, no matter what George sensed or thought. Lighting incense and staring at my navel while Robin got this life's lesson rammed down his throat via an axe through his neck or a sword into his gut, that just wasn't going to happen. Unlike those of George, my pictures were small, colored with finger paints, and in the here and now.

"Caliban?" she said from the door.

My eyes still on the street, I didn't look, but she knew she had my attention. She was a psychic after all.

"I won't wait forever." Then the door shut on me, just as I'd once shut it on her. It wasn't a good feeling . . . no matter what side you were on.

It was two hours later, six a.m., and my turn to open the bar. Sleep—who needed it? The Ninth Circle kept irregular hours. Some patrons like the night, some the early morning, some all damn day long. Ishiah switched it around enough that everyone could find what they needed on one day or another. It made for weird hours, a weirder schedule, and no damn dental either. Figured.

Delilah showed up barely twenty minutes after I unlocked the door. She looked the same as when she'd healed me . . . goddamn amazing. Wild and exotic, polished and lethal as a sword. She sat on one of the stools, picking up a feather from the bar. No matter how often you cleaned the place, there were always feathers. This one was Cambriel's—Cam's, cream and copper. He had the same copper hair in a long plait and a scowl that could clear the bar in a second. He also molted like an ostrich with mange. Considering the peri temper, I didn't mention it . . . much.

"Pretty boy." Funny that I minded Sawney calling me a boy, but with her I didn't mind so much. She twirled the feather and smiled at me. Delilah's smile wasn't your usual smile. It was more that of the cat that ate the canary or the fox that ate the henhouse— then had the farmer for dessert. It was satisfied and more than a little wicked.

"Delilah." I was surprised. I hadn't been sure I'd see her after the subway fight. Not that I hadn't seen a lot of her then. A whole lot. "Come to give me my jacket back?"

"No. I like the jacket. I keep it," she announced.

I'd liked it too, but what are you going to do? She liked it, I'd seen her naked . . . it was a fair trade.

I shrugged. "It did look good on you." And damn, had it. "You want a drink?" Six a.m.. It was late for the vamps, early for the wolves, but you never knew.

"No. Want this." She dropped the feather, reached across the bar, pulled me closer, and kissed me. It wasn't like George. That kiss had been warmth and sun and the gentle silk of tongue. This was hot, with teeth and a taste like night under a bloodred moon. It was enough that when we broke apart I didn't have a clue how much time had passed. I didn't much care either.

Okay, now I was in the deep end of the pool. Auphe rug rat phobia and all, I hadn't had much experience in this area. Well, being hunted, and Delilah was definitely a hunter—that I had plenty of experience in. But this . . . it definitely wasn't a comforting warmth and a red and gold girl on a pedestal. It wasn't the clover and sweet songs of a nymph either. It seemed like I should've said something; I *know* I should've said something, but "holy shit" didn't seem appropriate. I said it anyway—with feeling and a stinging lower lip that I suspected had the faint dents of sharp teeth in it.

She smiled again. "You smell of her. One who could not run with you in the dark places." She slid off the stool. "You smell like her but now you taste like me."

And with that she left. There was the swing of the long silver ponytail as she moved and the shutting of a door. If you could say one thing about Delilah, it was that she said what she had to say, did what she had to do, and then she was done. Boom. Gone.

I said it again. "Holy shit." The kiss combined with the still very vivid mental picture of her nude in the tunnels had me glad there were only two customers so far and that the bar came up waist high. By the time Promise came in an hour had passed. Luckily.

Delilah and now Promise. I was Mr. Popularity this morning.

Promise came into the place dressed in a snug scoop-necked sweater, sleek pants, boots, and a matching hooded cloak to protect from the sun. Gray, violet, and black, it all had reminded me of her rug I'd sat on, the one under her piano. Also the one that was probably being cleaned quite thoroughly at this very moment.

She smiled, sat on the same stool Delilah had, carefully arranged her cloak on the one beside her, and started in on me about George before I could get a word out. Not that my word-slinging ability was so hot at the moment. It'd been one helluva morning.

"So." She tilted her head slightly. "What of Georgina? What did she tell you?"

I shifted my shoulders. "Nothing." The bar was filling up a bit and I handed off a drink to a vodyanoi in a trench coat, scarf, and hat that had him passable on the street, just barely.

"She wouldn't tell you a single thing?"

Running on absolutely no sleep, I gave Promise a weary glance over the bar. I was beginning to slouch, as you could be while still technically being counted as upright. "George isn't big on hints. Robin did something bad. Karma is kicking his ass. Lessons to be learned. Embrace the whatever. In other words, we get squat in the way of help. Why are you here anyway?" I asked curiously. "Nik is usually the one who likes to point out my tactical errors. You know, the where and why of how I fucked up. You're depriving him."

"I'm sure he'll discuss that with you later," she said with amusement and absolutely no pity. "Right now he's playing nursemaid to Goodfellow. Those pity-me eyes of Robin's." She cast her own upward in vexation. "He doesn't know how to stop, I swear. It's pathetic. I refuse to suffer any longer." She rested pearl-colored nails on the bar surface. "And I nursed in the war. I have put in my service several times over. I am done with that."

"Which war?" I straightened up a few inches with interest. Long enough ago and Promise could've drained as many soldiers as she tried to save. I didn't know when the vampires had started living hunt-free lives. It involved human-style nutrition, four food groups and all, combined with massive supplements of iron and several other elements. It worked . . . now. It wasn't something available over a hundred years ago. I would've liked to think that if the war had been before the nineteen hundreds, Promise had only taken the lives of those who would've died anyway. I liked to think, but what did I know really? Besides that, it was none of my business. "World War Two? The Civil War?"

"Asking a woman her age. You shame your gender. And, Caliban?" Sable lashes dropped over languid eyes. "There is not enough wine in this establishment," she said with an inscrutable smile. "Perhaps not in the entire city."

I thought about asking her of the little girl in the picture that had been placed so carefully on the piano, but I had a feeling the question wouldn't be any better received than the other. "Okay," I gave in, "no wine, then. You want some fancy morning thing with champagne?"

"Yes, a Bellini would suit, if you would be so kind." The bar had few windows and they were covered with blinds and curtains for the sun-intolerant among the clientele. Promise had used the opportunity to remove her cloak and shake her hair free. It wasn't often I saw it loose and unbound. It was something to see. The stripes poured and rippled down her back to past her hips as she sat . . . a tiger on a wooden perch.

By the time I returned with her drink, she was ready to reveal why she was really at the bar. "So"—she took the smallest of sips—"you got what you wanted, then. Niko told me where you were going, and once Georgina saw you, she would know." She studied me over the glass filled with sun and champagne. "And she did, didn't she? Does that make you happy, getting what you wanted?"

The words were uncompromising, but behind them I heard a reluctant sympathy. Promise knew my reasoning, but she also thought I was a twenty-year-old idiot hanging on to past teen angst for all I was worth—like a baby with a pacifier. She knew my reasons were valid, but she, like the others, thought there were ways around them. Vasectomy, contraception, cross your fingers and hope for a bouncing baby non-flesh-eater. Let's say I didn't trust any of the three. No one knew what the Auphe body was capable of regeneration-wise; condoms broke—as Sophia had once carelessly said, Niko was proof of that; and as for the last option: No. No way.

The only thing that would work, George wouldn't do. She wouldn't look. She wouldn't cheat. And as much as I cared for her, sometimes I didn't much like her.

"Yeah, I'm happy. I got exactly what I wanted." I didn't snap or snarl. I said it in a perfectly even tone, which in some way was worse than the other two would've been. It was true. I'd gotten what I wanted. George safe. Safe from me. Safe from monster offspring. Safe from the Auphe, because if I didn't care about her, then neither would they. If I didn't see her, then they wouldn't notice her. It was very much in her best interest not to be noticed.

She dipped her head in apology. "I, who never have the slightest urge to meddle in anyone's personal affairs, cannot seem to help myself with you." She extended a hand to lay it across mine. "After all, Caliban, you are family." She'd said that, done that, the hand thing, once before and I hadn't reacted very politely. I tried to do better now. I left my hand under hers for three seconds (I knew . . . I counted) and then turned it to clasp hers briefly before quickly letting go. Like I'd said to Niko, I wasn't good at this shit. I just wasn't, but I would try. For Promise, I would try.

"Want another Bellini?" I asked gruffly, ignoring the fact hers was still three-fourths full.

She pondered the glass gravely, then said before taking another small sip, "Perhaps in a moment."

A hand abruptly landed on the junction of my

shoulder and neck. It wasn't a friendly grip either. "What now, boss?" I said with a groan. "I haven't impaled a customer in days."

"No," he agreed with bunched jaw. "You did, however, serve a vodyanoi a margarita on ice."

"So?" I shrugged, not seeing the problem.

"With salt," he added.

"And?" I twirled my fingers in an impatient come-on-already gesture.

"*And* half his face melted onto the bar." He bent slightly to put his head even with mine. "Salt tends to do that to them."

"Oh." I winced. I hadn't done it on purpose, although it was a good one to remember. As a matter of fact, Robin had mentioned that once the last time we'd dealt with them—salting them like a garden slug—but I'd thought he'd been joking.

"But, honestly, how can you tell about his face? I mean, come on." I grimaced. A vodyanoi was not pretty by any stretch of the imagination. Mythology says they look like scaly old men with green beards. In reality, they appeared more like humanoid leeches. Neckless, they did have a sketch of a human face to draw in their prey. A mottling of colors. Small liquid eyes, a dark mark on gray flesh to imitate a nose, and a sucker mouth they used to slurp out your blood. Quick in the rivers and lakes, they were slow and awkward on land, which is why they rarely left the water. Why this one had donned a coat and hat and lumbered his rubbery way to the Ninth Circle for a drink, I had no idea, but I would've thought he would at least know what salt looked like . . . for facial preservation if nothing else.

A wad of rags and a spray bottle of industrial

cleaner were slapped on the bar beside me. "I'll supervise," he announced with stony impatience.

I nodded a good-bye to Promise and headed down the bar. It curved like the bow of a ship and by the time we reached the end of it, I could hear the shrill keening coming from the unispecies bathroom down the hall. "Jeez, he's not still melting, is he? That'll be one helluva mess, and you can bet your ass it won't go down the drain in the floor." Actually, I did feel bad . . . a little. A vodyanoi would eat you if you dipped as much as a goddamn pinky toe in his particular watery territory, but this guy had been here for a drink, nothing else, and I'd melted the poor son of a bitch.

"You worry about the cleanup. I'll worry about the vodyanoi." Ishiah watched me wipe a slick, snotlike substance from the bar before I began working on the set-in gray-green stains. After a few minutes of watching me apply the elbow grease, he said grimly, "Robin was shot, wasn't he?"

You had to hand it to the peris; if it was worth knowing, somehow they knew it. It came from running bars. If there was information available, it was going to pass through a bar before anywhere else.

I raised my eyes to his. "Why you asking if you already know?"

"Exercise your social skills for a moment, would you?" He leaned across the bar, nose to nose. "I know he survived. I know he walked away. What I don't know is how badly he's hurt."

"Not bad." I continued scrubbing and snorted, "The son of a bitch was wearing a bulletproof vest. Can you believe it?"

"So he *was* shot and by a human." He moved back,

eyes distant and speculative. "I guess that solves that, then."

That stopped my cleaning. "You mean you know who the hell is behind this?" The cloth, heavy and ripe with vodyanoi flesh, fell to the floor. "You *know*?"

"The sirrush, the Hameh birds, now a human." The wings were out in full force. "Robin Goodfellow once did a . . . he did a thing that was not quite ethical. It was a long time ago and he's grown since then. Changed. I hope." The wings waved, disturbed. "And it was so very long ago that I can't imagine anyone seeking retribution now, but . . ." He shook his head, scar whitening at his jaw. "Obviously that isn't the case."

"Let me get this straight. You know who's behind this and Robin doesn't?" I said with disbelief.

The wings disappeared instantly as control returned to face and body. "He knows. He may even have known before he was shot, suspected at least. But he's certainly not going to tell you or your brother."

"And why the hell not?" The question may have sounded belligerent. It should have; it was.

"He respects the two of you," Ishiah answered slowly as if he couldn't quite believe it himself. "He considers you friends—Robin Goodfellow who has had very few of those in his life. He doesn't want to change that. He doesn't want to disappoint you."

Now, there was a concept to boggle. Robin didn't want to disappoint us? Robin who chased my brother relentlessly before Promise staked her claim. Robin who lied, cheated, and picked pockets just to stay in practice, who had killed a succubus in cold blood because she wouldn't give him the information we needed? Robin who sold *used* cars? That Robin didn't want to disappoint us?

I liked that Robin, I'd finally been forced to admit to myself, but did I think he'd worry about disappointing us? No. I didn't buy it. Unless . . .

"Just how not quite ethical was this thing he did?" I asked with apprehensive curiosity.

"You do not want to know, and, regardless, it's not my story to tell." He folded his arms across his chest. "I would give you more information on at least who these bastards are, but general knowledge isn't specific. Knowing the why and the very broad who doesn't get us any closer than if I knew nothing at all." The control flickered and I saw more than wings. I saw light and fire and my ears ached from the pressure, and then it was gone. "Go. Ask him. Maybe you can convince him where I can't. Stubborn bastard."

Jaw still a little loose from the light show, I was suddenly alone as he disappeared into the back room. I peered over the bar expecting to see smoking footprints burned into the floor, but there was nothing. Peris.

I still had to wonder.

Having given the unprecedented go-ahead to cut out of work early, Promise and I did just what Ishiah suggested. We arrived at her apartment at ten a.m. to find out from Robin what Ishiah wouldn't tell us. We walked in, I told him what Ishiah had said, and waited for the response. He was completely cooperative. Threw buckets of info at us faster than we could soak it up.

Yeah, right. He wasn't telling us shit.

"I have no idea what that canary with the overactive pituitary gland is on about," Robin said loftily from the sofa as he pointed the remote at the television that was normally discreetly hidden behind a reproduction of what was Waterhouse's *Windflowers*, or so I was told. It was a woman with blowing brown hair, a violet and ivory dress, and flowers all around her bare feet. It was Promise, I knew it was. She had been the model. Maybe not sketched or painted outside on that sunny morning, but she'd been the inspiration.

"Porn, where is the porn?" Goodfellow complained. "Does the woman not have a single exotic entertainment channel in her package? Unbelievable."

"Robin, we need to speak with you. Pay attention." Niko, playing part bodyguard, part nurse, removed the remote and tossed it with brisk force over his shoulder to me. Fortunately, I both expected and caught it or I would've choked on it. Not one moment of one day could I hope not to be tested at my brother's slightest whim. It was second nature to us both, but it didn't stop me from tossing it back. Niko ducked gracefully and it bopped Robin in the forehead.

"Charon's pasty white balls." Robin glared and rubbed a faint red spot above his eyebrow, but turned the television off. "Nothing happened in some forsaken sand-ridden land, and I have no idea who might want to kill me. Well . . ." His eyebrows twitched. "Let's embrace reality. I have no idea who might want to kill me as a concerted plot. How about that?"

"You're lying," said Niko. There wasn't a single doubt to be heard in his voice.

"And how do you know?" The head tilted, chin lifted, eyes narrowed—all in challenge.

"Because you always lie," Nik said with dark exasperation. "Why would that possibly change now?"

"Ah." Robin slid down a little on the couch and folded his arms. "Good point."

"Then stop being an asshole and tell us already," I demanded.

"Or what?" he asked mockingly. "You'll hug me?"

"You son of a bitch," I growled. Niko caught me as I lunged, still cursing, toward the couch.

Cunning fox eyes grinned at me, but the actual curve of his mouth was uncertain, as if that half-assed hug was so far outside his world that he barely recognized it for what it was. Yeah, you and me both, pal, I thought as I glared at him over Nik's shoulder. Learning how to be a friend was a bitch and a half.

"Robin, just tell us. If you tell us, we can help stop this. I would think you would want that." Niko pushed me back with a warning glare of his own. His glare was more of an implication . . . a level glance, but I knew it for what it was.

"No."

Niko turned back to Goodfellow at the puck's response. "No? You . . . no?" I hadn't seen my brother at a loss for words often. If not for the situation, it would've been entertaining. "No, you won't tell us," he went on, "or no, you don't want the attempts to cease?"

"The first." Robin aimed the remote and turned the television back on and the sound up. "Now, why don't you run along and find your Scottish pal? While you're wasting time here, he's probably scarfing up a busload of kiddies as we speak."

It was a low blow, and it was meant to be.

"Robin," I growled.

"No."

"Goodfellow. . . ," my brother insisted.

"No."

"You tiny-dicked piece of shit." I curled my fingers into a fist.

"Not very inventive, proven false, and no."

"This is a serious matter." That was Nik again with the calm reason.

"No."

"Loman."

He looked at me, but he didn't say no this time. He didn't say anything at all. There was nothing but silence from him until we gave up and left. From a *puck* . . . silence.

Which meant, for now, we were shit out of luck.

17

After a few hours of needed unconsciousness, I woke that evening, took a shower, and went where Niko was sitting on the couch looking at the paper spread out on our battle-scarred coffee table. He must've gone out to buy one, because he didn't tend to swipe the one from that asshole downstairs like I did. Always bitching to the manager about the noise, and I had to admit when you hit the floor after being thrown over your brother's shoulder, that does make some noise. So I played loud music when we sparred to cover up the floor pounding, lamps breaking, and tables overturning, but apparently he wasn't a fan of alternative music either. The manager came by and squawked at us once a week or so and the asshole under us lost a paper or three. Niko didn't approve but as Thou Shall Not Steal wasn't kissing cousins with Thou Shall Not Kick Your Brother's Ass in Sparring, I ignored him.

"What's up?" I asked. "You looking for 'Ninja needed, soy-eating, anal-retentive required' in the classifieds?"

"No." He didn't raise his eyes from the paper. "It

seems Sawney finally received some publicity after all."

I sat beside him and took a look for myself. The picture wasn't so bad. Just a gurney and a full body bag. That's a helluva life to lead, isn't it, when a body bag is just one of those things? No big deal. The headline made up for it, though: EIGHT SLAUGHTERED AT MANHATTAN PSYCHIATRIC CENTER. "Oh, shit," I murmured.

It seemed two security guards and six of the mental patients had been killed. Two more patients were missing. Four were decapitated and the other four had their throats slit. All were sliced to hell and back. "Hell, we knew the son of a bitch does have a taste for the psychiatrically challenged." And for me. I read the rest of the article. The two missing patients were assumed to be responsible for the deaths . . . with what? Their damn fingernails? Those poor bastards had been taken away either dead to be eaten later or alive for Sawney's fun and games. I hoped for their sakes they were dead. "Want I should take a smell around?" I didn't see we could do anything else except make sure it was Sawney.

"I think that is an excellent idea." He refolded the paper and slapped it against my chest. "Take that down to Mr. Arnold. He's no doubt been looking for it."

My brother, occasionally he did surprise me.

We waited until around midnight until dressing in black—jacket and coat, shirt and pants—and took the train up to East Twenty-fifth Street. Niko had done some research online about the place, but standing across the street looking at the fence topped with concertina wire, I didn't get a warm fuzzy feeling thinking about the mental health field. At least seventeen stories tall, the building was a brown looming mass straight out of a Stephen King book. Hundreds of glowing hungry eyes masquerading as windows, the double doors that took you in never to spit you out again, and the Kingster himself doing the body cavity searches. Then off you'd go to the double-lockdown ward where criminally insane was already preprinted on your name tag. *Hi, my name is Cal! I like to knit and kill, and I have father issues.*

I kept looking up at the place, hypnotized, then shuddered slightly and looked over at Nik. "Okay, if there's undercover work involved here," I said, "Sawney can eat everyone in the damn city."

Niko snorted and we crossed the street. There was still yellow police tape fluttering here and there, but the cops had come and gone. The hospital was bound to have upped the security, but if we couldn't avoid them, then we were in the wrong job. We found an area where the tall security lamp had a shattered bulb . . . courtesy of a silenced shot from my Glock. The Eagle I was saving for Sawney or any revenants. I doubted I'd need it—they'd come and gone, but you never knew. Niko pulled a pair of bolt cutters and we were through the fence in less than a minute. The grounds weren't all that big in and of themselves, but the building was huge. It took a while to circumnavigate the place while dodging the occasional guard, some of who looked pretty damn scared. Couldn't say I blamed them. Whether the killers came from inside or out, I doubted the scenario had been in the employment brochure. We were more than halfway around the place before I smelled him . . . Sawney and the revenants. I pressed close through the bushes, put a hand on the cold stone, and looked up.

"See it?" I asked.

"Yes," Niko responded. "I see."

About five stories up was a brand-spanking-new window. Crisscrossed with wire the same as the others, this one was a little more clear, a little less clouded with age. They had gone through there and back out again from the smell. The scent was strong, stronger than a one-way trip. "Did you want to ninja your way up the wall or something?" I dug my hand in my pocket. "I think I have some double-sided sticky tape in here. You could wrap it around your hands and—" I dodged the elbow only to end up with the heel of a calloused hand millimeters from my nose. Busted cartilage, bone shards into the brain . . . lesson learned for the day.

"You don't play fair," I grumbled.

"Have I ever?" He dropped his hand and kept looking up at the window. "And there's nothing up there to see." He was probably right. Only freshly scrubbed tile floors and grout stained a bloody brown that wouldn't come clean again no matter how much bleach housekeeping used.

"Can you follow their scent? See where they left?"

"I'm not a supernatural Lassie." Hell, I wasn't even as good as your average beagle, much less bloodhound, but—"I'll give it a shot." Keeping an eye out for the guards, I moved across the grass. There was more than Sawney and the revenants to track; there was blood and lots of it. Soaked into the ground and the fading grass, it made itself known just as well. It led to the north side of the fence. Up at the top you could still see the mottled stains of blood on the concertina wire. "Up and over."

We went through, and from there I wavered. The slaughter had happened last night. A lot of people had come and gone since then. "Okay, you're going to have to offer me a Snausage or something, because I've lost it."

"Try harder."

"What?" I demanded. "No 'I know you've got it in you'? At least give me some sort of inspirational speech."

"I did." He repeated it: "Try harder."

Great. I scowled at him and did exactly that. I tried harder. To my surprise I picked up something . . . a faint spore. Blood, bone, and Sawney's coldly cheerful insanity. I only caught traces of it every fifteen or so feet for a block or so and then nothing. I stopped and looked down.

"Ah." Niko crouched and touched fingers to metal. "He's gone to ground."

More exactly, underground. It was a manhole cover.

More cold concrete, more water, more darkness. I exhaled, wished Sawney'd had a thing for tree houses instead of caves, and pulled the Eagle. Using the bolt cutters Niko pried up the cover, jumped several rungs down, and hung on the ladder for a split second, then kept climbing down. I followed, pulling the cover not quite in place, but enough to fool the casual eye.

It had rained a few days ago and I could hear the rush of water beneath us. It wasn't much better than the tunnels had been—NYC wasn't known for its pure mountain streams—and the only things I could smell didn't have anything to do with Sawney and everything to do with courtesy flushes. It was a storm sewer, not a waste one, but the things water swept off the streets weren't always lemony-fresh. I breathed through my mouth and kept moving down.

When I hit the bottom, the water was cold, knee high, but it wasn't filled with floating dead body parts. In comparison to the SAS tunnels, we could grab a canoe and call this a vacation.

Still, dead body parts or not, Sawney might use the sewers as a home base. Cold, dank—it was a possibility, which was more than we had before. Now that we'd been at the Second Avenue Subway construction, he was bound to have left there. Sawney wanted his spider-hole secret. We didn't know whether he'd actually settled on that location or not before we'd shown up, but regardless we'd spoiled it for him.

Niko switched on his flashlight. "Do you remember when you were five and flushed your fish?"

"He was dead and that was in South Carolina." I sloshed through the water.

"Mmmm." The light dipped and I saw a sinuous shape beneath the surface of the water move past us. It was barely three feet long and it was not Freddy. Good thing too. Freddy had been a piranha.

We kept moving and truthfully I was surprised when we didn't come across any pieces of patients. Sawney wasn't the neatest of eaters. Unless he'd invested in a bib and a course in table manners, then this wasn't home or home was much farther down. I was really tired of tramping through tunnels and sewers, but it looked like this wasn't going to be an easy one. "Jesus. We might have days of this ahead of us," I said. "We'll have to get more help, bring paint to mark the off branches we cover, more lights." I turned and shot the revenant behind me in the stomach. "And get some rubber boots. My goddamn feet are freezing."

It fell in the water with a gurgle of blood and water rushing from its mouth. Its abdomen was pretty much gone—a bloody ruin of shredded flesh and the cartilage that passed for their bones. But there were still arms, a head and neck, part of a chest, and a frantically thrashing set of legs still joined, just barely, at the pelvis.

"I was beginning to wonder if you were ever going to shoot it," Niko said, "or were thinking of giving it a piggyback ride instead."

I rolled my eyes. "Asshole. There's no pleasing you." I nudged the legs with my foot as the head went under water. "I think I should've used the Glock."

"It would've been more convenient for questioning purposes," Nik pointed out with mild exasperation as he dipped his hand under the water, grabbed the neck, and lifted the head up out of the water. "We would like to have a word with you, if you're not too occupied at the moment."

The head whipped back and forth, arms moved in jerky disjointed movements, the upper torso dripped fluid. Been seeing a lot of that lately. It was getting boring. "I can question the bottom half if you want, but unless it can do sign language with its toes, I think I'm out of luck."

An even more exasperated gray glance hit me, then turned back to the revenant. "Where is Sawney?" The gurgling turned to a scream, then a wheezing laugh. "Traveler."

There was another gurgle as the head went back under the water. Niko sighed as he held it under. "I'm a patient man, but this is all getting to be rather annoying." Corpse gray hands clawed at Niko's arms. He ignored them. "And if you can't use your explosive rounds responsibly, I'll have to take them away."

"It could've been Sawney," I defended. "I can't smell shit down here. Okay, that's not technically true. I can smell shit down here, but it really is sh . . ."

The gaze narrowed and I holstered the Eagle without finishing. "Yeah, anyway, he's looking a little more cooperative now," I said, nodding toward floating arms and a lack of air bubbles.

The head was jerked back up and shaken briskly by the neck. Water gushed from its mouth and over its chest. "Now"—Niko's fingers tightened around the neck—"you're obviously going to die. Regenerating is not much of an option for you, missing one-third of your body. However." He smiled, and even I felt the ice creep down my spine at the sight of it. "You can die now or you can die later. I think you'd much prefer now."

"Human." The word bubbled through the blood and water. "Worthless meat. I don't fear you."

That was all revenant there. A little bit arrogant and a whole lot stupid. He went back under. "I doubt that he knows anything," Niko said absently as he tossed me his light and used his other hand to draw his shorter sword—the tanto blade. "If he did, Sawney wouldn't have let him fall behind."

"Maybe the revenants are showing some more will now," I offered, catching the flashlight and holding it on the revenant. "They're not that bright and they've got an attention span . . ." I waggled my other hand back and forth.

"Much like yours, you mean," Niko suggested.

I glared but went on. "Sawney's feeding them

some good stuff right now, but I doubt they're much into planning their future. He might be losing some of his control."

"Hmm. Interesting thought. Let us see."

It took a while.

I didn't think it was so much loyalty for Sawney as a hatred of humans. It'd be like a big-eyed lamb coming out of a field, kicking my ass, and making me its bitch. Revenant arrogance just couldn't believe it or give in to it. Not for a long time. Freddy and some friends showed up now and again to carry chunks of newly found fish food away in their mouths.

When it did talk, and with Niko it really was only a matter of time, it didn't have much to say. Yes, they'd taken the patients through here. We knew that. They were already dead when they'd been dropped into the water. It was the best that could be hoped for. As for the sewers and Sawney, it didn't know. Didn't know if he planned to stay or go. Didn't know if this was home or just another look at curb appeal.

It had wandered off from the others with a piece of flesh to gnaw on, gotten full and sleepy, and never followed the others on. Revenants were the same as people. There were smart ones (relatively), average ones, and there was this guy. Dumb as a fucking rock. But to give it credit—posthumous, but credit all the same—even a smart revenant might not be on to whatever Sawney was up to. That twisted brain— he would give an Auphe a run for its money. Murder, mayhem, and madness, and that was just what he saw in his rearview mirror. What was ahead, I don't think any of us could know.

But when we came back to the sewers we might just find out.

18

The next morning—actually, the next sunup. Sunup is not morning. It's hell and not fit for any human being, but Niko, having ascended to a higher plane of existence beyond simple things like time, wasn't human when it came to exercise. He dragged my ass out of bed and off we were to run a thousand laps around Washington Square Park. Okay, maybe not a thousand, but it felt like it. Washington Square Park was the nearest park to our apartment, but it was not a very big park and we had to run a lot of laps for Niko to feel like we'd gotten a good workout.

There would always be things we couldn't outrun: vampires, the wolves . . . Delilah would catch me in five seconds easy, but Niko made damn sure I could outrun things like revenants. He ran me at least once a day; morning, afternoon, night—it varied. He ran all three times, which made him faster than me and less likely to have his lungs turn inside out. Good for him. Me? If I could've figured out a way to get out of the one run, I would've. That's why I had a gun. Shooting is easy; running with Niko was hard. He always ran me into the ground, until I was soaked in sweat and couldn't take another step without my legs folding beneath me to dump me on the ground. Because that was real life for us—running to save it.

I still hated it.

After that and a shower, Niko and I sat in the kitchen and tried to figure things out regarding Goodfellow. Finding Sawney was something we were leaving to the end of the discussion, friend before foe and a better subject than dwelling on the Psychiatric Center slaughter.

Niko started by grilling me on the guy who'd shot Robin. He grilled me yesterday after the attack, but between my job at the bar, hoping Robin didn't grope him when he took in ice packs, and the killings at the Psychiatric Center, we'd been a little busy for a repeat grilling. He was hoping I'd remember something new and I did.

"Black hair and dark eyes. Skin a little darker than yours. What I think was some kind of Arabic accent. Faint, though. And he kept saying his task was done. That he was honored to die." Well, he got his wish there. "He also called Robin a betrayer. He didn't get into any specifics there. Wouldn't say if he was alone or not and I gave him plenty of reason to speak up." And I wasn't sorry for one damn bit of it. "Oh, wait. Hell, there is something else. The son of a bitch used some fancy move to throw me off of him—one that you've definitely never taught me," I said before popping the tab on the Coke and taking a swig. "Holding out on me, Cyrano?"

He frowned. "A move I've never shown you? Describe it." He had some soy, rice-powder, mud-colored drink he was nursing. He'd long ago learned not to offer me one. It was all I could do to keep my own down watching him drink his.

I got up and went ahead to illustrate the move a few times from the floor. He helped by assuming my role, straddling me with a finger pointed under my chin. Finally when he was satisfied, I returned to my chair. "Hmm. And an Arabic accent, you said." Niko moved over to the groaning bookshelf against the living room wall and scanned the contents. He chose a book, sat, and thumbed through it. After a few minutes of reading, he said with satisfaction, "*Varzesh-e Pahlavani.* An ancient form of Iranian martial arts, although in those days it would've been called Persian arts. It's well over two thousand years old."

"The accent, Persia, and Robin definitely twitched when you mentioned Babylon a few days ago." I wrung a note from the metal of the can. "I think we have a location pinned down." It was all right, this. Just me and Niko—like back in the old days. Research, learning crap I didn't care about, practicing obscure moves. Yeah, the old days . . . the days before I had to worry about an obstinate car salesman who couldn't be bothered to worry about himself.

Damn it.

Within seconds Nik was back with another book. Under his breath he was muttering names . . . Tammuz, Utukku. I drank my Coke and let it drift in one ear and out the other. When he hit on something, he would let me know. He didn't. Sighing, he closed the book. "We'll have to push Robin on it again, but now for Sawney." His eyes darkened to match the grim curl of his lips. "I think I have something."

"Yeah?" I said, surprised. "What?"

"I called the TA who shares the office with me while you were showering. I wanted her to pick up more classes for me until this is done. She had news."

"Good or bad?"

"Bad." He replaced the book on the shelf. "But informative. Students are disappearing at Columbia. Several. It hasn't hit the papers in a big way yet as they are students. Prone to wandering off after parties and not showing up for a day or two. But Shannon said she heard these students were reliable, not the kind to take off without telling someone."

"That could be anyone. Could be your average serial killer." I knocked the salt and pepper shakers together. "Sawney's not the only predator around."

"True. But I have a feeling about this. There's something about Columbia I can't put my finger on. Something I think I read once and have forgotten. We need to look into this."

"More so than the sewers?" I said skeptically and rapped the shakers again. I was equally skeptical that Niko forgot anything he ever read, but it was possible. He had a lot of information crammed in that head. "It's a *college*," I went on. "I doubt he's shacking up in the dorms."

He took the clanking shakers out of my hand and put them out of reach. "Trust me, and it'll certainly take less time than roaming more miles of sewers."

There was no doubt Niko was hell on wheels when it came to tracking and finding predators. That we hadn't found this one yet bugged the hell out of him . . . he'd gone from Zen to ice-cold and that didn't spell well for Sawney. "We'll need some sort of in. The police might not be there in full force, but the students will be on edge. Faculty too. I'm too young to pass for a cop." Although it'd be easy enough to get the fake ID. We'd been getting it since I was sixteen and Niko eighteen. Any Rom worth his salt could find a way easy enough and we had. Our clan might not accept us thanks to my Auphe half, but Sophia knew the tricks. And from watching her all those years we knew them too. "And you're too . . ." I shrugged.

"Too what?"

"Hell, you're like a James Bond villain. Cool, collected, lethal, and not a donut in sight. No one would buy you as a cop either." Besides, even though at twenty-two he could pass for twenty-six or twenty-seven easy, that was still too young for him to be convincing as a plainclothes detective. And his chin-length hair would immediately brand him as an imposter if he were in a uniform.

He snorted. "When I start drinking my soy-milk shaken, not stirred, then we'll talk. As for an in, if there is one, Promise will know."

And she did. Between her rich dead husbands and being a vampire, Promise was prominent on the social/charitable and nonhuman scene. If it was a fat, feebleminded rich guy you needed or a man-starved socialite, she just had to pick up a phone. The supernatural world was a little trickier to navigate because of trust issues, alliances, and creatures that didn't think there was a damn thing wrong with murder. But in the end she came through for us.

A long ride uptown on the A train later, we were at Columbia Presbyterian talking with a Japanese healing entity, O-Kuni-Nushi, known to his oblivious human colleagues as Ken Nushi, doctor and special seminar instructor for the premed upperclassmen at Columbia University.

A healing spirit, more powerful than a human

healer by far, would've come in handy not so long ago, but he didn't know Promise at the time and vice versa. He knew of someone who knew someone who knew someone and so on. As it turned out, he could still do us a favor. First, he was actually willing to pay us. Second, he was able to confirm the students were missing and the college was more concerned than the cops were at this point.

"You are correct. Two students have disappeared on campus over the past two days, also a maintenance man." Behind his desk, Dr. Nushi steepled long, thin fingers, two of which were banded with jade rings. One was white, one red. He had a face that was oddly monkeylike—large ears, black hair in a widow's peak, broad nose, and soulful eyes. Even more oddly, indifferent student that I was, I happened to remember a mythology lesson from years before. In the Japanese mythos, monkeys were thought to bring good fortune. If you needed a doctor, good fortune would be a nice bonus along with a cheerful bedside manner.

"I cannot say what has taken them," Dr. Nushi continued. "But there is something here. A predator, human or not, I can't say. But there is a stillness . . . an air. . . ." He looked at me, then opened his hands in a "who knows?" gesture. I had an air about me too, he seemed to think, but he remained silent on that subject. Luckily. Niko cared for comments about my Auphe heritage even less than I did. "I cannot put a finger on it," he said, "but I know. Death is here. A good physician recognizes it. This is walking, talking Death and it is using our campus as a feeding ground. Human or non, I want it gone. This is a place of knowledge, not death. But I didn't know what to do with the police saying we must wait forty-eight hours. I didn't know who to contact, not until Mrs. Nottinger called with the offer of your services." He nodded his head toward Promise.

"Sawney Beane." Niko had bowed to Dr. Nushi before he'd taken a seat. Now, in black on black, he sat straight in the deep blue brocade chair with face impassive. "It may be the one we're looking for hunts here now. It may be, as you say, a human. Either way, we will look into it." He looked at Promise, then back at me. "The tunnels and sewers might not be to his liking. He'll no doubt have several prospects going at one time, trying to find the best possible location for his true home. Once he settles on one he'll stay there, but I don't think he has yet. He could be hunting here and taking his victims back to whichever location he's trying out now. Whichever cave."

"If that is true, you will certainly be more help than the police," Nushi said.

"The police aren't here, then?" Promise asked. We knew they wouldn't find Sawney, if he was hunting here, but if they were patrolling the campus in force, they could make things difficult for our investigation. There should've already been rampant speculation about a serial killer with as many bodies as Sawney was leaving around.

But the thing was, bodies *weren't* being left around. We'd seen that, having checked the paper for several days after finding the bodies in the trees. There'd been nothing until the slayings at the mental institute. No stories on the ones in the trees or on the various body parts floating in the tunnels that could've been stumbled across by the construction crews. Mysteries. We had too much on our plate already, but it was something we'd need to come back to—eventually. Right now . . . it could wait, but we'd look into it. Maybe in a few weeks . . . or months. After Sawny, a vacation was the only thing I wanted, not mysteries.

"They are peripherally involved, but as I said, the students are adults legally, as well as is the maintenance man, and it has not yet been two days. They are investigating, but as there are no signs of foul play as of yet . . ." He spread his hands wider, then placed them on the desk. "They are certainly not here in force." The brown eyes sought out us all one by one. "This is my home, but I am no warrior. Mrs. Nottinger has said you are for hire. I will pay whatever you require to take care of this situation before it worsens."

Someone was actually going to pay us to risk our lives. Hot damn. It made horrific, near-death experiences a shade less annoying. I shoved my hand into the pocket of my black leather jacket and fingered a well-worn rip. I'd given Delilah my good one, but I liked this one too. I couldn't replace it; it was a classic, but I did need to replace the Glock, and explosive rounds for the Eagle didn't come cheap.

"Results will not necessarily be immediate. We will do our best, but Sawney is a one-creature slaughterhouse, quite literally," Niko cautioned. "And if the killer is human, the police would probably find him before we did."

"Then your best is all that I can ask." Dr. Nushi bowed. Nik bowed. And the meeting was mostly over. Except for Promise politely but firmly asking for Nushi's home address for billing purposes. She flashed a bit of fang in either strong incentive or flirtatious behavior. With vampires it was hard to tell. As the tips of Nushi's large ears flushed pink, I went with flirtatious.

We were given false student ID that would pass anywhere on either campus if we were stopped for any reason. Although I couldn't imagine why we would be. I looked the twenty-year-old punk-ass kid that I was. Niko, twenty-two, looked twenty-six, and could pass for a grad student or the TA that he was easily enough. Promise . . . Promise had an ageless quality, but no one would stop her because they thought she was a serial killer.

One student had disappeared on the way to French class, one while doing laundry in the basement of one of the dorms, and the maintenance man was a mystery. He'd gone out on a call, but taken the documentation with him. No one confessed to putting in a request and no one knew where he'd gone.

We separated to cover the most ground, mingling among the potential meals and looking for dead bodies and/or monsters. I took a map. Niko navigated by either the stars or his innate sense of place on the planet. It was past seven and dark; Promise carried her cloak over one arm and drifted. Two seconds later I'd lost sight of her. She knew how to move. I only knew the direction she'd vanished by the turning of male heads and one or two female ones.

I looked down at the map, considered it for a second, and then wadded it up to toss it into the nearest trash can. It wouldn't help me find Sawney. Smelling him would and thinking like him would. I wasn't entirely happy with the fact that I thought each would be an identical exertion. I'd been a happy-go-lucky maniac myself for over a week once. It wasn't difficult at all to remember the curve and slide of that particular thought pattern. Far too easy, in fact. One jump and you were on the ride, whizzing along with the wind cackling like insane laughter in your ears.

I tried my nose first. It felt safer.

Columbia is bigger than it looks, and it looked plenty big enough. We were concentrating on the Morningside Heights campus, where the students and employee had all disappeared. Nothing had yet happened at the med school and hospital fifty blocks up. There was Morningside Park bordering one side of the campus and Promise said she would inquire of any nonhumans within, a polite way of saying she'd ask the local yokels if they'd seen a new monster in the neighborhood.

I went from building to building, and first I thought it was going to be easy, because I smelled him right off the bat. But it wasn't long before I realized that, yeah, his scent was present . . . everywhere. Rank and unmistakable. He was hunting here all right. From what I could tell he'd roamed every nook and cranny of the school. Keeping to the shadows, avoiding the security lights, but *owning* it . . . every inch.

Hot damn. We were finally on to something. From the smell of it he was here almost if not every night. Every night . . . but not that many students were missing. This couldn't be it, could it? One of his possible locations? Or his new home? He liked caves, and there wasn't much cavelike about this place. Still, something was going on. All we needed to do was find the bastard, slice off parts, and ask him what.

But finding him was a problem. With his smell literally everywhere, I wasn't sure how to pinpoint it. It's never easy, is it? "Well, shit." I stopped and crouched on the long strip of grass between Broadway and Amsterdam that connected two sections of the campus.

"Pretty boy." A hand tickled behind my ear. "Frustrated?"

Delilah.

"You could say that," I grunted, surprised. I hadn't heard her coming; she was Kin after all, but I'd smelled her behind me. Wolf and vanilla, but what in the hell she was doing here I had no idea. I turned my head and looked up at her as she twirled a lock of my black hair around her finger. "That son of a bitch Sawney."

She wrinkled her nose, eyes turning new-penny bright. "He is here. He is everywhere. The stench of insanity." Which was true. He definitely had the stink of crazy all over him. Of course he had the same to say about me. She sat beside me. "Rabid, but that is normal for him. Stop looking." She shook her head disapprovingly. "He will eat you." Her face, her mouth moved inches from mine. "Let me eat you"—her tongue touched my lower lip—"instead."

Okay, that was even more of a surprise than her showing up—not so much the offer, as the timing. I wasn't Robin—Jesus, who was?—but I knew when someone was interested in me or at least interested in parts of me. And my parts and I felt the same way about her, although half of that combo felt guilty as hell about it. Not that that mattered. This wasn't the time or the place. Two students passed, girls, blond and brunette. They looked at us and hurried on, their long legs striding faster. I might look like a punk-ass twenty-year-old kid and Delilah a cross between a model and a kick-your-ass biker chick, but we still didn't pass in the human world. Not really. Those girls wouldn't know why they felt the way they did about us, but they sensed the difference in us somehow.

"Little girls," Delilah said with a derisive toss of her ponytail. "Scared of monsters in the big bad woods."

I hung my head for a moment. She didn't mind being different. I wondered why I did. "How'd you know I was here anyway?"

She sat beside me, her own long legs clad in leather. She stretched and reclined on her elbows in the grass. "Called Promise. Puck answered. Says Columbia. From there." She touched a finger to her small, straight nose. "I find your scent."

"And what do I smell like?" I asked with a reluctant curiosity. "Flay didn't seem to care for it, whatever it is."

The copper of her eyes darkened back to light brown as she puzzled on the question. "Strange. Interesting. Good and bad. Right and wrong." She gave an acquisitively hungry smile. "Sweet and sour."

I reached over and ran a thumb along the lower curve of that smile. "I hope that's about sex and not making me a meal. You wouldn't be the first werewolf that tried to make me dinner, and you wouldn't be the first one I killed."

She wasn't impressed, snorting. "Pups."

"Not all of them. Cerberus was no Red Riding Hood reject." Never mind that it had taken all three of us . . . Flay, Niko, and me . . . to take him down. We'd done it. I wasn't sure anyone else could have.

"Cerberus." The smile was completely different now, dark and gloating. She lifted the snug white shirt she wore to bare her scars. "Not fit to bear his cub. Flay and I, our family, to Kin Alphas we are not good enough. Not high enough in pack. Not pure. *We* are better than pure. *We* are Wolf." She rested a hand on her flat stomach. "But Cerberus said there would be no cub." Her lips tightened and she pulled the shirt back down. "No cubs ever now."

I could think of absolutely nothing to say at first, although I'd suspected before from the extent of the damage that could be seen that she wouldn't be making her nephew, Slay, any little cousins. Sorry seemed wholly lacking, and I finally went with my instinct. "He died painfully, in one god-awful bloody mess."

It was the right thing. The smile returned, blazing bright as her eyes. "Sex. Now." She took my hand, stood, and yanked me up with such strength that both of my feet almost left the ground.

Not that it wasn't nice to be wanted, to be used and abused, but the screams that ripped through the air emphasized that some things have to wait. Hey, I'd already gotten laid once this year . . . okay, once in a lifetime. What was my hurry?

One of the girls who'd walked past us came running back. She was alone this time, with blood on her face and jacket. I didn't bother to ask what had happened. It was self-evident enough. Sawney or a revenant had come creeping out of the shadows for an evening snack. She kept running past us with white-rimmed, unseeing eyes. I ran in the direction she had come from. Delilah followed, more out of boredom than any desire to save a human, I thought. She stayed in human form, but kept up with me easily regardless. As we ran, I pulled out my cell phone, gave Nik the terse facts, and tried for more speed.

We passed several students going in both directions. They veered away from us; it was obvious we weren't jogging for our health. We covered the length of the grass-covered walk, vaulted the small iron pole and chain fence that framed the grass, and followed the blood. It was the only way we found her . . . by the smell of her blood. It was thick in the air, as thick as the inescapable scent of Sawney and revenants.

And it was a revenant that had her, not Sawney. While Sawney's spore was hours old, that of the revenant was as fresh as the girl's blood. Both came from a building of red brick, narrow windows, and chimneys. It looked like a house, not a campus building. It was surrounded by low hedges and that's where we found them—the victim and three revenants. In a crook of hedge and building, shadowed and protected from a casual glance, they were feeding on her. One was at her throat, one at her chest, and one at her stomach, and there wasn't a damn thing we could do for her. The revenants had made scraps of her in a matter of minutes. It was the dark-haired one. Her short cap of hair didn't show the blood, but what strips of skin remained did.

I growled and kicked the head of the revenant from her throat. I wasn't wearing sneakers today. I was wearing scuffed black combat boots, thick-soled and heavy, and I broke the bastard's neck instantly with the blow. Not that that stopped him. His body staggered up and toward me while his head was bent at an acute angle. I'd broken the bone, but the spinal cord was still intact. Damaged probably, but not enough to make a difference in the primitive organism that was a revenant. Delilah, apparently forgoing the wolf this time, took one out with a knife. Took him down, out, and had him in pieces within sec-

onds. Why worry about losing a perfectly good set
of clothes in the transformation for a mere three
revenants—I could see her point. The leather
pants . . . and what they contained . . . yeah, that
would be a crime . . . *shit*.

I worried less about my hormones and more about
the third revenant that jumped me with claws and
teeth as sharp as any knife and a lot less hygienic. I
ducked and he slammed into the one with the catastrophic crick in his neck, and they both tumbled
down. I didn't use my gun. It was difficult enough
scuffling in the middle of campus without being noticed, even at night, and I used my own knife and
took one head while Delilah took the other.

"And you leave me nothing. You are an inconsiderate brother, to say the least."

I looked over my shoulder at Niko, who stood with
katana drawn. "You're getting slow, old man. Get a
scooter and we'll talk about saving you some ass
to kick."

I barely saw the swat, but I certainly felt it. Resisting the urge to rub the back of my shoulder, I
looked down at the dead girl, then away. "Our new
boss isn't going to be happy." I didn't blame him
one bit. I wasn't happy either.

"No, he won't be. They're getting bolder." Niko
knelt beside the girl. "They dragged her off the path,
but where did they come from? Here?" He looked
up at the building.

"Kinda small," I commented and it was true. It
simply wasn't large enough. If revenants and Sawney
had set up shop there, someone would've noticed. It
wasn't like they could hide out in ye olde attic like
first cousins' flipper kids.

"Yes, it is," he said absently, standing. "But seeing

is not always believing. Tell me what you smell." He glanced over at Delilah. "You as well."

I inhaled deeply as Delilah did the same. It reeked. The whole goddamn place stunk to high heaven of Sawney and the revenants, far more so than any other place on campus, which was saying something, and far more than any other place he'd been: the warehouse, the sewers, the Second Avenue subway. That was it for the sewers, then. It was kind of a relief that there'd be no more trudging through water. "This is it all right," I confirmed, trying not to gag.

Delilah agreed with a nod. "The Den. They come here. Go from here. Live here."

Not exclusively, but from the sheer concentration of odor, here more than anywhere else.

"Well then, Alexander Sawney Beane." Niko smiled, that rare, anticipatory smile that didn't bode well for whoever was at the end of his sword. "Knock, knock."

We had left campus before any students or security spotted us. Promise and Niko notified Dr. Nushi of the events and the bodies—which I suspected would soon disappear. Sawney or more revenants could come for them or that mysterious whatever that seemed to have a license in body collection. Nik and Promise went back to our apartment for research and other things. And for once, other things were in my schedule as well. Damn, twice in a year—where were the Guinness people when you needed them?

Delilah had an apartment . . . of sorts. Wolves weren't really all that good at things like rent and damage-deposits and utilities. Not your average wolf anyway. That's what Alphas were for. Alphas took care of the pack. Told them where to live, found the food to take down . . . the members of an Alpha's pack were, in a way, his children. In werewolf society, especially in the Kin, the Alpha of a particular pack would buy up a building or two—yeah, they had that kind of money—and take care of the power and water. Then their pack would move in. They might settle in one corner of a warehouse or they might settle in a series of apartments, moving from floor to floor every month or so. It depended on the wolf.

They always looked abandoned from the outside with blackout curtains or blinds on the windows to keep up the impression. The doors were also kept chained, but if any homeless happened to be smart enough to find another way in . . . well, yummy manna from doggy heaven.

Delilah's place had once been a school. There was a rusty chain-link fence and graffiti everywhere. Old graffiti. Any newer aspiring artists wouldn't do any better than the homeless. She used the key to open the chains and relocked them through a small hole fashioned in the steel-bar-enhanced safety glass. Sniffing me quickly, she nodded. "Come."

Before we'd gotten within ten blocks of the place, she had produced a small spray container, like a tiny perfume bottle, and squirted me liberally with it. "From the puck," she had said. And I remembered it from our previous run-in with the Kin. "Will make you smell different. Not like you. Not human food. Not Auphe." Not human, because someone might want to join in on the meal. And not Auphe, because . . . hell, that didn't need explanation.

She had chosen a room on the third floor and we made our way quietly up darkened stairs, stopping if she heard any other wolves. I might not have the scent of a human or an Auphe, but I had to *be* something, and if they saw me, they would know it wasn't wolf. Managing to avoid that, we reached her place. It was a big room that had once been two. A wall had been knocked down with a sledgehammer from the looks of the ragged concrete frame. The institutional walls had been painted an umber color, smoldering in the low light of the occasional lamp. The shades were light reddish brown glass run through with hundreds of random fractures, Tiffany in a postmodern world.

There was no couch, only cushions. A nest of six large cushions made up what I guessed to be the equivalent. Three feet by three feet, they were forest green, deep brown, rusty red.

"Nice place," I said politely and then got to the point. "You don't eat people, do you?" For nutrition, I meant. I knew the vast majority of the Kin did as well as some nonKin wolves. "I might have issues with that."

"People." She slipped off her jacket, then her shirt. She wasn't wearing a bra and suddenly people pitas seemed a little less important than they had been. But I held on, because it *was* important. I wasn't Auphe and I wasn't sleeping with someone who would do the things Auphe would do. "No challenge," she dismissed. "I am a hunter. *Hunter.* I am not jackal like some Kin."

Okay, that was good to know. There was another pile of cushions, slightly larger across the room, and they were white, every one of them—the barest shade paler than Delilah's hair. "You sleep as a wolf, don't you?"

She peeled my jacket off me in one smooth motion.

"Wolf dreams." Her eyes were bright. "They are richer, sharper. You taste, smell, hear, touch. The very same as this world here." She shrugged, which did interesting things to very interesting parts of her. "Maybe that is the world. Maybe this is only the dream."

"Dreamtime." I considered the holster, then slipped out of it. Robin would no doubt say she'd like me to keep it on. Kinky and all, but shooting off your own balls during sex is more kink than I cared to think about. And was I babbling in my head nervously? Yeah. So what? It was my second goddamn time. I could be nervous if I wanted. "Sounds similar to something that Aborigines in Australia believe. Nik told me about it once, said it was . . ." Great, I was babbling outside my head now.

But it was the last word I said that night as I was tackled to the floor. Last string of coherent words anyway. I did say a few single explosive ones. Delilah was no nymph. She wasn't soft and slow, meandering and mild. Delilah was a whirlwind of wants and needs and demands, and before the night was over, she taught me how to be the same.

I was glad, though, that she couldn't smell me through Robin's concoction. Couldn't smell the lingering doubt under the savagely sharp pleasure. The faint remorse beneath the sheer *holy shit* spine-knotting euphoria.

The touch of guilt behind every bite, thrust, and caress.

The regret.

19

The New York Metropolitan Museum was big. I knew that. But it was something I knew in the back of my head . . . like that the sky is blue. That fire burns. That a man can't get it up in fifty-degree water no matter what Robin thought. Basic, commonsense knowledge.

So while I knew the museum was big, I never thought about it—not until early the next morning when I was lost in the basement under the main building. I had gotten Sangrida's permission over the phone to be there, just checking for more sirrush, I'd said, and she'd made sure the same door to the basement was unlocked, but that was it. And it wasn't as if I could request a security guard to help me find the mummy. First, I didn't know which men were hers and not your average rent-a-cop, and, second, I didn't know if she was aware that Wahanket had made a burrow under her feet.

I didn't think pissing off the mummy would be a good idea. I'd seen the cold rage lurking behind the yellow glow that filled those eye sockets. He hadn't tried to kill us, but he still wasn't what I'd call an easygoing guy. And if he lost his home, I damn sure didn't want him sleeping on my couch.

Robin had led us confidently through a maze of stacked crates and dusty, forgotten exhibits. I'd paid attention, but apparently not enough. And now, lacking a trail of bread crumbs, I was thoroughly lost. The lights were back on this time, and I wandered through row after row of delicate gilt furniture covered with heavy plastic drapes, canvases of all shapes and sizes, marble statuary, dramatic black-and-white masks, and grime-covered case after case of weapons. Swords, daggers, even axes. It was amazing. You didn't even need to be a puck to get itchy fingers at the sight of it.

But that would be wrong, and, more importantly, difficult to smuggle out past the guards at the entrance. Now, that was a Robin thought and it brought me back to the reason I was there. Time to stop window-shopping and get to it.

Neither he nor Nik would be happy to know where I was or what I was doing. Robin because I was poking my nose where he'd made it very clear he'd as soon chop it off. Nik . . . Nik would not be enthusiastic—*strongly* not enthusiastic—about the fact I was roaming around the location of a sirrush attack. There could be a hundred of those damn things down here; there was room.

Finally stopping beside a Japanese screen, I gave in to the inevitable and called out, "Wahanket."

Nothing.

I tried again, louder this time. "Wahanket!"

This time there was a rustling and there was a sense of motion in the corner of my eye. I turned, gun in hand. Sangrida had left one of her guards'

9mms for me at the basement entrance I'd used, under the stairs. It wasn't the Viking broadsword I'd expected, which was fine by me. They were heavy as hell. During the museum's working hours, getting my own gun through security wasn't feasible, but this one would do.

The motion and flicker I'd seen materialized into a small figure. It was cat-sized, no doubt because it *was* a cat. It sat and stared at me with black-and-white eyes. Painted eyes. The rest of it was a deep tarnished bronze with the glimmer of gold around its neck. It stared for a few more seconds, then stood and disappeared smoothly into the shadows with the clink of metal paws against the floor. It was an invitation and I accepted it.

An animated metal cat. It was bizarre and then some. How could it move? Was it alive or some sort of ancient Egyptian sorcerer's mind trick? I didn't know, although I was leaning toward the latter. I believed in monsters—hell, yeah. But magic? If there wasn't some form of flesh or bone behind it, I had a hard time buying into it. I did know that I preferred the walking statue idea to the thought that it was some dried-up cat mummy.

Fake magic or real, it led me to Wahanket. With his preoccupation with technology, I should've pictured him surfing the Net or watching cable, but I couldn't. The mental image was too incongruous. It was much easier to imagine him plunging an ancient dagger into the chest of some poor schmuck writhing on an altar. Or maybe dragging his foot and moaning as he shambled toward his prey. Shamble, drag. Very shambolic. Was that even a word?

Probably not, but I was right about one thing: He

wasn't surfing the Net. He was . . . dissecting something—a rat, I thought. A really big rat. Huge. I made a face and drawled, "Supper?"

"You, uneducated baboon, should not mock the ways of your betters." The curdled shadows instead of a sickly glow in his eye sockets must have meant he was feeling mellow. "Which would be everyone inhabiting this infested world, including my new pet." He indicated the rodent with the flourish of an antique scalpel.

Pet? And I realized he wasn't taking it apart; he was putting it back together. I wasn't sure if that was less disturbing or more so, and I decided to ignore it altogether. Shifting my gaze slightly away from the bloodstained crate doubling as an operating table, I said, "I'm here about Goodfellow."

"The puck." The scalpel was discarded for a needle threaded with a fine silver wire that gleamed between hard black fingers. "His tongue is impertinent, but his gifts are acceptable. What have you brought me?"

Fortunately I'd thought of that. Unfortunately that early in the morning the street vendor supplies had been skimpy. "Yeah, about that . . ." I looked down at the gun in my hand. Normally I didn't make a habit of giving up a weapon to a creature I barely knew and didn't trust, but I'd be fooling myself to think Wahanket would need a gun to try to kill me. Or to take me apart and put me back together in some sort of hideous parody of Cal Leandros. "Here."

The dark hand curled around the grip, and I felt the brush of skin harder than horn. "Ahhh, such a pretty toy. The modern equivalent of the flintlock." He abandoned the rat for a closer examination. "I have seen many images, but there are no examples of such recent firearms down here in my domain." The teeth gnashed in a grin. "Man's enthusiasm for killing his own kind still pleases me, even after all this time."

As my eyes drifted back reluctantly, behind him I thought I saw the rat twitch. No, I was sure of it . . . with belly still gaping half open and eyes blankly empty, it twitched. I looked away again and decided breakfast wasn't the way to go today. "Great. I'm glad you're happy. Sorry there's no bow and ribbon. Now can we talk about Robin?"

"Baboons were never one for patience." He pulled out the clip as if he'd done it a thousand times. "Interesting."

The rat squeaked. It was faint and raspy and no-where near being on my list of latest frigging greatest hits. "Goodfellow," I emphasized sharply. Hearing my own voice was better than hearing the alterna-tive. "Someone's trying to kill him. You know any-thing about that? You know who might be gunning for him?"

The clip was slammed back home and a tongue as weathered as beef jerky clicked against the teeth. "You ask much of me. I hold the secrets of Osiris, the knowledge of Thoth, the death rolls of Anubis, but a list so long? You request the impossible."

That was the standard line. Your poor, your hun-gry, your huddled masses yearning to kill me, that was Robin's motto. "How about you narrow it down to the top twenty or so? Think you could do that?" There was the scrabbling of paws and the moist thump of what I hoped was a tail against wood. "Come on, Hank. I gave. Now you give, and you can get back to your Franken-rat, okay?" Poor damned trash muncher. I was no rodent fan, but Jesus.

"Twenty?" The weapon was placed carefully, almost lovingly, on top of a glass case containing a stuffed baboon, which, by the way, did not look like me. "As I have said, impossible. You ask me to separate twenty grains of sand from the desert's mighty stretch. Such a task cannot be done." There was a hole in his chest. I hadn't noticed that before. A sunken hole and the shine of gold and turquoise deep within. "Perhaps I could thin the wheat from the chaff and give you a hundred creatures who wish death upon the puck." Arms of bones and ropy flesh wrapped with brown wrappings crossed. "Go. Return in seven days and I will have the information you seek."

"Seven days . . ." I started to protest as there was a louder thump, wet and horrible, and then the skitter of racing paws. I looked down; I couldn't help it. Hurriedly, I looked back up, tasted bile, and hoped I never saw a rat, dead or undead, again as long as I lived.

"Go." The glow was returning to Wahanket's hollows of bone.

I went.

A week . . . I only hoped Robin lived that long.

I went back into the maze, wandered far enough away from Wahanket that I felt a little more comfortable, and then I did it again . . . once more doing what I'd told Nik I wouldn't. I sat on the dusty floor, cross-legged, and held out my hand. I focused, twisted that focus, and it came. I kept it smaller than a full-sized gate as I had before, but went for just a little bigger this time. From the size of an orange to that of a basketball. And I then focused harder. The gate, nothing but the gate. No thoughts of Tumulus or the Auphe. No thoughts of feeding someone to them. No thoughts that weren't mine. It wasn't going to happen. I wouldn't let it. Maybe I wouldn't even admit to having them in the first place.

The gray light swirled and eddied like a particularly dangerous riptide and it glowed like flesh-melting radioactivity. It was still ugly as hell and clamped down on the base of my brain like a vise. It hurt, it felt cold and wrong, and here I was doing it anyway.

Why? Because like I'd thought before, it could save my life someday. It could save Niko's life. That made it worth doing. It made the pain, the blood, and the sense of teetering on a chasm hungry for just one misstep worthwhile. The Auphe had never given me a damn thing I wanted to have or know, but if some genetic trick of theirs could ever save my brother or anyone else I cared about, then some good would come out of the horror show they had tried to make of me and the world.

I really wanted that bit of good. I'd saved Robin and myself before. I wanted to be able to do that again if push came to shove. Niko lived a life of monsters and madness because of who I'd been born. And he held his own—we both did, but if I could have that emergency exit available, I'd feel better. I'd feel maybe a fraction less responsible for the mess the Auphe had made of both our lives.

If only I could get a little goddamn better at it.

Despite my determination, the chasm whispered at me. It said things . . . bad things. It wanted things too, things even worse. I could almost touch those things, taste them, feel them. . . .

Shit.

With a massive effort, I shut them out. They were gone and I felt a slight sense of satisfaction . . . a very wary satisfaction. I wasn't stupid.

The pain spiked and with a hiss at the sharp ache, I closed the doorway. The light faded away and I wiped my nose with the dish towel I'd brought for the occasion. It worked better than the paper towels had. As I did, I thought it was nothing. Just things I imagined the Auphe thought and felt. I was in a creepy as hell basement doing an even creepier thing and who wouldn't imagine some crap in that situation? It was a fluke the first time and my imagination this time.

The blood kept coming and I wadded the cloth and held it against the flow for nearly ten minutes before it stopped. My ears were okay. Only that big gate I'd made to escape the sirrush had set them off. Wiping my face thoroughly, I fished the Tylenol out of my pocket and swallowed two. The headache, the blood, it was all still there. Practice didn't seem to be making perfect. That super gate I'd opened while fighting the Hob months ago had definitely gotten down and dirty with whatever I used to open those rips in reality. I could almost feel the blockage in my brain. Like a damaged area, hardened . . . thickened like scar tissue. I'd have to get around it or push through it.

Or, as Niko had said, my brain would come oozing out my ears. Either or. If he found out what I was doing, that might just be the least of my concerns.

I made my way back upstairs, getting lost about as many times as I expected. Once there I kept my head ducked down and made my way to the nearest bathroom to check for any leftover blood on my face. Ever try to check your reflection without actually looking into a mirror? Not so easy. I took some paper towels and soap and scrubbed first, then took a look that lasted about a fraction of a second before quickly turning my head away.

It was nearly as huge an accomplishment as shredding a hole in space itself. Phobias are tricky things. I knew a demon wasn't going to come out of a mirror and take me. I knew because I'd killed that demon, but that was the first glimpse I'd had of myself in a mirror since Darkling had crawled out of one to gobble me up.

How did I look?

Guilty as hell. Niko was so going to kick my ass.

When I showed up at Promise's apartment twenty minutes later, I'd tucked the guilt far out of sight with the natural acting skills Sophia had shown her marks over the years. In other words, I pasted a big fat lie on my face. If I was half as good as she'd been, I might just pass. At the apartment door I pulled up half a step behind Robin's housekeeper, Seraglio. She took one look up at me, shook her head, and fished in the pocket of her coat to hand me crackers and peanut butter in machine-wrapped cellophane. "A stiff wind would blow you over, sugar, and we're about to face a big gusty hot one now. Eat up." She had a small suitcase with her. Some of Robin's things, I thought, but . . .

I opened the crackers eagerly, took a bite, and said around it, "Where are the rest?"

"The taxi driver is bringing them up, all five of them," she sighed as she knocked on the door. "And for one mess of change, you'd better believe. God forbid he should help a lady out of the goodness of his tiny shriveled heart." Shaking her head impa-

tiently, she had lifted a small fist to knock again
when the door was flung open and out came Ishiah
in one hell of a temper. That wasn't the surprise. He
was always in a temper, a hot-blooded guy to look
as if he should be sporting a halo. The surprise was
that he was there—that Robin had opened the door
for him. Wings out of sight, he moved between Seraglio and me, didn't look at either of us, and strode
down the hall toward the elevator.

Shrugging, I took the suitcase from Robin's housekeeper and followed her into the apartment. Robin
was in a robe, probably one that had belonged to
one of Promise's past husbands, eating breakfast.
"Your crap, sir." I flopped the suitcase on the dining
room table. "Tips are appreciated, you cheap
bastard."

Fork suspended halfway between mouth and plate,
he looked at the case and demanded instantly,
"That's just the hair care products. Where's the rest?"

Seraglio was already leaving, preferring to meet
the cabdriver halfway rather than to deal with her
employer. I didn't much blame her. Changing my
mind about breakfast, I sat at the table and snatched
a honey-dribbled croissant from his plate and ate it.
"I saw Ish in the hall." He'd been trying to talk sense
into Robin, have him tell us what was going on, I
knew. Ishiah wouldn't tell us himself, but he could
use his time to endlessly prod Robin into telling us
himself. "He seemed pissed. Even more pissed than
usual." Which meant Robin hadn't cooperated.

I licked my fingers clean of the sticky sweetness
from the bun. "He also seemed worried about you.
Seriously, Robin, who is he? He knows you, and I
mean really knows you, the good and the bad. Not

many people can say that." Niko and I couldn't, not entirely—not with Robin holding back on us.

He hesitated, pushed the food around on his plate, then exhaled. "What is he would be more appropriate. A recruiter for the good and noble life, you could say, one with a moral code even more stringent than that of your brother." He gave a mock shudder at the thought. "It's uncanny. Unhinging might be the better word. Far too many Boy Scouts in the world." The mild annoyance deepened to something darker. "We have a history, Ishiah and I do. One of him pushing and pushing and utterly pissing me off. He'd have me give up everything that makes me the magnificent specimen I am."

"The lying, the cheating, the screwing everything in sight?" I asked with a grin.

"Exactly." He took a bite of eggs, outraged at the thought.

It was hard to imagine the guy with the balls to try and recruit Robin Goodfellow to the straight and narrow. Even harder to imagine why. "He really did seem worried as hell about you," I said again. He'd been angry, but controlled because I hadn't seen his wings as he'd stalked off. There'd been only a pale gray leather jacket, blue shirt, and faded jeans. His blond hair had covered the scar, so it didn't give anything away. Blond hair . . . but pale, not the more familiar darker shade I'd seen every day of my life. Overcast blue-gray eyes in contrast to pure winter sky, fair skin to Rom olive, an inch or two taller, but . . .

The realization prickled in the back of my brain, not quite made but worming its way up. Robin liked Niko, a helluva lot. He had chased him relentlessly in the past before Promise showed up. Hell, chased him a little bit after that too. And Ishiah . . . Ishiah looked like Niko.

No. No, that wasn't it at all. Niko looked like *Ishiah*.

Robin, already gathering in the creaky workings of my brain, looked me up and down and took in my rumpled clothing for a quick change of subject before I could open my mouth. "Again . . . in one year? How can you bear the exertion?" he drawled. "Just remember, once you go furry, you never have to worry. Well, technically that's not true. She could transform halfway through and eat you . . . have a cookie with her nookie. Or worse yet, have you seen those nature channels? Romulus's hairy sac. You could be stuck for hours. Next time be sure to take the crossword, just in case. Or a crowbar and some WD-40."

That effectively ruined my appetite. "I hope your ribs hurt like hell," I grumbled as Niko and Promise appeared in the room. The Ishiah matter wasn't forgotten, but I shoved it on the back burner as Niko had something on his mind. I figured that out when he shoved me in the bathroom, slapped a bar of soap in my hand, a towel over the mirror, and bought that big lie I was still wearing. After the quick shower, he was pushing me out the door past a sweating and swearing cabbie toting what had to be a one-hundred-and-fifty-pound steamer trunk. Poor bastard. Better him than me.

By the time we hit the street, Niko finally spoke. "We need to check on Boggle."

I was actually rather relieved to hear it. I felt . . . hell, I wasn't sure what I felt. Boggle was a killer and a predator, but we'd gotten her into that mess.

If she died because of it . . . it wasn't a good thought. "Okay. Wanna bring some lollipops for the kiddies?"

"And," he added, ignoring the wiseass remark, "Promise and I have verified Sawney's new 'cave.' "

"Yeah?" I said with grim interest. "Is it in that building?"

"More or less. Under it would be more precise. It was what I'd forgotten reading after all. That building is Buell Hall, the last remaining structure of a former insane asylum as they called it back then."

Oh, Jesus. It made sense. It made perfect sense. The slaughter at the mental institute, his fondness for the more psychologically damaged homeless, his fascination with the taste of Auphe craziness that he was so sure was in me. Sawney was all about insanity . . . twenty-four-seven. It made absolute goddamn sense he'd hole up in the ruins of an old asylum—as much as I didn't want it to.

But that neat, quaint brick building? It looked like the house of someone's grandmother. Cookies and milk, not electroshock and straitjackets. "You're kidding. Tell me you're kidding," I demanded.

He wasn't kidding. Where Columbia now stood had once been the New York Lunatic Asylum, renamed the Bloomingdale Insane Asylum years later. From 1808 to 1894, it had stood before moving to the New York Hospital in White Plains.

Frigging fascinating.

It wasn't creepy enough that the revenants were ravaging the campus; they and Sawney were also roaming the underremnants of an insane asylum from the eighteen hundreds. In addition to Buell Hall, there was the asylum tunnel system, once used for steam or coal transport, that ran beneath the campus. Tunnel upon tunnel. It would be perfect for getting around the place and popping up like a hellish jack-in-the-box without being seen in transit.

It was the perfect cave.

"It was said to have been quite a beautiful sight in its day. Lovely grounds," Niko said as we walked. I wasn't sure if he was yanking my chain or not, but either way, I didn't bother to hide a shudder.

"Yeah, beautiful. Jesus." Nothing like a brisk walk around the asylum with the loonies to get your day going.

Gray eyes gleamed at my discomfort. "Too many horror movies when you were young have warped your view of the mental health system."

Right. Scary movies when I was a kid, that was the problem. Not that the Auphe as a race were raving homicidal maniacs or that Sawney kept on like I was a lunatic-flavored lollipop. That had nothing to do with it. "So we can get into the tunnels there—at Buell Hall."

"Presumably."

It was getting colder and I stuffed my hands in the pockets of my leather jacket. Zipping it up wasn't an option, not if I wanted easy access to my holster. "And if we go down there and find his nightmare ass, what then? We haven't had too much luck so far. Guns don't work. Swords don't work. Hell, boggles don't work. Where does that leave us?"

"I've been thinking about that. Extensively." The last of the leaves were beginning to fall in the park and Nik caught one that wafted down in front of him. He turned it over with long, sinewy fingers, then held it up. "What color is it?"

"Red, I guess," I said, having no idea where he was going with this. "With some orange."

"No." He held it up and admired it before letting it drift away. "It's the color of fire."

I got it then. "And Sawney's no fan of fire."

"No. Being burned at the stake will tend to do that." Niko didn't seem too sympathetic. "All we need to do is recreate that."

"Without the army they had the first time," I reminded him.

" 'Weary the path that does not challenge,' " he quoted. "Hosea Ballou."

" 'I like things easy,' " I countered. "Me. Want to write it down? I can repeat it."

"That won't be necessary. After twenty years, I do believe I have it." He tugged at my ponytail. "I have an idea. One I'm surprised you haven't thought of, but we'll discuss it later."

I looked at him warily. "What are we going to discuss now?"

"I want to talk to you about Delilah and the nymph and the others who'll come after them," he answered, giving one last tug on my hair as the teasing humor faded from his eyes.

All right, I knew we'd had this particular talk with added stick-Auphe figure illustrations when I was ten. Here's Cal. Here's a girl. Here's their flesh-gnawing baby eating the neighbor's dog. I didn't believe Niko was setting up for a repeat performance. I was right.

"You have to be careful." The wind blew at his hair, but it was tightly secured and it barely ruffled.

"You know I am." If anyone knew that, it was Nik. If anyone knew what I'd given up to *be* careful, it was him . . . and George.

"That's not what I mean. I know how cautious you are in that respect. I know how much you've given up." There was a strong grip on my shoulder. "I'm talking about the Auphe. They are out there. We haven't seen them in months, but they will be back. There is no escaping that. You need to watch yourself . . . if I can't be there to do it for you."

There it was, his concern, and it was a valid one. I was on my own more now than I'd been just a year ago. In the past, I was either with my brother or with Robin. Now on occasion I was with those who didn't have the same loyalty to me as my brother, Promise, and Goodfellow did. Would they have my back like those three if the Auphe came for me?

"I'm growing up, Mom." I curled my lips and gave him a light punch. "It was bound to happen."

He stopped walking, but the leaves kept falling. "You're my brother, Cal. You're my family. You are my *only* true family. Do not leave me out of stupidity or carelessness." Then, as I turned to face him, he said something I only very rarely heard from him. "Please."

The last time he'd made that request he'd shaken me nearly senseless. He'd been furious, and behind that fury had been concern. This time the situation was less urgent, but the concern was the same.

He had raised me. My brother. I wouldn't insult him by calling him mother or father, not after the ones I'd had, but he'd filled the roles. Brought up my ass and kicked it when it needed it. Truthfully, he hadn't kicked it quite as often as it needed it. He was tough, but he knew what my life was. And what it wasn't—what it could never be. Normal. He'd cut me slack, more than I deserved. I was alive because of him. More importantly, I was sane because of him—no Bloomingdale Insane Asylum for me. Without Niko, I couldn't have said that with such absolute faith.

"I'll be careful. I promise." I said it with that same faith and I meant it. For Nik, there wasn't much I wouldn't do. Shit, there wasn't *anything* I wouldn't do.

"Good." He walked on, the leaves seeming to drift with him. "I'm glad banging your head against a trailer wasn't necessary this time."

"You're all about the love, Cyrano. Don't let anyone tell you different." I grinned.

Boggle, it turned out, disagreed with that.

Strongly disagreed.

It took a while to cross the park and through the particular grouping of trees to arrive at the clearing that held Boggle's home. The boglets were in the trees all around us. Their orange eyes blended in with the last of the leaves. Their muddy hides were also good camouflage against the bark of limbs and trunks. They were completely quiet, the only sound the occasional flake of mud tumbling down to the ground, and only Niko was ninja enough to hear something like that.

But at least I spotted the eyes and smelled them. That saved me a punishing swat and fifteen blocks extended onto our daily run. "What are they doing?" I asked quietly.

"Guarding their mother," he answered as softly, not bothering to look up at them or draw his katana. I had the odd feeling he didn't want to insult them by "spotting" them. "They're honorable children."

He was right, in both respects. When we reached the mud at the edge of the water, they flowed, after leaping from tree to tree, down the trees to surround us. Still in silence, they stalked back and forth, keeping between us and the pit. "We apologize," Niko said, raising his voice this time, "for the harm done to your mother."

The silence ended and the growling started. A pack of gators with longer legs and arms, more agile, smarter, and far more pissed off than your average swamp dweller. "I don't think they accept." I pulled the Eagle. "And you sounded really sincere to me."

I didn't blame them for being less than forgiving. I didn't think boggles loved or liked or had any emotions besides "hungry now" and "bright-shiny." But even without what we might consider affection, Boggle had raised her children, fed them, kept them alive. As boggles went, I thought she probably qualified as a good mom. And we'd sent her back to them skinned alive. If someone had done that to my family, done that to Niko, inadvertently or not, I wouldn't have been too goddamn happy myself.

"Boggle." Niko swung his blade lazily in the air, sketching a silver line in the metaphorical sand. Do not cross. "We don't want to engage in violence. We only wish to see that you're recovering and find out if you learned anything about Sawney while doing battle with him." Ever the practical one, Niko, mixing compassion with curiosity.

There was a moment when I thought his words weren't going to mean a damn thing—to the smaller boggles or the larger one. The boglets were slithering closer and the thick crust of mud remained unmoving. It looked like someone was going to have to go down, and, half-grown kiddies or not, it wasn't going to be Nik or me. I aimed the Eagle and put pressure on the trigger.

"Leg?" Niko murmured.

"Do my best," I muttered back. Mary Poppins with a gun, that was me. If a spoonful of sugar didn't do the trick, a legful of lead just might.

That's when Boggle finally came up for air. One clawed hand thrust up through the mud and water, then the other. Using the edge of the solid ground, she pulled herself up through the thickened surface. Mud coated her peeled chest, but it seemed looser there than on the rest of her . . . as if there was more liquid. As if her skinned raw flesh was weeping. Jesus.

Sawney—he had done that. It was good to keep that in mind. If anyone was to blame, it was him. Boggle had been paid, she'd agreed to the task and the price. She had understood the dangers. I lowered the gun. "Look, kiddies. Mom's up. Let's everybody calm down."

The orange eyes were dulled, but there was still a spark behind the film—a murderous gleam that made her offspring seem like a litter of playful pups. "You. You come here. You dare."

"We were concerned." Niko's grip had firmed on his sword. "Remember that Sawney is the one that did this to you, not us."

He was echoing my thoughts, but Boggle didn't seem to buy it. She came on to solid ground; slowly, but she came. The boglets gathered momentarily, growling and hissing, then scattered. "I am hurt. I will not heal for many days. Many that I cannot hunt, because of the Redcap." The gums were mottled an unhealthy gray with the black, but the teeth were the same as they'd been before. Impressive. "Because of you."

All our best intentions were fast heading down the tubes. We could retreat, but she could follow, as could the brood. We would have to hurt someone, most likely kill someone. It wasn't what we wanted, but it looked like that's what we were going to get. "Boggle," I said, "don't do this, okay? Just fucking don't." I'd almost said Boggy. I'd almost forgotten for a second this wasn't our old boggle.

She lowered her head, chuffing a humid breath and ripping the earth to deep furrows with random strokes of her claws. "Can't hunt. Can't *hunt*."

Food wasn't the problem. The kids were capable of bringing in all the muggers needed. They were old enough and big enough, but, as I'd thought before, this boggle wasn't like the last. She wanted to hunt, *needed* to hunt, and in her eyes we'd screwed that up for her. Temporarily certainly. And right now, she was tempted to deny that fate with us.

The hand flexed again and more dirt flew. "Can't hunt." It was said mournfully this time, and she deflated as the eyes shifted from my gun to Nik's sword. The puffing of muddy scales settled and she decreased in size by a third, not that she wasn't still huge. "Cannot hunt. Cannot roam. Cannot be."

Now I really did feel like shit.

"You will heal," Niko said. "You will hunt again."

Her homicidal mood shifting, Boggle settled onto the ground. "He cannot suffer enough. Never enough."

"I think you'd be surprised how much we can make him suffer." Niko lowered his blade in slow, wary increments. "He was burned at the stake once. We'll make him wish for that day again."

The orange eyes burned with sudden clarity through the clouded lens. "He cannot be killed. Cannot."

"We will kill Sawney," Niko countered with certainty. "That, I promise you."

Then he told her how.

20

Niko's promise and the information turned out to be enough for Boggle. We ended up walking away. I had my suspicions there was more to it than actual forgiveness, faith, and goodwill. I thought that Boggle didn't want to lose one or more of her children. Whatever the reason, it didn't matter. We walked away and no boglets had to die, and that was a good day.

We hadn't learned anything new about Sawney, but that had been a long shot anyway. Boggle had roamed the tunnels separate from us, looking for him, but nothing had caught her attention other than a few bodies floating in the water. I didn't ask what she'd done with them, if anything. They were dead already. No one except Boggle who could use what was left of them. It sucked for them and their families, but there you go.

On the way back, we discussed Robin and came to the conclusion that if we didn't catch whoever was after him in the act, we were up the creek. I'd thought it was possible the guy hit by the train might've been the only one behind it all, but from the way Ishiah was pushing the puck, it now seemed less likely. With the Sawney situation, Robin's problem couldn't have come at a worse time. He also couldn't have picked a worse time to be a stubborn asshole about it, but that was Goodfellow for you.

Ishiah had said Robin had done something not quite ethical in the past. No surprise, right? But from the way he had said that, from the way Robin refused to talk about it, not ethical, in reality, probably didn't begin to cover it. Not for the retribution it had put into motion. We didn't even know how long ago whatever had happened had taken place.

I did know it was a mess, and if we hadn't needed him fighting with us so badly, I'd have been tempted to leave him at Promise's with Ishiah to keep an eye on him. But we needed everyone we could get. Hell, I planned on asking Ishiah if he'd close the bar for a night and take on Sawney with us. And if he could bring another peri or two with him, that would be fan-frigging-tastic.

It didn't turn out that way.

"No," he said in flat refusal. "I'm sorry."

He didn't sound sorry as he stood behind the bar, arms folded and looking a little too much like Niko for my peace of mind. Now that I'd had the thought, it was a done deal. I couldn't unthink it, and I had no desire to be roaming around Goodfellow's subconscious cravings, sexual or otherwise. None at all.

"I thought you wanted to help Robin," I demanded. I'd stopped by the bar as Niko went on to check out that idea he'd had regarding Sawney. It was a good idea, damn good. Here was hoping it worked.

"I do want to help Goodfellow with his problem from the past, but Sawney Beane is not that problem. I have to prioritize."

He actually said it. Prioritize. An insane mass murderer, unknown assassins, creatures with wings, a man with genes far more demon than angel, talking birds, talking *mummies*, dead wolves, revenant after revenant, skinned boggles, and he actually had the stones to say prioritize.

I was . . . well, hell, not to be repetitive . . . boggled.

"But you can have the night off," he added politely. "I'll consider it a personal day. Your check will, of course, be docked."

Forget boggled, now I was just pissed.

"Sawney could kill Robin as easily as whoever's after him. So you're saying you'll be okay with that?" I leaned across the bar to emphasize the accusation.

"Priorities," he said, unmoved, "and I also have a prior commitment. Not that that's any business of yours." Thick dark brows lowered. "I would think that you would be more concerned about preparing for the battle than berating your employer. And if you keep mutilating the customers, you won't have one of those for much longer."

I managed to leave without taking a swing at him, but it was a near thing. As Ishiah had a temper every bit as bad as mine, he would've swung back. He might look like a Nordic version of Niko, but there the resemblance ended. No matter how long-lived Ish might be, he was hell on wheels. He might be the most moral son of a bitch in the city, according to Robin, but right now, he wasn't any damn help.

That would turn out to be a theme of the day.

Delilah turned out to be unavailable, per Promise. In other words, she couldn't find her with a bloodhound—her or any other wolves willing to go up against Sawney again. Boggle was down for the count and Nushi was, as he'd said, a healer, not a fighter. Once again it was down to the four of us. Four against countless pseudo corpses and one genuine corpse returned to life, bringing his scythe and a hunger that couldn't be sated.

Two . . . no, three students now, and one maintenance man. I knew better than to think that would feed all of Sawney's new clan. They hunted some on campus, but I knew they were bringing home more bacon than that. Using Columbia as a central location and the asylum tunnels as home, they were bringing them in more than groups of two and three. Revenants had a hunger to almost match that of Sawney. Hunger to hunger, obedience and madness, a large clan of sheer starvation and raving insanity . . .

Four of us against that. Why the hell not?

"Don't forget the head shot," Niko said at my shoulder.

We stood just inside the front doors of Buell Hall—an empty Buell Hall thanks to Dr. Nushi. He'd cooked up a fumigation for a rat infestation scheme that had kept the place locked up for the day and now the night. He'd claimed he'd seen a few of Mickey's wayward cousins at a recent speech to the pre-med club and they couldn't close down the place fast enough.

"There's nothing like a head shot to distract a guy, I'll give you that," I said. "Just don't forget how fast he is. I'll do my best, but . . ." I gave a shrug and a cold grin. "At least I can promise to hit part of him. He might be able to walk around with a fist-sized hole in him, but I'd like to see him do it with sixteen or so of them."

"Always the optimist." He slapped me lightly on the back. "You restore my faith in the human condition."

I didn't bother to open my mouth on that one.

One comment on how I was only half of the human condition would get me a painful nerve pinch. I let it go. "I try," I snorted, hefting the Eagle. I had a handful of extra clips on me, this time all explosive rounds. Revenants, Sawney, I didn't care which I blew apart tonight.

"You do realize I'm still in utter agony, a virtual cripple that you've dragged to near certain death." Robin was immaculate in copper shirt and brown slacks. His sword's hilt was chased with matching copper and small emeralds. It was a beautiful and graceful creation, but that didn't make the edge of the blade any less deadly. I wondered what excuse he'd given Seraglio to pack that up and bring it to Promise's apartment. Showing off his weapons collection maybe. That would work. Living as a human car salesman didn't stop "Rob Fellows" from being one helluva show-off.

"Yes, when you attempted to sexually assault my cleaning lady, your pain and suffering was abundantly clear." Promise's heather eyes narrowed and focused on a small gold hoop decorated with one tiny emerald drop that hung from Robin's ear. "Is that my earring you are wearing?"

"It matched the sword," he dismissed. "And it gives me a piratical look. I both pillage and I plunder. In fact, I all but invented the concepts," he said as he raised one wicked eyebrow. "Besides," he added carelessly, "you'll get it back."

"*If* you survive that near-certain death you spoke of?" she reminded with sweet poison.

"I'm sure you'll pluck it from my cold, clammy earlobe, Mrs. Nottinger-Granville-Schoenstein-Parsons-Depry. You seem to be quite adept at that."

A few days at Promise's place had disintegrated

the truce the two had once had. Rooming with a friend never worked out when it came right down to it. Mild affection could turn to homicidal fury from one towel left on the floor or, in Robin's case, one orgy in the living room. Credit where credit was due, the majority of them did seem to be nurses. Or at least they were dressed like nurses. I didn't notice any of them treating his cracked rib before Promise began throwing them through the front door, but the medical field is an arcane business. I might have missed it.

"After I'm done with you, you won't have enough molecules joined together to form an earlobe," she snapped back. The Egyptian dagger Niko had given her was in her hand and ready to taste blood.

"We never should've had two kids," I said to Niko. "One would've been plenty."

He had doffed his duster and was hefting a backpack over his long-sleeve gray shirt, the steel bands around his wrists barely showing. There was no room on his back for the sheath of his katana and he was carrying it in one hand. "Do not put this on me. I've raised one already."

Identical looks of contempt hit us both. "Okay," I said hurriedly. "I'm ready. Nik, you ready?" How much worse could Sawney be than a pissed-off vampire and puck joining forces against us? Then, all joking aside, I asked, "Robin, seriously, you up for this?" He'd insisted that he was. The poison had passed from his system days ago, the rib was cracked and ached, but it wouldn't hold him back in a fight.

"Up for it? Kid, I was on the beach at Troy. By the way, Achilles? Everything they say he was." He lifted his chin, gaze unwavering. "Believe me, I can handle this."

Poisoned, shot, nearly an extra in Hitchcock's *The Birds*, why would he want to handle it after all that? I didn't want to admit it, had been struggling with it for a long time, but I knew the reason. He was our friend. My friend. Jesus, I was such a girl. When the hell had I gotten so damn soft?

"Just don't get your ass killed, okay?" I ordered gruffly. I didn't wait for an answer. We'd scouted out the upper building and it was clear. Now it was time to head downward, and I did. I moved down the hall to the basement-access door and hit the stairs.

There was nothing there. Not if you didn't count the stench of Sawney and the revenants. It was enough to have me breathing through my mouth. "Where's the tunnel entrance?"

Niko had obtained a map of the tunnel system from Nushi, memorized it, gone over it with me several times, and then drawn it in permanent ink on the back of my hands and on my forearms. Following that, he'd stuffed the map in my pocket, saying, "In case we're separated. It's not enough, I fear, but it's the best I can do." Brothers believe in you, but they also know you. I know east from west, but that was the most I could hope for.

"In the southeast corner, beside the furnace."

Which would be one reason the smell was so strong. It was literally cooking against the surface of the furnace. I followed Niko and then helped him pry up the metal trapdoor in the floor. It wasn't locked, but it had been. The remnants of a padlock lay off to one side. The metal was heavy as hell in our hands and we eased it down soundlessly to stare into the depths. More stairs, but these were much older. Splintered wood framed with iron, they disappeared into the darkness. One whiff was all I needed and I nodded. "Home sweet home."

Robin stared over my shoulder and sighed plaintively, "At least the beach at Troy was warm. There was sun and sand."

"Bloodstained sand," Niko pointed out as he started down.

"It was still sand." Robin followed him. "In my life I've learned you take the small pleasures where you find them."

We weren't going to find any of those below, I knew. No small pleasures—only the very large satisfaction of putting Sawney down, this time for good. I waved Promise on. Having her at Robin's back might keep him more on his toes. Danger from all sides, that would keep the adrenaline pumping and the senses sharp and ready. And if I enjoyed the hunted look he threw over his shoulder before he melted into the murk, hey, that was just gravy.

When Promise vanished below, I turned on the flashlight I carried in my left hand and went down after them. Gun in one hand, torch in the other, I walked down the steps with care. As creaky as they looked, they were sturdy beneath my feet.

"All clear." Niko's low murmur came drifting up past stone and plaster walls. They once would've been completely covered with plaster and painted. Over the years that plaster had been soaked time and time again and had rotted. Handfuls were gone in some spots and in other areas nothing but stone remained.

There were splatters on the steps, the stone and the filthy plaster. Brown and dried. Blood. One helluva lot of blood. Sawney had picked his cave all right and it was a good one, up until a few revenants had gotten sloppy and poached from the campus. Then they'd actually killed and fed aboveground right at their front door. Sawney was insane, but he was smart. He wouldn't have ordered that or allowed it if he knew. You don't shit in your own backyard; every good two-legged predator knows that. That meant the discipline wasn't as all-encompassing as it seemed, at least not with all of them. It was a good sign. If we could take Sawney, the revenants might scatter. They would definitely be less of a threat if they reverted to typical revenant fighting skills. Every ghoul for himself.

At the bottom of the stairs the brown stains covered the entire floor, from wall to wall. I could picture it. The body, maybe only half dead, of the victim being tossed down the stairs like garbage. If they weren't dead at the top, I hoped like hell they were when they hit the bottom. What kind of world was it when that could be credited as an actual hope?

Sawney's world.

The tunnel wasn't as cramped as I thought it might be, but it made me claustrophobic nonetheless. There were no rooms, no alcoves, nothing—just one long range of tunnel. You could go forward or back, but that was it. There was no spreading out if someone caught you from the front and behind. It wasn't a good tactical position to be in. We were moving at a pace slow enough that I could walk backward with gun ready for any revenant that might be bringing home a doggy bag. It was a very real possibility. We'd chosen night for the assault as we hoped most of the revenants would be out hunting. Sawney might be as well, but if he was, once he caught dinner he'd come home with it. That's all we cared about—nailing him when he did.

If we'd come during the day, they all would've been down here. Not a good prospect for success. Revenants could and did pass during the daylight if they covered up with hooded jackets to hide slick flesh and wore sunglasses to conceal a milky flash of eye. If they kept their head down, they could slide through the crowds, but mixing with the populace was different than killing and dragging a body across campus. Nighttime was best for that sort of work.

This way we'd double our chances of coming across Sawney with considerably fewer revenants at his side. That didn't make the odds in our favor, but it did make them better. I'd take it.

"We're at the first split."

I stopped and turned to see the tunnel break off to the left and right. Both tunnels reeked, but the one to the left did just a little more. I jerked my head in that direction. "That way."

We moved and this time faster as I settled for snatching a glance over my shoulder every few seconds at the tunnel behind us. We had more space between us and the entrance now, as well as two tunnels for the revenants to choose from. They did use both from the smell of it, even if this was their main path of travel.

"He'll know we're coming," Robin said as his fine leather shoes trod silently on the brown, crusted path.

"How do you know that?"

He looked back at me, the stolen earring glittering in the beam of my flashlight, but it was Promise who beat him to the punch with the mildest of sarcasm. "Only because he has every time so far?"

"Good point," I admitted.

"He'll know, but he won't run," Niko said. "This

is his true cave. He will not give it up, and in his mind it is not as if he has anything to fear from us.''

That was the sad truth. Dead wolves, a skinned boggle, and the fact that he'd eaten a chunk of my chest were all proof of that. He had no reason to run. We were better than cable, the most entertainment he'd had in a long, long time. Several hundred years to be exact. The son of a bitch would probably be glad to see us—cackle insanely in glee. And why not? Where better to do anything insanely than in the subterranean leftovers of an asylum?

Something sparked brightly at the bottom of the wall to the right and I stopped to pick it up. It was an engagement ring. The diamond was small and surrounded by even smaller rubies. Pretty, but for the couple on a budget. I knew the others had seen it; their eyes were as sharp as mine, but they'd passed it by. What could you do? She was gone, whoever she'd been. Gone far from this place and maybe she was no place at all, I didn't know. I did know she wouldn't want proof of her lo . . . of her existence . . . hidden down here in the fetid darkness. I put the ring in my pocket. At the very least I could leave it somewhere up top . . . someplace in the sun. Promise's gaze was the one that turned back this time, her eyes soft. I scowled and looked away. It was corny and stupid, picking up that ring—two things I wasn't. I really wasn't. And I hated that I'd been caught in it.

We walked on and the tunnel seemed to get more and more narrow, but I thought that was more me than actual reality. We'd been underground a lot lately and it reminded me . . . of what, I wasn't really sure. Abbagor's cave? Although we'd almost died there more than once, I didn't think that was it. It was deeper than that, an abscess aching from a long time ago. No, not Abbagor, but maybe something more terrifying than even he had been.

The Auphe had had me for two years. I couldn't recall a single moment of those years spent in a world separate from this one. But there were times I woke up to the feeling of rock beneath my fingers and the sense of tons of the same hanging overhead. Caves, the monsters loved the goddamn caves.

"Cal."

I drew in a breath of tainted air, trying to clean away what barely qualified as the shadow of a memory, and moved past Promise and Robin to stand beside Niko. "Yeah?"

"We have a room." He indicated the door almost fifty feet down the hall. I couldn't make out any details. It was at the edge of the flashlight beam.

"Okay. I'm ready." With the Desert Eagle and the explosive rounds, I was designated distraction of the day. I needed to keep Sawney's attention on me while Niko put his plan into play. As the Redcap had already acquired a taste for me, it shouldn't be that hard. I went on ahead with Niko close at my back. When I reached the door, I noticed the faded printing on it. HYDROTHERAPY TREATMENT ROOM. I wanted to ask Nik what water had to do with the treatment of mental health, but kept silent as I moved a hand toward the handle. He could be there. Sawney could be right there, and I wasn't going to tip him off. I was ready for this to be over.

The element of surprise was lost with the screech of hinges almost rusted into a solid whole. That didn't mean it hadn't been opened recently. The metal was so old; it would never open easily again. Grimacing, I shoved at the door hard and with

Niko's help got it open enough to let a person slip through, and through I went. The room was small and empty except for a water-filled square in the filthy tiled floor. Five feet by five feet, it was too small to be a pool and a little too early in plumbing history to be a whirlpool tub.

"Why is there water in it?" I mused aloud. It was murky and impenetrable and it shouldn't have been there. Whatever it had been used for in asylum days, I would think it would've long dried up over the past hundred years or so. "And what the hell was it for?"

"In less educated days, mental health workers used to plunge people over and over underwater. It was some time before they came to admit that near drowning didn't seem to improve anyone's mood disorder." Niko regarded the flat surface of the water with disdainful repugnance. "I doubt Sawney is using it for a reason any more enlightened."

He was right.

A hint of white swelled under the water, breached, then sank again. An arm, it had been an arm. Christ. You'd think I'd be getting used to finding body parts littering the landscape in Sawney's wake. I wasn't. As we continued to watch, a leg appeared and disappeared, followed by a hand. All were disembodied, all white and drained of blood. The hand was a woman's, delicate with nail polish the exact color of a rose I'd once seen at a flower stand. Pink with the faintest touch of peach—the color of spring. It was beautiful and it was awful and I wondered if the ring belonged to her.

"Goulash," Robin said beside us. "Lovely. I'll never eat again."

"I have seen worse. So have you." Promise nudged him into motion.

"So I have," he exhaled. "Although I could've done without the reminder."

We all turned to exit the room. I'd taken one step when the cold hand fastened around my ankle and I was suddenly breathing water—black water that served as the broth for body parts. I choked and held my breath as I kicked at the iron grip that pulled me down. I felt the random bump of decaying flotsam and jetsam and kicked all the harder. It didn't help. There was the sharp scrape of a tile-edged opening at my waist just as I felt fingers on my wrist from above. Warm fingers. Niko. But as suddenly as his grip had appeared, I was yanked from it. I passed through the opening that I could only feel, not see. After that there was more water, the burning of my lungs, and that implacable grasp on my ankle.

Finally just as my breath threatened to give out, I was dragged out into the air feet-first. Not unlike my birth, I came out kicking and screaming. Or kicking and spitting waterlogged curses. A revenant had his teeth buried in my thigh. I kicked him off with my other foot and he looked up, grinning at me with a mouthful of mottled yellow and green teeth. I aimed the Desert Eagle there and blew his head off. There was more splashing of water and I twisted to see another revenant rising from the water. I fired again and the pieces of him sank beneath the surface.

Now alone on the tile floor—except for one dead revenant—I coughed up water and did my best not to think about what had been in that water. Around me was a room that was identical to the one I'd been yanked from. Great. More cutting-edge mental health care. I looked at the water one more time and then shook my head dog-fashion, sending the water flying. Nik wasn't coming. If he were, he'd have been here already. The other revenant must have closed some sort of hatch in the passage that connected the two tanks of water. Closed and locked it.

I set the flashlight on the floor to prop against my leg, which wasn't bleeding too badly, wiped at my face, and rolled up my sleeve. On my arm the map of the tunnels sprang into view. Niko's anal-retentive ways paid off yet again. I mentally traced a path that would connect the tunnel this room was off back to the tunnel where the others were. I knew Nik would be doing the same. Hopefully, I'd meet them in the middle. I grabbed the light and scrambled to my feet. The door to the room was half open and I slipped through into the hall, turning left.

And there was the bad news.

It was a concrete wall, one that wasn't on the map. It wasn't nearly as old as the walls of the tunnel. A recent addition, perhaps to keep trespassers and the more adventurous students out of a less stable part of the tunnels. Whatever it was, right now it was a huge pain in the ass. I holstered my gun, switched the light to the other hand, and checked the map again. There was another connect, but it was in the other direction and farther. I gave in to the inevitable and started a steady lope.

The air was cool and damp, reminding me too much of the water I'd just come out of. I closed my mouth against it and kept moving. The revenants were waiting. I didn't expect anything different. It was the ones that weren't out hunting . . . who were done with hunting for the night. They were well fed and a little sluggish for it, but sluggish for a revenant is still fast—just not fast enough. They came in twos and threes into the light. I went through half a clip, but it wasn't the revenants that worried me. It was Sawney. If he showed up, that was it. He'd handled all of us with a boggle and wolf chaser. If he caught me alone, ego and a smart mouth wouldn't help me one damn bit. I thought of making a gate over to the next tunnel, but if I did that, there was no guarantee I'd be able to do my part when the time came. There was no guarantee I'd be conscious to even walk through that gate—not after the last time. I couldn't take that chance.

I kept running, but I listened for a familiar insane cackle. I listened hard. And when I came to another wall, I did something else as hard.

"Son of a *bitch*."

This wall was the same as the other, and it effectively penned me in the same as a mousetrap. It was a little less than a humane one with the revenants running around, but a damn effective one. Couldn't these people update their maps? I had the explosive rounds, true, and if it had been a plaster wall, I could've used a clip to put a nice hole in it. But this wasn't plaster; this was concrete. If I used every round I had on me . . . maybe, and then what would I use to distract Sawney? Other than serving up myself as a buffet supper, not a damn thing.

I didn't want to go back in the water, but I didn't see any way around it. I didn't know if I could get past whatever obstruction was down there, but I knew I couldn't get past this one. We were losing time. The later it got, the more revenants would come home from the hunt, and that would only make things harder. They were hard enough already. God-damn it. I turned and this time, assuming I'd nailed all the revenants, I ran faster.

Assuming, it wasn't what I'd been taught. Niko has a quote . . . hell, Niko has a quote about anything and everything. This one had been about overconfidence or complacency, something to that effect. And then Niko had summed it up in terms I would actually remember. Assume, he had said, and *you* will get your *ass* kicked by *me*. It was slightly different than that old saying I'd learned in the sixth grade, but it got the point across. And I did remember Niko's version most of the time, but once in a while I blew it. Once in a while I had to say hello to Mr. Fuckup.

I thought I was alone. I was wrong.

"Traveler."

It stopped me in my tracks, that one single voice. I thought it was his at first, Sawney's, but the second time it came, I knew better. It was as gloating and predatory, but it wasn't coated with the oil slick of insanity. Instead it was coated with the dryness of dust and the grit of desert sand. I could smell the heat of a merciless sun rising from limestone tombs. Could all but hear the chanting of priests and the movement of a stone slab that would seal you in for human lifetimes.

My flashlight beam shot back and forth for several seconds before I spotted what I knew I would see. There was no cowboy hat this time, but there was the same resin-hardened flesh, blackened and with-ered lips, brown stubs of teeth . . . bandages, dry ones. He had been here awhile, then . . . waiting.

Wahanket.

The dusty glow flared in his eye hollows and the

leathery jaw cracked in a crooked, jagged grin. "Surprised, traveler? You should not be. On occasion every scholar should engage in field research."

"What are you doing here? How the hell did you even know we'd be here?" I asked warily as I pulled my gun.

"Knowing your movements, the most simple of things. I set my little pet to follow you." Pet? Oh, Jesus, that damn squeaking zombie rat he'd been putting back together at the museum. It'd run off in the shadows and I never thought about it again. "It was my eyes. I saw you come to this place before . . . above. I knew you would return here, below. As for what I want?" The corpse grin twisted. "Observing. Recording. That has been my life in that wretched basement for years upon years. I want to *participate*." Like a kid who wanted to be in the school play. Yeah, whatever.

"I want it to be as it once was when I created kings. As I have created one now. Awakened one, rather." It was said with gloating satisfaction. Dynasty after dynasty, Robin had said. Thousands and thousands of years, even a king maker and scholar could get bored—could want to get back in the game. Have a little fun. But it didn't matter what he wanted, because he wasn't going to get it.

The gleam of metal in my hand wasn't the only one. I saw another as the withered hand flashed upward. I'd forgotten the brittle basement-dwelling sage loved all things high-tech. And guns were definitely advanced technology, like the 9mm I had so moronically given him. I threw myself against the wall, dropping the flashlight and firing as I went. The plaster exploded beside me, but several feet down. Loving technology didn't necessarily translate into being good at using it. Target practice had been limited in the museum.

Although he wasn't a crack shot, he was quick for a bag of bones and scraps of flesh. He disappeared in the dark. "What is Sawney giving you, you bastard?" I snapped. He'd woken him up just as he had the rat. Wahanket had somehow triggered Sawney's reintegration. Given him whatever boost he needed to explode back to life. That traveling exhibition had shown up in the museum and the mummy had seen his chance to be what he'd once been, a king maker. But Sawney wasn't his puppet. Sawney wasn't ruled by anything except his own madness.

"Sawney Beane offers me nothing in the way of material goods. He offers me nothing at all. But he creates a newly interesting world," drifted the voice of the Sphinx. "I tire of this monotonous existence. Day after day, year after year. I tire of the bloodless quest for knowledge." There was a sly satisfaction. "Even if that quest gave the Redcap this place. His true home. I tire of it all. I am ready for change and this one brings it in splendid, bold strokes."

The gun fired again. The bullet came closer. I'd tossed the flashlight when I'd first fired the Eagle, not that Wahanket seemed to need the help. Could mummies see in the dark? Probably. Could they repel bullets?

We'd see about that.

I methodically sprayed the entire clip back and forth across the tunnel, side to side and top to bottom. Reading about gun battles on the Internet was different than being in one, although he was probably hell on wheels when it came to a bow and arrow or sword. A gun, though . . . overconfidence . . .

overconfidence was—damn, if only I could remember Niko's quote.

The smell of smoke filled my face, and my ears rang from the concussive blasts. I stayed close to the wall, felt around on the floor for the flashlight and switched it on, and held it at arm's length from my body to decrease my chances of being hit. I flicked it back and forth. Nothing. Okay, technically not true. There was something, just not the whole package. I moved forward and bent down to pick up Wahanket's gun, along with his hand still wrapped around it. As I made my way farther, I saw other bits and pieces of him. Not much, the occasional scrap of brown linen or blackened piece of dried flesh, but nothing substantial. It was a trail of bread crumbs, and they led back to the room, back to the pool.

The king maker had left the building.

Wahanket had changed his mind about being a participant after all. The role of researcher could be boring and monotonous, but the museum basement was safer than the real world. Wahanket had lost his edge a long time ago in those desert sands.

I looked down at the black water. "Once more into the breach," I murmured to myself. Or as Goodfellow would've said, once more into the breeches. I grimaced. It was as bad hearing it in my head as hearing it in person. Exhaling, I holstered the Eagle, pried Wahanket's gun out of his severed hand, and shoved it in my waistband before diving into the water. I was lucky; Hank had left the hatch open for me in his hurry to escape. It made the body parts bumping against me as I swam not so bad. Yeah, right. It was goddamn horrible, and when I reached the other side, I scrambled out as fast as I possibly could.

Wet footprints led away across the tile. Wahanket was running back to his basement. He'd think twice about leaving it again.

"Where the hell have you been?"

I looked up from the footprints to see Niko in the doorway. He was still wet from his attempt to pull me out of the water. "Correction," he said with narrowed gaze, "what took you so damn long to get back?"

"You worry too much, Grandma." I grinned in relief at the sight of beetled brows and irritable gray eyes. Niko's worry was always clearly expressed—as annoyance. "Did you see Wahanket?"

He ignored the question as he looked me up and down, but Robin, behind him, answered. "We saw a few wet footprints and a piece of linen. Wahanket, eh? Crafty corpse. But I suppose that explains how Sawney found a place so perfectly suited for him."

"And for that, perhaps we will deal with him later." Niko indicated where the material of my jeans was ripped over my thigh. "Revenant?"

As much as I hated to admit it, I had to. "Yeah."

"One?"

"Two," I said defensively, "and I was trying not to drown at the time. It's not my fault."

"It's amazing. The person who shows up at our sparring session looks so very much like you too." He said it as if he hadn't felt my hand slide through his in the water as I disappeared to God knows where. As if he hadn't run from one hall to another only to be blocked by concrete walls. We all had ways of dealing. When the situation had been reversed, I dealt the same, with sharp-edged sarcasm—once I'd killed everything that had gotten in my way.

"I'd say bite me, but I've been bitten already. Besides, Goodfellow might jump over you and take advantage of it," I grumbled, but curved my lips again. "And there was nothing over there but revenants and Wahanket. No Sawney."

"Then let's go find him," Nik said, waiting until I preceded him. Watching my back.

"By the way, you have absolutely nothing I want to bite," Robin snorted as he moved through the door. "Egomaniac."

Promise swallowed that one in silence, but it would make a reappearance later. I had faith. We exited the dead end of the room and started back down the tunnel. We walked a hundred feet before we saw it. At first, I saw only a glimpse. Pale, it flashed, disappeared, reappeared, and then vanished again.

"Travelers." There was the low hiss of several voices in unison. *"Trespassers."*

Great, a new refrain.

"They've learned a new word," I drawled. "How goddamn clever is that?"

"Several rungs below a brainless parrot," Nik responded with arctic bite, "and an utter waste of our time." More damn revenants and no Sawney. We were all disappointed. I knew I was tired of hacking at their stubborn, disgusting flesh. There was no honor in battle, no honor in killing. There was only necessity. Niko had taught me that. But if there had been honor, revenants wouldn't have entered that picture anywhere.

"Trespassers." What had been glimpses became a long look and then a close-up of one of the most freakish things I'd ever seen. *"Trespasserstrespasserstrespassers."* They boiled into the light, arms flailing.

They were wearing straitjackets, every last one of

them—left over from the good old madhouse days. No longer white, the grubby cloth was rotting and ripped. The overly long sleeves weren't fastened behind. Instead they flapped like the wings of maddened birds or wove through the air like a striking snake as the revenants ran. It was oddly hypnotic and not-so-oddly horrific. It wasn't enough that revenants looked like zombies; now they looked like zombies of the insane. Sawney wasn't happy just being mad himself or seeking it out; he had to dress up his goddamn pets that way as well. Talk about your hobbies we all could've done without.

"I've lived a long, long time and I've seen many, many things," Robin said, awed, at my back, "and I can confidently say that I have *never* seen anything quite like that." I didn't have time to respond. They were almost on us and I raised the Eagle and fired several shots.

Explosive rounds, they might not have much effect on Sawney, but they worked like a fucking charm on his boys. We didn't end up fighting them, but we did end up wearing them. I wiped a hand across my face, clearing it of pulverized flesh and thin, watery blood. I didn't wait for Robin's outraged comment about his wardrobe that had to be fast on its way. "Yeah, sorry about that," I said automatically as I heard his disbelieving gurgle behind me.

We moved on without further discussion. All in all, the best thing for me. We stepped over the bodies of straitjacketed revenants and dodged the two slow-moving ones that had craters in their heads. The spoonful of brains they had left kept them moving around, but not too aware.

Which is exactly how I felt when the ground disappeared beneath me.

21

This just wasn't my day.

I used to hate the sensation of falling, same as anyone else. But since I'd made a few gates and traveled through them . . . a traveler just as Sawney said . . . that had changed. I still didn't like it, don't get me wrong, but I sort of recognized the feeling. Walking through those gates was like falling, only not just down. It felt like falling down, up, and sideways—all at once. Hard to imagine, but that's how it felt.

So when the floor caved in under me and I fell, for a second I was confused. Had I opened a gate and not even realized it? One moment of confusion, but it was long enough to hit and hit hard.

I lost the flashlight. I didn't lose my gun. If the fall had killed me, I still wouldn't have lost the gun.

I'd landed on my side. I blinked dazedly into the blackness and realized . . . yeah, that wasn't an Auphe gate. You fell, asshole. Now get the hell up. It was easier said than done. I wheezed as I pulled air into shocked lungs and tried to move. That's when I felt the fingers on my leg. They crept up under my jeans and touched my calf, circles of ice on my bare skin. They moved soothingly, stroking my leg as they

sucked the warmth from it. Sawney. Only Sawney
drained the heat from you like that. I growled, low
and incoherent, in the back of my throat and tried
harder to move my arm, more specifically my hand
holding the gun. Oxygen-starved, I didn't have
much luck.

"Cal?"

It was from above. Niko. He'd managed to avoid
falling with me. Good for him. I wasn't surprised,
but I was a little relieved.

"Cal?" This time it came from beside me, along
with the crunch of boots landing on the debris of
shattered tile. There was light, a hand on my face,
and then the silver sweep of a sword. The frozen
touch on my calf disappeared just as the claws had
begun to puncture the skin. That trademark crazy
laugh went with them.

I let my arm relax. A futile tremor was all I'd gotten out of it anyway. In the flashlight's glow I could
see the Eagle resting in the dirt, my white finger lax
on the trigger. I also saw Niko's boots move closer,
and then, as I looked upward and he simultaneously
knelt, I saw his face. He was pissed as hell. "Sawney." He ran a quick hand over my arms, legs, and
spine. "I am going to enjoy killing him far more than
I should."

I'd gotten a few breaths in and coughed out,
"You . . . and . . . me . . . both."

With his help I managed a sitting position. I looked
up in time to see Promise and Robin jumping down.
It was about ten feet down from the tunnel floor, and
they managed it with ease. Certainly more ease than
I had. Promise seemed to float down while Robin
came down quickly and lightly, a hand bracing his
ribs. I knew how he felt. I hung my head and concen-

trated on breathing. Drowning, falling—I was getting tired of not breathing. "More tunnels?" I asked, shifting my shoulders against a blooming all-over ache.

"New tunnels with the tile replaced and fixed into place over them. Sawney must have had the revenants dig them," Niko said. Hands slid under my arms and hefted me to my feet. "An effective trap."

I wobbled, then steadied. "Sneaky fuck."

"Pithy, but accurate." Robin used his flashlight to scan the circumference of the pit. "Where did he . . . ah. There." There was an exit, one small enough you'd have to crawl through it while dragging your dinner behind you. "Wonderful. Crawling through dirt. Color me filthy and excited."

"Filthy and excited, and exactly how would this be different from your norm?" Promise asked with the perfect appearance of genuine interest.

"Well, color me annoyed as shit," I gritted before Goodfellow had a chance to fire a shot back. I twisted the crick out of my neck and started toward the hole.

Niko fisted a handful of my jacket, holding me back as he moved ahead. "My turn to go first," he said mildly.

He did it with more grace than I had. Soon we were all standing in a new tunnel. Nine by nine, it was carved out in the earth beneath the asylum tunnels. "Our little friends have been busy." Robin looked around, bent down to touch the dirt door, and came up with a finger wet with red mud.

"Very busy indeed," Promise added. "That is fresh. Tonight's kill."

"Good. That means we're close." Niko moved— fast, smooth, and still as coolly pissed as he'd been when he'd dropped down into the pit.

I hadn't thought of this whole mess from Nik's

point of view. Sawney had defeated him easily at every turn, had killed allies he'd enlisted, had attacked his brother with impunity and actually consumed part of him. Niko was not happy—in no way, shape, or form—and was determined to make this encounter with Sawney our last. My brother—he'd never learned to spread the blame around. It was our failure, not his, but he wouldn't see it that way. Couldn't see it that way. He'd lived the majority of his life under the weight of sole responsibility. There was no changing that habit now.

One damn good brother, but as I'd thought many times before, too good for his own good.

As we moved, we found more signs of Sawney's victims. There was no more jewelry, but there were clothes. Ragged and dirty. Knit caps and ancient coats. Shoes with peeling soles. So many clothes was bound to equal a whole damn lot of victims—the homeless we'd known he was concentrating on now.

He'd figured out pretty quickly that these weren't the days when travelers disappeared and it was considered a hazard of the day. He knew people would look for him if he stuck to your average New Yorker who had a job, wife, husband, children, parents . . . the ones that would be missed. But as we'd seen, the homeless were perfect and he wasn't the first monster to think so. They even traveled, pushing carts from here to there. I doubted that was a prerequisite for Sawney anymore, the traveling. When you lived in a city this big, you didn't need to wait for the wayward traveler moving across the countryside. And then there was his taste for the mentally ill, and that definitely tipped the scale. There was safe and there was madness-flavored fun . . . a win-win for our boy Sawney. We'd known that, but seeing it on such a large scale . . .

Jesus.

The clothes didn't litter the dirt floor. They were hung whimsically from the ceiling, like the gauzy curtains you'd see in a harem in an old movie. Some shirts were pinned to the walls with one arm pointing the way ahead and the other hanging limp. Shoes were lined up at the base of the wall to march in the same direction. When the shirts and shoes ran out, then came the hands and feet. The palms of the hands were punctured by nails pinning them to the packed dirt wall, and the index fingers pointed the way. In the same frozen march as the shoes were the feet with dirt plumping up between gray toes. I looked away. Even if I'd been completely human, I wasn't sure I could've stayed that way after what we'd seen in the past week.

This whole god-awful show made me wonder if he'd anticipated we'd come all along or if it was just more of his sick sense of humor played out for his own entertainment. Right before we killed him maybe I would ask him. At least the blood was less easy to see, soaked up by the earth beneath our feet. It was still there, though; the revenant proved that.

He was cut in half and left on the floor long past where the body parts finally ended. A chain was wrapped around him several times over and trailed off into the darkness. Sawney had taken away the bottom portion of the revenant with him and left a torso with a head, arms, and hands. The same hands that were feverishly shoving dirt into the gaping mouth. Red mud was oozing from the corners and I realized he was trying to suck the blood, nourishment, from the dirt. White eyes fixed on us hungrily and the hands sprang to a new task—dragging the revenant toward us with a greedy scrabbling of fingers. But the chain sprang taut and he moaned in despair.

"I believe we have another campus poacher," Niko said as he watched the form writhe. Like I'd thought earlier: Any good predator like Sawney knew you didn't kill in your own backyard. You didn't leave a neon-bright trail of bodies to your lair. Apparently the revenants just didn't grasp the concept.

"I guess Sawney did find out about their extracurricular activities." And from the looks of it, you didn't want to piss off Sawney because punishment was as inventive and harsh as what we'd done in the sewers. "Want me to . . ." I tapped the barrel of the gun against my leg. Put him out of his misery wasn't quite right. I didn't give a shit how miserable he was. He deserved to be. Put him out of *my* misery would be more accurate. This was every gory horror movie come to life and I could pretty much do without it.

"No need." Niko's sword swung and a head rolled. The teeth snapped and would for a while, but the light would fade from behind clouded-glass eyes and all would still. Eventually. If he'd been whole and fed, we could've questioned him. I doubted he would've talked, but we could've tried. But half of a starved revenant is in feed mode and nothing else. They need the nourishment to regrow the missing parts; thinking shuts down and instinct takes over. Unfortunately instinct didn't know that even a revenant couldn't regrow half of a body. He could've gone on existing that way for months and months, though, and I was sure Sawney would've given him every moment of that time to suffer.

"Not one wolf would come, eh? Hmm, I wonder why," Robin said, skirting the body and kicking the head out of the way while deftly avoiding the teeth. "The leg humpers have become more intelligent than I; if that's not a bad sign, I don't know what is."

"I'm beginning to wonder how even an army was able to take him." Promise had long put away her dagger and now had her own sword out. She tended to be fonder of crossbows, but this situation called for more sheer destructive power. Better to slash at a revenant than worry about aiming for an eye socket.

"Not a good thought." Valid, but not good. I stepped over the body and followed the chain into the blackness. Alice down the rabbit hole. She found madness; so did we. But we found the bodies first.

They hung from the ceiling, a forest of them. In reality, it wasn't more than twenty, but it seemed like a hundred when I caught the first glimpse of them. They hung from hooks fixed in wooden beams that must've supported the floor of the tunnels above us. Like the carcasses of cattle they hung. There was so much dried blood that the dirt floor had coagulated to a hard surface beneath my feet. The hall had ended in a cavern dug by revenant hands. It wasn't the same as a rock cave, but it was as close as you could get. Sawney had come home.

I looked up at all the naked limbs, slack faces, empty eyes and muttered, "Holy shit." Some were decomposing, some were stiff in rigor mortis, and some looked as if they'd been plucked off the street only hours ago. The smell of rot was so thick that it seemed you could've scooped a handful out of the air if you tried. I didn't put it to the test.

"Are you ready?"

I turned my head toward Nik and answered darkly, "More than."

"Be careful," he ordered in a barely audible voice—no giving Sawney any hints of what was going to happen. "Being a distraction doesn't mean being a dead one. Watch yourself. If he gets too close, move back and we'll try something else."

"Don't get killed. Got it." I gave him a grin, because what else could you do in the face of all this death? Grin defiantly or lose it altogether.

"Good. Now don't forget it." With that he moved off toward the left-hand wall. Robin headed for the right, Promise stayed at the entrance, and I went right down the middle.

I wove between the bodies, doing my best to not touch a single one. They didn't move; I know they didn't, but from the corner of my eye it looked like they did. "Sawney," I called. "You worthless child-killing scum, where are you?" The light of my flashlight bounced from dull eyes to white feet to shiny steel hooks. "You're not hiding, are you? Not from the likes of me, full of crazy."

"Sawney!" This time I shouted it. In this place where the silence was as thick as the smell, I dared to raise my voice to a shout and the body hanging beside me shuddered to hear it. It was a nightmarish thing, but it didn't shock me. Terrible or not, it seemed a reaction that belonged here, along with the death and despair. And because of that, it slowed me—only for a fraction of a second, but that was more than enough.

Sawney climbed over the top of the body with the

smooth scuttle of a scorpion to grin at me with blazing cheer. "A traveler come to visit." A hand flashed so quickly that I barely saw it move. I jerked back in reaction, but it was too late. I felt the score of a claw along my cheek. The ebon hand was raised for a taste. The red eyes brightened through the white and brown ropes of hair that swung over the black absence of a face. "I remember you, traveler. I remember your taste. Ah, so good. We could be brothers, you and I."

Of course he remembered me. The son of a bitch had been waiting, and he damned sure was no brother of mine. "Then you remember this," I snarled and fired the Eagle.

I missed.

Like I'd said, the bastard was quick. Quicker than me . . . maybe even quicker than Niko. As quick even as the Auphe, which was as quick as I'd ever seen. I hit the dead body, though, and blew it in half. I sincerely hoped the others were sticking to ground level as instructed and fired again as Sawney jumped to the next body. This time I hit him in the chest. In the double-fist-sized pit I'd created I saw a glitter as bright as glass. The hole I'd created in his side in the tunnel at the SAS was gone, as if it had never been. I fired again, but once again he was gone. But he wasn't getting away, not this time. One way or another this was the last time we took on this homicidal piece of shit. The absolute last goddamn time.

I went after him, pushing bodies aside with my arm, trying to hold the flashlight on his fleeing form. I fired again, hitting him in the back, and that's when he leaped from a body to the dirt and wood ceiling, flipped backward over my head, and cut me from behind. From the fiery pain, I could tell it wasn't a scratch, but neither was it meant to kill me. No, that'd be too easy. Sawney wanted to play. I'd figured on that. He was a playful kind of monster. He was already closer than Nik had wanted, but I wasn't ready to back off. This was it. This had to be it. No more dead little girls, no more dead women in love. No more.

Whirling, I fired, separating his leg at where I guessed the knee would be under the flowing imitation of coat. His enormous grin never faded. He snatched up the leg and disappeared. At least it seemed that way. I barely got an impression of the direction he'd gone—back the way I'd come.

"Promise," I warned as I ran.

She was ready for him, blocking the entrance with her sword. He gave an annoyed hiss, the first non-gleeful sound I'd heard from him, and sprang back to the ceiling and raced along it out of sight of my flashlight. I swore, spun on my heel, and headed after him. That's when I discovered it wasn't only human bodies hanging from the hooks. Leprous hands snatched at me as I ran. More rule-breaking revenants hung twisting on the metal. They clawed and snapped, maddened by their imprisonment . . . tortured by pain. Yeah, too damn bad for them. I didn't have any more pity than I had had for the one chained in the tunnel.

I pushed through them, ignoring the bloody stripes left across my face and neck. Sawney was the only thing on my mind now. "You're running, Sawney? You afraid your meal's going to kick your ass?"

I couldn't see Niko or Robin, but I knew they were hidden in the darkness waiting to make their move. Robin's job was the same as Promise's—keep Sawney in the cavern. Niko's was to take advantage the minute I got Sawney sufficiently distracted to hold still for a few seconds. All I had to do was make that happen. A couple of seconds . . . it had seemed a lot more doable when we were discussing it aboveground.

"Sawney," I started to yell again just as he came out of the darkness beside me and took me down. I twisted under him and fired again in his chest. There was a cracking, the sound of rotten pond ice splitting under a spring sun. Clear, cold glass peppered my shirt, fragments of whatever made up the core of the inner Sawney. They burned even through the cloth, like dry ice. I fired again, shoved him hard, and rolled beneath the swipe of the scythe. Not fast enough to save me a slice along my stomach, but quick enough to keep my guts inside where they belonged. I had to get distance between us or Nik would scrap the plan and move in, intent on saving my ass. I rolled again and pulled the trigger two more times, nailing him in the throat. Blood, with the clear purity of rain and the chemical bite of anti-freeze, poured out like a wide-open faucet. I skittered backward from beneath it and moved up to a crouch. As for Sawney, chest and throat in ruins—Sawney seemed to be having the time of his life. I noticed his leg was back in place, which seemed to add to his good cheer.

"Traveler."

He was drifting closer, his feet not touching the ground. I'd seen it before with him, but I'd already had my view of the monster world soundly shaken with this bastard—and this would've been nice to do without. I raised my eyes in the joy of denial and tried for that head shot Niko had asked me for earlier.

Too late. Sawney was gone. Not so fast this time, but I wasn't sure if his wounds were slowing him down or he wanted me to keep up to play a little longer. If I had to pick, I'd pick the one that screwed me but good. I followed anyway as this cavern passed into another. The entrance was hidden by a curtain of hooks and corpses. I pushed through them with distaste to find an identical space. More blood, more bodies, and more Sawney. And this time he kicked up the play to high gear. He slashed the moment I passed through the cold flesh. My blood was on the scythe along with the blood of tonight's victim or victims. Not exactly sanitary and the very least of my concerns.

I threw myself to one side and emptied the clip in his direction. It was a lot of bullets and I wasn't sure a single one hit him. His scythe hit me, though, carving a thin slice in my shoulder. Flitting away, he disappeared, reappeared, and sliced the outside of my thigh. I backed away, ejecting the clip and sliding a new one home. The slashes were painful and bloody, but superficial . . . just for fun. So far. But they would get deeper. Nik wouldn't hold back any longer. As a distraction, I was great. As for getting Sawney to hold still, I might not survive that long. He was too goddamn fast.

But then . . . I could be fast too.

Time to see if practice made perfect.

Breaking promises. I'd done it a few times now. But sometimes you break them little, and sometimes you break them big. This was going to be fucking huge.

"Traveler."

There. Slash. Gone again, but I heard the faintest rustle of bodies behind. Niko was coming, and I hadn't done my job. Not yet. But I would. I said I would, and I was keeping my word there even if I was breaking it somewhere else.

"Yeah, I'm a traveler." I could feel the sweat soaking my shirt and jeans. "One like you haven't seen before, asshole."

I saw him through the hanging bodies, the scythe duplicating his grin. "Travelers, they are all the same to Sawney Beane. Go here, go there. Horse, no horse." The smile, always with the damn crazed smile. "All the same."

"Not me." I gave a grin of my own—wild and savage. "Not this traveler."

So I traveled.

As before, I didn't build the gate before me; I built it *around* me, and I was gone. I reappeared behind him and nailed him in the back. Then he vanished and I vanished with him. I fired, missed, traveled, fired again. Sometimes I hit him, sometimes I didn't. But he couldn't shake me, no matter how he tried, because I was a nightmare. I was this monster's nightmare just as he'd been one to so many others.

I saw Nik from the corner of my eye now and again, and also occasionally saw Promise and Robin fighting off revenants. I wondered what I looked like to them, as I glowed with a sickly gray light and disappeared, reappeared, disappeared, reappeared . . . Maybe like a rapidly sped-up movie—a fast-forward of blood and metal.

I was bleeding again from the nose; I tasted the salt. The ears too, like in the museum, but I was also bleeding from my mouth. I swallowed the copper of it and went on, because that was fine; better than fine. It was just goddamn great. And I was laughing—because once I pushed through the pain, once I embraced the head-crushing agony—traveling was fun as hell. And I liked it far more than was good for me, because it tasted just like Sawney said I did.

The next time I faced Sawney I put one in his forehead and when I flashed behind him I emptied the clip in the back of his head. While grinning through blood-coated teeth, I fired bullet after bullet, blowing away the curve of skull to show the glassy mass within, taking that head shot Niko had once asked of me in the subway.

That's when Sawney turned his head completely backward to grin at me. In his mind, it was all fun and games, even if we both died. With the sound of bones cracking, his body turned at a slower pace to keep up with his head. The scythe rose high.

And this time I didn't flash out. This time my brain tied itself in an exhausted knot and the traveling flowed out of me, riding on the blood. But that was all right, because, for once, Sawney was standing still.

Which was when Niko set him on fire.

The flamethrower had been concealed in the oversized backpack Nik had been hauling. Although whether Sawney would've known what it was was debatable. Although Sawney knew a lot of things he shouldn't, thanks to Wahanket probably. Even without that help, he would've learned fast in this time and place. Yeah, one smart son of a bitch. Too bad for him that wasn't going to help him now. Too damn bad.

As I staggered back from him, the stream of flame enveloped him and he went up like a bonfire. Covering him from head to toe, Niko manipulated the fiery stream like a fire hose, and from the look on his face, he was enjoying it as much as he said he would. Sawney, however, was not. The insane laughter had turned to insane screams. The hooked revenants and the ones on the ground screamed with him. Sawney whirled in the air, bright as the sun, singeing and burning the bodies around him. The screams . . . they didn't stop. They went on and on as Sawney spun faster and faster. Niko kept the flame on him.

"Now, you bastard," he said quietly, "now comes your justice."

And while Justice was blind, she could give you one helluva sunburn. He burned for what seemed like forever. I watched silently as I used my hand and then my sleeve to mop the blood from my face and spat out the red stuff as well. The headache was fierce, but not as agonizing as it had been. I'd either broken through the wall or just flat-out broken period. Either way, I couldn't have cared less as I watched that monster begin to fall in on himself. The hair was gone, burned away. The crystalline spine and skull were naked to the eye and melting like glass in a furnace. In other places, the flesh, already black, was hardening, then crumbling to ash beneath him. And still the screaming went on. I was glad my ears were already bleeding. It saved some time.

"Prometheus, look what you have wrought," Robin marveled at my elbow.

The revenants that remained had turned to run, and I didn't have the energy to lift my gun to stop them. Without Sawney, they were little threat. Promise took the head of one in passing, but as for the rest . . . screw it. We let them go. They wouldn't be hanging around Columbia anymore, and like cockroaches there would always be more in the city. No matter how many you stepped on, they would always be there.

Sawney burned on. He clawed the air as his insides turned into a river of melting ice or evaporated with an ugly, chemical-tainted hiss. We didn't have a stake to roast him on as they had had in the fifteenth century, but twenty-first-century technology made up the difference.

"No, travelers. *No."*

There was only a black, twisted thing left now . . . small as a child and shot through with a glitter of smoked diamonds. When the plea didn't work, the laughter came back, a harsh caw through disintegrating vocal cords, but crazy as ever. "I will be back. From ashes and bone to flesh and murder. You cannot stop me. None can."

"Promise?"

She moved at Niko's rapping of her name and lifted a bottle from her bag. Smaller than Nik's backpack, it held one thing only . . . a glass bottle of sulfuric acid. "If you can come back from a few scattered molecules"—Niko's smile was cold and sure—"we'll certainly be ready and waiting to see it."

Either he smelled it or somehow sensed what it was, and for the first time the laughter and screaming combined into one sickening whole. Insanity wasn't so fun for Sawney anymore; true insanity was being pulled from the shores of mortality by a riptide of acid and flame. I hoped it hurt. God, I hoped it hurt, and I hoped he was as terrified as every one of his victims had been.

Especially one tomboy little girl who'd lost her sunshine barrette.

Then it was over. The small dark form fell in on

itself and the flames burned wildly on the ground. Niko kept the flamethrower going for another five minutes before finally switching it off. The embers flared, then dulled, leaving only ashes and blackened bone. It had taken him over five hundred years last time to come back from that.

It wasn't long enough.

Promise poured the acid in a steady stream over the remnants. They smoked and melted into the ground. It hadn't taken an army after all.

He was gone.

22

The trip back through the bodies wasn't any less terrible knowing the reason for all that death had been eliminated. The people were just as dead as they had been before. We killed the hooked revenants, but left them hanging. Cleanup on this scale wasn't something we were set up to do even if we were inclined. Ken Nushi would have to deal with that or, with the way bodies were disappearing lately, he might not. Instead of cobbler elves, could be there were little mortuary elves that cleaned up the scene of the massacre with tiny mops. It made as much sense as anything else. Something had definitely been at work cleaning up Sawney's first victims—the bodies in the park.

Right then I couldn't have cared less. Good for whoever. Way to take initiative.

Niko had given and would continue to give me hell for breaking my word about the traveling. I had weeks of humiliating ass-kickings in our sparring future. I grinned to myself and spat a last mouthful of old blood. Nothing said family like having the Kung Fu King wipe the floor with your butt. It was better than a card any day.

"Zeus, kid, you look like a nonunion-sanctioned human sacrifice." Once we made it through Sawney's tunnel and up to the man-made one, Robin got a good look at the blood drying on my face and grimaced.

"Been to a lot of those?" The bleeding had stopped, and, although my head still hurt, the pain was bearable . . . more so than it had been in the museum. Much more so. That meant something. I thought I'd wait awhile to find out what.

"Human, no." He still had his sword out to deal with stray revenants and used it to salute me with a happy leer. "But I had a virgin or two tossed my way."

"That's right, because you were a god," I snorted, remembering his drunken rambling from the bar.

"Yes, because I was a god. Did you expect anything less?" The normally sly grin had abruptly turned into something tired and old.

I felt the same way. It had been one long night. My head ached, the multiple scythe slashes burned, and I wanted a shower. I wanted to sluice away the blood and the taint of the black water. I wanted to be clean again. Then I wanted to sleep, a nice utterly satisfied sleep.

But people in hell want a really good antiperspirant too, don't they?

The stairs up to the basement rocked under my feet, from one side to the other. It took me a second to figure out it was exhaustion and not an earthquake. We didn't get many of those in New York, but you never knew. I rested a hand against the wall and used it to brace myself every third step or so. Halfway up, I felt a small hand at the base of my back supporting me. I looked back to see Promise looking up at me with a finger held to her lips. As long as she had lived, she knew all about the male ego. I tried to pretend that I didn't need the help, but I did get up the stairs quicker than I would have without it.

Ahead of us, Niko and Robin were already on the stairs to the first floor. Promise and I closed and padlocked the trapdoor. It would give Nushi the extra time he needed to get some sort of supernatural cleanup crew. It also gave me a chance to catch my second wind and make it up those stairs without Promise's assistance. The lights were low in Buell Hall and it was silent, peaceful. I could've dozed as I walked, but I kept the lids up and tried to stay alert. There could still be revenants. There could be security doing a sweep. Nushi would speak up for us, but that would put him in a position he'd probably sooner avoid. So, as we hit the small lobby, a gloom-shrouded two-story affair, I was as sharp as I could manage under the circumstances.

It wasn't enough.

I don't know what it was. It could've been I couldn't smell through the blood in my nose or that the smell was one that I expected here—just background. Cinnamon and spice and everything that was so nice about college girls. But it wasn't only cinnamon. It was cinnamon and honey, a scent I'd caught several times before. When she walked out of the shadows I made the connection . . . way too goddamn late.

Seraglio.

She wasn't alone. She was flanked on one side by three men and on the other by two more men and a woman. They all had the same glossy black hair and dusky skin. They were of average size compared to her small stature, but other than that, they all had the same look to them. It was more than an ethnicity; they looked related. Family. They all had guns as well. Those weren't matching, but what the hell?

"Seraglio." It was Robin. He said her name with resignation, and as I looked over at him, I could see that he was expecting this. Not her, no, but this. Once a human had made one of the assassination attempts, he'd known who was behind it. All of our pressing hadn't moved him to tell us, but he'd known. I didn't think he'd known that it would come so soon, though, and with us in the crosshairs with him.

She inclined her head. "The Herdsman." She bowed it again. "Tammuz." Then again. "Pan." Lifting her head, she smiled. "Our God. Our never forgotten, fleeing God. How we have missed you."

The Georgia accent was long gone, as was the bold snap of her eyes. Now there was only cold. Cold voice, cold eyes, cold satisfaction.

"Tammuz? The Babylonian god?" Niko's sword was up as was my gun, but we were thoroughly outnumbered in the weapons department.

Robin shrugged lightly. "Like you've never given anyone a fake name?" He settled back on his heels, dropping the point of his sword toward the floor. "What am I thinking? Of course you haven't." Cool and breezy. It was the Robin we'd first met, one who was so accustomed to hiding who he was and being exactly as his race was painted: shallow, thoughtless, full of uncaring conceit. It was easier to see your sins catch up to you if you didn't care, right? But he did. If he hadn't, he would've told us the truth. Whatever was going on . . . whatever this was, he felt guilty over it. He felt regret, and he cared a great deal.

"You really were a god?" I asked in disbelief. In

the bar he'd told me so while drunk as a skunk, but who'd believe that he was telling the truth more or less?

"*In vino veritas.* If you drank more, you'd know that." Then the facade fell and he rubbed his eyes wearily. "I'd ask what you want, Seraglio, but I think we already know that, don't we?"

"The Banu Zadeh tribe does not forget slights, no matter how old. No matter how many thousands of years pass. And the slight of a god is a shame to a people that cannot be forgiven or forgotten." Her finger tightened on the trigger until the knuckle paled to light gold against her darker skin. "Babylon is no more. Our tribe has dwindled to what you see before you, but we have you to thank for that. When you left us"—her voice became a hiss—"*deserted* us, the sickness came and the fury of the mightiest storm the desert had seen came. Within months, half the tribe was dead. You took your presence and you took your protection and now we are all but gone from the world. Because of you. All because of you. But"— her smile returned—"those ancestors that were spared have allowed their descendants to claim vengeance. We are all that is left of the Banu Zadeh, but we will be enough."

Robin could have said it was coincidence, the disease and storm, that he'd never been a god, only an imposter, but I wondered if his "abandoning" them was all there was to it. Particularly when the remnants of the tribe had chased him for thousands of years bent on vengeance. I could see how easily whatever it was had happened. When we'd first met him, Goodfellow was the loneliest son of a bitch I'd seen. Pucks didn't seem to stick around each other much. The ego seemed to be part of their genetic makeup from what I could tell from the two I'd met. No wonder they went their separate ways. The clash of narcissism would be explosive. And the majority of other nonhuman races hated and scorned pucks. Thieves, con men, egomaniacs, it was the accepted image. And, hell, it was true, but Robin had proven he was more than that. He stood with us and had since the beginning. He'd faced death with us more than once. It hadn't been sheer loneliness that had driven him to that, but that had been part of it . . . at least in the beginning.

I didn't think it would've been any different in the days of Babylon. I could see him coming across a desert tribe and being different enough that they were suspicious of him. But if he were a god, and I was sure he had a few Houdini-style tricks to dazzle ancient humans, then they'd welcome him. Embrace him. No contempt. No hatred. Just acceptance, friendship, worship. Who could turn down a little worship? Not your average person, and definitely no puck. Eventually Robin would bore and move on. It was his bad luck on the timing was all. Of course, if he'd still been there when disease and natural disaster reared their heads, it might not have gone any better for him than it was going now.

"You cursed us with your abandonment," she continued. "As our tribe has died, so will you."

"And you think you can kill a god?" Promise inquired with the perfect touch of dismissal. I didn't think it would cast enough doubt in them to work, but it was worth a try.

"Even gods can die." The dark eyes were unrelenting in their determination. "We've seen many things in our long search, my people. Generation after generation has seen wonders and horrors, and we've seen the deaths of gods. We have killed many ourselves. Your kind," she said to Goodfellow with a righteous vindication curving her lips. "They were never the right god, never you, but we killed them nonetheless. They were not you, but they were like you. Uncaring and undeserving of existence."

"Why didn't you simply shoot me in my bed?" he asked. "It would've been easy enough for you." Although it wouldn't have been. Robin would've heard the slightest out-of-place noise. He hadn't lived this long without picking up a thousand and one tricks of survival.

"First, we had to be sure you were the right one." With her other hand she held up a gold armband with what looked like lion heads carved on the ends. "One of the first things we learn as children. The one offering that you took with you. I searched your apartment and finally found it. You kept it all this time. The sentiment moves us." Yeah, why was I not believing that?

She tossed it at his feet. "I could've tried at the apartment, ended you there, but no. You come and you go. The days you spend at work, or so you say. Six nights out of seven you are gone whoring, fooling others into believing you'll never leave them as you left us. I never knew when you would *grace* me with your presence so that I and my brothers could be waiting. Besides, facing a god on his home territory where he is his strongest, we are more clever than that. And we've come to know through several other of your kind that you are all but impossible to poison. The sirrush proved that." I thought of all the food she'd given me and felt my stomach roil. "So we tried several times to kill you with the sirrush, the Hameh, our brother." Pain flickered behind her eyes. "I do not believe you deserve to see your death face-to-face, a warrior's death, not one of treachery for you are a treacherous creature. But now I see we acted as you did, cowardly and without honor. The same death you chose to inflict on my people. You destroyed us as a people and now as the last of our people we must face you to do the same. And we will be more honorable than you."

"There aren't many who aren't," he replied matter-of-factly before dropping his sword. It hit the arm-band with the musical sound of a bell ringing. "So, you will let them go, then the others . . . as you are honorable, and they've done nothing to you."

A self-sacrificing puck. The world would stop if it knew, but the world didn't know Robin like we did. He had it in him. Until this moment maybe even he didn't know, but it was there. What a hellacious way to find out.

"I sincerely doubt they would go, Almighty One. Even now they stand with you instead of shunning you as they should. They know what you have done now. Where is the shock and horror at your shame?" She shook her head. "No. They are not your kind, but they are like you. Take them as your servants into whatever afterlife a god claims." The smile was reflected by those who stood beside her, her tribe. Not one of the smiles was a pleasant one.

"How'd you find us?" Niko asked abruptly. "And how did you find Robin at the subway? We weren't followed." And we hadn't been. Any one of us would've picked up on that.

"A GPS tracker in his cell phone. The modern age is a marvel of technology. The following of a god becomes simplicity. A human outwits the divine. The world has come full circle."

"But finding Robin to begin with had to be a bitch." Kind of like her. "Over two thousand years. Way to hold a grudge."

"It's retribution. Only blood will answer the debt." It was hard to believe this woman had once made me breakfast. She and the others were all the same unyielding stone. I guessed if you were going to be a hard-ass, seeing your living, breathing runaway god before you would be the time for it.

"If you give a damn, I am sorry," Robin said quietly to them. "Whether you believe it or not, I truly am. Not for what you think, but I am sorry." Sorry for what he'd done and sorry for what was coming.

There was no give, in their eyes or their faces, and I realized: We were going to have to kill them. All of them. Humans. It didn't sit right. I didn't think it ever would, but it was getting easier. After all, I'd been more than happy to kill that bastard in the subway. Of course, here we might not get the chance to. We were good, but we were facing seven guns. Promise could take a number of hits and stay on her feet. The same wasn't true of the rest of us. At least one of us was going down; it was a fact, one that sat hard and undigested in my stomach. We were thoroughly fucked.

Unless . . .

Unless I could get behind them. Get the drop on them. It might make the difference.

And that's when I discovered another difference, the one Sawney had made, what he'd pushed me to. I guessed I owed that murdering bastard a favor, because the knot tied in my brain was gone as my mind got the second wind my body had. The effort to head him off, the mind-rending strain to be faster, the necessity of ripping reality time and time again had finally punched through the scar tissue that had held me back these past weeks. It was wide open. *I* was wide open.

And it was easy this time. It was so damn easy. There was no blood, no pain, and it was so right that I wondered how I'd survived this long without it. As Seraglio extended her gun with a "No, my god, we do not give a damn. Not for you or your apologies," I was suddenly behind them, and I felt good, really good, and . . . predatory. Content and hungry for violence, with a blood that felt as if it scorched my veins. As if it were a heat that only killing could cool. Then the feeling was gone, because I had more important things to think about, or maybe it wasn't gone. Maybe it just let me do what I had to.

Was it me? Was it not?

Who gave a rat's ass?

It *was* definitely me, though, who shot the first two in the back before two others turned. No honor. The only thing honor got you was killed. I saw Nik roll and come up from the floor to impale the man on the far side of Seraglio. Promise, although she took two bullets first, took out the woman beside him with a quick snap of her neck. Goodfellow produced two daggers and two more fell with metal in their throat. I saw blood bloom on Robin's neck, red dripping down Niko's hand, I saw Seraglio begin to pull the trigger of the gun aimed at Robin's head, and then I saw wings.

Wings, pale blond hair, and a blade moving as fast as he fell. Ishiah.

Seraglio's gun flew to one side immediately followed by her head. As her small body crumpled, I could've staggered with relief that I hadn't had to be the one to do it. She'd made me pancakes. She was a hunter and a psychotic killer, but she smelled like cinnamon and honey, and she'd made me pancakes.

Then I forgot about the pancakes and remembered the blood on Niko and Robin. I knelt beside my brother. Promise was there as well, ripping at his sleeve and getting blood on her hands in the process. "Later," Nik ordered, voice controlled. No pain. No panic. "Security. Police. We have to go now. Take Robin." He was right, I knew that, but seeing the blood still coursing down his hand, I opened my mouth to say we could take one second. "Cal, *now*."

Damn it. I shut my mouth and turned to Robin as Nik got to his feet and he and Promise moved quickly toward the door. Goodfellow was upright, hand pressed to his throat. He pulled it away to look at a palm wet and red. "Gods bleed." He gave a liquid cough. "Seraglio would be pleased." Then he dropped or he would have if I hadn't caught him on one side and Ishiah on the other.

"Jesus." He had blood on his lips and his eyes had gone unfocused and hazy. I slapped my hand over the torn flesh of his neck. "I thought you had a prior commitment," I snapped at Ishiah. It was easier to snarl at him than concentrate on the warm wetness pouring through my fingers or the drowned gurgle to Robin's ragged breathing. So much for the damn bulletproof vest.

"This was it." If there was any regret over killing Seraglio, I didn't hear it. I didn't expect to. He'd done it to save Robin. If he hadn't done it, I would've done it myself, and you wouldn't have heard any regret in my voice either. It was pointless to show what you couldn't change.

We dragged Goodfellow rapidly toward the door and out into the cool night air. "Nushi. We need to get him to Nushi to be healed. Promise?" I said with desperate demand.

"Hundred and ninetieth Street and Fort Washington, apartment number twelve-C," she said swiftly as both she and Niko looked back at the limp puck with grim worry. They didn't have long to look. Within a second he was gone, pulled upward and out of my hands. Ishiah took him. Powerful wings bunching with muscle, he lifted a now-unconscious Robin into the air and soared away. Going to Nushi. Right now he was the only one fast enough. And he would be.

He had to be.

23

"Did he let you in this time?"

"No. Stubborn bastard." Two days later I was spreading out the supplies on the kitchen table and gesturing for Nik to strip off his long-sleeve gray T-shirt. The six-month-old circular scar on his chest was still a bright contrast against his olive skin. It wasn't the best of memories and I looked away to the ugly furrow on the outer aspect of his biceps. It wasn't bad, not nearly as bad as I'd thought when I'd seen the blood coating his arm and hand. Still, one more not-so-great memory. "He wouldn't even answer this time."

My own wounds, Sawney's going-away present, ached as I moved, but they were much less deep than Niko's bullet wound. Thin slices, they'd heal soon enough. "Damn pucks," I muttered as I cleaned the wound.

"I think this situation applies to only one puck . . . ours," Niko corrected as I applied the antibiotic cream. "I don't think many others would be too ashamed to show their faces."

"They do love showing them off," I snorted. I put the gauze and tape into place and sat as he pulled his shirt back on. I pushed my half-empty glass of hours-old morning orange juice back and forth. "You'd think the son of a bitch would at least let us in long enough to see that he's okay."

"Ishiah and Nushi both said he was healed." He added with a sliver of humor, "And I would think the sheer volume of his cursing us to Hades through the door would reassure you. It's not the voice of a dying man."

No, it wasn't. Neither was the mocking of our fighting skills, lack of drinking capabilities, and pretty much everything about our personal appearance. It was razor-sharp, sliced as fine as Sawney's scythe, and was definitely not the voice of a sick puck. But I'd felt his unconscious weight against my arm and the blood pouring through my fingers. I'd sensed the cool slither of death sliding through him. That was hard to forget, almost as hard as the fact you'd inspired an entire tribe of people to hunt you through the centuries with the burning desire to kill you. As many times as we'd pounded on his door in the past days, he'd refused to open it, refused to face us.

A hand looped around my wrist. "He'll come around, Cal. He simply needs time to come to terms with what he did."

"And that we know what he did," I exhaled, with understanding.

Ishiah, with Robin's permission, had finally told us the whole story. I doubted Robin would ever tell us face-to-face himself, and as I'd suspected, there was more to it than just playing god. Had that been all there was, I was sure Robin wouldn't have been that ashamed. He was a puck, born to lie, steal, and fool. The storm and disease weren't his fault. He hadn't been responsible, no matter what the tribe and their descendants had thought, not for those deaths.

But there were two others. . . .

It wasn't boredom after all that had him leaving. It had never occurred to Goodfellow that the more attractive members of the tribe might not want to "service" their god. Who wouldn't possibly want some of that, right? He still had that attitude today, but now maybe it was tinged with a weariness I just hadn't noticed.

There had been one woman, particularly beautiful and with an even more particularly possessive husband. She had gone to the god as requested. She hadn't fought. She hadn't said a word. He was charming and handsome and he was her *god.* She'd done what her new faith said was her duty and she did it willingly . . . if a god wanted you, who were you to say no? To even think no? And when it was done and she had gone back to her husband's tent, he hacked her to death with his sword. Possessive, obsessive, maybe even insane, because he had tried to kill the god as well.

When Robin had left what he really had come to think of as his people, there had been two bloody bodies in his wake. Two deaths because of a puck ego. Two deaths that might still have happened had he not been there; abuse is abuse and insane is insane, but there was no doubt they had happened at that moment because of him. The tribe hadn't blamed him for those deaths, but he damn sure blamed himself. After thousands of years, he still blamed himself enough to not want to face us.

I understood that, but that wasn't going to stop me from kicking down his door tomorrow. Enough was enough. He was our friend. That pretty much said it all. No matter what he had done, he was a friend. Yeah, tomorrow, absolutely . . . foot through his door. I told Nik so.

"Which is probably exactly what he needs." He squeezed my arm and let go to frown at the table. "Leftover eggs and antibiotic cream. I could do without the mix. You're a hopeless slob, you know that, little brother?"

"Yeah, yeah." He'd spent the night at Promise's and this was his first look at my morning mess. I took a drink of the warm juice. "How's Promise?"

"Healing well." It was a myth that vampires healed immediately, but they did heal much faster than humans did.

As we'd stood and watched Ishiah and Robin disappear into the night, we'd heard the wail of an approaching siren. I'd built a gate instantly and taken us all back to the apartment. I couldn't take Goodfellow to Nushi. I'd never been in his place before . . . didn't know the way, and there was a way to every gate—twisting and true as an arrow to the heart. On the other side of our doorway, Promise's wounds, one high to the shoulder above her clavicle and one at her hip, had already stopped bleeding. The one to the hip was a through and through and best to just leave the other bullet in, she'd said.

Vampires, balls of steel or one helluva tolerance for pain—it was one of the two. With villagers chasing your ass with pitchforks and torches, you would've needed at least one of them.

As for the gate . . . that sensation, the Auphe-ness I'd felt with the first one or two, it hadn't returned with the very last one—our escape exit. Maybe because I was watching for it. But I was afraid it'd be back. Sooner or later. At least I wasn't Frodo, foaming at the mouth every time I put on the ring. I had to be careful, though, careful as hell. Even though I didn't want me to be—*it* didn't want me to be. "Nik," I said diffidently, "I think you might be right. No more gateways for a while might be a good thing." I pushed the glass away. As much as I'd denied it, I was my father's son. Because of that I couldn't let my guard down. Not as long as I lived. "No more traveling, Sawney would say. I think I might like it a little too much."

No one in the world could read me like my brother could. No one ever would. We'd grown up with the Auphe at our window and around every corner. We'd grown up with the monsters outside and the monster inside me. If I said I liked it too much, he knew what I meant.

"No more gates." Then he flicked my ear and offered easily, "Haven't I said that all along? Although don't think I didn't know you chose to ignore me."

"Know-it-all prick." I rubbed my ear. "If only I listened to your wise and sage advice, we'd be . . . oh yeah . . . dead now."

"That doesn't change the fact it was wise and sage." His eyes gleamed. "And you'll only wish you were dead when I'm finished with you. Get your gear. We're going to the park."

Time for a class in Butt Kicking 101. I was never going to graduate from that damn class. "Give me two hours. I have something I need to do."

George lived a short subway ride away. I walked it. It took forty minutes. I still had the engagement ring in my pocket, the diamond and rubies of a dead woman. I had told myself I'd bring it up in the sun for her, but it might be better to leave it where her fiancé could find it, if I could find him.

It had gone from cool to cold, an early winter. There were scudding clouds and the icy bite of an approaching snow. I used to like winter when I was a kid. We'd traveled around so much I'd seen it all. Places where it was warm in January and never snowed and then places with three feet of it. I'd liked the snow best. No school. Not that Sophia cared if we went, but my brother did. Snowball fights with him . . . got my ass kicked there too. I'd also liked the stillness and quiet of the snow, not to mention the fact you could see the footprints of anyone who'd hovered around your window with red eyes and metallic grins. You could be prepared . . . ready.

But then the Auphe took me at fourteen, and I'd come back with a profound dislike of the cold. Tumulus, Auphe hell, the place they'd kept me from what we thought, was a dimension of rock, charnel stench, and searing cold. I might not remember my time there, but I remembered Darkling's few hours of cooling his heels there. Somewhat. Bits and pieces through a blurred and hazy lens. That was my mind trying to protect me. It knew. If I remembered what happened in those two icy wasteland years I'd spent there from fourteen years old to sixteen, they'd have to pour me into one of those straitjackets we'd seen in the asylum ruins. I didn't like winter anymore, and I didn't like the cold.

But, hell, it's New York. What are you gonna do?

Suck it up and tuck your face against the wind. The subway would've been easier, warmer too, but I needed the time. Not to think . . . the thinking had been done on this for a while. I just needed it. You might have to jump from the third story of a burning building, but you needed to take a breath first. Because this leap wasn't one of faith. This was one of endings and a bad choice over a worse one. I needed that breath.

Sooner than I wanted to be, I was in front of her building. The steps were empty this time. I stood at the bottom one in hesitation. Five inches of concrete and it seemed like a mountain, one I suddenly didn't want to climb. She would know. The instant she saw me, she would know. It wasn't what I wanted, but it was what I'd planned. Until George was no longer a part of my life, she wouldn't be safe. She wasn't a warrior like Nik or near impervious to bullets like Promise. She wasn't Robin, sly and better with a sword than all the goddamned Musketeers and Zorro combined. She wasn't us. She was George . . . stubborn, determined, but gentle and vulnerable as hell. She'd fight if she had to and do it with courage and an unbreakable will. The rest of her, though, was all too breakable. To something even far less deadly than an Auphe.

And then there was me. Tainted right down to my DNA. I couldn't be with her. I couldn't be with any human woman. She wouldn't believe that, but she would believe something else. She'd believe in Delilah. Charm had been a one-night stand. A onetime thing for one particular thing. But Delilah was different. With her there was the potential for something else . . . something that could snare my emotions, the more primal ones, for a while. Something real—probably not especially healthy, but something genuine. That was the betrayal. And George would know it the moment she set eyes on me. Wasn't that why I was here?

Then I saw the white flutter of an envelope resting on the stone balustrade. It was weighted down by a small piece of polished glass, dusky topaz like her skin. I picked it up and saw one word written on it: *ring*. I opened the unsealed flap and pulled out a small slip of paper. It too had just one word written on it.

Good-bye.

She already knew.

Mission accomplished. Good for me. That had to be relief that burned in my stomach and if I walked stiffly up the steps to the lobby, well, it was cold, right?

I fished out the ring with fingers just as stiff and cold and slipped it in the envelope. Sealing it, I dropped it in George's mail slot and it was gone. Just like George was. Just as I'd planned.

I didn't remember much of the walk back. My hand held tight to the bit of topaz glass in my pocket, but my mind was as frozen as the weather as I flowed with the sidewalk crowd. And that was for the best. I didn't want to think, not about my choices, not about George. Not thinking, that would get me through this day. Committing Niko's cardinal sin— not noticing the unforgiving and dangerous world around me.

But then it noticed me.

I felt the gates open. One after the other. One, two, three . . . ten . . . fifteen. I looked up, and there they were—on top of my building. Marble skin, white hair, gunmetal teeth, they blended into the winter itself. You wouldn't have seen them if you didn't know to look. But I knew. I saw them. Lining the ledge like gargoyles, Auphe after Auphe after Auphe.

All looking down at me.

Oh, *shit*.

Read on for a taster of the next instalment
in the Cal Leandros series:

Deathwish

Coming in August 2012

1

Cal

Once, when I was seven, I was chased by a dog.

We lived in a trailer park then, my brother, our mother, and me. There were lots of dogs around, most of them running loose. I didn't mind. I like dogs. But dogs . . . dogs don't much like me in return. Puppies do. Puppies like everyone. They'd crawl in my lap, chew happily on a finger or the tattered edge of my sneaker. Dogs are different—one sniff of me was enough. The upper lip would peel back, ears would flatten, and the warm brown eyes would go glassy and slide sideways as they hunched away with tail tucked beneath their legs. Dogs don't just not like me; they're afraid of me.

Except for Hammer. Hammer wasn't right; not right being flat-out crazy. One hundred pounds of shepherd mixed with Rottweiler mixed with God knew what else, Hammer wasn't afraid to look at me as the other dogs were. No, Hammer liked to look at me. He liked to think about me. If anyone thought animals didn't think, didn't plot, didn't plan, then they'd never met Hammer. Two trailers down and one of the few dogs in the park kept on a chain, he watched me every day as my brother and I walked to school. He never barked. He never growled. He never even moved. He just watched.

Because of his lack of apparent aggression, any other kid might have been tempted to pet him. Not me. Even at seven, I knew a monster when I saw one. It didn't matter whether his owner had made him into one or he'd been born one like me. Hammer was Hammer. You didn't pet him any more than you petted a rabid grizzly bear. You just walked by and kept your eyes on the ground. You never looked. . . . Just as Hammer never moved.

Until he did.

Hammer was bad inside, *wrong*, and as I recognized him, he recognized me. And when drunk old Mr. McGee let the chain finally rust through, Hammer came for me. I had my dollar-store sneakers and a bagged lunch my brother had made for me, but I didn't have my brother. He'd gone ahead, although he was still in sight. He never failed to make sure I was in sight. I'd forgotten my backpack like kids do. I'd catch up. No big deal, until Hammer made it one.

He'd been lying in the same position he lay in every day. Bowl of dirty water, gnawed club of wood. That day, like every day, I wondered why he didn't like me. We were both twisted. Both wrong. So why? I didn't get a chance to wonder any further than that. There was a blur of fur, jaws clamped into my backpack, and my body was thrown sideways. He dragged me several feet before he tore the pack completely off me.

I didn't think. As I said, I'd seen monsters. You didn't hang around and ponder the situation. I got up and ran. While I'd seen monsters before, been followed, watched, I hadn't ever been chased by one. It was my first taste of death at my heels, my first taste of running for my life.

It wasn't my last.

In fact, I ended up spending a vast amount of my life running. Not just living my life on the run, which I had as well, but actually *running*. I wasn't seven anymore, but I was still flat-out hauling ass. Like the wind—like the fucking wind. Running from this, running from that—usually from something with teeth, claws, and the attitude of a great white on steroids. Things that made Hammer look like a toy poodle.

I hated it, the running. Hated it like poison. Which may be why I had finally decided I'd had enough and committed to staying in one place more than a year ago, and that place was New York City. A veritable Mecca for monsters like me, as well as monsters like Hammer—those that had me literally running for my life or the life of one of the few people I gave a shit about. There weren't many of those. Part-time bartender, private investigator/bodyguard/jack-of-all-trades to the nonhuman world, and one suspicious son of a bitch, that was me. Not precisely Mr. Social. It paid to be wary in a dark world thought to be nothing more than fairy tales and ghost stories by most people—most people being the blindly oblivious, the cheerfully clueless, the ever-so-lucky assholes.

The handful of people, humans and non-, that I did give a crap about had all ended up in New York, too—in the City That Never Sleeps, a good place for us creatures of the night. Everyone I cared about, and one in particular: my brother. He had been with me since the beginning, *my* beginning, and now had me running through the streets to make sure my beginning didn't bring him to an end.

The running—it always came back to that. A pity, because I was an inherently lazy son of a bitch. Burning lungs, knotting muscles, stuttering heart—I could do without any of that, thanks. But now I was running toward something, although there was plenty to run from. Death behind me; the unimaginable before me—an unholy situation, and it only made me run faster. The bus that nearly clipped me as I ran across the street? That wasn't even a blip on the radar. I had bigger, badder, and far more destructive things on my mind.

"Traitorous cousin."

The side of that bus brushed my jacket as I looked up at the sound of the icy hiss. For a second I saw it crouched on top, proving that mass transport wasn't just for hygienically challenged humans. I saw metal teeth, red eyes, and hair the color and drift of jellyfish stingers. I saw a killer. I saw a monster.

I saw family.

Then I saw something more immediately relevant— the front of a cab barreling at me. I dodged to one side as it braked. I rolled across the hood, taking down a bike messenger. Vaulting the cursing man, I ran on. I didn't look behind me. I didn't have to. I knew what was there. I knew what was coming, and I knew it wasn't alone. But that was the least of my concerns. What was important to me now was getting to the park, because I had other family. Real family.

My brother was at Washington Square Park, waiting for me. We were supposed to spar. "Spar" was a word Niko used when he meant he was going to beat the shit out of me for my own good. He kept me sharp and quick. He kept me evading monsters and taxis with equal alacrity. He was the reason I'd lived this long. The ones that followed me, the Auphe, knew that too. They hated him nearly as much as they hated me. And hate was like air to an Auphe. When something was as easy as breathing, you got pretty damned good at it. But the Auphe weren't good. No . . .

They were the best.

That's why I ran. Not because they were behind me, but because I suspected they were also in front of me. They'd been waiting for me at the apartment building at St. Marks's, where Niko and I lived. I'd come home to see them lining the roof, and I'd felt the internal wrench as they ripped holes in reality and slithered through. The dread was instant. If they knew for sure where I lived, they knew where I went. If they knew that, they knew the same about Niko. Months ago

they had said they'd kill everyone in my life before
they killed me. I believed them. Reapers and rippers
and older than time—living murder wrapped in cold
flesh. They didn't lie. Why would they when blood-
soaked destruction was so much more entertaining?

Yeah, it had been months, but they said it, I believed it, and now was apparently the time. Long
months of waiting, but, hell, I'd have been happy to
wait a little longer.

No such goddamn luck.

I came off East Eighth Street, crossed Astor, then
hit Broadway and kept running. This time I was hit,
a big, ancient black Lincoln, but it only grazed my
hip. There was the screech of brakes as I was knocked
to the asphalt. As I scrambled back to my feet and
kept moving, the skies opened up and dropped a wa-
terfall of icy rain. I was soaked instantly, but the cold
I felt on the outside couldn't touch what swirled inside
me. Once on Fourth, I was running through the people. The human and the non-. The blissfully ignorant
and the voraciously aware. The dinner and the diner.

Among the walking, talking snacks that were now
cursing the rain, I could see the occasional pale amber
eye, the gleam of a bared tooth. Upright Hammers.
And they knew me as Hammer had. Smelled me. Werewolves were good at that. Leg humping and sniffing out
a half-Auphe—it was all a piece of cake.

There were other monsters among the unwitting,
but I didn't bother to pick them out. I didn't have
time. I didn't have time for anything except getting to
Nik. It was a fifteen-minute run, going as fast as I
could. Fifteen minutes was a long time. I didn't let
myself think it might be pointless, that Nik had been
at the park for more than an hour now. I just gulped
wet air, tried not to think how much easier it would
be if I shot the people milling in front of me, blocking
my way, and kept running.

There were people in the park, but they were all

leaving—running themselves, although not as desperately as me, for shelter from the unexpected downpour. When it was cold enough to shrink your balls and wet enough to prune up everything else, it tended to put an end to casual walks and Frisbee playing. Niko would be on the far side of the green. There were bunches of trees gathered around the perimeter of the park. We worked out by a particular group of them in the northwest corner. As I ran toward it, I smelled the grass crushed under my feet, the mud, the dead leaves, the acid-free oil Nik used to clean his swords. . . .

And Auphe. I smelled Auphe.

Elf and Auphe, one and the same. Proof that mythology never failed to get it wrong. How it had gotten blond, prissy, silk-wearing elves from the world's very first monsters, I would never know. After pointed ears and pale skin, the resemblance stopped, and the steel teeth, razor claws, and lava eyes of a demon started.

I ignored the few people who gave me quick stares as they ran in the opposite direction, and tried to get more speed. I couldn't—I was giving it all I had and more. But then I was there. I was in the trees. The leaves had all fallen and the dark branches should've been bare as they split from the trunk to spread against the sky. They weren't. They were filled with Auphe, as pallid as the winter sky behind them. They were hidden enough by the rain that I could barely see them, but they were there. There had been no one behind me because they had beaten me here, the same twenty from the apartment building. From the roof to the trees—it was only a step for them. Open a door in reality, pass through, and there you were.

The one on the bus hadn't been following me. It had been playing with me. Homicide and humor—it was one and the same to the Auphe.

And Niko faced them all.

Revealing himself, he stepped from behind a glistening black tree trunk. Jesus. Alive. Fucking *alive*. And he was ready, with dark blond hair pulled back and katana held high in the pounding rain. The Auphe didn't blink, didn't move. "Gun," Nik said calmly.

I was already reaching under my jacket for the Glock .40 in my shoulder holster. My grip should've been tight and cramped with adrenaline, but I'd pointed one weapon or another so many times over the past four years that my touch was light and confident. The rest of me could've taken a lesson. Normally I was good at this—I saw monsters all the time and faced them head-on. Kicked ass, tail, flipper . . . whatever they had. But this . . . this was the Auphe. Half of my gene pool. They'd been not only the bogeymen of my childhood, but of my whole damn life. Outside windows at night, around darkened corners, trailing behind me from the time I was born until I was fourteen. Bad, right?

Wrong.

There was worse. They took me. For two years. I didn't remember those years and I probably never would, but inside, at a level I couldn't access, I somehow knew what they had done. Could feel it. Seeing just one was enough to have the taste of screams and blood in my mouth and a chunk of ice in my gut.

Seeing twenty of them was like seeing the end of the world.

Pointing a gun at the end of the world seems fairly goddamn futile. I did it anyway. "It's broad daylight, assholes. Seems bold even for you," I said tightly. I didn't freeze, not this time. I swallowed the bile, grew a pair, and kept the Glock steady. Two-headed werewolves, mass murderers, dead bodies hanging like fruit in a tree, I'd faced all of that—I'd face this. "Or did you get the weather report I missed out on?"

"Faithless cousin." Hundreds of titanium needle teeth bared at me as the closest one spoke. "The blind do not see us."

"And when your eyes are ripped from their sockets," hissed another, "neither will you."

Jesus, family. It was a bitch.

But maybe they were right. Even if the water falling from the sky hadn't been the next best thing to the biblical flood, it still might not have mattered. Because if you saw them, you'd have to be insane, wouldn't you? So instead, maybe you'd just turn your head and keep moving as your brain glossed over what simply couldn't be. Maybe your average human was smarter than I gave him credit for.

"We nearly wiped your race from the face of the earth." We'd also gotten our asses spanked and handed to us on a silver platter in the process, but Niko didn't feel the need to mention that. Show the enemy no weakness. A throwing knife appeared in his free hand as he continued without hesitation, "We finish what we start."

That's when they fell from the trees. Predators who had no equal. The hundred others we had killed had been a suicide run we'd unexpectedly survived. A big-ass explosion, a collapsing building, and the good fortune of several lifetimes; I didn't think we'd get that lucky again.

They were like lightning as they fell—that quick, that deadly, and that inescapable. I heard steel hit flesh as Niko swung his blade, and I also heard the thud of my back hitting a tree as clawed hands lifted and threw me before I could get a shot off. God, they were so damn *quick*. Another one snatched at my shirt, scoring the skin of my chest, and tossed me to the wet ground and then landed on me to pin me there. I could see my skewed reflection in the mirror of its teeth as I jammed the muzzle of the gun under an unnaturally pointed chin and pulled the trigger. The bullet hit nothing but the rain. The gate, one of twenty opening, gobbled up the Auphe just as it gobbled up the others.

They were just *playing* with us.

Blocking the rain, the gray light of the gate shimmered above me, hypnotic in the twists and turns of it. It slowed me for less than a second—I'd seen my share—but that was long enough. The hand came through to wrap around my throat, black nails snagging in my shirt and my flesh. I didn't wait for the muscular jerk that would yank me into the light. I emptied my clip into it instead. As the bullets vanished, the hand against my skin spasmed tight enough to cut off my air, then went limp. When it did, the gate closed, leaving a pale arm severed at the elbow lying across my chest. Dark blood pooled on my stomach as the arm suddenly twitched, fingers opening and closing before slowly stilling, this time for good. Dr. Frankenstein couldn't have done any better. "Shit." I pried it off of my neck and with a lifetime of revulsion threw it to one side. "Shit. Shit. Shit."

"So"—there was no whisper of drenched grass, no ghost of the faintest of footsteps, but suddenly Niko was looking down at me anyway—"other than that, how was your day?"

Actually the day had sucked ass before the park, during the park, and it didn't look to be getting any better.

We'd called Promise and Georgina to warn them about the Auphe. Niko spoke to both of them; my call wouldn't have been precisely welcome on George's part. She had cut me out of her life as of that morning. I'd worked toward that for a year now and I'd finally gotten what I'd wanted, although I'd never really wanted it. But I had bad genes, and not wimpy little alcoholic or schizophrenic tendencies either. I had the DNA of Dahmer and Godzilla combined, and I wasn't passing that on.

Promise was a vampire and George a psychic, when she wanted to be, and they weren't helpless against the Auphe. Not completely. It didn't make me feel any better. The Auphe were the Auphe.

Now we were here to warn the third person in our lives. He was a cocky, annoying, conceited, lazy son of a bitch. He was also a friend, one who'd had a few bad days of his own this week. He was currently holed up in his apartment and had been for three days. No one went out; no one went in. For a chronically social, not to mention horny, puck, that was alarming behavior.

I pounded on the door of his Chelsea apartment. I was slowly drying off; the rain had stopped not long after we'd left the park. "Goodfellow, open the hell up!"

There was silence, then a muffled but cutting reply. "How did *you* get in the building? You can't afford to piss on the topiary out front much less walk through the door. Go away." I heard something hit the door with a shattering of glass. "When I want to see belligerent, fashion-impaired monkeys, I'll go to the zoo and watch the feces fly."

That would be Rob Fellows, car salesman of the month, year, decade. Better known to us as Robin Goodfellow . . . Pan . . . Puck, whatever name he'd been passing off at the time. Immortal, stubborn, and could talk shit with the best of them. He'd also saved our lives more than once. That made his nonstop mouth a little more bearable.

"This lost its entertainment value as of yesterday." Niko folded his arms and leaned against the wall. "Kick in the door."

Unlike most siblings, I listen to my big brother. I kicked in the door. It was a good door—solid, thick. It took a few tries to get it open. There was quite a bit of damage—splintered wood, locks ripped free of the frame—none of which I planned on paying for. Goodfellow was right. I couldn't afford to piss on his bushes, and he had money to burn. Besides, tough

love was tough love. And right now that's what the
infamous Robin Goodfellow needed.

"Oh, good." Wavy brown hair disheveled, green
eyes bloodshot, the puck was sprawled on his couch
in pajama bottoms and an open, wrinkled silk robe.
"The Hardy Boys are here to show me the light."

I walked into the apartment, which was an unholy
mess. Considering his housekeeper, Seraglio, had been
killed just days ago, that wasn't much of a surprise.
As she had been trying to kill us all at the time, I
wasn't crying a river over that. On the other hand, I
still remembered how she'd made me peach pancakes.
It was a concept that was hard to fathom. Pancakes
and assassination. What a mix.

There were empty wine bottles everywhere I looked,
littering the floor, the granite counters, and there was
even one embedded in the screen of the plasma TV.
Damn, I'd loved that TV.

I nudged a bottle out of my path, moved closer, and
winced at the sheer volume of alcohol fumes seeping
through Goodfellow's pores. I had a good nose, as
good as your average dog, thanks to my Auphe sperm
donor. But even a normal human nose could've picked
this up easily. "Jesus." My eyes watered as I squinted
at him. "How are you not dead?"

"I was there when the first grape was fermented,"
he grunted. "It makes for a tolerance a fetus like you
couldn't begin to comprehend."

"So you were the one who taught Bacchus to
drink?" Niko asked with a gleam of skepticism in his
gray eyes that came from a year's familiarity with
Goodfellow and his . . . er . . . exaggerations. He
didn't wait for the answer, instead making his way to
the kitchen.

"Actually, I did. Of course, I think he's in AA
now." Mournfully, he lifted a bottle into the air, then
drank. "It is to weep."

"Yeah, I'm sure." I sat on the massive rock crystal

coffee table in front of him. "Okay, Robin, you deserved a little holing-up time, but now you've got to shake this off. The Auphe are back playing their games. They messed with Nik and me in the park. They could come here next. They were toying with us. They might be more serious with you. As in rip you open and get drunk on that alcohol you call blood. You have to be ready. Sober your ass up."

"*Gamo* the Auphe." Goodfellow had known the Auphe when people were still living in caves, gnawing on mammoth bones and picking fleas off one another. He had a healthy fear of and respect for them. Very healthy. At least up until now, apparently. "Bring them on." He took another drink. "Lead their pasty asses hither. I'll give them something to chew on."

I wasn't sure whether he meant his sword or himself, and that worried the hell out of me. He'd been through it, I knew, but I wasn't sure how to deal with a depressed and ashamed puck. I'd never seen him less than confident—brazen as hell. Cocky and way too willing to show you why that word was appropriate in more ways than one. Anything different from that, I wouldn't have been able to picture as of last week. Now . . . now I'd seen it and it wasn't right. It wasn't puck—it wasn't Robin. I didn't like it. Goodfellow had lived a long, long time. Now wasn't the time to give up.

I reached over and snatched the bottle out of his hand. "Okay, fine, you fooled some people into worshipping you as a god. And, yeah, their descendants chased you for thousands of years, wanting to kill you for deserting them. So what? They failed. Get over it already."

The glassy eyes blinked several times before he gave a slurred drawl. "You know, say it that way and it doesn't sound so bad." Of course it had been more than that. Two people had died—died very bloody, terrible deaths because of his massive puck ego, when he had been their "god." He hadn't meant for it to happen, but it had and that's what had him in the bottle, not being worshipped and nearly killed by the last of his followers' tribe. Speaking of bottles, he grabbed at it and missed. I'd seen Robin drink, but I'd only ever seen him drunk twice before. The first time had been when he'd met us, and the last time had been days ago. Both had been for only a few hours. This time, I would bet he'd spent every minute of these past three days like this.

"Look," I said sharply, "we don't care what you did back then. We only care what you do now. You're a friend, and you were a friend to us when any person with the sense God gave a mentally challenged rock would've run the other way."

He let his head flop against the back of the couch. Looking up at the ceiling, he exhaled, then reminded me with a faint note of nostalgia, "Don't forget that you threatened to slit my throat when we first met."

"And even that didn't dissuade you from talking endlessly." Niko appeared and deposited a plate on Robin's lap. There was a sandwich on it and what looked like homemade potato salad. I tried not to think how Seraglio had no doubt made it herself. "Now eat, sober up, and face up to the fact that what you did was wrong, but not wrong enough to justify your murder as penance."

Goodfellow remained motionless, either thinking about it or ignoring us entirely. Niko leaned in, planted a hand on each side of Robin's head, looked down at him, and asked silkily, "Did I or did I not say 'now'?"

Yeah, the tough love. Niko was all about it.

There was more silence, a grunt; then the puck straightened marginally and reached for the sandwich. "I hate you both." He took a bite, chewed, swallowed, and added grudgingly, "But I'm glad the Auphe didn't kill you. The massive hero worship you have for me brightens my day."

"Yeah, I can imagine." I pushed a few bottles off the coffee table and spread out a little while Niko distanced himself to stand at the other end of the couch from Robin. I doubted it helped with the alcohol reek, but I gave him credit for trying.

Making his way methodically through the sandwich, Robin looked us both up and down, and then asked between bites, "The Auphe came at you and neither of you have a scratch? How did you manage that? Are you carrying nuclear armament now, Caliban? Did you give up on the pop guns?"

"Like I said, they were just playing with us. Talking shit." I did have a few claw marks, but in our work if you could still walk and talk, that didn't count. "They were on the roof of our apartment building when I came home, and then they traveled to the park where Nik was practicing."

I often thought of going through the gates as traveling now. I'd been called "traveler" repeatedly by a homicidal asshole in the past two weeks. Sawney, mass murderer and one seriously crazy son of a bitch, was dead and less than ash now, but the term had stuck with me. It was as good a description as any for what the Auphe did . . . for what I could do. And as it also covered my other half—Rom—it fit.

"And you"—he grimaced—"*traveled* after them?" He'd gone through a gate with me on one occasion. It wasn't a pleasant sensation for non-Auphe; not unless you were into puking your guts out.

"No. I ran my ass off." Traveling, once difficult, had suddenly become easy. Too easy. It put me in touch with my homicidal Auphe roots more than was good for me . . . or for anyone around me. I'd told my brother I wouldn't do it again if I could avoid it, but if I hadn't been in the midst of a sidewalk full of people I would've done it in a hot second. He was a helluva lot more important than wrestling with the wrong half of my Jekyll-and-Hyde issue. He was worth losing a piece of my soul. . . . If I had one, it was only because of him anyway.

Still, it wasn't anything I wanted to talk about. How I felt the mental stirrings of a bloodthirsty heritage when I passed through the gray light wasn't my favorite topic right now. The Auphe nature wasn't mine. I wouldn't let it be. And if I said that to myself over and over and sprinkled enough frigging fairy dust around, maybe it would be true.

Clap your hands. Clap them goddamn hard and wish like a mother.

"But why—" He stopped when he saw Niko's eyes narrow fractionally, effectively ending the subject. When your overprotective big brother carries a sword, people tend to pay attention. "Moving on." Robin tossed the plate onto the table's surface, knocking over yet another bottle, and rubbed his eyes. "I need a new housekeeper."

I didn't say anything. He'd liked her; he'd lusted after her; he'd even respected her—a rarity for Goodfellow—and she'd tried to kill him. What was there to say in the face of that?

Actually, I did have something to say, although it was not about Seraglio. It was about what had happened in the park. I hadn't been completely sure then. . . . No, that was a lie. I had been sure, but I didn't know how I was sure and I didn't want to talk about that—that the only way I could know was because of my two stolen years. The Auphe were a subject I avoided, but discussing those two years—that I avoided at all costs. I was afraid—hell, terrified—that talking about it might one day peel back the darkness that swallowed those years, which would then swallow me. And I'd lose my mind. For good this time.

"Yeah, or you could pick up after yourself," I said

distractedly, then went on before his outraged laziness hit me in the face. "Nik, Robin, in the park . . ." I ran a thumb over the smooth stone of the table's surface and grimaced before going on. "They were all female. The Auphe." I tended to think of the Auphe as "he" or "it," because physically there was no difference between male and female to the eye and because I didn't want to give them the label of actual biological organisms. They were too goddamn horrific for that. Too alien.

Niko frowned, both at the knowledge and the fact I hadn't told him sooner, I knew. "What are they usually?" I could see he was annoyed with himself for never asking that question before. He was dedicated to knowing every fact about the Auphe that he could gather, because one day one of those facts might save me.

"I don't know." I gave a defensive shift of my shoulders. "I usually pay more attention to not pissing my pants and staying alive, so I guess they've just been a mix."

"How do you know they were all female?" Robin asked curiously, his reddened eyes slightly more alert. "It's not like the male Auphe keep them swinging in the breeze, and I assume they have something to swing or one couldn't have impregnated your mother." He considered the matter as he popped in the last bite of sandwich. "Perhaps they recede up inside the body. There are some animals—"

"Robin," Niko said matter-of-factly, "be quiet."

Goodfellow caught a look at my face, which, considering how much I wanted to hurl right now, probably wasn't the best it had ever looked. "Ah yes. Well. Sorry," he apologized sincerely before making a washing movement of his hands to scatter any remaining crumbs. "The male and female no doubt have a difference in scent."

He was probably right, but what the hell did it

mean? It didn't do jack shit for us if we didn't know what it meant. I said as much and changed the subject abruptly. "Where do we go from here? A rehab center for Goodfellow here?"

Niko was silent just long enough that I knew he would bring this up later when we were alone—whether I wanted to or not—but then he said smoothly, "Promise wants to talk to us. She may have some work for us." Most of our work wended its way through our favorite vampire. "That includes you, Robin."

The brown head dropped into waiting hands. You could virtually see the hangover forming. "Why? I'm highly looking forward to the alcoholic coma due me, thanks so much."

"Because with the Auphe reappearing, we all need to stay alert. And you"—Niko flicked the side of Goodfellow's head with enough force that I heard the *thwack* that was usually reserved for me—"you are not alert. Shower and dress. You have fifteen minutes."

"And we charge fifty an hour for babysitting," I added, "so grab your wallet." As green as Robin was when he swayed upright, I'd be happy just not to have a gallon of vomit hurled onto my shoes.

There was no vomit, but the fifteen-minute timetable went right out the window. Considering the shape and smell of him, I didn't mind waiting longer for a clean and slightly more sober Goodfellow to walk back into the room. He was as pasty as the Auphe ass he'd been referring to earlier, but he was moving under his own power. That had to be a good thing. When we reached the street he hadn't recovered any color and he had a faint wobble to his step, but that didn't stop him from leering at a passing woman. "Well, hello."

When she didn't respond, he switched his gaze to the man behind her. "Well, hello."

"Three days without sex," I snorted. "I'm surprised your dick hasn't deserted you for greener pastures."

Goodfellow glared at me as he swayed. Niko reached out to steady him and said reprovingly, "I wish, especially now, that you had not done this to yourself."

"Yes, yes. I'm sure you take your Metamucil shaken, not stirred," he griped. "But some of us like the grape." He walked . . . weaved, whatever. "We need a cab before I fall on my face."

By the time we reached Promise's building on the Upper East Side—60th and Park, another place too expensive for my bladder—Robin had sobered up more. Pucks—they have one helluva metabolism. It didn't stop Promise from taking a second look at him when we walked into her place. "You are well?" she asked dubiously.

"I'm alive," he said tersely. "I think that counts, but ask me again later." Trudging to Promise's ivory couch, he collapsed. "Perhaps I could get a little hair of the canine?"

"No," Niko replied firmly. Leaning in, he kissed Promise lightly. "If you have a key to your liquor cabinet," he said to her, "this may be the time to employ it."

She touched her fingertips to his jaw, and then turned to look at Goodfellow. She didn't say anything further, but I could see the sympathy in her eyes. She knew. She'd been there with us when Seraglio and her clan had nearly killed Robin. She was often exasperated with him, more often pissed as hell, but she was still fond of him—although somewhat less fond after he'd once turned her apartment into the scene of an orgy.

Robin looked away from her gaze. It was bad enough, I knew, that Niko and I had seen him so vulnerable. One more was too much. "I'm not here for an intervention or the entertainment, and I do have my own business to run. Can we move this alcohol-free ordeal along?" Yes, Robin Goodfellow, Puck, Pan, the Goat in the Green, did have his own business that he ran with a ruthless hand. He was worse than any monster. Worse than any beast from a mythical hell.

Like I'd said, he was a car salesman.

Worse still, a *used*-car salesman, the type of man that bragged that he could sell a condom to a eunuch or life insurance to the undead.

"I'll come to the point, then, so that you may return to fleecing the sheep." With a parting kiss to Niko's cheek, Promise walked to the darkly tinted window and pulled the curtains. In a gray silk skirt slit just above the knee and a scoop-neck sweater that was a soft shimmer of violet, she looked at us with equally violet eyes. Her hair, striped moon pale and earth brown, was pulled back in three braids, tumbling in loose waves at the crown and falling to the small of her back. "I have an old acquaintance. He wants to hire us."

She was generous with the "us." Promise, like the vast majority of vampires, didn't drink blood anymore, but she had gone through five very wealthy, very elderly husbands in the past ten years. However, I was sure every one of them had died with smiles on their wrinkled faces and gratitude in their shriveled hearts. Consequently, she didn't need the money we brought in; she did it for the love of the game . . . or the love of something else. Someone else.

"An old acquaintance?" Robin waggled his eyebrows. "The naked kind?"

Promise sighed, then ignored him. "Seamus. A vampire like me. He seems to have a bit of an interesting problem."

"Huh. A vampire. What's he want?" A vampire acquaintance, eh? Robin might not be so far off. Niko wouldn't be annoyed. He wasn't that possessive, and insecurity was only a word in the dictionary to him. But I was more than ready and willing to be annoyed for him. That's what brothers are for.

"Yes, a vampire." A finely arched eyebrow lifted. "As for his situation, this is something unusual, Seamus says. This is nothing completely . . . apparent. It's a subtle thing, and perhaps nothing at all. But to determine that I think we'll need a team approach."

"There's no *I* in 'team,' " Robin pointed out, starting to get up, "There's an *I* in 'intercourse,' 'iniquity,' 'illegal,' 'intoxication,' and did I mention 'intercourse'? But there is no *I* in 'team.' And I'm all about the *I*, which means that *I* will see you later."

"There's also an *I* in 'I'll kick your ass,' so sit down," I ordered darkly. "Maybe if you're lucky and finish sobering up, we'll tag your ass and turn you loose in the wild."

He gave a silent snarl, but by the time we got out of a cab at Seamus's place, an artistically clichéd loft in the artistically clichéd SoHo, he was sober. Despite that, he made no move to go back home. He might have had only a reluctant interest, but reluctant or not, it kept him there. "Art." He looked up at the walls of the loft, where the artist's work was liberally displayed. Not seeing any paintings of himself, he gave a disgruntled snort. "Theoretically."

Seamus slid his eyes toward Promise. "Humans and a puck. *Mo chroi*, I fear for your social standing."

Promise had said Seamus's problem was interesting, which was funny, because Seamus himself turned out to be just as interesting. Stick him in a kilt, paint his face blue, and he could've stepped into a Mel Gibson movie without missing a beat. Maybe because he'd actually lived through similar battles—the nighttime ones anyway. He wasn't tall, although hundreds of years ago he would've been. About five-nine, he was built with broad strokes. Wide shoulders and chest, muscular arms and legs; he wasn't your typical lithe and languid, ruffle-wearing vampire of pulp fiction. Except for one small braid that hung from temple to stubbled jaw, the wavy, deep red hair was pulled back into a short club at the base of his neck. That with the tawny eyes made him into a lion of a man, a giant cat walking on two legs. Which would make me a scruffy alley cat, an ill-tempered one who already had a headache from the Auphe situation. . . . It damn sure wasn't improved by the surroundings.

Seamus was an artist. His massive warehouse loft was wall-to-wall with his work. He liked bright, vibrant colors. Very bright, and vibrating right through my goddamn skull. After the day I'd had, this was like an ice pick between the eyes. I groaned and dug into my pocket for Tylenol, as Promise discarded her ivory hooded cloak onto a battered old chair to embrace Seamus lightly.

"Seamus, it's been a long time." Her expression was one of fondness, pleasure to see an old friend, and . . . something else. It was so brief I would've thought I'd imagined it, if I hadn't watched Sophia size up a mark thousands of times. Neither Niko nor I could hope to read people like our thieving mother had, but we held our own.

An old acquaintance, my ass.

I glanced sideways at Niko to see a perfectly blank face. No reason for him to feel threatened by Promise's past relationships, although this was the first one he'd come across where the participant wasn't dead and who hadn't been profoundly geriatric before he slipped into that state. I shook out two painkillers into my hand and then offered him the bottle. He bared his teeth for a fraction of a second, and I took that as a no. Putting the bottle back into my pocket, I popped the pills dry as Seamus welcomed us. Hands on Promise's shoulders after she pulled back, he leaned forward to brush a kiss across her cheek. "Paris was a cold and lifeless city without you, *leannan*. I'm glad our paths have crossed again."

"You're dusting off the Gaelic, Seamus," she said reprovingly. "Are the women not falling for 'lassie' any longer?"

He grinned, his strong white teeth gleaming a bright contrast to the copper shadow on his jaw. "You've caught me, then. The last pretty maid I tried it on branded me a cheesy pervert, I believe. Back in London. A feisty one, that, but I won her over in the end." Dropping his hands to his sides, he said, "But let us then get down to business, *mo chroi*."

"She's not your heart anymore, no matter what your nostalgia tells you," Nik said very mildly. There was no edge to the words, but there was one in Niko's sheath if Seamus wanted to make an issue of it. No jealousy, but a definite line drawn in the sand. And didn't it figure my brother would pick up Gaelic in his spare time?

"My nostalgia lasts longer than your lifetime, human," Seamus replied as mildly. "I shall be waiting at a finish line you will never see."

Promise didn't look amused by the exchange, and Goodfellow didn't help things any. "Men fighting over you," Robin said as he started opening cabinets and rifling through them, looking for that hair of the dog he'd mentioned earlier. Since he was sober now, I let it go. One or two wouldn't hurt him, and it might help us. "It's like old times for you, eh? Or it would be if both of them were dueling with their walkers."

She was even less amused now. Seamus repeated with a snort of disdain, "A puck, Promise? Sincerely, lass, what would possess you?"

"My company is my business, Seamus. Don't make assumptions on an old acquaintance," she warned. "You make it difficult to want to give you our assistance."

He gave her an abashed look from mellow whiskey-colored eyes. Curling his lips, he put a hand to his chest and bowed slightly. "I'm a poor client and a poor host. Forgive me."

Robin finally stumbled on a bottle of wine and toasted us. "You're forgiven. *Sla inte chugat*. Now where's your corkscrew?"

"As I have no brothel to offer you, Puck, a meager good health to you as well. And in the drawer by the stove," Seamus answered, suddenly good-natured . . . even toward an odious puck. He waved a hand at the couch and chairs, simple wood and natural fabrics that contrasted against the bold colors of the paintings. The Tylenol was beginning to let me see them as bold rather than eye-melting. "My apologies. Please."

I didn't believe the apology or accept it, but I did accept the invitation to sit. Sprawling in a chair, I looked over at Robin pouring a glass of ruby red. I held up one finger, cutting him off with the single glass. He rolled his eyes and ignored me. I may as well have been at work at the bar.

Promise sat on the couch, and Niko stood. Niko usually stood. You never knew when the couch might come alive and eat you. You had to stay alert. Constantly vigilant. Although after the Auphe attack, I didn't blame him. I dealt with it a little differently. Every cell inside me vibrated with the need to runrunrun. Sitting, slouching, watching Robin, looking at art I didn't get . . . it kept a small part of my mind occupied. Kept me from grabbing Niko's arm and tearing down the street. Getting out of town like the old days. Going anywhere. Anywhere but here. Anywhere the Auphe weren't. Just like a dozen times before.

Good times. Jesus.

It was also a helluva ride waiting . . . balancing on the knife's edge as I just waited. Waited to feel that heads-up, that gut twist of an Auphe gate opening. The sensation of theirs ripping open were a distant echo of mine, but I could still feel them. It was a nice alarm system, good to have. But it was no fun, the nerve-shredding anticipation. No goddamn fun at all.

"Have one, kid. It will do you good."

I looked up to see a wineglass in front of me. Robin was right. At the moment, one wouldn't kill me. The Auphe would, but wine wouldn't. "Thanks." I took it and had a swallow. I made a face. It was the good stuff. I didn't drink much—with an alcoholic mother, I didn't like to take chances—but I did know the better the wine, the worse it tasted. I liked the cheap stuff. The more it tasted like Kool-Aid, the happier I was. You could take the boy out of the trailer park . . .

Robin clicked his glass against mine and toasted. "As they say, it never rains; it pours. Pours liquid fire from the sky, sets us aflame, and scorches the earth to barren bedrock." Goodfellow's glass was now half-empty, but he stuck to the one-glass rule. "Cheers."

Niko shook his head when the bottle was held in his direction, as did Promise and Seamus, who said, bemused, "You are, without a doubt, the most grim and gloomy puck it's been my pleasure to come across."

No one commented. Aware he'd breached a touchy subject, he continued briskly, "On to my difficulty, annoyance that it is. It started nearly a week ago." He frowned. "I'm being followed. At least it seems that way. Ordinarily, I would know, but this . . . this is different. I do not see anyone tailing me, as they say, yet wherever I go, someone is there, already waiting. Someone who has far too much interest in me. Always in a public place where I cannot *discuss* the situation with them." White teeth, fangs and all, were shown in a humorless and savage grin. "And before I am to leave, they disappear. I turn away for a moment, and they are gone. It seems they know my intention before I do."

"Same guy?" I asked.

"No, which makes it more perplexing." He shook his head. "They're smart, whoever these sons of bitches be, but after four hundred years, I know when I'm being watched. I know when someone's a little too curious about my affairs."

"So you see the need for the team dynamic," Promise said, her hands clasped loosely over her knee. The oval pearlescent nails gleamed. "We can surround whatever curious gentleman shows up. He can't evade us all."

Well, if nothing else, it seemed easier than our last few jobs. No flesh-eating kidnappers. No fire-spewing serpents. No dead little girls. And with the Auphe back, something easy was all we could probably handle. If we even wanted to. Yeah, we needed the money, but trying to stay alive trumped that. I had doubts, serious doubts we could do both. I had doubts we could do even the most important one. I looked over at Nik and voted no with two words: "The Auphe."

Seamus's face slid into an expression of pure disgust. "Those *diabhail* creatures. What of them? I'd heard they were no more."

Promise hadn't told him I was half Auphe, and vampires don't have the sense of smell werewolves do. The wolves always knew. Seamus, however, didn't seem to have any idea about me, which was fine. I'd seen enough of those same looks of disgust shot my way. Disgust and fear. I was beginning to take a perverse pleasure in the last one. Not such a great thing to admit, but being hated for who you were right down to the genetic level leads to some defense mechanisms. Unhealthy ones, probably, but what the hell?

"Yeah, well, you heard wrong." I pulled the tie from my hair to let the dark strands fall free against my neck. I stretched the black elastic until it dug into

my fingers with a painful bite. "They have a problem
with us. And an Auphe problem is one fucking big
problem. We don't need the distraction right now."

Niko disagreed with me. "Job or not, Cal, we still
have a problem," he pointed out with inarguable logic.
I hated logic. It was never on my side. "They'll come
when they come; we can't change that. Whether we're
working a case or not. Putting our lives on hold won't
make us any safer."

Or any more likely to survive, I added silently. But
he was right, and it wasn't about the money. It was
about what I'd said earlier, keeping at least some of
your thoughts somewhere else. Not enough to be truly
distracted, but enough to keep from drowning in dread
and apprehension. I shifted my shoulders to loosen
the tension in my neck, and exhaled. "Okay, okay.
I'm in." Moving from kidnapping to extermination to
babysitting—our cases weren't quite heading in the
right direction. Thoughts for another time . . . like
when our asses weren't in such a sling. Or when we
were dead.

Plenty of time then.

So we took the job. Robin, unable to help himself,
jumped in to haggle Seamus up to an outrageous fee.
It was a wonder he left the poor bastard with the
tartan boxers on his ass. On that slightly disturbing
thought, I turned toward the door with the others,
leaving behind echoing spaces, powerfully raw art, and
Seamus . . . Seamus, who was staring at Niko's back
as I looked over my shoulder. Not at Promise as I'd
expected. But at Nik. Staring and staring hard.

This could be a problem.

ROB THURMAN

NIGHTLIFE

'There are monsters among us. There always have been and there always will be. I've known that since I can remember, just like I've always known that I was one ... Well, half of one anyway.'

Cal Leandros is nineteen. He eats junk food, he doesn't clean up after himself and he fights with his half brother Niko. It's a fairly normal life, but for the fact that Cal and Niko are constantly on the run. Cal's father has been after him for the last four years. And given that he's a monster whose dark lineage is the stuff of nightmares they really don't want him and his entire otherworldly race catching up with them. But Cal is about to learn why they want him, why they've always wanted him - he is the key to unleashing their hell on earth.

Meanwhile the bright lights of the Big Apple shine on, oblivious to the fact that the fate of the human world will be decided in the fight of Cal and Niko's lives ...

ROB THURMAN

MOONSHINE

'I was born a monster. Although truthfully, I was only half monster. Half monster or whole, in the end it didn't matter. I had my weaknesses, same as anyone else. And I was facing one of them now.'

Cal and his half-brother Niko's lives are settling back to normal after preventing their bloodthirsty relatives from bringing about the apocalypse. They've found a new apartment and even gainful employment by starting an investigative agency in partnership with a glamorous Upper East Side vampire. Of course, their clientele tends to be a little . . . unusual, but their money spends just the same.

Their latest job is undercover work for the Kin - New York's werewolf mafia - to sniff out proof of a set-up by a rival. The location is Moonshine, a gambling club for the otherworldly and Cal figures it will be an easy in-and-out sort of job. But as Niko likes to point out, nothing is more dangerous than overconfidence and when a brawl gets out of hand, it looks like he's right. Are Cal and Niko being set up themselves? And by people whose bite is much worse than their bark . . .

HUNGRY FOR FRESH

 **BLOOD** ?

Then come and join us at
www.facebook.com/BerkleyUK,
where we're dedicated to keeping you
fully up to date on all of our SF, fantasy
and supernatural fiction releases.

- Author Q&As
- Exclusive cover reveals
- Exclusive competitions
- Advance readers' copies
- Guest blogs from our authors
- Excellent reading recommendations

And we'd love to hear from you, email
us at **berkleyuk@uk.penguingroup.com**